D1565723

The
BLACK HAND

(CRNA RUKA)

*

ANDREW STACK

ISBN: 978-1-7349682-0-0

Book Cover Design by Rafael Andres
Book Editing by Elizabeth Ward
Book Proofreading by Michael McConnell
Interior Design and Formatting by Lorna Reid - Reedsy

Author's Note:

This is a work of fiction. Names, characters, places, and incidents either are the product of the author's imagination or are used fictitiously, and any resemblance to actual persons, living or dead, events, or locales is entirely coincidental. References to historical facts, people or places were meticulously researched and verified by multiple sources.

Dedication

To William Charles Stack. Enlisted to become a man at eighteen, blessed to become a father at twenty one and honored here with the title of "Dad" to live on forever.
November 17, 1934 – February 25, 2010
United States Marine

CONTENTS

Part I
"8/9"

ONE

EXACTLY ONE YEAR AGO

August 9th, 2020 – 1:11am, Hawaii-Aleutian Time
Four-hundred-and-fifty miles northwest of Honolulu, Hawaii

The black hands on Kenneth Gibbs' watch read 10:45, August 9th. Five minutes later it read 11:50, August 8th. An hour and twenty one minutes after that he glanced at the device one last time. 1:11, August 9th again. A miracle of time travel? "If only," thought Gibbs.

Head Coach Kenneth Gibbs and the players of the United States Olympic Men's Basketball team were on their return flight from Tokyo. Hours earlier they defeated China to capture the gold medal at the XXXII Olympiad.

Gibbs, a historian by education, was a master of dates. What a fascinating phenomenon it would be if he could go back in time. He would change so many things. Especially on the date of August 9th. Which August 9th would he alter first? 1945, 1974, 1990, 2014? Definitely 2014. But August 9th of the year 2020 was not to be denied and was having nothing to do with the silly notion of time travel.

The device on his wrist measured his heart rate and tracked his sleep as well. His pulse never varied more than a beat per minute from one date, to the previous and back again: 140. Slumber: zero in the last twenty-four-hour period. There must have been a defect in the instrument, as such readings would indicate someone quite ill. Almost terminal.

The date changes were not a phenomenon at all. They occurred by flying over the International Date Line and crossing from night to morning after the timepiece reached midnight. The entire experience was a hoax. An illusion created by nonexistent demarcations of time and location. Lines drawn by men over the centuries meant to separate and make something lesser or greater than the other. Much like other invisible lines drawn by men to do the same to people, not time.

Kenneth Gibbs considered himself a man of action and of language, not only a historian. Whether during his sixteen years in the Army or as a basketball coach, his place was leading young men on a battlefield or on a court of competition. Also, his words were the language of war and sport. Simple to deliver and in theory, easy to follow. "Defend, attack, cover, move, shoot. Kill," he'd said often throughout his career.

Yet at the most critical times of his life, all he did was stare and say nothing. Paralyzed by grief, muted by fear. In the vernacular of combat, he froze. In sport, he choked. But today, August 9th, 2020 was different. His history of freezing and choking was about to end. His days of living were about to end, too.

"Goddamn America. God bless the Crna Ruka," Gibbs said. He raised his right hand. The barrel of his weapon was inches from Alphonso Detandt's forehead. Without hesitation, Gibbs pulled the trigger of a Browning FN, model 1904 pistol. Serial number 19074.

The bullet hit dead center of the brow of the 31-year-old point guard from New Orleans. After entering the skull, the bullet shattered into hundreds of pieces. The frontal lobe died first. Detandt's problem-solving skills and motor functions disappeared in a millisecond. The part of his brain that made him an all-star basketball player was history.

Next to expire was the parietal region. The sugary taste of a beignet from Café du Monde touching his lips was gone forever. Lastly, and simultaneously, the occipital and temporal lobes hemorrhaged out his sight and sound. No more images and rhythms of the combination of light and music coming from the jazz bars of Bourbon Street.

Detandt was dead before the bullet casing hit the aisle. No one on the aircraft witnessed the shooting, but hundreds of millions of people around the globe did. A minute later, another bullet entered a man's skull. It was that of Kenneth Gibbs. The time and date on Coach Gibbs' wrist as his dead hand fell to the deck of the airplane read 1:14am, August 9th.

By 2020, the ruse of time travel was more deceptively perpetuated by technology. For in 2020, time and travel meant nothing. Everyone was everywhere at the same time. No one cared about clocks and maps. The automation responsible for the deception on August 9th, 2020 came in the form of a computer worn on a wrist, a near super-sonic aircraft and a camera paired to the social media platform Facebook Live.

There was no defect in Kenneth Gibbs' watch. However, one major flaw existed somewhere. It resided in the heart of Kenneth Gibbs. A tragic glitch synced with his brilliant mind. Only fifteen souls would ever come to know and understand the two life-giving vital organs of Kenneth Gibbs. It took the soul of an entire nation to figure out his life-taking Black Hand.

***

PRESENT DAY

August 9th, 2021 – 8am, EDT
Russell Senate Office Building, Washington, DC

Sara Gujic is the chairperson of what is informally known as the 8/9 Commission. One year later to the date of August 9th, 2020, Gujic is leading a two-day briefing before the Senate and House Homeland Security committees, the Senate Cyber Security and Emerging Threats subcommittees and House Counterterrorism and Counterintelligence subcommittees. Six other 8/9 Commission members have joined Gujic to answer questions regarding their specific areas of expertise.

Also in attendance are members of the President's National Security Council and the directors of all seventeen U.S. intelligence agencies. The briefing is also being broadcast live to over 100 million Americans.

The 8/9 Commission is officially named "The National Commission on the Terrorists Attacks of August 9th, 2020 from Within and Upon the United States." The task force was formed to provide as detailed an account of the events leading up to that tragic day as well as the aftermath of the days, weeks and months following.

Sara Gujic is sitting at the center of a table in the Kennedy Caucus Room. She clicks "Play" on her computer.

***

"Goddamn America. God Bless the Crna Ruka."

"Coach, what the hell are you doing?"

3

"Dad! He's got another gun. Kill him!"

***

"Honolulu Control, this is Bombardier, November, niner, eight, seven, come in."

"November, niner, eight, seven, Honolulu Control, go ahead."

"Honolulu, niner, eight, seven. Requesting emergency landing, runway two six right. We are 340 nautical miles out."

"State your emergency niner, eight, seven."

"We have eight dead passengers on board. Repeat, eight fatalities. We are requesting immediate clearance to land."

"Niner, eight, seven, copy. Eight fatalities. Squawk seven, five, zero, zero, if required. Change to channel 121.5."

"Honolulu, niner, eight, seven, Emergency channel 121.5. Radio check?"

"Niner, eight, seven, Honolulu Control. Five by Five. Niner, eight, seven, are you being hijacked?"

"Honolulu, negative, repeat negative, we have not been hijacked. First Officer Williams and crew are in control of the cabin. I am in control of the aircraft."

"Niner, eight, seven, please maintain course and speed and await further instructions."

"Honolulu, copy that."

"November, niner, eight, seven, Honolulu Control."

"Honolulu, go ahead."

"Niner, eight, seven, please confirm on your flight manifest, General Orlando Quinn is among your passengers."

"Honolulu, General Quinn is on board. He is alive. Repeat, General Quinn is confirmed alive and uninjured. As are the remaining passengers and crew. We believe the general may have been the shooter. First Officer Williams has possession of his firearm. He ordered the general and the other passengers to the rear of the aircraft. Fatalities are seven players of the Olympic basketball team and the team's head coach. Now 290 nautical miles out. Request permission to land."

"You are cleared to land runway two six right. Be advised. Two F-22's from Hickam en route to your intercept. They will provide escort until you have entered the circuit.

"We've received orders from NORAD and you will be met by ground escort upon landing. Do not taxi to the terminal. Please follow to Joint Base Pearl Harbor-Hickam. Army CID regional office will be on station upon arrival at Hickam. Upon landing change channels to 121.9. Copy?"

"Copy. Will contact Honolulu Ground on 121.9 after landing. Cleared for landing runway two six right."

"Niner, eight, seven. Honolulu out."

***

Sara Gujic clicks "Pause" on her computer.

"Ladies and gentlemen, that was every word recorded from inside the cabin and cockpit of Flight 9 8 7, on August 9th, 2020. Flight 9 8 7 was an aircraft on loan from the National Basketball Association. The flight departed Tokyo on the evening of August 9th and was scheduled to land in Los Angeles eleven hours later.

"The passengers on Flight 9 8 7 included the men of the US Basketball team, its head coach and the father of the team's star player. The father was Army Major General Orlando Quinn, deputy director of the National Geospatial-Intelligence Agency in St. Louis, Missouri.

"It is those words and the tragic events of that day which brings us together, a year to the date later. The first four lines were recorded on Facebook Live. The remainder is the complete oral communication transcript taken from the cockpit flight recorder between the pilot and Honolulu International Airport.

"On August 9th, 2020, America was under attack. However, unlike September 11th, 2001, domestic terrorists – American citizens – carried out these attacks. The result? Hundreds of innocent civilian deaths and casualties in cities across the country. The destruction of critical government assets and potentially disastrous exposure to enemies, the likes of which the country has not endured since World War II and the Civil War. Concurrently, on August 9th and the days following, America was being defended. But not by our national intelligence community, elite military units or law enforcement.

"A small, unsanctioned, clandestine team of twelve men and three women devised a counter-terrorism plan so deceptive in its design and effective in its execution, America was spared the loss of hundreds, if not thousands of additional lives. Probably many more over the course of the days and weeks following August 9th. Maybe another civil war. All fifteen were ordered to take life, to kill. They did so knowing a nation's freedom often depends on just that. They were also prepared to sacrifice their own lives if necessary. Nine of the fifteen did so.

"Esteemed members of Congress and Americans everywhere, the goal of this commission over the next two days is to provide a detailed briefing without political biases or conjecture. We will present the facts as we discovered them. We as a nation must judge how those facts came to be and what we must do to prevent repeating the tragedies that befell our nation on August 9th, 2020.

"The work of this commission was classified at a Top Secret – Acknowledged – SAP level. The purpose was to not compromise the integrity of our investigation and the report itself. In short, prior to today, only a handful of people was aware of this commission's findings. Under executive order from the president, I am authorized to make public the now-unclassified contents of our report without redaction.

"At the request of the president, everyone in this briefing received the full 612-page investigative report written by this commission. I apologize for its length and depth of detail but we left no stone unturned. The same report is available for download free to every American citizen at www.89.gov.

"Also at the president's request, we received instructions to write a second report but in a narrative form. Much shorter, but more engaging, more insightful hopefully. A 'novel', if you will. One written to capture the attention of every American. The objective is to tell the compelling account of August 9th and not the mountain of details, people, dates and places.

"I will present this story over the course of the next two days. The historical references of dates, people, events and places are, to the best of our knowledge, correct. It is only in the dialogue of this narrative where we took some artistic liberties. We ask you to trust we have done our best to be as accurate as possible, with some assumptions applied.

"As I said earlier, the audio file I played for you was recorded on August 9th, 2020. A video of the first moments is out for public view, but we felt no need to include it as most people watched multiple times. To show it again would be gratuitous.

"And though the recordings are from August 9th, 2020, our story has a much deeper history. Included is the date August 9th, 2014. A day six years earlier, when a tragic death, violence and chaos erupted in a previously unknown town outside of St. Louis, Missouri. A town called Ferguson.

"In 2014, two simultaneous events took place in Ferguson, that changed America forever. One personal, tragic and secret, the other public, widely-documented and criticized. As a result of the 2014 events, two parallel destinies emerged and ran so closely together as to be undetectable without far greater investigation.

"One, a destiny of two families. The other, of an entire nation. Six years later, on August 9th 2020, those parallel destinies turned abruptly on each other and exploded into what we all now refer to as '8/9'.

"This briefing will be delivered in five parts. Part One will be a complete accounting of August 9th, 2020 itself. This will include, I'm afraid, disturbing verbal testimony and additional video recordings. Evidence most of America has not heard or seen prior to today. A day on which billions across the globe celebrated the conclusion of the Summer Olympic Games in Tokyo. An event meant to demonstrate a world at peace, but violently interrupted by a series of lethal attacks that stunned our nation into a state of paralysis.

"Part Two; we will tell America about the key characters involved in both the attacks upon and the defense of America. We will share their stories, and their histories. We found one of the shortcomings of the 9/11 Commission Report was its failure to tell us why 9/11 happened. That commission reported extensively on the planning and operational aspects of the 19 hijackers. The 9/11 report also included detailed descriptions of how scores of first responders knowingly put their lives in grave danger by heading into the destruction, not away.

"But again, the report did not tell us why. What sickness inspired the murderers to carry out such horrible attacks? They did so willingly, knowing September 11th would be their last day on earth.

"How did our first responders, with families, loved ones and futures, cast aside those binding elements of society and find the courage to run face-first into certain death? We believe by sharing the backgrounds of those involved with August 9th, we can answer the questions of why the men and women did what they did.

"Part Three, we will present our findings on a group known as the Crna Ruka or the Black Hand as translated into English. This includes the formation, objectives, command structure, strategies, financing and recruitment of members. Right up to the final day of the Olympics. A day the U.S. Basketball team won the gold medal, and then most of that team lost their lives.

"Part Four will be the immediate aftermath of August 9th, 2020. The days and few weeks following what some refer to as the longest day in American history. For, in effect, it was. The events we will describe to you began on August 9th in Japan where the date was still August 8th in America. Within a span of thirty six hours, one date on the calendar seemed to last an eternity.

"The final part will be only the beginning of our epilogue. Our final act remains unfinished. Are we stronger and more unified? Have we learned our finest and final lesson on the subject of America once and for all? That our great nation was constructed for two underlying principles and while mutually dependent upon each other are not equally weighted.

"To embrace, encourage and celebrate our differences but not at the expense and priority of defending, with our lives, the unifying and common values which make America truly unique and exceptional.

"This commission will take questions throughout this presentation if further clarification is needed. We have also opened up a bank of 200 recorded phone lines for citizens to have their questions heard. We have teams of operators standing by to screen questions for appropriateness, availability of time and verification of callers. Questions can also be texted to '892020'. Before we begin, any questions from the Senate or House committee chairpersons?"

"Madam Chair, sorry to dive into the details so early, but Crna Ruka is obviously not English. Please explain to those who may not know what that phrase means. Also, how do you properly pronounce it?" asked the chairman from the Senate Homeland Security Committee.

"Sir, the phrase is Bosnian, my native language. Its literal translation means 'black hand.' The best way I can describe how to pronounce it is to imagine the letters T and S in front. The word begins with a nasal 'TS', like a sneeze and ends with a guttural 'chirna'. 'Tschirna.' I hope that helps. You can use Google Translate for a better listen.

"Crna Ruka was the name originally taken by a secret paramilitary organization formed in the early 1900s. Members of this clandestine group planned and successfully assassinated a royal figure. That one murder led to one of the deadliest conflicts in world history – World War I. We will refer Cnra Ruka and its English equivalent frequently throughout the next two days. In the context of our report, sometimes the Bosnian version is appropriate. The same is true for the English version.

"In fact, we will share many foreign words, phrases and complete sentences. You will also learn of different names, both proper and informal, honorifics, titles, pejoratives, slurs, code names and nicknames.

"For in the end, this is foremost a story about language. How we identify with those we love and those we don't. About interpretations and misinterpretations. In the end, our story comes down to a single word and that word's legacy and currency.

"For your convenience, we have published a list of all foreign language words and phrases used in this report. We also provided a list of all the relevant individuals in the order of their appearance. You will find both in the appendices of the full report you have in front of you."

"One more question before you start. The president and vice president; why are they not here?" asked the chairwoman of the House Committee on Homeland Security.

"Ma'am, they are indisposed at the moment and apologize for not being able to attend. Let us begin."

8/9 Commission Chairperson Gujic begins by displaying photographs of all the primary characters on television monitors positioned throughout the room. Everyone present and watching at home instantly recognizes those pictured. Included is a picture of Sara Gujic herself.

TWO

SEVENTY-SIX YEARS AGO

August 9th, 1945 – 9:00am Japanese Pacific Time, Nagasaki, Japan

"Is it going to rain today, Mommy?" asked the six-year-old Japanese girl as she boarded her school bus.

"Possibly. It's cloudy enough to rain."

"Oh, I forgot my umbrella."

"Don't worry, sweetie. A little rain never hurt anyone."

The mother was right. A little rain never hurt anyone. Unless that rain came in the form of eight kilograms of Plutonium 239 with a blast force of 42 million pounds of TNT. Which was what the atomic bomb named Fatman carried as it descended toward the city of Nagasaki, Japan. Forty-five-thousand residents were hurt by the little rain as the mushroom cloud that delivered the pain rose to eight miles high. The definition of hurt meaning: dead.

Miraculously, the six-year-old schoolgirl lived. Seventy-five years later on July 24th, 2020, that little girl, now eighty-one, lit the flame to open the XXXIII Olympic Games in Tokyo, Japan.

***

ONE YEAR AGO

August 9th, 2020 — Men's Basketball Gold Medal Game, XXXII Olympiad, Tokyo, Japan

"Coach, you gotta put the other guys in. I'm dead," Ronan McCoy said during a time out.

"Stop bitching, McCoy. If you hadn't been out all night fucking around, you'd be OK," said head coach Kenneth Gibbs.

"What about Jayden? He's not playing, and he's our best player. What the hell are you thinking?"

"I'm thinking you need to shut your mouth and play basketball. All you've done this entire trip is whine like a stuck pig. If you prefer, I'll sit you as well."

"No, Coach, I'm good."

"Put my son in the game!" came a scream from a dad in the second row behind the American bench. The yelling was from General Orlando Quinn, and he was referring to his son, Jayden Quinn.

"Mind your own business, General," Gibbs yelled back.

***

Back in the United States, the entire country was wondering what the hell Kenneth Gibbs was thinking. Ronan McCoy was right; Jayden Quinn, arguably the best player in the world, had been sitting on the bench most of the game.

At halftime, the United States trailed by six and the majority of the starting players had barely broken a sweat. For some reason, Coach Gibbs had gone with a smaller and less capable lineup than he had all throughout the Olympics.

Andrew Beutel, Daniel Kreinbrink and Davud Novak, while serviceable NBA players, were a notch down on the talent scale compared with the perennial all-stars who sat on the bench. Besides skill level, the three shared one other characteristic. They were white. By adding a fourth, Ronan McCoy, the starting lineup consisted of four white men and one African American; starting center, Charles Mwangi. The remaining "second stringers" were black.

The game ended much closer than many expected and the U.S. eked out the win. Final score USA 82-China 79. Ronan McCoy carried the load throughout the game and nearly collapsed from exhaustion when the final buzzer blew. He finished with forty-four points, fifteen assists and the game-winning three-pointer as time expired. An amazing athletic accomplishment given the fact that he'd slept the same amount of time the night before the game as he'd spent on the bench during it; zero.

He'd been out the night before enjoying his own private "Carnaval do Rio de Janeiro" with Brazilian twin volleyball players and arrived at the arena moments before tip-off. He reeked of sake and the traditional South America dish called Moqueca. A pungent, blood-red, fish stew. However, when his team needed him the most, he played his best. Twins or no twins.

***

The American television network commentators were not only dumbfounded that the game was so tight, they yelled at the cameras with outright anger.

"There's something going on here that is completely inexplicable and out of character for Coach Gibbs. To have his best players sitting, who all happen to be black, while the team struggles is wrong. I'm not one to use this word lightly but I will tonight. This is some kind of statement about race and it couldn't be more obvious," said the court-side reporter within ear-shot of Coach Gibbs. Gibbs stared at him.

"What an idiot. He has no idea," Gibbs said to himself.

Many fans watching the game back in the States became so disgusted they turned it off. They wouldn't know the final score until the next morning. And by that time, no one cared what the final score was. There was bigger news.

The game started at noon on the ninth in Tokyo, meaning a 10pm start on the east coast of the U.S. on August 8th. Moms, dads and kids alike, idolized the super-star players like Jayden Quinn, Darnell Cary, Mattox Jabbur and Iver Koch. Individually, the four regular starters averaged less than ten minutes of play-time. Between those four, a combined eleven NBA Championships and seven NBA Most Valuable Player awards was riding the pine.

"I thought we were done with this crap," one dad in St. Louis, Missouri, told his son as he turned the TV off at halftime. "Come on son, we're going to bed."

Based on the final TV ratings, more like 50 million dads around the country were done with this crap as well.

Unfortunately, the announcers couldn't turn off the cameras and go to bed. They were forced to stay and report on what they observed. "Never in my history of announcing Olympic Men's basketball have I been so surprised by what I witnessed tonight. Yes, the U.S. came out with the victory but at what cost? This is far more embarrassing as a nation than the 2004 Games in Athens," said one announcer.

He was referring to the United States team that came in third in the 2004 Olympics in Athens, Greece. That American squad of NBA All Stars lost to teams from Puerto Rico, Lithuania, Argentina and was fortunate to beat host country Greece. Who knew Puerto Rico was a country, much less a basketball powerhouse? The Americans ended up finishing the tournament in third place. Bad enough for the bronze medal.

***

In 2020, social media and other rogue news outlets across the globe weren't so polite with their language and assessment of what was wrong with the way the tournament concluded in Tokyo. The blogosphere, Twitter sphere and ionosphere lit up computer screens and televisions like the nuclear bomb Fatman had done to the Nagasaki skyline seventy-five years earlier.

"Blatant racism at its core. Time for another revolution my brothers," said @MalcolmZ on Twitter.

"Like the old days. The way things should be," replied @3kaywhiteknight.

The final basketball game of the XXXIII Olympiad and the decisions made by the head coach of the US Olympic Team would have been the talking point of the week to come. That is, until ten hours later when most of the country forgot about the Olympics.

While the players took some pride in their gold medal victory, many voiced their frustration with the personal show of disrespect. They decided as a group not to participate in the closing ceremonies, and wanted to leave Japan right after the gold medal ceremony.

At least, eleven players wanted to leave. Ronan McCoy, the star point-guard from West Virginia was fast asleep on the team bus five minutes after he got his medal. He was perfectly comfortable staying right there for the night. It took a couple of players to wake the guy to board the flight home.

***

Of the three and a half billion people worldwide that witnessed the 2020 closing ceremonies, only 25 million were in the United States. Overall the games were a disaster for the broadcaster and worse for the US Olympic Team.

It was the lowest-rated American viewership in forty years. The requests for refunds from disappointed advertisers were certain to start flooding in the next day. A few network executives contemplated hari-kari, the Japanese ritual of suicide by disembowelment, but none had the required Samurai knife or courage.

The historical dominance the US had become accustomed to in sports such as swimming, gymnastics and track and field was over. The US team finished fourth overall in the medal count behind China, Russia and host country Japan. Most surprisingly, the tiny West African country of Sierra Leone sent over seventy athletes and took home thirty medals. A first in that nation's history.

***

"Congratulations, you should be proud of the accomplishment," Coach Gibbs said, shaking the hand of and presenting a gift to each of the players as they boarded the plane. The team had performed above the coach's expectations and he took in the final moments with nothing but joy and appreciation in his heart.

"We are not done yet, men. We represent our country until the moment this plane touches down on American soil," the coach added.

"Some balls this guy's got," McCoy said to Andrew Beutel as they boarded and took their seats. "What did he give us? Oh! Look, one of those Apple watches. He probably installed a GPS tracker to know where the hell we are all the time. Treats us like his kids. Bullshit."

Settling in for the return flight with Coach Gibbs were ten players that represented the most gifted athletes the coach had ever seen. Two more senior players, Beutel and Novak rounded out the squad of twelve.

That was fine with Coach Gibbs as he'd selected the older players to add an element of leadership to the team. They also happened to be the only other white players besides Ronan McCoy and Daniel Kreinbrink.

Coach Gibbs chose all four, in large part, to serve as a neutralizing factor to a volatile racial climate that had manifested itself once again. Many political leaders and leading sociologists suggested tensions were getting worse in the United States in 2020, not better. But how was adding more white players supposed to help address that?

***

The Bombardier Global Express is considered the most luxurious, long-range business aircraft in the industry. This particular model was configured to carry twenty passengers, all in first-class style. The US basketball team was allowed to fly on the jet, to and from the Games, courtesy of the National Basketball Association.

The plane had ten rows, with one fully-reclining leather seat on either side of the aisle. The aircraft galley was stocked with the finest foods and alcohol the NBA could afford, which was anything. It was staffed by a flight crew of four, including two of the most stunning flight attendants Ronan McCoy had ever laid eyes on. He would have to ask for their cell numbers before landing.

When flying on a private plane, Coach Gibbs and the team drove on to the flight line, grabbed their gear and left. No need to be hassled with long check-in lines or, by his former military standards, incompetent TSA employees. Coach Gibbs sat in the first row on both flights. Sitting in the seat across the aisle from him was General Quinn. His best friend for the past few decades. The two flight attendants sat in the last row near the galley and the rest was open seating for the twelve players.

Ronan McCoy and Jayden Quinn sat in Row 2 in accordance with an unspoken rule about seat assignments. Best players sit up front. The two oldest players sat next to each other toward the back of the plane leaving the remaining eight to pick with whom and where to sit.

"On behalf of the entire flight crew, we congratulate you all on your gold medal victory," announced the captain over the plane's PA system. "Tonight our cabin crew will be serving a delightful meal courtesy of General Quinn. A one-pound A5 Grade Kobe beef ribeye and a 20-piece sushi combination roll from the world-famous Sukiyabashi Jiro restaurant in Tokyo. $540 a platter, and General Quinn's favorite meal from his favorite restaurant. He hopes you will enjoy it. Let's give a hand to our generous soldier."

Everyone clapped.

"I think they bought it," said the general to Coach Gibbs.

"Amazing, how naïve and easily manipulated the entire media industry can be."

"I can only imagine what's being said and written about the two of us.

Zivjeli (cheers) my friend," said the general in Bosnian as he raised his double Beefeaters martini.

"*Fee Sahatik*," (to your health), Coach Gibbs said in Arabic. "'Us', what do you mean 'us'? I'm sure the writing will be all about me. You're the hero, remember? By the way, I love you. You have been and always will be my best friend, Orlando." It was the first time in his life Coach Gibbs did not refer to his friend by the title of General and Orlando was happy.

"Ken, you are the bravest person I have ever met. I love you too and am honored to be your friend."

Orlando reflected on the moment. It had been such a long time. Six years, he thought, since he and his friend put aside all the troubles of the world and did nothing more than share a drink.

His friendship with Kenneth Gibbs was so important to him that years after the tragic death of the coach's daughter, he still hurt terribly for his friend. He would have done anything to ease his pain. He knew this date hurt more than all the others. For it was the day Coach Gibbs' only daughter Melissa took her own life. August 9th, 2014. What an amazing and tragic coincidence most would have thought. His most glorious and tragic day on the same date. It wasn't a coincidence.

"Can't we remove the date August 9th from the calendar?" Orlando asked his friend as they shared their private moment. "They got rid of the thirteenth floor from every hotel. Why can't we do the same with a date?" Coach Gibbs heard the general's brilliant question but didn't answer.

After dinner, Orlando spent the next hour or so catching up on work and signed in to the secure network at National Geospatial Intelligence Agency (NGIA). He was the deputy director and worked at the agency's complex outside of St. Louis, Missouri.

Approval of the provisioning of satellite imaging in multiple sectors across the world. Routine stuff and something he approved hundreds of times a week. Thirty-one requests were in his work folder. Other intelligence agencies, local and national law enforcement agencies, military installations, all requesting up-to-the-minute detailed imagery and analyses of sectors of interest. He approved all but six.

One final work to-do; send all approvals to the National Reconnaissance Office who reposition the satellites as requested. He hit send on the requests and signed off from work. A quick login to Facebook to send a message to a friend overseas and he was done.

"Mission accomplished," he said to himself sarcastically. A phrase he learned to hate upon hearing it for the first time in 2003. To the general, with over 30 years of service to his country, it seemed as if the mission was never accomplished. Always more war. More death. He turned a last time before falling asleep. A tear from each eye rolled down his cheeks.

"Happy birthday, my son," Orlando whispered to Jayden sitting one row behind him. Only four people in the world knew it was Jayden Quinn's birthday and not one of the four was the birthday boy himself.

All the black players except for Jayden huddled together to enjoy one last celebratory toast before calling it quits. A blue, syrupy concoction from a chilled bottle with the name "Hpnotiq" on it.

"Never tried it," the general said as he closed his eyes.

It took but a few hours for the flight attendants' exceptional service to have the desired effect. The two surveyed the cabin. Most of the passengers slept, except one or two still on their computers. This allowed the attendants a few hours to gossip about which superstar they thought was cutest and after serving everyone, grab some sleep themselves. They both voted for Ronan McCoy. It was supposed to be an easy flight to Los Angeles. It turned out to be one they would remember for the rest of their lives.

Three and a half hours after takeoff, the plane was 750 nautical miles north of the island chain of Hawaii and near where the Japanese fleet had been on December 7th, 1941. The flight was turning out to be longer than expected as the leading edge of a Category 2 Typhoon named Ignacio was in the western Pacific and caused the flight to take a much more southerly route than the filed flight plan. Forecasters were projecting the storm's eye would be over the mainland of Japan within twenty-four to thirty-six hours.

The team was fortunate the plane had taken off at all. Within a few hours after departure, Haneda International Airport was closed due to storm winds in excess of seventy miles per hour. Spectators and athletes scheduled to leave Japan on commercial flights on the morning of August 10th had no choice but to ride out Typhoon Ignacio. Japanese authorities took what means were available to secure athletes and spectators in the Olympic village dormitories and neighboring hotels.

Coach Gibbs looked at his watch and pressed the function to show the time in St. Louis. It was 5:11 am on the 9th in Missouri and 1:11 am, start of the 9th in Hawaii. He rose up from his seat, grabbed his toiletry bag from the overhead compartment and went to the lavatory.

Besides General Quinn and Coach Gibbs, everyone else on the plane appeared to be asleep. Ronan McCoy, awake for the previous forty-eight hours, was snoring like a bear. The food, cocktails, forty minutes of basketball and those twins had wiped him out.

It took less than two minutes for Coach Gibbs to take care of his business. As he walked back to Row 1, he looked at his best friend and recalled the many wonderful years they'd spent together. He said a short phrase in Arabic. "*As Salamu Aliyyakum.*" (Peace be unto you.)

"*Wa Aliyyakum As Salam,*" General Quinn said back.

Coach Gibbs pressed the "Record" button on a device strapped around his head and a small light switched on. He walked past most of the rows on the aircraft until he arrived at Row 9. Alphonso Detandt was in seat 9A and Daniel Kreinbrink in 9B. Standing directly in front of Detandt, Coach Gibbs took two seconds to speak eight words he'd never spoken in his life and never would again.

"Goddamn America. God Bless the Crna Ruka."

David Kreinbrink, sitting in the seat across the aisle from Detandt didn't hear the pistol fire as Coach Gibbs pulled the trigger, and he didn't wake. Again, too much food, alcohol and basketball.

Prior to leaving the lavatory, Coach Gibbs had loaded the gun's magazine with thirty-one bullets designed by US Air Marshals in the 1970s called Devastators. The purpose of them was to be able to incapacitate hijackers while limiting the potential danger of passing through a person and penetrating an aircraft's fuselage. The bullets were engineered to explode on impact.

With a noise suppressor attached to the end of the pistol, the firing of such bullets produced only ninety decibels of sound. Equivalent to the amount generated by jet engines inside an airplane's cabin at cruising altitude. The sleeping passengers didn't wake from the shots fired.

Gibbs continued making his way back to the front of the aircraft, stopping at each row and firing his pistol with accurate effect into the heads of each of the seven African-American basketball stars. He was about to shoot an eighth.

"Coach, what the hell are you doing?" screamed Jayden Quinn. He grabbed the coach's arm holding the gun and pushed him back toward the first row, knocking the gun free from his hand. The gun slid a short distance and stopped beside General Quinn. He picked it up. Coach Gibbs began to reach inside his blazer.

"Dad, he's got another gun. Kill him!" Jayden ordered his father.

General Quinn followed that order and fired one shot from a distance of three feet. It was deadly accurate and into Gibbs' forehead. The last image and sound captured by the camera and seen on Facebook Live was a picture of the barrel of the pistol pointing back into the camera. The suppressed flash and explosion of the cartridge as it left the weapon, smashing the camera and entering the brain of Coach Gibbs was perfectly clear. He was dead before the casing hit the aisle.

The light on Gibbs' head was that of a GoPro Hero 7 HD video recorder. While in the lavatory, Gibbs had paired his GoPro with his iPhone and the aircraft's satellite internet and signed on to Facebook Live. He captured, in live video stream, every moment of his murderous cabin service. He also tagged every player's Facebook account to the video. Within seconds, the post went viral to hundreds of millions of followers worldwide.

Viewers gasped at his words, condemning the country he'd proudly served while in the Army for sixteen years. One of his last acts was to tag the video with the Cyrillic script Црна рука. "Crna Ruka". There it was, that phrase again. What could it possibly mean?

The TV network executives and every other form of media earned all the ratings they wanted on August 9th, 2020 and no refunds to advertisers would be necessary. Within a few hours, the 200 million or so American adults who didn't see the team's final shot in Tokyo, were mesmerized and horrified by the final shots of the team's coach.

***

Fifty-six years earlier in 1964, it had taken billions of dollars in investment, thousands of employees working at the National Aeronautics and Space Administration (NASA) and hundreds of tons of equipment to broadcast live, for the first time across the globe, the XVIII Olympiad from Tokyo, Japan. Coach Gibbs was able to replicate the same technological marvel with a $400 smartphone and a $199 camera. Combined weight: less than one pound.

The soldier in him recognized that the advancement of technology was not always benign. Countless wars throughout history resulted in utter devastation when man's ability to comprehend the power of technology was not synced with its ability to kill. Coach Kenneth Gibbs knew his history tragically well and applied its lessons accordingly. As an educated historian and combat veteran, he both marveled and wept for man and machine's efficiency on delivering death.

***

August 9th, 2020 – 11:15am, Central European Time, Facebook Content Moderator Remote Office, Sarajevo, Bosnia

"What the hell now?" said Ratko Mulic in Bosnian to absolutely no one as the screen on his laptop pinged him, indicating incoming work-related activity. "All I want to do is watch the game."

Mulic was watching a rebroadcast of the Olympic Bronze Medal Men's Basketball game between his beloved Bosnian team and in his words, "the bunch of infidel goat-fuckers" from the country of Serbia next door. But duty called. He pressed pause on the TV remote.

Tens of thousands of contract employees work around the clock in the Facebook Community Standards division at home-based and office locations around the world. The duties of these teams is to review and block any content, photos or videos that violate the company's policies against hate speech, illegal behavior and violence.

Mulic worked at the Bosnian/Serbian Language department from his rather meager apartment outside of Sarajevo. The ping he received regarded viral activity on the Facebook timeline of Jayden Quinn.

"Understandable," he thought, "for the most popular athlete in the world." But why was he alerted when his duties only included posts made in the Bosnian and Serbian languages?

The notification on his screen regarding Jayden Quinn's post read "Crna Ruka" in Cyrillic script. To Mulic, the meaning of the words besides their literal translation seemed familiar but he couldn't recall why. He didn't bother to open the post.

Five seconds later, he had no choice. Artificial intelligence and content monitoring algorithms immediately alert reviewers when a post exceeds

100,000 views or responses. The post automatically opens on the screen of the reviewer and requires some action when responses exceed 250,000. Facebook established the rule in the event a viral post violated Facebook's Community Standards. It would then be deleted by an employee before it continued to spread across the platform.

A post of a one-minute video that originated from a Facebook subscriber named Kenneth Gibbs from St. Louis, Missouri with the two Bosnian words tagged and shared to Jayden Quinn's account, had garnered over 300 million views, 7 million responses, 2 million comments and 10 million shares. An all-time record for any single post in Facebook's history. All in a matter of a few minutes.

Mulic's first and most important duty was to block the post but he did not. He watched the massacre with wonderment and horror three more times. By allowing the post to remain online for another three minutes, the Facebook numbers increased five-fold. He finally clicked delete, but by then it was too late.

He read the tagged Cyrillic words. Each time, more slowly and shocking than the previous. "Црна рука. Црна рука. Црна рука." "CRNA RUKA, CRNA RUUKA, CRNA RUUUKA." "The Black Hand." His heart momentarily stopped pumping blood to his brain.

A flashback to his high school history class appeared, not on his screen but in his head. He remembered the Crna Ruka. He also knew something was dreadfully wrong. He needed to tell someone in authority.

Two minutes later, Mulic's screen went blank.

"What the hell is going on?" While he sat on hold waiting for tech support to answer his call, he watched the remainder of the game. The Eastern Orthodox hircine fornicators from Belgrade defeated his Bosnian team 101-77. "*Sranje*," (shit), he said again to no one.

***

The date and events of August 9th, 2020 joined a pantheon of other seminal moments in modern American history that oddly, but not always coincidentally, occurred on August 9th.

August 9th, 1945. The bombing of the city of Nagasaki. Over 45,000 killed. The use of nuclear weapons ended one war and began another; The Cold War.

August 9th, 1974. For the first time ever and on live television, a president of the United States resigned his position. It took years before the country's elected officials restored the faith of the American people.

August 9th, 1990. Two undocumented immigrants, making an arduous journey toward freedom, were shot and killed by an American army lieutenant assigned to a border patrol unit. A third immigrant survived the shooting and grew up to become one of the most recognized figures in the world.

August 9th, 2007; a French bank refused to buy or sell hedge funds tied to the United States home mortgage market, causing a freezing of money in the global financial markets. The lack of liquidity amongst the largest financial institutions in the world led to the worst economic crisis in American history since the Great Depression.

August 9th, 2014, due in large part to an over-militarization of local police departments around the country, the small town of Ferguson, Missouri erupted in protest over the shooting of an 18-year old African-American man guilty of stealing a cigar.

And, most devastating to Kenneth Gibbs, head coach of the Olympic Men's Basketball team and former Lt. Colonel in the US Army, August 9th, 2014 was the date his daughter, Melissa, was brutally raped and took her own life as a result of the attack. The assault also took place in Ferguson, Missouri.

History has a long, cruel and bitter sense of timing. August 9th turned out to be the most cruel and bitterest date of them all. And August 9th, 2020 was far from over. Nineteen hours remained in Gibbs' hometown of St. Louis, Missouri.

***

PRESENT DAY

August 9th, 2021 — 9:20am EDT, Russell Senate Building, Washington, DC

"Madam Chairman, ah, chairperson, Miss Gujic? Excuse me, how should we refer to you? I'm sorry," asked the congressman from Illinois.

"You can call me Sara."

"Thank you, Sara. How did the coach bring a loaded weapon on an airplane? How did he go through security, both in LA and in Tokyo and why wait until the flight back? Many times the coach accompanied his team where he could have done what he did."

"Sir, there is no full security screenings on private chartered aircraft. Coach Gibbs, his best friend Orlando Quinn and the players walked on the tarmacs at both airports, boarded and left. It was that simple."

"Well, do you believe that should change? Should we require full TSA screening for private planes?"

"I said at the start of this briefing, it is not the job of this commission to represent or propose any policy or position on anything. Report the story as we wrote it, based on facts. Any changes to policy should come from our elected officials.

"However, let me answer the other part of your question about why Coach Gibbs waited until they were on the plane. He understood America's obsession and paranoia about air travel. He wanted to send a statement so powerful, so horrifying, so as to inflame our wildest fears. It is the goal of a terrorist, to inflict paralyzing fear on the survivors.

"We all saw the events of 9/11 unfold on our TV screens and the horror of that day changed the world. And now this, broadcast live, the deaths of seven superstars – our heroes, if you will – all on Facebook. Textbook terrorism. Tragically yet brilliantly delivered to the computer screens and smartphones of billions of people around the world.

"We spend billions on staff, training and equipment at our airports. For what? To protect passengers and crew from a weary mother trying to sneak a third bottle of breast milk on a flight?

"I ask this question rhetorically and on behalf of the president regarding our nation's security strategy. It is not meant to be interpreted as a political statement. But a question worth pondering.

"Yet all other manner of soft targets go unguarded. Our schools, offices, churches, clubs are, at best, lightly manned. Even getting into this building today, with so many esteemed attendees, the security I went through doesn't compare to what I've been through at the airport. Are our resources being used in their best capacity?"

"It sounds very much like you are presenting a political position Miss

Gujic," the congressman says, and stops calling her Sara.

"No sir, I'm asking a question based on fact." Sara continues by holding up an unloaded pistol she grabs from her laptop bag. "I brought this in today knowing I would be escorted through a private entrance." The audience gasps. She puts the gun on the table for security staff to retrieve.

"I told the president I would do this as a demonstration if the opportunity presented itself. One of the president's secret service agents loaned me the gun on the drive here today after unloading it."

"Sara, you stated earlier you would provide more information on the meaning of the phrase 'Crna Ruka'. Can you share with us now what that means?" A question from the second highest-ranking naval officer in the room.

"Crna Ruka is the name of the paramilitary organization responsible for the assassination of Archduke Franz Ferdinand and his wife Sophie, the Duchess of Honenberg.

"On June 28th, 1914, members of the Crna Ruka, trained assassins, positioned themselves at various locations around the city of Sarajevo, Bosnia. The Archduke and his wife rode in a motorcade on an official visit to the city. A young man by the name of Gavrilo Princip was the fatal trigger-man. He is considered by many to be a hero of the effort to unify the Balkan states. That unification movement resulted in what was once the former country of Yugoslavia.

"Many others in the region and throughout history, have considered him to be no more than a terrorist and murderer responsible for the start of a war that killed over 20 million people. World War I."

"Was Gavrilo Princip the leader of this Crna Ruka?"

"No. The leader was a Serbian army officer by the name of Dragutin Dimitrijevic. But for years, no one except his most trusted lieutenants knew his true identity. He went by a code name and was referred to by it in all manner of communications. No one in the Crna Ruka ever used his real name. His code name was Apis. It means 'Holy Bull'."

"And why did Coach Gibbs adopt this name 'Crna Ruka' as some sort of rallying cry for his murders? What's the significance? Was Gibbs their Apis? Their leader?"

"Admiral, let me answer the hard question first. No, to the best of our knowledge, Coach Gibbs was not the modern day Apis. We still have yet to determine the person's true identity. There's a question whether he exists. I doubt he does.

"According to our interviews, possibly two people know his identity. One of those two was Kenneth Gibbs himself, who is of course dead, and General Orlando Quinn. Whenever we inquired from him who this mystery man Apis is, he recites the entirety of the Code of the United States Fighting Force. In other words, Orlando Quinn is neither confirming nor denying 'Apis' is real.

"The adoption of the phrase 'Crna Ruka' was nothing but a ruse. A maneuver by Kenneth Gibbs to deceive and confuse. To make us believe there was more meaning to his actions than the obvious."

"And what was the obvious?"

"That people would die. Famous people. Men we idolize. Like those idolized in the early twentieth century. Royalty. Except America's royalty aren't called kings or queens. They're called professional athletes. Even the gun Gibbs used in the shootings, the Browning FN 1904, serial number 19074, was part of his deception."

"What do you mean? What about the gun?"

"It is the exact gun used by Gavrilo Princip, the Bosnian shooter in 1914."

"You mean the same model gun?"

"No, the exact same gun."

THREE

August 9th, 2020 – 7:28am EDT, the White House, Washington, DC

"Sir, wake up. We have a big problem here," said Secret Service agent Thomas Chalk.

"I'm well aware Agent..." the president stopped. He couldn't remember his lead agent's name. "I know we have a problem. I was informed about the tragedy of the Men's Basketball team an hour ago. I'm trying to sleep."

"It's not that, Mr. President. There was another attack. Please join me, sir. You'll be back to bed soon."

"Goddamn it."

***

Now in the John F. Kennedy Conference Center, otherwise known as the "Situation Room," in the basement of the West Wing of the White House, the president asked of his National Security Council members, "What's going on? What now?" The one digital display working read "DEFCON THREE."

"Where's Sec Def – where's Charlie?" asked the president as he shook off his sleep.

"I'm right here, Mr. President," said the Secretary of Defense sitting next to the president.

For the next thirty minutes, the president heard from each of his top aides what new and disastrous developments had occurred in the one hour he'd slept. When they finished, he had some questions and orders.

"What do we know about the terrorists?" Each member stared at the other, waiting for an answer.

"To hell with this, I'm going back to bed. I'm declaring a national state of emergency starting now. Order an emergency session of Congress. I want the Senate and House back in DC now. Agent... Agent, wake me up at noon."

***

An hour prior to the president being awakened by agent Chalk the first time, an alert on the workstation of Navy Petty Officer Third Class Timothy Wheeden woke him up as well. Wheeden worked the night shift at the National Reconnaissance Office (NRO) in Chantilly, VA.

He and the entire crew were on high alert status after hearing of the attack on an American registered private aircraft. Numerous high profile, celebrity team members of the United States Men's Basketball team had been murdered, and it was still unclear to many within the intelligence and defense agencies whether another '9/11'-like event was in the making. The National Reconnaissance Office is responsible for designing, building, launching and maintaining America's intelligence-gathering satellites.

While all electronic security camera eyes and a formidable array of defensive weaponry looked out and up toward the roads and skies, a deadly attacker successfully entered the NRO building undetected. The killer wiggled his way through a ¼ millimeter fiber optic cable buried under the building, and he unleashed hell.

The ping on Wheeden's terminal and corresponding message read, "Virus Detected. Activate Anti-Virus software." Five seconds later, Wheeden's screen went black.

Consecutively and with increased speed, his work associates' screens did the same. Within moments, the entire office sat in the digital dark. The anti-virus software did nothing to prevent the attack.

The National Reconnaissance Office is one of seventeen different member agencies that make up the United States Intelligence Community. Other members include the more recognized Defense Intelligence Agency, Office of Terrorism, National Geospatial Intelligence Agency, Hollywood-darling Central Intelligence Agency and the National Security Agency.

All the agencies are linked together through a series of joint command, control and communications networks. The networks were designed accordingly as a result of the 9/11 Commission claiming the intelligence communities worked in silos. By establishing shared networks, agencies more easily exchanged analyses, resources and recommendations with the White House and Pentagon brass.

But now, because of those networks, one agency after another lost the use of its workstations and intelligence-gathering capabilities at an alarming speed. Each time the information security systems administrators thought they'd controlled the virus, a small mutation allowed it to live on.

By 6:18am EDT, August 9th, 2020, the sun peeked its bright eye over the nation's capital. But the country's national intelligence gathering capabilities remained in the dark, and immobile. Later in the day, it would be deaf as well. The President of the United States was still asleep comfortably in his bed, not to be disturbed for another hour.

On August 9th, 2020, America's vision at the National Reconnaissance Office contracted such a bad case of pink eye, that it was blind for days. Its eardrums at the National Security Agency burst from the percussion of a single but lethal thunderbolt and its spinal cord of connected networks received a blow so fierce as to suffer a C-4 fracture of the nervous system, rendering it a complete quadriplegic.

The American people, after seeing what was shown on Facebook Live and what was about to play out in America's streets, country clubs, beaches and towns, if given a choice of handicaps most would choose blindness. A disability to which most Americans grew accustomed.

***

The best way to describe how the social media giant Facebook designed and operated its business model is to use an antebellum southern cotton plantation as an example. Thousands of black, enslaved machines, worked around the clock at farms until the point of obsolescence or failure. Discard, purchase younger, better, stronger units and put them back into production.

The farm consists of tens of thousands of these slaves caring for, gathering and putting out to the market little fluffy balls of pliable product to be weaved into whatever fashion the market finds profitable. In 1820, it was clothing. In 2020, it was data.

In July 2020, Facebook launched its first ever Low Earth Orbit (LEO) satellite from the Kennedy Space Center in Cape Canaveral. While fiber optic cabling was still the gold standard in delivering fast, reliable broadband internet, in many remote areas and due to expense, this was not a financially viable option.

Facebook and other large tech companies competed aggressively with each other to own their customers' internet service, and not only from server farms to the hubs of large telecom companies. They wanted to own the last mile as well. The last mile is the nearest point of a network that pipes into homes and businesses. Anywhere that internet is provided by a wire or nearby hotspot.

By launching its LEO satellite, hundreds of millions of new subscribers could connect to Facebook for the first time without wires anywhere throughout the network. In Obljaj, Bosnia, a village of twenty-two inhabitants in the Dinaric Alps qualified as one of those remote areas.

At 11:45am on the 9th, in that small Bosnian village, a man no longer alive by the name of Petar Princip posted to his account using Facebook's new low-earth orbit satellite. The post consisted of Cyrillic lettering, much in the same vein as the post from Coach Gibbs on the flight back from Tokyo.

The post read, "Уједињење или смрт." (Unification or Death). No pictures, no memes, no videos. Only a hyperlink back out to the internet. The post was also shared to the account of Jayden Quinn, Coach Gibbs and the seven players killed on the flight back to the US.

Eager to see more than a few men getting murdered on an airplane, hundreds of millions of users clicked on the hyperlink. By doing so, a creature with the genetic ability to multiply by ten to the infinite power was let out of its cage. The beast and its digital offspring began eating through computer hard drives at astronomical speeds. The virus also wormed its way onto any mobile device registered on a user's account.

One second after that, the dolts who clicked on an unknown hyperlink from Facebook or shared it with their friends, which was practically everyone, were shut down. The last mile proved as difficult to own and control as always.

For the approximately 200 million American Facebook subscribers, they wondered how they would communicate with each other, post back-to-school photos of the kids or, most importantly, "Mark Myself Safe." They couldn't, they shouldn't and they weren't.

Stay-at-home moms and stray-away dads could have picked up the phone and called their fake friends and fantasy lovers. However, because Facebook succeeded at blurring the lines between the real and the make-believe, most didn't know who to call first. By the time most Facebook subscribers could log back into their accounts, they didn't want to ever again.

FOUR

OVER TWO YEARS AGO

July 1st, 2019 – St. Louis Country Club, St. Louis, Missouri

"Sir, I have an application to submit for possible approval," said the membership director at the exclusive golf and tennis club.

"Where's he from and what's his lineage?" asked the club chairman.

"Well, his application says his name is Calvin Heyward. He's from Tennessee and a church pastor. But I couldn't find anything when I searched him. He's forty-nine, African-American and..."

"Stop. Did you say African-American? I thought I told you we have one of those already. Until that guy dies, we don't need another. Is that clear?"

"Yes, Mr. Walker."

***

ONE YEAR AGO

August 9th, 2020 – St. Louis, Missouri

"Retreat transportation departs at 11:30am, sharp – O'Fallon Park Recreation Complex. Arrive twenty minutes early," read the text message sent via the WhatsApp account of the Unified Church of God Pastor Calvin Heyward. Thirty-eight recipients responded with "Praise god."

At the exact same time, in five other branches of the Unified Church of God (UCG) across the country, similar messages went out from pastors and were received by their congregation. Now, 175 men nationwide boarded one form of transportation or another.

The six pastors had planned this event for over a year and the excitement of it all coming together in one special day was palpable. Most of the participants were younger than twenty years old and had never participated in an event of this significance.

The night before the retreat, Pastor Heyward sent a message to all the attendees with the following instructions: "Dress in all white, do not bring your cell phones, do not bring food or water and shave your entire body from head to toe." A baptism and a spiritual cleansing, maybe.

A charter bus for the retreat arrived at the rec complex at 11:15am for its scheduled pickup. All the participants who signed up for the St. Louis retreat arrived on time and ready to go. They boarded as Heyward and one other man loaded four duffel bags of supplies in the undercarriage compartments of the bus. He then instructed the driver to depart.

The destination of the retreat, as filed with the charter company, was to be the Lady of the River's Shrine located forty-five minutes north of St. Louis along the banks of the Mississippi River. Pastor Heyward told the bus operator his group planned a day of reflection, fellowship and camaraderie. The plan included finishing with a group baptism in the cleansing waters of the filthy river. The bus company didn't expect them to return for six hours.

As they pulled away, Heyward attempted to text his five associates across the country once again to confirm all had left on time. The WhatsApp text, for some reason, didn't go through.

"God, I hate social media messaging. Why can't we use email and regular phone texting? Like the good old days," he asked the person sitting next to him.

The quickest route to the shrine was to head due north. Pastor Heyward asked the driver to head west on I-70 instead.

"I'll have to call that into the office. The management monitors my driving route via this GPS," said the driver.

"No, you won't and please turn off that GPS," said Heyward. Feeling the cold metal of a Glock 9mm against his temple, the driver decided Heyward's route to be better and that he didn't need to call it in, after all.

"Where am I am going?"

"Do you know where the St. Louis Country Club is?"

"No idea," said the portly and elderly black bus driver. "Never heard of it."

"I'll get you there. Go south on I-170 in ten miles."

Within twenty minutes the driver, scared, confused but obedient to Heyward's directions, pulled into the luxuriously-kept grounds of the country club in the tony town of Ladue, Missouri. As the driver looked into the rear-view mirror he saw the entire busload of people donning bandanas around their faces and St. Louis Ram's caps on their heads.

"Fuck the Rams. Let 'em rot in LA," the driver said as he put the bus in park.

***

The exclusive St. Louis Country Club had been founded by George Herbert Walker, a successful businessman and one-time president of the United States Golf Association. He was the great-grandson of Thomas Walker.

The elder Walker was a wealthy British merchant mariner who profitably transported over 15,000 slaves from the coast of Sierra Leone to the British West Indies and the United States before he was beheaded at sea by his crew in 1797. George Herbert Walker was also the maternal grandfather and great-grandfather of the 41st and 43rd Presidents of the United States. George Herbert Walker Bush and George Walker Bush, respectively.

The country club had a long history of racism and anti-Semitism and in its entire existence had admitted one African-American. Reportedly, it had admitted the one black man on the grounds that the club was threatened by the IRS. It could lose its designation as a non-profit organization and therefore its tax-exempt status. Apparently the only thing the rich white members and descendants of former slave owners seemed to hate more than blacks and Jews was paying taxes.

The city of Ladue in 2020, where the club was located and with an average annual household income of over $250,000 made it the wealthiest municipality in the St. Louis region for the 84th consecutive year.

The bus stopped immediately in front of the entrance to the club. The fat driver exited first with his legs already churning at full speed when he hit the ground.

Heyward, seconds earlier, had told him that when they park he should leave the keys, get the heck out of there and, "Oh, by the way, God bless you."

"Let's go. WASP season is open!" Heyward said, referring to the acronym for 'White, Anglo-Saxon and Protestant'. Heyward exited the bus with the same sense of urgency as the driver; but with a destination.

He grabbed the four large bags from underneath the bus and with the help of others unloaded twenty five AK-47 assault rifles, ten CZ Zen automatic sub machine guns, an assortment of hand guns, a dozen Russian-made F1 hand grenades, Molotov cocktails and a GoPro 7, head-mounted video recorder for himself. He donned the GoPro and pressed record.

The first people to see the horde dressed in all white coming at the front doors were three young men working as valets. The look on their faces was that of absolute terror. As soon as the marauders passed the young men, they dropped the keys to the members' cars and ran like hell. They passed the gasping bus driver at the 200-yard mark.

Once inside, Heyward spotted an armed security guard standing near the foyer of the restaurant. The former police officer instinctively drew toward his holstered sidearm. Heyward, even with his mostly-masked face, gave the guard the same look a father gives his son seconds before the kid is about to do something incredibly stupid. That look that says, *"Really? Are you really going to do this?"* The guard understood the look. He had a dad. He also understood Heyward's cock of his head backwards that said, *"Leave now."* The guard obliged. He caught up to and passed the panting bus driver at the 400-yard mark but never came near the young valets.

The murderous group broke into smaller squads and made their way through and around the country club as if they knew exactly where to go. Because they did. The men and women locker rooms and the pool area where moms and kids were enjoying the last days of summer came under full, lethal assault. Mothers attempted in vain to protect their children by shielding them as they got dressed or while in the pool. Their shields didn't work.

The tennis area, where smartly-dressed couples played mixed doubles had no way out of the fenced-in courts and made for easy targets. And lastly, in the club's lounge and restaurant area, the esteemed members froze in such disbelief of what was occurring they remained seated and accepted being murdered, scores at a time.

"Bloody Mary's and Bloody Marty's for everyone," one of the terrorists declared as he entered the bar, shooting.

One squad of men, only three in size, aimed their instruments of terror not at victims but at walls, doorways and ornate paintings of former members. They didn't carry sub-machine guns. Their weapons were cans of black spray paint. Throughout the posh club, they sprayed the letters, 'Crna Ruka'. A calling card of the organization responsible for this day.

Pastor Calvin Heyward didn't personally kill anyone. He'd devised a special assignment for himself. As he doled out the weapons, he strapped a carpenter's belt around his waist with two tools. A small hatchet and a hammer. In the belt's pocket was a box of nails.

As he stumbled around the dead members, he used the hatchet to lop off as many right hands of the victims as he could, given the time allowed. He nailed each of the twenty-five bloody hands to the foyer wall where the photos of club board members had hung moments before.

Heyward couldn't take credit for the gruesome idea. He'd got it after watching season three, episode three of *Game of Thrones* titled "Walk of Punishment". He told the men with the spray paint, "Paint them all black and make sure you write 'Wall of Punishment' above them."

"Hurry up, we only have another minute or two. Everyone gather at the front door. Group photo." Heyward thought it would make an excellent social media post. The murderers dressed in all white with large blotches of fresh, red, WASP blood made for terrific color contrast.

"Smile and raise the Crna Ruka." No one's smile could be seen through the bandanas but each member wore a single, black shooter's glove. To Heyward, the image conjured up memories of the famous photo of track and field stars Tommie Smith and John Carlos who likewise raised black-glove covered hands in protest at the 1968 Mexico City Olympics.

The spiritual retreat of reflection, fellowship, camaraderie and now-bloody massacre took seven minutes. Not six hours, as the bus company planned. The total body count ended up being better than Heyward expected. Almost 300 dead and another 150 severely injured. "We're truly blessed," he told his church members as they re-boarded the bus.

By the time the first City of Ladue Police squad car arrived on site eight minutes after fifty 9-1-1 calls, 275 members of the prestigious club had terminated their lifetime memberships and the building was in flames.

In 2019, the official annual report of the City of Ladue Police Department recorded one murder. The annual report for 2020 would have to include a murder rate 275 times greater than that of 2019, making it the #1 city in America in homicides for the first time ever. Surpassing neighboring St. Louis City, which had held the top spot four years running.

The bus left the St. Louis Country Club one minute before the cops arrived and took a more circuitous return route. It took thirty minutes and carried one less person; the driver. Along the way home, Heyward and his fellow murderers could hear scores of squad cars, ambulances and helicopters from multiple municipalities heading in the direction of the St. Louis Country Club. Surprisingly, none of those first responders passed directly by the bus as it made its way back to the rec complex. It was as if Heyward knew the routes the cops and paramedics would take. That's because he did.

Not surprisingly, a regional response to this type of emergency was a jumbled mess. The St. Louis region is comprised of ninety-six different towns, villages and cities all with their own police departments, fire departments and command, communications, control and information systems protocols.

By the time many of those departments learned to be on the lookout for a charter bus, Heyward and his group had pulled back into their neighborhood in North St. Louis City. As they drove into the parking lot of the rec complex, Heyward tried in desperation to upload the video and group photo of the massacre from his GoPro and phone camera to the social media account of Archibald Moore. The app didn't want to open or sync with the camera.

"What the hell am I doing wrong?" he asked the person next to him. The post was all ready to go with two tag words, 'Crna Ruka'. He checked his signal strength on his phone. It was fine, but the post wouldn't load. He pulled up the speed dial number of a newspaper reporter he'd saved in his phone the day before. He attached the video, but before he could hit send he was interrupted.

"Stop. I told you. Do not use normal text messaging from your phone. You're going to put us on the grid right away. They'll be able to track us."

"I don't give a damn. The world needs to see what we did today." He hit send.

"You're fucking insane."

***

It took hours for authorities to locate any of the five fleeing witnesses. The most important, the bus driver, was found in a grocery store restroom downing a fifth of Jack Daniels three miles from the crime scene. Only the second 5K the bus driver had ever run and while his time was unofficial, he'd set a new personal record of twenty-seven minutes.

With the help of one of the scores of municipal police departments, St. Louis City authorities determined the bus to be operated by Cardinal Charters. When asked to describe the person who rented the bus, the front desk clerk said, "I can't remember, some scrawny little white dude."

Records at the bus company indicated the UOD Islamic Center had ordered the rental with an address of 5000 Gravois Ave, St. Louis. Method of payment, cash and main point of contact: UOD Islamic Center Imam by the name of Nathan Bedford Forrest. Point of contact phone number: 615-350-3309.

Upon calling the number, investigators sat dumbfounded upon hearing, "Thank you for calling the Tennessee State Penitentiary. Please listen carefully to the following menu as many of your options have changed. Early parole for third time offenders isn't one of them."

The address of the Islamic Center led police to an ornate water fountain in a small pocket park in South St. Louis City called a sebilj. This particular sebilj was erected and presented to the city of St. Louis by the president of Bosnia in 2013.

The forensic lab at the St. Louis Police Department found no meaningful evidence. There wasn't a clean fingerprint, hair fiber or morsel of discarded food anywhere to be found on the bus that could be traced to any potential suspects.

The security camera video footage of the shooting clearly showed the attackers entering the club. Their faces could not be identified as the bandanas hung below the eyes and above the noses. Even their recently shaved heads were covered. They were all wearing caps that read St. Louis Rams.

The investigator from the St. Louis Police Department almost said, "Fuck the Rams. Let 'em rot in LA," when he noticed something odd from the security footage. The video he was reviewing was from the outside camera near the front doors. It was the entire group of killers posing for a photo.

"Sergeant, come here. Take a look at this. Notice anything weird?"

"You mean besides all the blood? No, nothing weird."

"Look closely at the person in front, left of center. Look at the shirt. What do you see?"

"Tits. Big ones. What are those doing there?" Other video footage from multiple cameras confirmed the same. Even with the woman's face obstructed, there was no doubt.

It took the rest of the day and well into the night to identify the victims of the St. Louis Country Club massacre. Included in the list of dead was the governor of the State of Missouri and a U.S. Senator who was his guest. There was also a long time member with the last name Walker.

The governor was a rising star in his party and was strongly considered to be the president's next vice-presidential running mate in the upcoming November elections. The most recent vice president had resigned his position in early June after his wife was diagnosed as being terminally ill. The president intended to announce his choice of running mates at the upcoming convention to be held in Charlotte, North Carolina in late August.

The United States Senator had been elected to his position less than two years earlier and was considered a local hero in the St. Louis region. His death was hardest felt among the many local citizens who'd come to love and respect the man immensely. Senator Green, dead at fifty-eight.

The victim named Walker was the direct descendant, nine generations removed, of Thomas Walker, the 18th century slave trader.

The Walker who wasn't beheaded in 1797 but was behanded in 2020 was also chairman of the membership committee for the club. The same Walker who'd denied Pastor Heyward's membership application a year earlier.

The local TV news stations, on location moments after the first responders, reported that no African-Americans or people of Jewish faith had died at the St. Louis Country Club.

FIVE

S t. Louis, Missouri was not the only city that was under direct assault. In fact, two other horrendous attacks killed hundreds in Silicon Valley near San Francisco and in New York on Long Island. All perpetrated by an organization that referred to itself as the Crna Ruka.

Authorities discovered that at least three other planned attacks either went sideways in their execution, were unfortunate enough to be in the right place at the right time or were thwarted by police. In Southern California and on the Eastern Shore of Maryland, nearly forty terrorist members of the Crna Ruka cells died before arriving at their targets.

***

The Los Angeles cell of the Crna Ruka, comprised of nineteen young men, perpetrated their own demise by a simple matter of poor dexterity and typical driving and weather conditions in LA.

"Men, listen up," said the first lieutenant of the LA cell as the group settled into their seats on an old school bus. "We're heading up to the Los Angeles Country Club but that is not the target. The club is closed for renovations and it's to be our rally point only. Don't get distracted if you happen across some contractors or a maintenance worker. Move on fast."

"Group A, you have to double-time up the backside of the golf course to the Playboy Mansion. It's less than a mile away and you need to get there in under ten minutes. There's a Breakfast-with-the-Bunnies fundraiser starting now and the newspaper said over a thousand will be in attendance. Hit as many as you can in five minutes and high tail it back to the bus.

"Group B, same deal. You'll be heading to Rodeo Drive. Less than a mile. It's usually packed with people having their Mimosa brunches, waiting for the shops to open. Pay special attention for any Hollywood stars. Hit them first. No longer than five minutes and then get back to the rally point.

Are we clear? Any questions?"

"I got one," said a young man. "Where the hell is Pastor Smiley? Why isn't that old dude here? He's supposed to be leading us."

"I don't know. He said he'll meet us. Don't worry about him. He's too old to make those runs anyway."

"And what are these for?" a second young man asked, holding up a small, three-ounce vial of blue liquid.

"If you're in the process of getting caught or if you get shot, take that. That's an order. You'll be dead in a minute. Now put on your bandanas and hats."

Like the cell in St. Louis, the LA group all wore white and had shaved their entire bodies, but instead of donning caps that read St. Louis Rams, their hats said Los Angeles Rams.

"Can you believe the Rams went to the Super Bowl last year? Love the Rams. They were rotten in St. Louis," said one young man to another.

Right as the stolen school bus was turning on to the west bound lanes of Interstate 105, or 'the 105' as the locals called it, the bus hit a pot hole and one of the men dropped his vial of poison. The glass shattered and spilled the liquid onto the bus floor. The bus came to a crawl as traffic, even on a Sunday, was horrible.

The liquid was harmless until the inside of the old bus reached eighty degrees. Which it did pretty quickly in the morning heat of August in Los Angeles. This particular liquid has a nasty habit of turning gaseous when it reaches its boiling point of seventy eight degrees. About normal room temperature.

Within a few minutes the three ounces of fluid was now enough gas to fill the entire cabin of the bus. The attackers inhaled the gas and died within a minute. The bus came to a slow, crashing halt on the inside jersey wall, blocking two lanes of traffic. Only adding to the almost daily woes of the universally-feared 105.

No lecherous but generous donors at the Playboy Mansion were harmed. Not a drop of champagne or blood from the thespian shoppers on Rodeo Drive spilled. The city of Los Angeles did not feel the long reach of the Crna Ruka.

As far as the whereabouts of Pastor Smiley? He had every intention of joining the group on August 9th but the night before, he underwent cosmetic surgery and hadn't recovered. He lived up to his name and had a second grin added to his head that ran from one ear to the other, under his chin.

***

"Good evening, bastard," said the thickly-accented man as Pastor Smiley answered his door.

"Please come in," Pastor Smiley said, thinking the old man standing in front of him had said, '*Good evening, pastor,*' How can I help you, sir?"

"I have a gift from my grandson, Charles Mwangi."

"Charles Mwangi the NBA basketball star? How wonderful. But what's the occasion for the gift?"

"He wishes you 'Happy August 9th' a day early." The 81-year old, native-born Kenyan, Simba Mwangi then pulled a Samburu tribal knife from his belt and sliced the guy's throat as wide open as the Cheshire Cat's grin. Simba took a long drink of the man's blood. It tasted good and made the old man feel like a young lion. Which was also good, as Simba means lion in his native language of Swahili. The bastard-pastor Smiley never smiled again.

***

The twenty-one members of the Baltimore Crna Ruka cell fell victim to a series of thunderbolts. The odds of being struck by lightning once are astronomical. The odds of being hit four times in a matter of seconds was beyond mathematical calculations. Or was it?

The deliverer of death was not a mythical Norse god named Thor. This god's name was Buff and she carried her hammer of mortality on the bottom of the United State Air Force's most feared aircraft. The A-10 Thunderbolt.

***

The last unsuccessful cell was from the birthplace of Martin Luther King Jr.; Atlanta, Georgia. Thirty men in another chartered bus headed east to copy-cat the St. Louis attack by hitting Augusta National Golf Club. Their bus was pulled over by the Georgia State Police on the Carl Sanders Highway on a bridge above Lake Oconee. But not by a lone patrol.

In front of them, a UH-1 Huey helicopter with a 20mm machine gun and two multi-rocket pods on each side. Behind them, three armored personnel carriers with a .50 caliber machine gun mounted on the top of each.

The loudspeaker from the helicopter announced, "You have thirty seconds to come out, unarmed, or we will open fire." The bus was empty in twenty seconds. Their protest march ended like many of the peaceful ones conducted by the great Civil Rights leader in the 1960s. Nonviolently, but with a bunch of guys getting locked up.

***

PRESENT DAY

August 9th, 2021 – 10:07am, Russell Senate Building, Washington, DC

"Ms. Gujic, the amount of detail in your presentation is appreciated as it communicates an effective understanding of potential soft spots in our national security strategies. Specifically as it relates to targets of opportunities for terrorists," said the congresswoman from California.

"But your style of interjecting sarcasm, even attempts at humor if you will, feels at odds and not in keeping with the spirit of the tragedy that befell this great nation on August 9th, 2020. Did you and the rest of your commission take into account how this style might be hurtful to many families of the victims?"

"Madam Congresswoman, my team and I took into great account the sensitivities surrounding the events which I now describe to you and the nation. Our conclusion was, and I mean no disrespect, to hell with the sensitivities.

"Our mission today is to provide straight talk insight and if someone's feelings get hurt along the way, well, I can only say, 'grow up'. These are serious issues we are dealing with and to add a little sarcastic and comic flavoring to an otherwise horribly depressing situation is one of the few outlets we have that can help us from being driven nuts. It's cathartic."

"So you find atrocities like racism, suicide, even murder to be funny?"

"Not at all. All three acts you mentioned are either despicable and should be dealt with in the most severe manner possible or, as it relates to suicide, that's tragic. But comedy is situational and when used in proper context, it helps us heal.

"If I were a family member of one of the terrorists who died that day on the LA freeway, I'd weep for them the rest of my life and pray that they may be forgiven by God. If my loved one died while enjoying a swim at the St.

Louis Country Club, no, not funny, nor will it ever be. But, sitting here a year later and thousands of miles away thinking about how ironic it is that those men died for no other reason but for a pothole and a sweaty palm, well, that's funny. When my staff and I finally discovered the facts behind the demise of the terrorists and Pastor Smiley in Los Angeles, we couldn't stop laughing for over an hour."

The congresswoman isn't laughing but millions of Americans at home are. Gujic is 'killing' it.

"Don't worry, Madam Congresswoman, we'll get serious enough again soon."

***

ONE YEAR AGO

August 9th, 2020 – 9am PDT, Menlo Park and San Francisco, California

Gujic was right about the getting-serious-enough part. What occurred 350 miles north of LA and on Long Island in New York was deadly serious. Starting at 10:01am local time, Silicon Valley was looking more like Bekaa Valley in Lebanon in the mid-'80s than home to America's largest tech firms. Meschutt Beach on Long Island, New York, looked like Omaha Beach in the north of France on June 6th, 1944.

A beautiful and temperate California coastline was being attacked by a band of men who left from an origination point in East Oakland. By 10:30 am fire and smoke filled the morning air and was as thick as a mid-winter fog over the San Francisco Bay. Palo Alto and Menlo Park was the destination of one bus of Crna Ruka members.

There was to be a second bus of men with plans to attack the Pacific Heights neighborhood in San Francisco, but that bus never left Oakland. Their leader, Pastor Tyrell George, like his associate to the south, was a no-show. The young men waited a full thirty minutes but after no George, no go. They went home instead.

"I can't believe I shaved off my dreadlocks for this bullshit. It took me ten years to grow them. Ten years!" yelled one of the men from the group that left for home.

Back in Menlo Park, and even with its $30 billion endowment, Stanford University was taking a frontal assault on its storied campus very poorly. Students had yet to report back for classes so it was more the buildings themselves being targeted with homemade fire-bombs and hand grenades. Stanford Memorial Church, Jordan Hall, the Hannah-Honeycomb House, designed by Frank Lloyd Wright and the School of Computer Science were all ablaze.

After ten minutes at Stanford, group one, on their return trip stopped at the headquarters of the social media giant, Facebook, four miles away. They had enough munitions to set afire three of the eighteen buildings that made up the tech campus.

The newest addition to Facebook's massive real estate footprint, a building referred to as MPK 21 was heavily attacked. Even on a Sunday, hundreds of employees were working and were shot on sight by the attackers. The victims received death and destruction delivered to them Amazon Prime-style. Same day and free. In total, 295 employees died. Scores more were injured.

The lead lieutenant of the attack on Silicon Valley tried desperately to log on to his Facebook media account. He was ordered to post the video of the slaughter, but like Pastor Heyward in St. Louis, he couldn't do it. He was literally standing in the center of the social media world and there was no connection.

"They need more tech support...less Feng Shui," he said.

Neither of the Oakland groups planned much of an escape route other than simply walking away as one group did. The group at Facebook didn't spill the poison. They drank it. Dozens of squad cars and three SWAT teams made it to Menlo Park in time to encircle them in the courtyard of Facebook's headquarters. They were all dead within a minute.

Pastor George, unlike Smiley to the south, had no plans whatsoever to attend the attacks. His plan was to get on I-80 and drive as far away to the east as his BMW i8 Roadster could take him before the attacks actually began. Someplace in the middle of nowhere. Maybe Truckee, California or even Winnemucca, Nevada he thought. He got to the first stop sign on his street.

As he rolled through the intersection, a Ford F-650 owned by NBA All Star Mattox Jabbur broadsided his Roadster at forty miles per hour. Jabbur's twin sisters, Maxie and Minnie Jabbur exited the massive truck and added injury to injury by shooting Pastor George five times each. All ten shots coming from twin Glock 9mms. About to leave, Maxie turned and shot the man an eleventh time.

"You always have to one up me, don't you?" Minnie said to Maxie as they left.

***

In Manhattan, New York, authorities received a credible alert of a possible attack on the city to occur on August 9th and likely to come from two different directions. From the east, the Little Egypt neighborhood in Astoria, Queens and from the south, from Brooklyn.

The anonymous tip about the potential attacks referenced an exact time and a reason behind them; 1:01pm, and the thirtieth anniversary of America's involvement in Operation Desert Shield. A buildup of troops, armaments and permanent military bases in the Kingdom of Saudi Arabia after Iraq attacked Kuwait on August 2nd, 1990. Another 9/11 possibly, authorities thought.

But unlike September 11th, 2001, the New York National Guard and the New York City police department stood ready and waiting. The governor and the mayor ordered roadblocks, barricades, bridge closings, helicopter sorties and armored personnel carriers along all major routes on to the island of Manhattan. Attackers could expect to be met with a lethal response if they dared show their faces. They didn't.

It being Manhattan and August, none of the real movers and shakers stayed in town on a Sunday morning. The squad of Crna Ruka killers knew that. The Wizards of Wall Street, Marketing Masters of Madison Avenue and the WeWorkers who don't really work were enjoying their weekend in the Hamptons.

Instead of taking a bus to their targets like in other cities, twenty-three men met at a small private marina in Brooklyn and boarded a fishing charter at 7am. At gunpoint, they instructed the captain and two mates to head to the rich fishing grounds of South Hampton. Sure it was a good six-hour, one-way trip, but they promised to tip well and not to kill him if the captain could run the boat at full throttle. He did as ordered.

The boat entered Shinnecock Bay and headed due north to Meschutt

Beach. The place was overloaded with tourists on the hot summer Sunday and the Crna Ruka men on board the Blue Dolphin fishing boat looked forward to a successful outing.

After a quick docking and leaving two armed men behind to make sure the captain didn't report them, the others made two quick passes up and back down the beach. Killing as they went. The fishing was good and the killers limited out on beachgoers when their guns ran empty. One hundred and ninety three "keepers" were freshly dead and the bay water was now red with the blood of the victims.

This group, unlike the men across the country in San Francisco, planned their escape well. At 1:30pm, a CH-47 Chinook helicopter touched down on the beach. The men jumped on board. They waited a full two minutes for the other men holding the captain and mates hostage, but they never arrived. The helicopter took off without them. Sitting in the co-pilot's seat was their cell leader, Edwin Morton.

Back on board the Blue Dolphin, the two hostage takers figured that an elderly captain was not likely to be armed or courageous enough to do anything stupid. They paid him no mind. What they failed to figure was that a retired thirty-year veteran of the New York City Police Department was very likely to be armed and more than courageous enough. They were unaware that Captain Scott was that. A retired cop. And retired or otherwise, once a cop always a cop.

As the two Crna Ruka members watched the attack from the starboard gunwale, Captain Scott grabbed his .357 magnum from the wheelhouse cabinet and walked up behind the two terrorists. Thirty seconds later, he and his mates were dropping the bodies overboard. As the mates were cleaning the mass of brain matter off the deck, Captain Scott ordered, "Put that in that white bucket. It will make for good chum for the stripers and blue fish on the way home." Once a fisherman, always a fisherman.

At the controls of the Chinook was a New York National Guard Major and a charter member of the New York chapter of the Crna Ruka. The major's original orders were to provide air cover back in Manhattan starting at noon in anticipation of a credible threat that had been called in by an anonymous source. It was the major himself that called it in with specific, but false, details of the attack, locations, strength of numbers, time and so on.

The helicopter left the scene of the mass shootings within two minutes and landed an hour later at a tiny, isolated community called the Woodcrest Bruderhof in Rifton, New York.

Months prior to the attack, Edwin Morton had arranged a three-day cultural exchange program for his men at the modest, almost Amish-like, Christian community in a remote village in the Catskills Mountains.

The welcoming committee from the Bruderhof arranged housing, meals, and fellowship for the visitors from the low-income church in the Bronx. The Elders of the Bruderhof never questioned why they arrived in a $25 million helicopter.

It took a few days for the Bruderhof residents to hear of the attack as they do not watch television, use the internet or cell phones while on the property of their village. By the time they knew something was fishy, the Crna Ruka members had made their way back to New York City.

The plan worked beautifully and Pastor Morton expected to be rewarded greatly by Calvin Heyward – if only he could reach him. The communications plan of using WhatsApp messaging and Facebook to update each other and to post videos of the successful attacks was completely botched. "Never trust a woman to do a man's job," he said to his members.

From the cells that reached their targets on August 9th, 2020, they killed over 750 American citizens. Hundreds more would have certainly been killed if the attacks in Los Angeles, San Francisco, Atlanta and Maryland had been successful.

The day was recorded as the third bloodiest day on American soil, not counting the Civil War. Only September 11th, 2001 and December 7th, 1941 surpassed it.

But the day was not over. It was only 12pm CDT when the attacks took place. There was still twelve hours to go and if Calvin Heyward had calculated correctly, the number of fatalities on August 9th, 2020 would far surpass those other dates in history. Not to mention what he had planned for August 26th, two weeks later.

***

PRESENT DAY

August 9th, 2021 – 10:18am, Russell Senate Building, Washington, DC

"Ms. Gujic, a couple names that are familiar were mentioned regarding events in LA and Oakland. Charles Mwangi and Mattox Jabbur. They were two of the Olympic players killed on the plane by Coach Gibbs. How did they know these pastors who were murdered by their family members and what did they know of the planned attacks?" asks the senator from Georgia.

"As I mentioned in the start of our briefing this morning, I will be covering all the details of the events leading up to August 9th in Part II. That will be later this afternoon. It is out of context to comment on that now. I ask for your patience.

"However, I can tell you that in your home state, the police in Georgia received a tip from well-known and respected members of the Ebenezer Baptist Church in the Sweet Auburn neighborhood of Atlanta. The members were able to provide exact details of the plan and the cops took it at their words to be true and accurate," Gujic said.

"You know that was the church where Martin Luther King, Sr. and Jr. were pastors. Who were these 'well-known' members of one of the most famous churches in the country?"

"The President of the United States, the best player in the National Basketball Association and..."

"And who?"

"The Savage Warthog."

SIX

ONE YEAR AGO

August 9th, 2020 – Warfield Air National Guard Base, Middle River, Maryland

"Wire transfer complete. $2 million. Bank of Haiti. Operation Thunderbolt is a go for August, 26th, 7pm EDT," read the WhatsApp text on Colonel Maretta "Buff" Sowers's phone.

"Thousands of Haitian kids thank you for your kind and generous donation. Your receipt for tax purposes is attached. Now go fuck yourself," the colonel texted back. Not a nice way to talk to such a benevolent donor, but thoughtful to include a receipt.

Colonel Sowers had no intentions of waiting until August 26th for the commencement of Operation Thunderbolt. She was already at her base and had been for hours prepping for her mission. Final inspections of the landing gear, weapons systems, navigational instruments and calculations of fuel requirements. She climbed into the cockpit of an A-10 Thunderbolt, fired up the twin turbofans and taxied to the end of the runway.

The A-10 Thunderbolt as it is officially called is a killer of an aircraft in every way imaginable. Bombs, missiles, rockets and a 30mm cannon rivaled by no other. The pilots that flew the aircraft preferred to call it by its nickname, the Warthog. Thick, mean and able to bring incredible lethality from either high altitude bombings or low altitude cannon strafing. The plane is as ugly as it is lethal, and earned the nickname of the ghastly animal accordingly.

In the case of Colonel Buff Sowers, she matched the temperament and physical characteristics of the airplane perfectly. Ornery, powerfully strong and facial features as hideous as the African savanna pig itself.

Sowers's cantankerous personality developed over decades of being told all the things she couldn't do and then having to prove people wrong. Her strength was the by-product of her championship-level weight-lifting career. And her face, at least the left side, had been sculpted by flaming aviation fuel from a helicopter crash in 2004. The combat injury left her badly scarred with permanently damaged muscles along her jawline.

"Tango 2 1 7, clear for takeoff, runway 33. Turn left, heading 2 0 0. Climb and maintain altitude 1000 feet. Contact BWI ATC on 119.4," said the air traffic controller.

"Roger, Tango 2 1 7, clear for takeoff, runway 33. Turn left, 2 0 0. Climb to one thousand. Tango 2 1 7 out."

"Have a nice flight, Colonel Sowers."

Sowers lifted off and banked hard left to heading 2 0 0. She pulled a couple G's and loved it. The official flight plan she filed with Air Traffic Control put her final destination as Naval Air Station Pax River – Live Firing Range located 100 miles south of Baltimore. She would fly nap-of-the-earth with waypoints at the historic Fort McHenry in Baltimore and the Chesapeake Bay Bridge near Annapolis. Twenty minutes of flight time once reaching her top speed of 400 knots.

At her current speed of 200, Sowers reached her first waypoint – Fort McHenry – in three minutes. As she approached the old fort, she saw a large group of people gathered at its entrance. Not tourists, but protestors. They blocked cars from either entering or exiting the fort's grounds and set them afire.

"It's working," she said to herself.

She also saw a small group of men removing a historic replica of the Star Spangled Banner that had flown gloriously over the fort since 1800. They lit it on fire like the cars. It was a replica of the same flag seen by Francis Scott Key during the War of 1812. Famously, Key wrote a poem about the flag that became the country's national anthem.

In an attempt to acknowledge the crowd, Sowers buzzed the fort at 200 feet and wagged her wings from right to left and back again several times. A friendly pilot's way of saying hello. She looked over her shoulder as she passed. Several rioters were waving hello back to her.

"What nice people," she said.

Back at an altitude of 1000 feet and at 400 knots, she screeched across the runways and terminal building of Thurgood Marshall Baltimore/Washington International Airport. The airport was named after the first African-American Justice of the United States Supreme Court. *How fitting*, she thought. She was about to adjudicate some African-American justice of her own.

A few more miles and there it was. The multi-building complex with fields of satellite and radio antenna pointing in all directions around the globe. The intelligence behemoth known as the National Security Agency (NSA). Sowers went weapons hot-cannon.

The A-10 Warthog is equipped with the GAU 8 Avenger autocannon loaded with 1300, 30mm shells. The firing capacity of the cannon is 3600 rounds per minute. A-10 pilots often joked that the Air Force built a $5 million gun and for fun wrapped a $30 million airplane around it.

She pressed the trigger. The first 30mm High Explosive Incendiary round from the Gatlin-style cannon penetrated the copper-lined window on the ninth floor of the Director of the National Security Agency offices in Building 2A. The sixtieth round was a few meters to the right of the first. It hit the building one second later.

Being that it was a Sunday and the offices of the highest-ranking staff at NSA, none of the head brass were at work. The only fatality was the building and it was decapitated. In total, 500 rounds hit the target, which went up in flames.

Her next pass was on the Domestic Electronic Intelligence Directorate in Building 1B. She had 800 rounds left and she intended to use every one of them. But unlike the headquarters building, this building was staffed on a Sunday with thirty American spies. The word American didn't just indicate their nationality. It also indicated their targets of espionage.

She counted all thirty people running out of 1B moments after they watched the fighter jet light up Building 2A. She fired a quick salvo of sixty rounds over the heads of the fleeing employees. An angry pilot's way of saying, "Mind your own fucking business from now on." By the time her gun was empty, Building 1B was engulfed in more flames than 2A.

She switched her weapons to the six Maverick air-to-ground missiles loaded on her outer wings. Each was targeted for one of the many large arrays of satellite and radio antennae positioned throughout Fort Meade. She scored a direct hit with each missile, destroying a total of fifteen antenna. She was still armed with five GBU-12 laser-guided bombs.

From Fort Meade, Sowers turned southeast. For her bombing run, she needed more altitude and less speed. She climbed to 2000 feet and was crawling at 150 knots. With the US Naval Academy insight, she banked hard left, now on a heading due east along Highway 50 to the Chesapeake Bay Bridge. There they were, as promised. The A-10 Thunderbolt was ready to bring the vengeance of Zeus upon his enemy.

Parked across the east-bound lanes was a Maryland State Highway Patrol car with an officer leaning against it, enjoying a cigarette.

"*Allahu Akbar Ibin Sharmuta*!" (God is great, you son of a bitch!) she screamed as she pressed the release trigger. The bomb missed hitting the cop on the top of the head by three feet.

"Sorry, Dad," the air force pilot said, looking up to the wild blue yonder, "I need to work on that." Fortunately, with a blast radius of a baseball field it was close enough to vaporize both the Statie and his cruiser instantly.

The second bomb was for a fire truck, overstuffed with eighteen fire fighters. The truck was making its way up the first third of the east-bound bridge. She pressed release on Number Two. A direct hit on a moving target going ninety miles per hour.

"Someone call 911!" was the collective last response from the First Responders.

Her third target was to be a single guy standing on the rail at the highest point of the west-bound bridge. A jumper, or least pretending to be. There he was. Right as Sowers pressed the release trigger, the guy pressed the jump trigger. He was no longer a pretender. Off he went from the side of the 200-foot high span.

The fourth bomb caught a second state trooper on the eastern shore side of the bridge running for his life. The bomb didn't hit him on the head either, but caught the wide brim of his Stetson hat. Like his partner on the western side, there wasn't anything left of him, or the Stetson.

Her designated landing area was a few minutes away so she detoured slightly and slowed down even more, almost stall speed. She turned the plane on its side and peered down upon the stage of the Red Eye's Dock Bar at the Kent Island Narrows. It was Bikini Contest Sunday, and she wanted a look.

Buzzing the stage at fifty feet, she was able to see the whole, spectacular show. "Dem some fine lookin' white women," she said in her finest southern, black and lesbian accent as she passed overhead.

She had one bomb left under her wing but was never assigned a fifth target. She came up with one of her own. Turning due south, she headed toward the private summer residence of General Bartholomew Massie. He was the Adjutant General of the Maryland National Guard. Sowers liked to refer to him as "BM".

BM had a shitty habit of teasing Sowers about her sexuality. Even in front of her subordinates, he made hurtful comments he thought were hysterical. Sowers thought they were only moderately funny. One such wise crack came a few months ago. "Colonel, when's the gender reveal party? Are you a boy or a girl?"

There it was, as the satellite photos from the National Geospatial Intelligence Agency indicated it to be. A well-polished 50-foot sailing yacht docked at BM's home with the name 'Maverick' painted on her stern.

"Jackass," Sowers said. "Guy doesn't even know Maverick was a navy man, not air force." A reference to the movie *Top Gun*.

She pressed the trigger for the last time. As she did, she yelled out, "Get ready for the big reveal everyone!"

The bomb exploded on impact.

"It's a giiiirl!"

Prior to take off, Sowers used some of her pre-mission prep time for her and an ordnance tech to remove 95 percent of the bomb's high explosive material. She replaced it with fifty gallons of pink paint. Like Tom Cruise's acting career, the boat was history. It took months to remove the Cradle Rose semi-gloss from what was left of the general's dock and back yard. "I thought I ordered Pigtail Pink," she said.

Sowers touched down and rolled to a stop on a small dirt road on the Eastern Shore. She grabbed a can of spray paint from her flight bag and painted some words on the left front of her aircraft, short of the nose. She took a picture and texted it to her fellow pilots who used to ridicule her about being a lesbian. It read "ALONE, GAY."

Sowers thought for a moment, that words are like mathematics. Rearrange the components and get different results. The homophobic and ignorant fly-boys would never understand the anagram she painted.

She took the first name of one of the most famous aircrafts in United States history and reversed it. The ENOLA GAY. The name of the B-29 Bomber that dropped the first nuclear bomb on the city of Hiroshima, Japan seventy-five years ago this week.

As she stood rubbing the smooth and hairless pig of a plane, a single tear rolled down Sowers's jet-black face. The emotional composition was divided for a love lost on an icy evening on the Baltimore/Washington Parkway and another loss on August 9th, 2020 in the cornfields of the Eastern Shore of Maryland. Buff would never again feel the gentle embrace of her wife who'd been killed in a car accident in 2017, nor jam her muscular, thick torso into the crowded cockpit of a United States Air Force fighter jet.

After kissing her Warthog goodbye, as she'd done with her wife three years ago, Sowers walked a short distance to a crossroad. She stopped at Greenbriar Road outside the town of Madison, Maryland. There she read a historical marker designating the 1820 birth site of a slave by the name of Araminta Ross. Sowers raised her right hand and gave the most proper of military salutes.

Araminta Ross was a slave who'd escaped to Pennsylvania and established a secret network of safe houses located throughout the antebellum south. The purpose of the safe houses was to shelter other runaway slaves on their long and lonely journeys to freedom.

Ross became the chief engineer of the Underground Railroad and her name became immortalized in the 400-year struggle for the African to live free and equal in the United States of America. After Ms. Ross became a free woman, she changed her name to Harriet Tubman.

Buff began her own long and lonely journey, but she wasn't going to Pennsylvania like the slaves Tubman freed. She was going to Pennsylvania Avenue in Washington, DC. 1600 to be exact. And she was going to set herself free.

***

PRESENT DAY

August 9th, 2021 – 12:30pm, Russell Senate Building, Washington, DC

"Madam Chair, we have a recorded question from an Air Force Major stationed in Mildenhall Air Base in the U.K. We'd like to play it for you now and await your response," asked the communications manager in charge of running the open phone lines.

"By all means."

"To all, this is Major Jack Sheehan, F-15 Squadron Commander, Mildenhall. Can the commission provide the final numbers on the loss of civilian life from the attacks on 8/9? Thank you," asked the major.

"This is an emotional question for me to answer, as it is for anyone," said Gujic. "First, I'd like to thank the major for his call. But I challenge the question as it relates to numbers. It's easy for us all to fall into the trap of a numbers game. It helps to put aside the mental and emotional picture that forms if we were to see the faces and hear the stories of those that perished.

"The majority of those killed on August 9th were much like you and me. Ordinary Americans going about their Sunday spending time with family, enjoying the freedoms we often take for granted. We must never forget that.

"That being said, counting those that succumbed to their wounds, 1,153 civilian victims died. In our full report we've included a short remembrance note written by a loved one of each of the victims. I suggest to everyone to read those."

"Excuse me, Miss Gujic, but those numbers are incorrect. You've understated the number of victims by twenty-one lives," said the director of the FBI.

"Yes ma'am, it may appear that way. But they are accurate. You may be including the people killed on the Chesapeake Bay Bridge."

"Why did you not count them?"

"Sorry ma'am, but they were not civilians. They were Crna Ruka."

***

Part II
"Identify: Friend or Foe"

SEVEN

"THE QUINNS - FRIENDS"

June, 1964 – St. Augustine, Florida

"Honey, look at the bullet hole right here," said Martin as he stood outside his vacation rental.

"Can we please leave? This place gives me the creeps," said his wife, Coretta.

"Give me a few weeks. I think LBJ's ready to do a deal. Andy will be here in a couple of days and with some media attention, we will be ready to go."

***

"Last one in is a rotten egg," said the young African-American to his friends, as he belly-flopped into the pool. Within seconds, all four were enjoying a swim on a hot summer day at the Monson Motor Lodge in downtown St. Augustine, Florida.

"Out of the pool now or I'm calling the police," screamed the owner.

"Go ahead and call the cops, see what we care...Marco?"

"Polo."

"Let's see how you like swimming now," said the owner as he poured acid into the pool to encourage the young men and women to leave. The five were dragged out and placed under arrest by the local police.

***

One year shy of its 400th birthday, the city of St. Augustine, Florida was a lightning rod for the Civil Rights movement. Martin Luther King Jr. and Andrew Young joined protestors who made marches through the city protesting Jim Crow era laws. During King's visit, an attempt was made on his life when his guesthouse came under fire.

Five of those protesters jumped into the "whites-only" swimming pool at the Monson Motor Lodge. There, the owner, James Brock, lost his cool and began pouring acid into the water. The images and story made the national news. The next day, President Lyndon Johnson secured enough votes in the Senate to pass the Civil Rights Act of 1964.

Orlando Quinn was born a year later in America's oldest city on November 17th, 1965. His parents chose his name a minute after his birth. His father read the newspaper announcing the Disney Corporation planned to open a new theme park near the city of Orlando, Florida. A few hours' drive south of St. Augustine.

Orlando's father loved the original park in California and had suggested naming his son Disney. His mother spared her son the ridicule that would come with that name. For his middle name? That was different. The hospital filed the official birth certificate at the county courthouse. Orlando Disney Quinn.

Six years later, on the opening day of Disney World, the Quinns waited first in line. Orlando's dad took his wife by the hand, put his son on his shoulders and sprinted to the 'It's a Small World' ride. They rode the attraction endlessly and listened to strange-sounding, foreign words from around the globe that none of them understood.

Back in St. Augustine, Orlando grew up hearing many other strange words as well. Not foreign, but still not understood.

"Dad, why do you keep driving when we've passed miles of perfect beach?" a seven-year old Orlando asked his father one summer outing.

"Well, that part of the beach is for "whites only", son. We go down here to Butler Beach. Where everyone is welcome."

"That makes sense, Dad."

Butler Beach is a strip of coast line near St. Augustine purchased by Frank Butler. Butler, a real estate investor grew tired of being told blacks weren't allowed on any stretch of beach between Daytona and Jacksonville. Over a hundred miles. By purchasing the land, Butler welcomed all to his property regardless of the depth of a person's tan.

By eighteen, Orlando grew tired of a place that didn't make sense. He decided to leave the small town and begin exploring the small world. His favorite subjects in school were foreign languages and geography. He figured the best way to learn more of both was to experience them firsthand.

***

"Join the Army," the recruiter announced at Orlando's senior class assembly. "Travel to foreign lands, learn new languages, eat exotic foods, meet a world of interesting and different people...and then kill them." Other than the killing part, Orlando bought in. He signed up that very day.

Orlando completed Army Basic Combat Training at Ft. Leonard Wood Missouri. While at basic training, he scored excellent results on an exam called the Defense Language Aptitude Battery. From Missouri, he was assigned to study at the Defense Language Institute and Foreign Language Center in Monterey, California where he studied Arabic.

***

January 3rd, 1984 – the Defense Language Institute, Monterey, California

"*Marhaban bi, al Luga al Arabia al Fussha*," ("Welcome to Modern Standard Arabic"), said Orlando's Arabic instructor, Mr. Gharfa.

"*Shukran Usstath*," ("Thank you Professor"), responded the class of eight confused uniformed service members.

The Defense Language Institute (DLI), considered one of the finer language schools in the country, housed and taught students from all five military service branches, the State Department and numerous intelligence agencies.

Orlando first studied Modern Standard Arabic at DLI. The middle-eastern language's equivalent of the Queen's English. Proper, precise and true to its grammatical and phonetic rules. Modern Standard was perfect if Orlando intended to do nothing but listen to radio and television broadcasts for the rest of his career.

After the one-year Modern Standard class, Orlando completed another year learning Egyptian, Syrian and Iraqi dialects. Now he could actually talk to people. At least in Arabic. English was a different story.

***

July 6th, 1984 – The Boom Boom Room, Fillmore District, San Francisco

"Hey, you want to dance?" asked then-Private First Class Orlando Quinn.

"I don't work that way," said Tracy Beckette snidely. "You need to buy me a drink. After we talk for a while, I determine whether I want anything to do with you. Now, back over there with your friends and try again."

Orlando met his future wife during his language studies. He spied her on the dance floor and witnessed a grace and athleticism he'd rarely seen before. While a decent athlete himself, this woman was at a different level.

It wasn't only her ability to keep beat with the unpredictable rhythm of jazz. It was the determination in her eyes to read the band's movements and be one step ahead of them. He attempted to join her on the dance floor. She declined the attempt.

After sending numerous drinks her way and she repeatedly handing the drinks to the women next to her, she finally capitulated. She waved her finger at him to join her. He hurdled two dancers twirling on the dance floor to arrive quickly.

Tracy Quinn knew a thing or two about hurdling. She won the NCAA Women's 100-meter and 400-meter championships while at nearby Stanford University. She went on to win two gold medals at the XXIII Olympiad held in Los Angeles in July of '84.

After the games, they celebrated with a short drive across town for a visit to Disneyland. Orlando couldn't have been happier. Disneyland, like Disney World, also had the 'It's a Small World' ride and they rode it endlessly.

Orlando and Tracy Quinn became husband and wife a year later to an audience of 500 people in Tracy's hometown of Oakland. Four hundred and ninety five sat on her side of the church, five sat on his. A typical wedding.

Orlando accepted an Army bootstrap opportunity to earn both his bachelors and masters in Military Science and Geography as well as his officer's commission from the University of San Francisco. Tracy graduated valedictorian from Stanford and number one in her class with a degree in computer science.

Five years later, their only child, Jayden Fillmore Quinn entered the world at the King Faisal Hospital in Riyadh Saudi Arabia during the elder

Quinn's first combat assignment in the Middle East. Or at least, that's what Jayden's birth certificate said.

***

September, 1991 – Officer's Club, Fort Hood, Texas

"December 21st, 1989. That's my story and I'm sticking to it" Tracy Quinn started telling the other military wives. Tracy was sharing her account of the exact date when she became pregnant with Jayden.

"Given that my big shot Army husband always has some place more important to be than home, it had to be the evening of the 21st during a commercial break of *The Cosby Show*. Between 7:45 and 7:50," she finished. The ladies all erupted in laughter.

Orlando had a different version of Tracy's story but never shared. He recalled a different date his wife became pregnant. The date was never, and if he told his version, it wouldn't get many laughs.

***

August 9th, 1990 – Route 85, the village of Hafar al Batin, Saudi Arabia
Seventy miles south of the Kuwaiti and Iraqi borders

First Lieutenant Orlando Quinn was part of a leading American force deployed to the Middle East in August of 1990 during the buildup to Operation Desert Shield.

The Iraqi Republican Guard invaded Kuwait on August 2nd and demonstrated hostile intent toward the Kingdom of Saudi Arabia. Orlando joined an observation unit along the border comprised of a small squad of American soldiers and Royal Saudi Army officers. It was during his six-week duty assignment when he witnessed the miracle of the birth of his son.

Most fathers, upon seeing their son's faces for the first time claim the event as the happiest and proudest day of their lives. "Manly" men break down and cry at the moment of delivery. First Lieutenant Quinn was no different when it came to the crying part. He wailed when he first looked into his son's eyes. But they weren't tears of joy. They were tears of misery and regret.

If he could relive it, he would wish Jayden had never been born that day, and that he'd never become his father.

***

"Take the shot, Lieutenant." The order crackled over the handset of Quinn's radio.

"Cannot confirm enemy combatants. A small unmarked pickup, two targets, bed is loaded with fuel containers and other supplies, please advise again," said Quinn as he switched his M-16 from safe to semi.

"Iraqi scouts without question. Take the shot. Command indicates your sector is clear of non-combatants. If target of opportunity presents itself, take the shot Goddammit."

"Roger that."

Lieutenant Quinn assumed a prone position on the roof of an out-building in the tiny village. He identified two people as the vehicle stopped within his immediate line of sight. The two tall occupants' silhouettes filled the small frame of the windshield, but the shadows blocked any facial details.

"They must be Republican Guard," said one of the Saudi officers lying next to him.

While not trained as a sniper, he was capable of hitting the targets as they stopped thirty meters away. He would kill the driver first and then set his sights on the passenger. The first shot landed as true as he aimed. The bullet entered the driver's skull and exited the back window. "Kill number one," he whispered in Arabic to the two men.

The target in the passenger seat had but a second to move in the direction of the driver when a second shot shattered the windshield. This one blew through the passenger's neck. Both bodies slumped over the seat. "Kill number two."

As he and the two officers slowly approached the vehicle, weapons at the ready, he detected a faint wailing in Arabic coming from the passenger side. But not Iraqi dialect. Something closer to Egyptian. Certainly not a dialect he expected in the eastern sector of the Saudi desert during a time of conflict. Even more to his surprise, a woman's voice.

"*Istayquith Zowgi, Istayquith Zowgi.*" ("Wake up my husband"). Her husband didn't wake as she begged him to do. He was dead, not asleep. The wife, still alive but life gushing from her neck ounces at a time. Quinn searched her body more closely for weapons.

"No, this can't be. She's pregnant," he said. Probably seven or eight months, he concluded.

"Leave her," the two others said to Quinn in Arabic.

"We can't. We're bringing her with us."

"*Sakhif mejnuun.*" ("Fucking crazy.")

Quickly, the three carried the woman to their vehicle and headed back to their camp. Orlando tried hopelessly to stop the bleeding.

"*Kaifa Hal? Kaifa Hal?*" ("How are you? How are you?)

"*Ana jayyidin jiddan, Ana mumtezzan.*" ("I'm very good, I'm great.") No, she wasn't. Orlando knew she didn't have long to live.

They arrived at the meager medical tent set up to treat minor injuries and heat exhaustion. Not a pregnant woman with a bullet hole in her neck.

"Can you save her, Doc?"

"I can't stop the bleeding. She's going to die. But maybe I can save the baby. I have to cut it out now."

And cut was exactly what the Army medic did. Without formal surgical training, much less on how to perform an emergency C-section, he operated as gingerly as possible. The mother, nearly unconscious, moaned modestly with pain.

"I got him. He's breathing and the cord is stitched off. Get him to Riyadh now."

Orlando took the child and lifted him so the mother could see her son. She said her final words in Arabic, "His father wanted to name him Jayyidin. It means 'good'." She died a few seconds later.

Out the tent and into a chopper, Orlando was cleared to fly to King Faisal hospital in Riyadh. Chief Warrant Officer One Scott Baetzel lifted the aircraft from the ground and opened up the throttle as wide as possible.

"Lieutenant, we're looking at almost two hours flying time. Hold on tight. I'll go as fast as possible."

"How can this be happening? Why the hell were they there?"

The duty assignment was scheduled to be six weeks. Only a week in a combat zone and Quinn had already killed two people. He prayed to God he wouldn't have to again. His prayer was answered for exactly thirty years, until he was ordered to kill again.

His last kill came not while at the rank of lieutenant or general. On

August 9th, 2020, he earned the honorary rank of 'Kaishakunin'. A title bestowed upon him by the very same man he would end up killing.

***

When asked by officials how the American came to be in possession of a newborn baby, Orlando lied. He told them he discovered the child abandoned in a house. None of the officials believed the lie but the country faced more important issues as Iraq aimed its SCUD missiles at the Riyadh and other cities. They let it go.

Every night of his remaining five weeks in Saudi Arabia, he talked for hours with his wife Tracy about something crazy. Should they adopt the baby?

"Are you for real, Orlando? Could this happen?" Tracy begged for it to be possible. They both suspected she was unlikely to ever be able to produce children.

When they were first married, Tracy confessed to her new husband and an Army doctor that while in college she used steroids to train for her track and field competitions. The drugs had left her as barren as the Saudi desert.

"But I don't want to name him Jayyidin. People will make fun of his name because it sounds Arab. I want to name him after my father. Something that sounds more American."

"No. We're going to name him as his father wanted. We'll call him Jayden. Does that sound American enough for you?" asked Orlando.

"OK."

***

How does a man go about adopting a child whose parents he killed? It turned out to be much easier than Lieutenant Quinn thought it would be.

The passports and some letters from relatives retrieved from the vehicle indicated Sudan as the country of origin, not Saudi Arabia. Earlier in July, they'd taken a ferry from Port Sudan to Jeddah. They first traveled to Mecca where they participated in the Islamic ritual of Hajj.

From Mecca, they'd continued on the long drive towards Kuwait City where they planned to live with relatives. They did so even though they did not have the required Kuwaiti resident visas in their passports. They were trying to enter the country illegally.

But then out of nowhere, the war in Kuwait started and the southern borders along Saudi Arabia were closed. Stuck in a deserted village in northern Saudi Arabia, they scrounged for food and water to survive. They possessed neither the money nor gasoline to return to Sudan.

It made sense to Orlando as he considered how tall the mother and father were. They were likely of Dinka tribal descent in Sudan where men often grew to seven feet and women six feet and higher.

Authorities at the hospital informed Orlando that if the child was to be left in an orphanage, he would likely never be adopted. Saudis were not very welcoming toward African Muslims. Less so of those who were Shia and not Sunni. In simpler terms, they said, "You want him? He's yours."

After a few weeks of working the system both in Saudi Arabia and with US officials, Orlando Quinn flew home for a one-week leave with something "good" for his wife. He had all the proper paperwork including a perfectly legal birth certificate issued from King Faisal Hospital on the day of the adoption.

Some of the information written on the document was true. Most of it was lies. Name: Jayden Fillmore Quinn - Truth. Date of Birth: September 24th, 1990 - Lie. Father: Orlando Quinn - Lie. Mother: Tracy Quinn - Lie. Country of Origin: United States of American - Lie. Race: African-American - Truth. The boy was conceived and born of African parents. He was raised and loved by American ones.

One dead and one live father had chosen the name Jayden. Tracy picked the middle name Fillmore after the place she'd met her husband. The horrible realities of war picked the last name: Quinn. Tracy never told her son or anyone the story of how he came to be Jayden Fillmore Quinn.

"It's better if people don't know, right, Orlando?"

"Yes of course, dear, but it's pretty obvious he's not ours. Look how dark his skin is compared to ours. How do you plan on explaining that?"

"His skin is only a shade or two darker. Besides, tell a lie often enough and people will believe."

"I'll try to remember that."

***

From 1990 on, and unlike most American service members, where Orlando Quinn went, so did the family. Even if he paid for housing out of his own pocket. He wanted his wife and son to be as close to his duty assignments as possible so he could sneak away on a one or two day pass to go see them.

While Jayden grew to love the diversity of food, culture and language, Tracy hated it. To her, the isolation, gates and fences at foreign military installations were prisons. As much about keeping her in as it was about keeping the bad guys out.

Jayden's relationship with his father was quite different than most he witnessed as a kid. Orlando took a more hands-off approach with his son. Partly due to his frequent absences, but more so to help Jayden find his own way in life.

That's not to say Orlando didn't impart the guidance that only a father can. Through words sometimes, but mostly through actions. Especially relating to doing one's duty and being willing to make the ultimate sacrifice in the commission of that duty.

Orlando never encouraged his son to follow in his footsteps and join the military. But if Jayden one day decided to do so, he would support him. The general saw the result of far too many young men and now women being put in harm's way and he secretly wanted his son to have nothing to do with war.

In 2020, Jayden would be called upon to defend his country. Not in a desert or mountain range thousands of miles away but in the country of his origin. The one listed on his birth certificate. He would defend America from itself and the call to serve came from the least likely of people. His own father.

EIGHT

"THE PIG AND THE COBRA - FRIENDS"

August, 1987 – Jonesboro High School, Jonesboro, Arkansas

"We pronounce our state Ar-Kan-Saw, Miss Decosimo, not Ar-Kan-Sas," said Mr. Whitt, the senior English teacher. "And if you don't mind, please stop referring to me as Missus Whitt? I'm a man. You should use the word 'mister' as the proper gender salutation."

"S's pronounced as W's. He, she, him, her, Mister, Missus...English is bullshit. Or is it cowshit?"

"No, you're correct. Bullshi...Ahh. Take this note and go to the principal's office," said Whitt, at his end. The W in Whitt pronounced as a W, not an S. Thank goodness.

***

Theresa Aguilar Decosimo was a five-foot one-inch, 100-and-nothing pound Filipina immigrant when she arrived in America at the age of fifteen. Her height and weight held true to those dimensions her entire life.

She was born on June 12th, 1971, in a small village on the island of Palawan, Philippines. June 12th was the 73rd anniversary of that country's independence. A perfect date for her. Theresa was both Filipina and fiercely independent. By the age of ten, she spoke both her native Tagalog and English as it had been taught since kindergarten at her all-girl catholic school. However, she was always challenged to understand the nuances of timing and place with regards to when English profanity was appropriate or not. She defaulted to using it all the time.

She also struggled with gender-specific pronouns and other words denoting gender. The traditional island language of Tagalog, like other

Austronesian languages in the Pacific Islands, did not use them. A bull and cow, hen and rooster and many other gender-specific words in English, are the exact same words in Tagalog. The same was true for people. A person was a person. No "he, she, him or her" were used, as the words didn't exist. That is until the Spanish, and later, Americans, occupied the island nation and introduced them. Many villages in the remote regions never made the change to "Tagnish" or "Taglish" as the combined languages were referred to in the bigger cities.

As an intelligent 14-year old junior in her high school, Theresa had been selected by the Catholic Diocese to participate in an international exchange program that would send her to study in America. Upon hearing of her acceptance into the program, she giddily fantasized about the glamour of Hollywood and New York and the majesty of Washington, DC as she watched on TV. She was assigned to attend a public high school in Arkansas. She did not see the glamour of LA or New York for decades. And by the time of her first visit to DC, its majesty was fading.

***

August, 1988 – Arkansas State University Admissions Office, Jonesboro, Arkansas

"A free college education and see the world," read the sign on the Army ROTC recruiting table.

"What's this all about?" asked a naïve Theresa.

"Arkansas State University and the army will pay for your degree."

"What's the catch? It can't be that easy."

"Complete an application today and if you qualify for the program, it is that easy."

"Can I still go to nursing school?"

"Yes, the Army needs hundreds of nurses. We have hospitals in places like Hawaii, Greece, and the Philippines."

"To hell with the Philippines, I want to go to Greece." Theresa fell for the sales pitch hook, line and suture. She enrolled in both the nursing school and the ROTC program.

It was during Theresa's sophomore year in college, while attending a goodwill basketball game against the United States Military Academy, that Cadet and third-string point guard, Kenneth Gibbs first saw her. He had plenty of time to look. He was riding the pine and found scouting the crowd more interesting than a game he wasn't playing in.

There among the hundreds of blond and brown-haired natives was a woman with jet-black hair, a perfect Pacific Islander complexion, Asian eyes and a feminine physique that caught his attention. During half-time, Gibbs approached her.

"Were you staring at me during the game?" asked Gibbs.

"I wasn't staring at you dumbass."

"Let's start over. Hello, my name is Ken Gibbs. What's your name?"

"Theresa Aguilar Decosimo."

"Well, Theresa Aguilar Decosimo, I was wondering if you will join me and my team for dinner after the game."

"Sorry, but I don't like men."

"Oh? OK."

"Not like that. I like the way some men look and I'm sure there are nice ones. I don't trust them. You only have three things on your mind."

"What's that?"

"Killing each other."

"And?"

"Keeping your bellies full and your balls empty."

"Well, at least join me in filling my belly."

"Ok, but don't ask me about the other thing."

At dinner, Ken did most of the talking. Theresa did most of the staring. Earlier at the game, he'd been correct. She had looked at the man. Tall, perfectly-cropped military hair, an athlete's physique and the most remarkable blue eyes. She very much liked the way this one looked.

Even with the concerns Theresa had with the males of her species, there was a blazing desire inside her to find true love. It burned constantly. If she wasn't studying biology or anatomy, she was consuming romance novels by the dozens.

She knew somewhere out there was her English knight, Viking god, Nubian prince or Celtic warrior. The hero who always returns from battle to proclaim his true, undying love for the faithful woman waiting for him.

Theresa Decosimo settled for a pine-riding, West Point cadet basketball player by the name of Kenneth Gibbs. Three years after meeting each other, Theresa Decosimo and Kenneth Gibbs became husband and wife. Two-hundred-and-seventy days later they became parents.

Theresa was born Catholic and she intended to go out that way. Abstinence before marriage, an unwavering commitment to one person after and mandatory church service on Sundays. While every curse word in the English language was fair game, the phrases "Goddamn it" and "Goddamn you" were strictly prohibited.

Upon hearing it, whether in private or in public, she would spit so much verbal poison at the perpetrator as to leave the victim speechless and paralyzed. Hence, the nickname bestowed upon her by her husband: 'The Cobra'.

Her friends challenged Theresa on her devotion to Catholicism as she also professed to be an atheist. Her response was always the same; "You don't need to believe in God to be a devout Catholic."

After four years of college and nursing school, Theresa Gibbs wasn't in Hawaii, Greece or the Philippines. A few months after giving birth to their daughter Melissa, Theresa was in a Somalian soccer stadium-turned army field hospital. As part of an Army surgical team, she spent her days not sipping ouzo in Santorini, but squeezing life-saving IV bags of blood and medicine into soldiers injured during the siege of Mogadishu in 1993.

It was during those days when Theresa saw how America could be all that it could be. As the wounded rolled into the stadium, it wasn't just American soldiers she was expected to care for, but fighters from many different nations including that of the enemy. Somalians, who hours before were trying to kill Americans, were now having their lives saved by that very same nation.

From those days on, whenever someone began to bash America, the Cobra would once again rise up, spread her hood and direct her poison in the direction of the scoundrel. She believed the possibilities in her new country were endless. Theresa served out her eight years in the Army yet continued to work as a surgical nurse at trauma centers across the country.

Her final nursing job was Director of Nursing at a trauma unit in St. Louis. The family moved there in 2006 after her husband abruptly ended his Army career and was fortunate enough to land the job as head coach at St. Louis University. Kenneth Gibbs, with sixteen years in the Army, was four short of full retirement benefits. Theresa never questioned her husband's decision and was happy to see he was finally out of harm's way.

Coach Gibbs, even with multiple combat assignments, had never lost contact with the game he loved. While in the Army, he spent two years as the assistant coach at West Point during graduate school. After that, no matter where he was stationed, he lobbied for and was often selected to be the post's head coach.

It was surprising how good some of those teams in the military were. As talented as many colleges and in some cases, better. Having 10-or-15-thousand young, athletic and fit men to select a team from didn't hurt.

As a full-time coach at the St. Louis University, Gibbs still found time to lead the army team at Ft Leonard Wood, Missouri. The playing seasons were different and while staying at a summer house at the Lake of the Ozarks, the fort was nearby. He did the job for free. Part of his own commitment to continue to serve.

His teams at St. Louis University never won a national championship but his teams at Ft Leonard Wood were worldwide military champions multiple times. During exhibition games between his college and the fort, the team of soldiers won on many occasions. By 2020, four of those former grunts whom Gibbs coached were legitimate perennial all-stars in the NBA; Darnell Cary, Mattox Jabbur, Alphonso Detandt and Carl Wilson.

NINE

"THE GIBBS AND QUINNS - FRIENDS"

August 9th, 2007 – Vashon High School, St. Louis, Missouri

"Man, don't take that shit from nobody. If he fouls you again, knock him into the bleachers," said Jayden Quinn's high school teammate.

"But then I'm going to get teed up."

"Who gives a damn? This game doesn't mean shit and that brother is knocking the crap out of you. You got three inches and thirty pounds on the dude. Mess that boy up."

It wasn't until 2007, when Jayden Quinn was seventeen, that he experienced his first full taste of the American way of life. It came in the manner of his favorite sport, basketball. His dad was promoted to the position of deputy director and site commander at NGIA in Missouri.

Jayden played his senior year of ball at Vashon High School in St. Louis City. The Vashon Wolverines were a perennial state and national basketball powerhouse with a reputation and playing style as tough as the neighborhood in which it was located.

The Quinns could have sent Jayden to any of the more prestigious private schools located throughout St. Louis but his mother insisted he attend Vashon. Tracy Quinn understood that in order for Jayden to be the best, he needed to play with and compete against tomorrow's stars. Playing at Vashon exposed Jayden to some of the most gifted high school players in the entire country.

It was in one of his first games, when his school was playing a summer friendly against an equally talented team from East St. Louis High, that his mom earned her nickname. The game broke down into a series of fights among the players and parents. Leading the charge for the parents on the Vashon side was none other than Tracy Quinn. After watching her son getting pushed around, she started doing some pushing herself.

It was her bloody and vicious bite on the arm of an opposing father that turned the auditorium into an all-out brawl. Her bravado and gnashing teeth earned her the moniker, "Mama Wolverine" by the booster club. It was the only nickname she ever liked.

His father had a slightly different reason for Jayden attending Vashon. Being the son of an Army general, Jayden had lived his entire life abroad and was not exposed to the unique perspective of growing up African-American. In fact, Jayden had no perspective of being any kind of American.

Jayden's transition to living in the U.S. for the first time was difficult. His social life consisted of gatherings with friends of the family in upscale neighborhoods. His school life consisted of shakedowns, fist-fights, teen pregnancies, drug overdoses and the occasional stabbing or shooting.

His mother, having grown up in East Oakland, was keenly aware of the perils of urban high-school-aged boys. She closely monitored Jayden's academic, athletic and personal life and was quick to reel him in if she felt he was being negatively influenced by others.

As a player, he was athletically more talented than the rest. However, his style of game needed some adjusting as he'd grown up playing a more gentlemanly game in other countries. His senior year season stats were decent but not enough to draw the attention of big-time college recruiters. Twelve months later, those same recruiters were scratching their heads and explaining to their athletic directors how they'd missed such a talent.

It was as a spectator when St. Louis University head coach Kenneth Gibbs first noticed Jayden. The young man was leaner and taller than the other boys but possessed a fluidity in his glide and unparalleled quickness to the basket. Combined with his feather-soft shooting skills and instantaneous transition back to defense, Jayden looked more like a combination of a tall ballet dancer and an Olympic-caliber fencer than a basketball player.

The coach also took note of Jayden's demeanor while on the bench. Quiet, focused, yet on-edge, ready to return to the game. Like a lion, his muscles were taut and ready to attack when asked to do so. A little research and Gibbs discovered the young man wasn't on any of the radar screens of the more prominent basketball powerhouses.

"Mrs. Quinn?" Coach Gibbs asked Tracy.

"Yes."

"Hello, my name is Ken Gibbs and I'm the head coach at St. Louis University down the street. I'd like to talk to you about your son coming to play for our school. Has he considered any of his options yet?"

"What options? Not a single school has made him an offer. He has a private try-out in a few weeks at my alma mater, Stanford. We'll see how that goes. The other schools don't know what they're missing out on."

"Ma'am, I see exactly what they are missing out on. Is it too forward to invite you and your family over to my house for dinner? A chance to talk about our program at SLU."

"Not too forward at all. Yes, and thank you for asking."

***

"The St. Louis University Billikens couldn't be happier with our announcement today that Jayden Quinn, forward from Vashon High School, has accepted our offer to come play at St. Louis University. Jayden, welcome to the team," said Coach Gibbs as he placed a St. Louis University hat on his new recruit's head.

"Thank you, Coach. I'm thrilled for the opportunity to play for the Billikens. One question. What exactly is a Billiken?"

Orlando Quinn was also thrilled. His son would be home and attending a Jesuit university as he did years earlier at the University of San Francisco. Orlando expected his son to add the classics to his list of languages. Latin and Greek. Tracy was not thrilled. She was livid. Stanford University, where Jayden applied and tried out weeks earlier, never returned her phone calls or emails. Jayden received a form letter from the Dean of Admissions claiming something to the effect of, "...unable to verify the academic rigor of your high school achievements."

***

After Jayden started attending St. Louis University, the Quinns and the Gibbs were inseparable. They shared twice a week dinners and family weekends all summer at the Lake of the Ozarks a few hours west of St. Louis.

The first two weeks of August each year were extended stays prior to the start of the school year, and therefore basketball practice.

During Jayden's junior year of college and Melissa Gibbs' senior year in high school, the couples decided instead of renting all the time, to go halves on a lake house. Coach Gibbs was feeling a bit out of sorts, expecting an equal share of the vacation home's expenses based on what the income of a two-star general in the Army to be as compared to that of a Division I basketball coach.

"What's wrong with this country?" Ken complained to Theresa. "I'm making so much more coaching a game than a guy willing to give his life for his country. Our priorities are all screwed up."

"Get the hell over yourself, and this country is just fine. She is more than capable of making up his own mind and if we can see them more often as a result, then I'm happy with that."

"Don't you mean 'he'? 'He' is capable?"

"Oh, whatever. I hate this 'he', 'she' crap. What's the difference?"

***

June 12th, 2011 – Gibbs/Quinns Shared Vacation Home, Lake of the Ozarks, Missouri

"*Masae alkhar sawdeequii alafdal, Kaifa halaka?*" ("Good evening my best friend, how are you?") asked General Orlando Quinn.

"*Ana jayyidin jiddan, wa anta Lewwayi?*" ("I'm very good, and you, General? "), replied Coach Gibbs as the general and his wife entered the kitchen.

"Speak English for shit's sake," Theresa Gibbs ordered.

"The Cobra strikes again! And on his, slash, her birthday no less," Coach Gibbs joked. Reminding the friends of Theresa's trouble with understanding gender pronouns.

The four parents shared so many common values and interests, Theresa casually suggested to Tracy at dinner that if the wives ever switched husbands nothing much would change. The men smiled at each other with sheepish grins. The Cobra spat, "Minds out of the gutter, boys. You're both *baboy*. (Pigs)"

As the general said, the two former army grunts were the best of friends.

Yet Coach Gibbs, whose highest rank was Lt. Colonel, always referred to his best friend as 'General' in any of four different languages. Orlando pleaded with him to call him by his first name but Ken always refused.

"General, to call you anything but that is like calling my dad by his first name. I'm not sure I know what my dad's first name is."

Speaking Arabic was how many conversations started between the general and the coach. They'd both spent years in the Middle East throughout their Army careers. While General Quinn was formally trained, Coach Gibbs was self-taught.

The general spent many days helping Gibbs with his vocabulary, verb conjugations, pronunciation, writing and diction. After a few years as his tutor, Gibbs' language comprehension and use progressed to be as equal to, if not better than, many of the students Quinn studied with while at the Defense Language Institute.

As close as the general and coach were, the wives were closer. The two ladies didn't travel much which meant more time together back home in St. Louis. Tracy adored Theresa's spunky, straight-forward, no-bullshit way of talking. Although 'bullshit' was one of Theresa's favorite words.

Theresa, in turn, loved the common bond of the two families' military service and was in awe of Tracy's intellectual and athletic brilliance. She was equally in awe of Tracy's physical appearance.

While medium in height, Tracy's arms, legs and abs were sinewy. Her face was chiseled, symmetrical and she had an adorable mole right between her eyes. Two or three shades darker than her already dark skin. She also was surprisingly more buxom than Theresa thought an Olympic athlete would be and often teased Tracy about it. Tracy curved in all the right places and made many men turn when passing. In return, Tracy reminded Theresa that she was also quite gifted in the upper regions, and as a joke made t-shirts for them for a breast cancer awareness walk.

The front of the shirt read, "Big or Small, Save Them All." The back read, "The Double T's with the Double D's." It was a joke they both came to regret, as their husbands referred to the two of them in the collective as The Double D's, not the Double T's.

But what impressed Theresa most about Tracy was the woman's intellect. Tracy was the personification of a supercomputer. Her microprocessors seemed to always be running at a speed Theresa could not compute.

It was a wasted talent, Theresa thought. Because of the frequent military moves, Tracy struggled to find consistent work while her husband continued his ascension in rank. Tracy could have owned the tech world if only given the opportunity.

Theresa and Tracy weren't always joking with each other. Their conversations often took on a more serious tone. They discussed the issues of racial stereotypes and how each of them experienced it in similar ways.

Tracy, raised in a poor neighborhood in East Oakland and educated at Stanford confirmed Theresa's belief that anything in America was possible. Tracy's take on America was different. She'd always questioned why she was only able to gain admittance on the basis of an athletic scholarship under Title IX of the Higher Education Act, though academically she proved to be gifted. Sure, she attended a public high school but she aced her advanced classes and scored a perfect 1600 on the SAT's.

Theresa shared stories with Tracy about arriving in the United States only to land in a small town in Arkansas where she determined the Filipina population to be somewhere around one.

While a hit with the boys, the local girls were not so positively attentive. Not taking into account the girls' obvious ignorance of geography, Theresa was called a Gook (Korean/Vietnamese), Chink (Chinese) and Nip (Japanese).

It wasn't until her sophomore year in college when she was denied admittance to a sorority when someone finally got the geography right. The senior sister explained to Theresa that "we don't allow any Flips in our house." Geography notwithstanding, nothing felt right about that comment.

TEN

"THE MONGOOSE AND MAMA WOLVERINE – FOE"

Fifty-seven years ago
August 20th, 1963 – Accra, Ghana, West Africa

"You are aware of my feelings on this big Civil Rights march scheduled for next week," Dr. Du Bois said. "A little less complaining and whining, and a little more dogged work and manly striving, would do us more credit than a thousand civil rights bills or marches," Du Bois said to his friend Kwame Nkrumah. "And another thing. Was there ever a nation on God's fair earth civilized from the bottom upward? Never. It is, ever was, and ever will be from the top downward that culture filters. The talented tenth rises and pulls all that are worth saving up to their vantage ground."

"But you must be in favor of Dr. King's preaching of non-violence and civil disobedience. Are you not?" the president of Ghana asked his Harvard-educated guest.

"I think I've been clear about my position on preaching and for that matter, religion in general. Poppycock. And please, Mr. President, please do not refer to Martin Luther King as 'doctor'. A degree in Theology does not qualify him for the honorific."

August 27th, 1963 was the last day on earth for the 95-year old William Edward Burghardt Du Bois. W.E.B., as he referred to himself and "Dr. Du Bois", he insisted from everyone else. He was the first African-American to receive a doctorate degree after finishing his studies at the University of Berlin and Harvard University. He became a professor of sociology and economics at Atlanta University. He also founded the National Association for the Advancement of Colored People (NAACP) in 1909.

Du Bois died in Accra, Ghana on the west coast of Africa twenty-four hours before the start of Dr. Martin Luther King Jr's. Freedom March on Washington, DC and his famous "I have a dream" speech.

While DuBois' legacy became legendary in African-American history, he also proved to be controversial for his writing of several studies critical yet insightful of the sociology of African-American religious organizations.

One study titled "The Negro Church" was published in 1903 and while critical of faith-based organizations in many ways, shone light on the bonding effect black preachers had on communities of color. Particularly those communities in large urban areas throughout the south and Midwest.

Specifically, DuBois wrote, "The black preacher is the most unique personality developed by the Negro on American soil. A man who found function as the 'healer of the sick', the 'interpreter of the unknown', 'the supernatural avenger of the wrong' and the 'one who could most aptly express the longing disappointment and resentment of a stolen and oppressed people.'"

The African-American church is comprised of seven major protestant denominations. While similar in size and culture, slight variations in biblical interpretations and applications exist. The Civil Rights leader Martin Luther King, Jr. was Baptist and his message of non-violent protests and civil disobedience rang true with many of his faith. There were many still that believed otherwise.

***

Thirty-two years ago
November 11th, 1988 – Memphis, Tennessee

"Can I help you, officer? What did I do wrong?" said Archie Heyward as he rolled down the window.

"You didn't come to a full stop at that intersection back there. I need to see your license and registration please," the police officer requested. "What is that I smell? Have you been smoking marijuana?"

"Ah, no sir. I picked the car up from the shop twenty minutes ago," Heyward lied, trying to devise a reasonable alibi for the rancid odor of home-grown pot.

"Son, step out of the car please."

***

Archibald Heyward was born in 1970 and raised by his father in the Shelby Forest neighborhood of Memphis, Tennessee. Shelby Forest, with a crime rate ten times the national average, was another example of the urban decay that had infected many of America's inner cities for decades.

His dad named him Archibald at birth after his favorite boxer, a famous light-heavyweight champion named Archibald Moore. He even called his young son by the boxer's nickname: "The Mongoose".

As a kid playing football, Heyward would bury an opponent into the ground and stand over him saying, "Fear the Mongoose". The opposing team's coach, while clearing the dirt from his young player's face-mask, asked the referees, "Aren't mongooses five pound African rodents, not 200-pound sixth graders?"

By his eighteenth birthday, Heyward had developed into a man among boys. He measured six-feet-five-inches tall and weighed 270 pounds. Tall, thick, muscular and surprisingly athletic given his size. His physique was a perfect combination for either a champion boxer or a dominant football player and Heyward didn't disappoint. He became both. It wasn't just his body that was suited for violence.

Excited about taking his game to the next level and celebrating his team's recent city championship, Heyward was responsible for picking up the night's party supplies for the team. After being pulled over for rolling through a stop sign at three miles per hour, a cop found three ounces of marijuana in his glove-box. He was arrested, arraigned and assigned a public defender. Heyward decided to skip a trial and pleaded guilty to the charge of conspiracy to distribute a controlled substance.

His court-appointed attorney was apparently unprepared to address the severity of the charges. Heyward was unprepared as well. How could he be? After eleven-and-a-half years in the Greater Memphis School District education system, Archie Heyward could not read. He was sentenced to four years at the Tennessee State Penitentiary in Nashville.

The date of the arrest was first in a long string of incidents of bad timing for Heyward. The day before getting busted, he and his dad celebrated his eighteenth birthday. A day later, Heyward was old enough to be tried as an adult.

***

December 24th, 1990 – Tennessee State Penitentiary, Nashville, Tennessee

"What the heck is that?" Heyward asked himself as a single coin rolled across the concrete floor of his prison cell. He picked it up. An engraving with a bald eagle and a burning cross was on the front of the coin. "And what do these letters 'SYMWAO' and 'MIAFA' mean?"

"It means, 'Spend Your Money with Americans Only' and 'My Interests Are for America'," said one of the six white-hooded guys standing at the entrance of Heyward's open prison cell.

Just seventy-five miles south of Nashville is the small town of Pulaski, Tennessee. Few Americans know about the historical significance of this town, but a gang of fifty white prisoners of the Tennessee State Penitentiary did. Exactly 125 years earlier, on December 24th, 1865, the first Chapter of White Knights of the Ku Klux Klan was founded there. General Nathan Bedford Forrest, a former slave owner and hero of the confederacy was the organization's first Grand Wizard.

On the 125th anniversary, six of those fifty wizards entered the cell of Archie Heyward with the intention of celebrating in the savage tradition of the KKK. Heyward, not feeling as festive as the men surrounding his bunk, took out three of them with fist-blows so fierce, one was dead before hitting the ground.

Heyward succumbed to the attack after strikes to his head from the remaining three Klansmen. They owned the tactical advantage of brass knuckles and a baseball bat. Heyward spent two months in the prison infirmary due to his injuries and another nine years in prison when a voluntary manslaughter conviction was tacked onto his sentence.

During his eleven years, Heyward pursued two areas of study and two personal hobbies he enjoyed more than others. Reading and the bible became his academic pursuits. He was prolific at the first and gifted at citing passages and interpretations from the second.

By the time he left prison, he memorized every chapter and verse in both testaments with a preference to the older book. He and five other inmates who'd become his friends formed a bible study group with Heyward as their main preacher.

When Heyward wasn't reading or preaching, he was learning the art of persuasion from his favorite televangelists and working on his boxing skills. To Heyward, the two skills were not mutually exclusive. He learned that if a preacher couldn't con money out of his congregation with his tongue, a boxer could beat it out of them with his fists.

In 1988, Archie Heyward entered prison as a frightened, confused and illiterate boy. In 1999, he exited not only with a new-found sense of confidence and purpose and a liquid-smooth tongue, but also with a new name. Calvin Heyward.

He chose the new first name 'Calvin' as he studied everything written by the famous 16th Century French theologian and pastor named John Calvin. Heyward read that Martin Luther King Jr. was originally named Michael King, Jr. But after Daddy King visited Germany in 1934, the father of the civil rights leader changed both his and his son's name to Martin Luther. A tribute to the leader of the Protestant Reformation. Heyward did the same as a tribute to the other leader of the Reformation but decided to take the man's last name for his first.

***

September 12th, 1999 – Trans World Dome, St. Louis, Missouri

"The Rams are going to be the real deal this year, don't you think?" said Calvin Heyward to the three young men he'd invited to be his guests at the opening game of the 1999 season.

"No doubt. Maybe even the Super Bowl. Funny how good they are. They were rotten in LA," one of the 18-year olds replied.

That opening day game was the first official service of the new Bi-State Unified Church of God in St. Louis. Heyward had moved to the Gateway to the West upon his release with two purposes in mind. Grow his following and grow his bank account statements.

He started small, with four young men he met playing pick-up basketball at the local YMCA. The five of them met almost daily at Crown Candy Kitchen on the north side of town where Heyward enticed the men with promises of spiritual salvation, burgers and chocolate shakes. After witnessing the volume of cash the famous little restaurant was pulling in, Heyward offered his guys a better incentive than milkshakes.

"Take this," instructed Heyward as he put the loaded gun into the hand of one of his young followers. "They close at eight. The cops who always eat there will be gone. Go through the back service door and ask the owner for a donation. Make sure he donates everything."

That one gift produced over four grand. How generous of the café owner. Heyward and his men never went to Crown Candy Kitchen again. It was a shame as the place made the best sandwiches and shakes in town.

And so it went as Heyward grew his church. As his former prison prayer group gained their releases from the Tennessee State Pen, he assisted them in setting up their own operations in select cities. He helped file the required paperwork to become an official non-profit, as defined by the Internal Revenue Service.

The requirements for becoming a branch leader was first to sign the church's constitution and oath of allegiance. After that, Heyward expected each of his five pastors to build a following of congregants loyal to the same. By 2010, the Unified Church of God had operations in Atlanta, Baltimore, Los Angeles, New York, San Francisco and St. Louis.

He also required each pastor to establish methods of financing the church's activities. Heyward's list of fund-raising efforts included the familiar. Passing the collection plate, weekly bake sales and neighborhood car washes.

He added a few more suggestions; drug-dealing, prostitution, armed robbery, money-laundering and embezzlement. The latter part of the list proved much more successful than the former. He and the group of pastors went on to create a unique level of giving called the "Truly Blessed". For a tax-deductible gift starting at $25,000, the Unified Church of God added contract killings.

Technically, any type of quid pro quo for a charitable donation is frowned upon by the Internal Revenue Service according to the rules written under IRS Section 501(C) 3. "Murder for Hire" most certainly fell under the definition of quid pro quo. Heyward, by way of a brilliant accountant and attorney found ways around the tax law. And hundreds of other laws.

Within a short time, all six locations of Heyward's operation were pulling in serious cash and all tax-free. Anonymous donors giving tens of thousands. The money was laundered through deposits into the church's accounts. The money flowed back out to the church leaders in the way of homes, cars, international travel and in some cases, legitimate businesses.

It was silly, as many in his following reminded him, that Heyward had started the UCG in St. Louis because of a boxer and a football team; more accurately, a single player. St. Louis was the childhood home of the famous boxer Heyward was originally named after; Archie, "the Mongoose" Moore. It was also the current home to the St. Louis Rams professional football team.

Heyward grew up a lifetime fan of the Los Angeles Rams, then the St. Louis Rams, and once again back to Los Angeles. It wasn't the uniforms that Heyward loved. It was the game-changing defensive lineman by the name of Roosevelt Greer. More affectionately called Rosie.

To Heyward, Rosie was him and he was Rosie, with a twist of good and bad luck added to each respectively. Both born of a poor family in the south, each a mountain of a human, a bone-breaking football player and then a minister, spreading the word. Plus there was something about the name. To Heyward, the name 'Rosie' evoked feelings of kindness, love and beauty. Feelings he didn't experience very often, growing up in a violent Memphis neighborhood.

When deciding where to stake his cross, build a following and launch a criminal enterprise, Heyward thought, *why not St. Louis?* By the year 2011, his church had grown to over 400 legitimate, god-fearing members. His crime ring grew to over fifty.

He also grew himself. He was even more of a mountain of a man. By the age of 41, he weighed in at 300 pounds. He kept himself well-groomed, muscular and fit all through the years. A by-product of working out every day.

***

November 2nd, 2011 – Chaifetz Arena, St. Louis University, St. Louis, Missouri

"Squish your tits together and lift your back leg," Calvin Heyward panted to a drunk Tracy Quinn as he tried to remove her overstuffed bra and undersized jeans.

"My tits are too hard and I don't have a back leg."

"Then lift your front one."

"Lay down. I'll do it."

***

The first time Tracy Quinn formally met Calvin Heyward was at her son's first basketball game of the 2011 season. The St. Louis University Billikens were beating up on some unheard of university called Cardinal Stritch.

Heyward sat next to Tracy in the near-empty arena as he recognized her from the numerous times he'd attended Vashon High School games in Jayden's earlier years. He liked what he saw and put his smooth-talking tongue and a smuggled fifth of bourbon to work. Likewise, Tracy recognized Heyward. How could someone not recognize a man of his size?

By halftime, the two newly-acquainted and intoxicated Billiken fans were in the back of Heyward's car where he put his smooth tongue to work in other ways. Calvin Heyward was scoring more outside the arena than poor Cardinal Stritch University was scoring inside.

Tracy convinced herself there was nothing wrong with some old-fashioned fun. That is, if tearing at Heyward's flesh like a "mama wolverine" could be considered old-fashioned. It certainly was fun.

The Billikens went on to have their best season in decades due in large part to having one of the nation's best players as the team's starting forward. Jayden Quinn. Tracy Quinn went on to have the best sex she'd had in decades. Due in large part to having a six-foot-five, 300-pound muscle-head as her lover. Calvin Heyward.

Tracy was enraptured by the pleasure of spontaneity and brute love-making for the first time in twenty years. Tracy's infidelity was out of character with who she thought herself to be, but her insatiable desires for the physicality of making love were not.

Once an athlete herself, and at the highest competitive level, Tracy needed her body to be tested, engaged, pushed to the limit and ultimately left satisfied and exhausted. At her age, she no longer could compete at the Olympic level but she could put her finely-tuned body to use in other ways.

Over the many years, Tracy's willingness to uproot Jayden and move to countries in or near where her husband was deployed was because she needed Orlando in the most physical of ways.

But the call of duty was a much stronger urge for Orlando. No matter where or when his country called upon him, he was there. In all of his assignments, he was never once ordered to go. He raised his hand for any mission, no matter how remote or dangerous.

The result was years of being absent from the family while Tracy raised their son. Tracy thought Orlando would be home more by taking the full-time assignment as the deputy director of the NGIA in St. Louis, but she was wrong. He averaged over 200 days a year on the road.

Calvin Heyward became a ready and willing resource for Tracy's desires. He was local, available and her physical equal. She succumbed to his body and his blessedness. She was again in love but in a manner she'd never experienced with her husband. Tracy found religion. It was none of the seven major African-American denominations. It was Calvin Heyward.

Unlike Tracy's new-found salvation, Heyward had no such reciprocal feelings. He was, after all, pastor to a congregation that was seventy-five percent women. Many of them young and without a man in their lives. Being a minister to such a heavily unbalanced population made for a target-rich environment.

Over the years he'd lost track of the number of salvation-seeking, single mothers he'd bedded and blessed. Or was it the other way around? He'd also lost track of the number of children he'd sired. But by 2011, there was an unusually high number of Calvins and Calvinas around the neighborhood.

But Tracy did have something Calvin wanted, and it wasn't her body. She was the wife of a two-star general and site commander of one of the country's most valuable intelligence agencies. An agency that could provide real-time imagery, emergency management response conditions and detailed assessments of national assets deemed vulnerable to criminal or hostile malfeasance.

Most importantly, NGIA provided up-to-the-minute analysis of local police department command, control, computers, communications and intelligence systems (C4I) protocols. All helpful when running a national crime organization such as the Unified Church of God was becoming. It only took him three months for the first "big ask."

"Tracy, I need maps. Detailed maps and the analyses that go with them."

Calvin Heyward asked Tracy Quinn to join him in becoming a felon. His logic for being so brazen in his request? If she did this one thing, he had her for life. If she refused, by his oath to his church, he'd kill her. Tracy was quick and unwavering in her response.

"Yes, I have access."

Besides her body, Tracy shared stories with Calvin of a game she and her husband played on a regular basis over their years of marriage. A game designed not for fun but for concern for the security of a nation.

Throughout the general's career he maintained a Top Secret-Sensitive Compartmented Information security clearance. The highest level of clearance with the broadest range of access to classified information. He was well aware of Tracy's technical prowess in the world of computers and assigned her a recurring task.

"Hack it," Orlando had commanded her.

"What are you talking about?"

"I want you to try to break into our systems. I want to know our degree of vulnerability. The way I figure it, if a stay-at-home housewife with a low-end retail computer can hack into our sensitive systems, so can the enemy."

"Don't you have people for that?" Indeed the general did.

His first order of business when he took the assignment at NGIA was to hire two equally qualified teams of the brightest programmers he could find. Some of the programmers were world-renowned computer hackers in their own right.

The jobs of these two teams changed every month. Team One: Design the next version of the anti-viral and firewall software upgrade of the NGIA's systems to such a level of security that Team Two could not break it. At the end of the month, switch roles. Team One then attempted the hacking. Team Two; the upgrades. The whole process was no different than top-flight athletes competing against each other in practice, thus making them better at how they performed come game time.

Simultaneously, and secretly from his two teams, was a third team with only one player. Tracy Quinn. The general gave her network access to a sandbox copy of the database software. Something Tracy could play in but without the sensitive and classified material of the live version. Allowing her into the sand box was still a major violation of multiple regulations and federal laws, but the general was more concerned with national security than a few outdated rules.

Could Tracy break into the system regardless of which of the two teams upgraded the software? Her batting average – 1.000. Every single time. Tracy was able to get in and, in some cases, in less than a few days. Once inside the firewall, planting viruses was easy. She was that talented on a computer.

In the entirety of his career, Orlando never met anyone as naturally gifted as his wife. She transformed her athletic ability on a three-dimensional track to a two-dimensional field called a computer screen. She was winning gold medal after gold medal.

To finish the game, Tracy provided the precise computer code, line by line that she wrote to penetrate and infect the secure systems of the National Geospatial Intelligence Agency.

But in 2012, Tracy Quinn became a free-agent, switched teams and was playing for someone else. She was named the Chief Information Officer of an organization called the Unified Church of God. She was unaware she carried such an esteemed title and the job came with no salary. Her only compensation was eight more years of infidelity. She accepted the position whole-heartedly and without a provision from her boss for resignation, only termination.

***

PRESENT DAY

August 9th, 2021 – 11:28am, Russell Senate Office Building, Washington, DC

"Miss Gujic, are we supposed to believe a stay-at-home mom was some sort of computer genius? I think that is hogwash," comments the twenty-term congressman from Arkansas who is chairman of the Senate Cyber Security and Emerging Threats subcommittee.

"Our nation spends billions on cyber security and we hire some of the best and brightest minds out there. Are you sure Mrs. Quinn didn't have additional hackers working with her during this supposed game she played with her husband?" asks the 76-year old congressman responsible for being knowledgeable and up to speed on the latest cyber security technology.

"Sir, do you know of an organization called the International Subversives?"

"No. Should I?"

"As the chairman of your committee I would have thought so. The

International Subversives, as sinister as that name sounds, started with a teenager living in a remote town in Australia. That boy, working from his home PC and with limited internet access successfully hacked into and embedded computer viruses into some of the most sophisticated networks in the world.

"The quiet, blond-haired, blue-eyed 16-year old became one of the world's most notorious hackers. He even hacked into the systems at the National Security Agency and the Central Intelligence Agency as recently as five years ago. Do you remember who I'm speaking of, Mr. Chairman?" Gujic asked.

"Of course, that son of a bitch Julian Assange." At least the old man kept up on some of the tech world.

"Well, Mr. Chairman, the only difference between Mr. Assange and Mrs. Quinn was that she was a better hacker than he was. During the many years of being at home while her husband was elsewhere, she and her son Jayden became champions of the computer, as they were in sport. They didn't learn foreign languages. They were fluent to the highest levels in computer languages. Dozens of them."

"So, Tracy Quinn was responsible for the computer viruses that disabled our intelligence community network and brought down the social media giant Facebook?"

"Well, I'll cover that later in this briefing but if you need to know the answer now? Yes and no. Tracy Quinn's fingerprint and the code she wrote infected our networks and Facebook but it wasn't Tracy Quinn who planted the virus.

"In fact, the entire crime organization relied on those systems being accessible. And Tracy was under orders from Heyward to see that they were. It was their means of real-time intelligence and communication. The actual person responsible for disabling those systems was close to her but was operating under orders of his own."

"Who was that, Ms. Gujic, and who issued those orders?"

"Her husband of course. And the man issuing the orders? Someone known only by his code name. Apis," Gujic finished.

ELEVEN

"THE SENIOR AND THE FRESHMAN - FRIENDS"

December 26th, 2011 – Quinn/Gibbs vacation home, Lake of the Ozarks, Missouri

"So now you notice me. What about years ago, when I had the biggest crush on you my freshman year in high school?" Melissa Gibbs said to Jayden Quinn.

"You were fourteen, I was seventeen. There are laws against that kind of thing."

"Well some laws are worth breaking."

Nine years later, Jayden would find out how true that statement was.

***

Jayden first met his future fiancée, Melissa, in 2008, his senior year in high school. At the end of a game, Coach Gibbs introduced himself and his daughter to Jayden when they were watching him as a potential recruit. Three years later, Jayden confessed that he had no recollection of that first meeting, and why would he? She was a freshman and three years younger. Seniors never looked at freshmen. At least until college.

Throughout his playing years at St. Louis University, Jayden and the entire team attended twice a week dinners at the Gibbs' home. It was at these regular dinners that the star player of the Billikens once again met Melissa Gibbs, but this time he remembered. She was about to become the love of his life.

By the end of her senior year in high school had Melissa blossomed into a strikingly beautiful young woman. Black-as-night hair, olive-colored skin and an hourglass figure from her mom. Rounded eyes, with the same deep blue shade he remembered of the Mediterranean Sea, from her dad.

It was also that same year that the two mothers began noticing subtle hints of trouble. Mothers have a sense of their children's emotions most fathers, especially absent ones, never pick up on.

At the regular Quinn and Gibbs family get-togethers and weekends in the Ozarks, Theresa and Tracy picked up on the glances, subtle smiles and time spent watching sunsets together on the back deck. Jayden and Melissa were falling in love. It was less than a year later, during the summer between Melissa's high school graduation and the start of Jayden's senior year in college that the relationship became family-wide knowledge.

"Wait, what?" a clueless father asked his wife. "How in God's name did this happen?"

"You're such a dumbass." Theresa said. "What did you think would happen? Take two young horny kids and put them in constant and intimate proximity of each other."

"Has she...?"

"Stop. He better not have."

"Don't you mean she better not have?"

"Oh, whatever. Fucking English pronouns."

Theresa knew they had not. Melissa and Theresa shared the same daughter-and-mother relationship that millions before them had. Melissa was in love with Jayden and was tempted by their mutual desire to be with each other. How could she continue to resist? Theresa's advice to her daughter was always the same. The advice was both treacherous and metaphorically ridiculous.

"Honey, think of sex as an ice cream cone with three giant scoops of your favorite flavor on top," Theresa said. "While it can be shared by two, it can only be held by one. You. If you decide to share it with any stranger that happens to take an interest, then eww, disgusting. Don't do that.

"However, if you find the one person you trust and want to share the joy, then ask yourself, when do we dig in? The answer is in the ice cream itself. When you finally take it out of that freezer, those first few bites will be moments of wonder.

"But as time passes, the ice cream begins to slowly soften, and while the flavor is exactly as it was when you started, the appreciation begins to wane.

You may begin to be bored with it. Upon those last few bites, the two of you will recognize its coming to an end and once again, take complete and utter joy in its deliciousness. My point Melissa is that the longer you can wait, the more pleasure you will have. Does that make sense?"

"Not at all Mom," Melissa's eyes glazed over but the constant repetition of the lesson over her years of adolescence and early adulthood had the desired effect. She would not take out that frozen cone until her and Jayden committed to each other for the rest of their lives.

Upon hearing the ice cream story from her mom for the hundredth time, she felt comfortable enough to ask her, "Mom, where are you and Dad on the ice cream cone?"

"We're finishing the second scoop and your father, the baboy, keeps slobbering it all over my hands." They laughed and loved as only a mother and a daughter can.

Just across the street at the Quinn home similar conversations were being had between Jayden and his father. Even now, as a soon-to-be senior in college, he'd never experienced a woman to her fullest. Come to think of it, he hadn't experienced a woman at all. He was utterly clueless.

With the constant moving to foreign countries the opportunity had never presented itself. Oh, he heard many courtside and locker room conversations, starting in his senior year at Vashon, but he also saw the depressing outcomes of teenage and college promiscuity.

Teenage girls and young women hamstrung with newborn babies and no support to finish their education, and the fathers, too young and idiotic to understand the life-long and devastating effects of their behavior. Jayden decided he wanted no part of it and would wait until he found his true love. With his true love now squarely in his sights, he asked his dad, "Why should we have to wait until marriage? We both love each other hopelessly and plan on being together forever."

Two-star General Orlando Quinn, leader of warriors into mortal combat, protector of his nation's freedom, proficient linguist in seven different languages took a deep breath and said, "Son, think of sex as an ice cream cone...." Theresa Gibbs had taken the time to educate the otherwise-clueless general on the appropriate response at one of their many couple's dinners.

Tracy Quinn took a different position towards her son's relationship with her best friend's daughter. She didn't like it. Not one bit. It wasn't part of her plan.

"Jayden, think about what you're doing. You have one more year of college ball and the world is going to open up to you. The sports media is already talking about your draft prospects. Number one or two for sure. Why do you have to rush into things?

"Once you hit the NBA, your life is going to be radically different. Instant fame, instant fortune. So many possibilities, stardom. Now how is Melissa going to be able to handle that? I'm thinking about her well-being." Tracy was lying once again and was now a master at it.

"Let me ask you something, Mom. Where is the on and off button for a person's feelings? I can't help how I feel. I'm not stupid. I know how some athletes behave. Babies with four or five different women. All these women serving themselves up to players so they can touch fame. Melissa and I are not like that."

"I thought the exact same thing when I married your father. When I won my gold medals at the Olympics, I had so many opportunities that I passed up on. Sponsorships, commercials, first class international travel. Maybe long-term fame. I threw it all away because of young, foolish love."

"And how is that love today, Mom, still foolish?"

***

June 28th, 2012 – National Basketball Association Draft, Newark, New Jersey

"The number one overall pick for the 2012 NBA draft, from St. Louis University, please join me in congratulating Jayden Quinn," read the NBA commissioner.

Jayden, his mom, dad, as well as the entire Gibbs family were in attendance for this monumental event in Jayden's life. His mom was right. His life was changed and almost overnight. Everywhere he went there seemed to be a camera, an audience and an abundance of women present.

Even back in St. Louis, where professional basketball is not a sport on many people's minds, he was asked to pose for photo ops, conduct interviews and make himself available for sponsorships, endorsements and social events.

He did his best to maintain a balanced lifestyle but his mom was a public relations machine. She managed his schedule, his travel and most importantly his time with Melissa. Which wasn't much. Within a short time, Jayden found a way around his mother's roadblocks. He decided to take Melissa with him.

Melissa changed her enrollment and major at Washington University to their newly-offered online degree program. Everywhere Jayden went for away games, Melissa was on a flight right behind him. Tracy was furious, and let Orlando know it.

"This is all her doing. She won't let him be himself. She's destroying his career opportunities," she said to her husband.

"Tracy, I'm going to say this as nicely as possible and I hope it doesn't come out the wrong way. Shut the hell up and leave them alone! Who do you think you are to interfere with their lives? I've listened to your complaining for over a year and I'm done with it. Oh, sorry honey. Did that come out the wrong way?"

***

Tracy Quinn thought it did come out the wrong way and she wasn't going to stand for it. She was prepared to end the romance by whatever means necessary. Mama Wolverine was gnashing her teeth again, and hiding out in her lair waiting for the right time to attack.

***

July 5th, 2012 – Gibbs/Quinn Shared Family Home, Lake of the Ozarks, Missouri

"I think I caught the flu or something yesterday. I feel like shit," Theresa confided in Tracy as the two prepared breakfast.

"Maybe the Irish flu. Have you never been hungover before?"

"Maybe on my wedding night. But I thought that was a side effect of..." Theresa whispered, "S. E. X."

"So wait, every bad word in the dictionary is OK to yell out but you whisper S. E. X.?"

The two friends laughed.

It was during the 4th of July festivities at the lake when the most astounding of coincidences about their husbands' pasts came to light. After completing dinner and on their fifth bottle of wine, the couples retired to the back deck to enjoy the shimmering sunset over the lake.

They were all talking about how fortunate they were in life and how blessed they were to have such great friends and beautiful children. Then the conversation turned more serious.

"Tell us some war stories, boys. Ken's never shared a single moment about her combat tours in Bosnia or the Middle East," Theresa said with a slight wine-induced slur. "All these years together and still keeping secrets. I told you men couldn't be trusted."

Tracy followed, "I think you mean 'his combat tours' but whatever. Same goes for the general here. Both of them have those Purple Heart medals but I've never heard how either one of them earned it. Orlando threw away the citation that came with it. C'mon Ken, fess up."

"So, I'm at Al Asad Air Base, Iraq. August, 2004. Hottest place ever, in more ways than one. I'm ordering supplies and the next thing I know, I'm watching this British helicopter take off. It gets hit with an RPG to its tail.

"The pilot starts trying to gain a little altitude to find a safe place to set it down and..."

The general interrupted mid-sentence. "...And the helo runs into a weather balloon line?"

"Who told you about that?"

"And the chopper crashes, bursting into flames? Eight passengers were pulled out of the wreckage by two soldiers. In the end, everyone on board died."

The former Lt. Colonel, outranked by three levels, ordered the two-star general to tell him how he knew this.

"Ken, the other guy with you that day was me."

Gibbs dropped his wine glass. The wives looked at each other with that 'WTF?' look on their faces.

"We're best friends, why didn't you tell me? How long have you known it was me that was with you?" asked Ken.

"I've known for all of thirty seconds. When I received my award, the After-Action report did not include the name of the other soldier with me. There were enough other witnesses to the crash and our attempts to rescue the victims; the brass gave it to me anyway without your report."

"My After-Action report was similar except I testified seeing part of the name tag of the soldier with me. All I could remember reading was 'Qu. ' You know how many people have a last name that starts with those letters?

"General, you're wrong about one thing though. There was a survivor, a U.S. Air Force A-10 pilot. Her name is Colonel Maretta Sowers. She was a light colonel back then. She's a full bird now and stationed in Maryland somewhere."

"Only one promotion in eight years? Who did she piss off?" asked the general.

Unlike the wine, friendship and amazingly coincidental story, there was something else not shared that night. It was the fact that Orlando had two Purple Hearts on his military record, not one. One from Iraq, the other earned during a short temporary duty assignment with the 14th Infantry Division in October 1993.

The unit was in need of Arabic linguists and Orlando had volunteered for the assignment. He received a near-fatal wound on the morning of October 4th but ultimately survived the shooting. Within a few weeks, he made a full recovery. He'd never told Tracy about the incident. He also felt no need to share it with Ken and Theresa.

***

The two went on for an hour, recounting the event, their injuries, their units, how they both ended up in that one place in time together. They ignored their wives. The ladies were fine with that, as they were spellbound by the story.

"I was told by members of my staff that the soldier with me was injured after the side door of the helo fell off its hinge and broke his leg," the coach said. The general pointed to the scar on his leg where the compound fracture had pierced his skin.

"And likewise with me. When I asked about you, witnesses said the back of your uniform was on fire." The general didn't need his best friend to show his burns. The scars had been visible while water-skiing together on the lake. But in keeping with the Army way, he hadn't asked how he'd got them.

The fact two soldiers had been in the same place, and were injured during the same attack was not so uncommon in a combat zone. It was also not so remarkable to be sent to different field clinics hundreds of yards apart on a base with 15,000 uniformed personnel.

The denseness of the smoke from the burning helicopter had been thick enough that the two soldiers were not able to identify each other. The fog of war was also thick. It always is during the moments of combat and immediately thereafter.

What was remarkable was that they somehow ended up recounting the same story, enjoying the same wine in a place 7,000 miles removed from the battlefield. Even more remarkable was that their friendship could be any stronger than it already was. The shared experience only made it that much more so.

"Well, what about the Air Force pilot who lived? Ken, have you met her?" asked Tracy.

"I spoke with her numerous times but it never worked out. I was kind of going through some personal issues after Fallujah 2.0 and never followed up with her."

"I can handle that. I'm head of an intelligence agency for goodness sakes. I'll track her down," said Orlando.

***

"I found her," Tracy announced at breakfast the next morning.

"How did you do that?" asked Theresa.

"Through my superior technological intellect and Sherlock Holmes-like investigative skills. I Google searched her." Tracy had actually done what the general said he would do the night before. She'd got on the NGIA system and found her.

"There are countless stories about a woman being the first African-American fighter jet pilot to receive the Purple Heart. All the details matched last night's story. Her name is Colonel Maretta Sowers, but she prefers to be called Buff. She has a PhD in mathematics, has never been married and this is my favorite – she can deadlift 350 pounds. She's a former Georgia state high school weightlifting champion. She and I are now friends on Facebook."

"What's Facebook?" asked Orlando. "We should try to meet her in person sometime."

"Done deal. I already talked to her. The two of you are flying to Baltimore next week for a little reunion. You're staying at her house. She insisted," Tracy finished.

TWELVE

"THE WARTHOG - FRIEND"
TWENTY-SEVEN YEARS AGO

November 22nd, 1993 – High School Weightlifting Championship, Omni Colosseum, Atlanta, Georgia

"C'mon Buff, you got this. Those 45's are nothing. Just feathers. C'mon girl, you can do it," encouraged Mr. Sowers of his high school senior daughter.

"*Rrrruh*," grunted Maretta 'Buff' Sowers loudly as she began her third and final try. The six 45-pound plates and 45-pound bar slowly lifted off the ground. Like a 747 rolling down the runway at Hartsfield Airport. Sowers needed to square her shoulders and lock her knees and it would be over.

A final, vicious scream to generate the needed thrust and she nailed it. Three hundred and fifteen pounds. A new Georgia state high school record. The weights came crashing down to earth the moment the referee signaled a legal lift.

"Way to go, my baby!" screamed an excited father. "With hard work, you can do anything." He squeezed his daughter tightly with nothing but love. Maretta Sowers was happy she won the championship but disappointed for not succeeding on the first try.

"Sorry, Dad, I need to work on that."

***

Maretta Sowers was born in Atlanta, Georgia and grew up in the U-RESCUE Villa Housing Project until she graduated from high school. U-RESCUE was an acronym created by dim-witted politicians and stood for Urban Renewal Emergency: Stop, Consider, Understand, and Evaluate.

Later in life, Sowers attempted to create a mathematical formula to quantify the level of stupidity it took to come up with that one. She couldn't. The housing projects were leveled in 2008.

From an elementary school age, Sowers was identified as an exceptional mathematics student. Her test scores ranked her in the 99th percentile nationwide every year. Her skills were not a result of superior schools or access to private tutors. She had to work at it. Sowers grew up in a poor household but learned the value of hard work from an early age.

Her mom and dad worked multiple jobs to make sure she had food on the table. The last twenty years of her dad's life, he worked sixty hours a week as a baggage handler at Hartsfield Airport. Her mom worked the same number of hours a week as a nurse's aide. During Sower's senior year, her mother contracted tuberculosis from a sick patient and never recovered.

Sowers loved math and spent many of her waking moments playing with it. She particularly liked how, depending on the ordering of the components of an equation, it led to different solutions. Mathematics was an understandable representation of life. Change the order while maintaining consistency with the components. Different results.

If Sowers wasn't solving Calculus problems, she was in the high school weight room. By her senior year, she set a second state record with a total combined weight of four lifts of 905 pounds. It was in the weight room where the football players gave her the moniker "Buff." She loved the nickname instantly and introduced herself accordingly for the rest of her life.

After high school, Sowers accepted a full academic scholarship to Bethune-Cookman University in Daytona, Florida. Sowers chose Bethune-Cookman for two reasons. To escape the violence and poverty of U-RESCUE and because of the school's exchange program with neighboring Embry-Riddle Aeronautical University, to which she was at first denied admission.

She received a bachelor's degree in Advanced Mathematical Computations and her Masters in Aeronautics. She continued her studies years later and received her PhD in Mathematics from Johns Hopkins University in Baltimore.

It was as a child, while accompanying her father to Hartsfield Airport, she would sit and watch thousands of aircrafts taxi, takeoff and land. She decided she wanted to be a pilot. By the start of her junior year in college, the aeronautical department at Embry-Riddle found someone very gifted and approached her with an opportunity.

***

"Ms. Sowers, the Air Force is looking for top Aeronautics students to consider a career in flight. We have a number of slots available for students such as yourself to enroll in our ROTC program. Are you interested?" asked the Air Force ROTC recruiter on the campus of Embry-Riddle.

"I'm in. Sign me up. I'm going to be flying fighter jets."

"Well, don't rule out transports or tankers. They can be rewarding as well." The recruiter was as typical as most recruiters. He was lying. He knew the odds of a woman flying fighter jets was pretty low. But Sowers had grown up beating the odds her entire life. A year-and-a-half later Sowers, now a first lieutenant, was flying A-10 Warthogs over Baghdad. She was the first African-American woman to do so.

Flying jets was more thrilling to Sowers than she had anticipated. The physiological stressors of experiencing multiple G's while performing high-angle banks and climbs required the same concentration and exertion of strength as dead-lifting 300 pounds. She loved it.

Sowers stood low to the ground at 5 feet, 4 inches, a smidge tall enough to meet Air Force minimum height standards. With her dark skin, powerfully thick neck, chest and legs, she could think of no more appropriately named aircraft for her than 'Warthog'. Air Force brass tooted its own horn endlessly about a new culture of inclusiveness and equality. It meant nothing to Sowers, until years later.

***

Sowers celebrated her eighth year in the United States Air Force in traction at the Landstuhl Regional Medical Center at Ramstein Air Force Base in Germany. A month earlier, while riding as a passenger in a British helicopter at Al Asad Air Base in the Al Anbar province of Iraq, an Iraqi insurgent located off base fired one round from an RPG, striking the tail rotor of the aircraft.

Within seconds the aircraft crashed, killing everyone on board with the exception of Sowers. She was pulled from the fiery wreckage by two nearby soldiers. She had a broken neck, two broken legs and severe third-degree burns on her lower jaw and neck.

After recovery, she returned to flight duty but now as a stateside member of the A-10 squadron with the 175th Wing-Maryland Air National Guard located in Middle River, Maryland. While technically no longer attached to an active duty Air Force unit, Sowers retained her rank of full bird colonel and full-time work as her Air Force Specialty Code (11FX4) was in high demand. 11FX4 standing for Fighter Pilot-Highest Skill Level.

***

July 12th, 2012 – Home of Colonel Maretta "Buff" Sowers, Savage, Maryland

"Sorry for the informalities boys but come here, you two. I want a love hug," Buff Sowers said after opening the door for her American heroes.

"You're breaking my back, Colonel," Ken said.

"What's with the titles? You need to loosen up and learn to talk like my brothers. 'You breakin' my back, bitch.' Go ahead, give it a try."

"Sorry, force of habit. West Point bleached the street lingo right out of me. I'm sorry, Colonel. I should have made a better effort to come see you."

"I didn't want to say anything until you both got here but I've met you before Orlando. A long time ago. Way before Iraq."

"Where?"

"Well, after Tracy called and told me who you two were, I did a little research. Turns out you and I are members of the same church. The Ebenezer Baptist Church in Atlanta. You wouldn't remember me, but I attended Youth and Government summer camps there starting at age seven. You were quite a bit older and you were one of my counselors-in-training. Can you believe it? I didn't know you grew up in the Atlanta area?"

"I didn't. I grew up five hours south, in St. Augustine. My dad joined the church after meeting the head pastor back before I was born. A guy by the name of Martin Luther King, Jr. After King was murdered, my dad took me up there every summer. I stuck out like a sore thumb. Not being from the area and all. But after a few days, everyone treated me like one of their own. I loved it."

"That's funny. My dad wanted to name me after MLK. But my mom wanted to name me after his wife, Coretta. They compromised. Maretta."

"What was going to be your name if you were a boy?"

"Cortin." They all laughed.

"First, I find out you saved my life and now this. Crazy. I did the math, impossible."

"Nothing's impossible. It's a small world, Buff."

The three spent the entire weekend together and it was as if they'd known each other their entire lives. In many ways they had. So many similar experiences in a life in the military. Ken and Orlando couldn't remember a weekend they'd enjoyed more than their time with Buff. Buff not only enjoyed it, she was transformed by the two men.

"Why no stars yet, Buff?" asked General Quinn as Buff drove the two men to the airport at the end of the weekend. "I specifically remember pulling out an airman with bottle caps on her flight suit. Lieutenant Colonel, same rank as I was."

"General, unlike the Army that hands out stars like kindergarten teachers, the Air Force is a bit more selective. But I'm up for a slot in a month's time. I'd love it if you could put in a kind word for me."

General Quinn regretted asking the question the moment it left his mouth. He had other suspicions of why she wasn't promoted along with her peers. After dropping the two men off at the airport, the general turned to his friend, Ken Gibbs.

"She's a lesbian, right?"

"Whoa, hey now, General, I don't care and you don't either. What made you bring this up?"

"You're right. I don't care. But many in the upper ranks do care and I hope it hasn't prevented her from moving up in her career. The military can get a little weird about things like that. How do I know she's a lesbian? She told me last night when we were drunk as hell and you were in the bathroom. Her exact words, 'Would you be my beth man at my wedding? I'm getting married to the moth beautiful woman in four month'." The general was mocking Sowers's drunken lisp.

"So that explains why she asked me, 'Would you be my wifth maid of honor?' while you were in the bathroom."

The two friends laughed gaily and lisp-fully.

***

November, 2012 – Air Force promotion board hearing, Pentagon, Washington, DC

The Air Force spends over $30 million per A-10 Warthog, $5 million on its gun and spends another $5 million a year for maintenance, ordnance and pilot training. The increase in flight pay from a field grade officer to a general officer in the United States Air Force in 2012 was $200 a month. The base pay increase from full bird Colonel (O-6) to Brigadier General (O-7) was another $2100 a month. Sowers did the math, in her head.

It would take 127 years for the Air Force to have to spend the same amount of money on a promotion to Brigadier General for Sowers as it did for the equipment she was responsible for every day. To her, the promotion was a lock. She was the most qualified, educated, combat experienced, Purple Heart recipient candidate in the group of candidates. In fact, she was the only Purple Heart recipient in the group.

"Colonel Sowers, thank you for coming to today's promotion board meeting. We have reviewed your application for nomination to the rank of Brigadier General with great interest and admiration. Your accomplishments both on and off the battlefield are commendable to the highest degree. Your professionalism and exceptional performance reviews demonstrate your commitment to service."

Sowers was ecstatic and certain about what she was going to hear next.

"Unfortunately, at this time, the board has recommended two other worthy candidates for nomination. We have submitted those recommendations to the Chief of Staff of the Air Force. Due to a limited number of slots available, we are unable to approve your application at this time."

That was not what she was certain to hear and she was no longer ecstatic. To Buff, hearing those words felt like she'd failed to deadlift 135 pounds. Impossible for her to comprehend.

But she maintained her professional composure and asked the ranking board member, "Well sir, thank you for considering my application. May I ask, was Colonel Foster one of the two accepted nominees?"

"No Colonel, she was not. Thank you again for coming today and you are dismissed."

***

Since the Vietnam era, African-American women have served in the military at a higher percentage of the overall civilian population than any other racial demographic group. While many Americans loved to profess their patriotism, black women practiced it.

Sowers was personally familiar with the career path of another black woman with similar qualifications, flight ratings and combat experience as her. Like Sowers, she was turned away from promotion on multiple occasions. Her name was Colonel Adrian Foster. The two colonels were well acquainted. They were lovers.

"Can you believe it, hon? Both of us denied again?" asked Colonel Foster. "What does a lesbian black woman need to do to be promoted in this white, heterosexual man's Air Force?"

They both faked out a laugh.

With the exception of being denied promotion time and again, Sowers was happy. She had three loves. Foster to fill her heart, flying to push her body physically and mathematics to sharpen her mind. The couple purchased a home in Savage, Maryland, equidistant from Sowers duty station at Middle River to the north and Foster's at Andrews Air Force Base, near DC to the south.

At Andrews, Foster was assigned to the 113th Wing of the District of Columbia Air National Guard and was one of five African-American women to ever pilot the F-16 Falcon in combat. Though she loved flying fighters, her dream job was to become the first female black pilot of the much slower, four-engine, Boeing VC-25A, otherwise named Air Force One.

The two Air Force Colonels quietly married at the Howard County Courthouse on January 1st, 2013. The first day it was legal to do so in the State of Maryland. Their ceremony consisted of the two of them and five witnesses. Foster's dad, Tracy Quinn as the flower girl, Theresa Gibbs as the ring bearer, Coach Gibbs as Foster's maid of honor and Major General Orlando Quinn as Buff's best man. The entire wedding party wore white and it was January.

Just a month after they were married, an incident that began years earlier led to Foster receiving a Uniform Code of Military Justice – Article 15. An Article 15 is a form of non-judicial punishment in which an airman's commander can initiate an investigation.

If deemed appropriate, the commander is then within his or her authority to pass final judgment and administer any form of punishment within certain guidelines. Denying promotion or a reduction in rank are within those guidelines. In civilian terms, the service member's commander is the prosecutor, judge, jury and executioner.

The specific incident that led to Colonel Foster's Article 15 started in 2009, while she was deployed in Iraq. Foster befriended a twelve-year old Iraqi boy seen on base providing personal services such as shoe-shining, ironing uniforms and running errands. Foster gave the kid a few bucks here and there and genuinely liked him. Upon rotating back to the States, Foster wrote and became Facebook friends with him to see that he was still alive and well.

In late 2012, then fifteen, the boy joined a terrorist organization known as ISIS in western Iraq and was detained by American forces. Somehow, Foster's squadron commander found out she had a personal relationship with a terrorist and it led to her Article 15.

Upset by the outcome of the hearing – a reduction in rank to Lieutenant Colonel – Foster stopped at the Officer's Club before heading home. She downed a few belts of vodka to take the edge off. Driving home at a speed more resembling that of an F-15 than an automobile, she hit a patch of ice and then slammed into a tree on the side of the Baltimore-Washington Parkway. She was killed instantly.

It wasn't until a few months after Foster's death that a defense contractor named Eric Snowden released classified information about the National Security Agency's clandestine and illegal operations. The NSA was intercepting American citizens' phone calls, emails, text messages and Facebook messages. It was then that Buff realized how her wife had been identified as associating with the young boy in Iraq.

The country Sowers and her wife Foster spent their entire lives defending was spying on them and tens of millions of other Americans. Not all of the high-powered, listening antennae and satellite communication intercept equipment at Fort Meade were pointed at foreign locations. Some were pointing inward on America's own people.

There were hundreds more attendees at Foster's funeral than there were at her wedding. The casket bearers, all current or former military service members, wore their dress uniforms. Much more fashionable.

The evolution of modern warfare did not go unnoticed by Coach Gibbs and General Quinn. Sowers survived an attack from a weapon fired yards away from its target. A hand-held, rocket-propelled grenade.

Foster died from a weapon launched by a young boy in Iraq thousands of miles away. *"Ana jayyidin jiddan, lakin Allahu Alakbar."* ("I am very good, but God is greater.") A message on Facebook hit the target with deadly success.

THIRTEEN

"DEAD HANDS - FRIEND"

May 24th, 2000 – Milton, West Virginia

"Happy birthday, boy. How do you like your gift?" Mr. McCoy asked his youngest son.

"Ouch, Dad. It hurts. Tell this guy to take it easy on me. He's going too fast. I was hoping for a new basketball," Ronan McCoy answered as the tattoo artist began to create his art on Ronan's stomach.

"Be quiet. What, you some kind of faggot or something? Besides, you have ten basketballs already."

"Oh shit, I think I screwed up," said the meth-addict tattoo artist to Ronan's father.

***

Ronan McCoy, a scrappy and often-times troubled young man, grew up in an environment much different than the typical path to the NBA. On the surface he was the complete opposite of Jayden Quinn. McCoy was born, neglected, abused and later abandoned in Milton, West Virginia in Cabell County. The county's claim to fame was its ranking as being the #1 county in the entire United States where a citizen was most likely to die of a drug overdose.

Ronan grew up in a mobile home licensed by the state to sleep five but required by eight, all with the last name McCoy. All with dark red hair the shade of an over-ripe strawberry. The McCoys' upbringing was such as to guarantee their necks blended well with their heads.

The father was a raging, punching and later absent, alcoholic who blamed his problems on his heritage. The family was Scotch-Irish, an immigrant group who had settled throughout West Virginia in the late 18th and early 19th centuries. The Scotch-Irish evolved in America to be hard-working, god-fearing and gun-toting American patriots. It wasn't his Scotch-Irish heritage that made Ronan's father an alcoholic. It was his love of his two favorite whiskeys, Scotch and Irish.

The one saving grace of Ronan's home life was the dirt basketball court his dad had leveled off in the backyard. With four older brothers and one sister, Ronan had a basketball team with a referee to spare. Being the youngest and shortest boy, Ronan never developed an inside game. He relied on perimeter shooting and relentless defense to beat his older brothers.

By the time Ronan received a preferred try-out at Marshall University, he led his high school to two state championships and was a near 60% three-point shooter. He made the Marshall team and by his senior year in college was leading the nation in three-point scoring and was considered a top prospect for the NBA.

By modern NBA standards, Ronan McCoy was not particularly tall, fast or black. He could do nothing about his height and speed but he was working constantly on the black part. By the time he joined the league, over 50% of Ronan's body was covered with one tattoo or another. Most of the tats were nonsensical or offensive images and phrases Ronan's dad had inked when the boy was in his teens. For twenty bucks and a fix, the artist always inked as requested.

Ronan's first tattoo started at his belly-button and in a counter-clockwise fashion ran around his entire torso. The tattoo was meant to read, "You can take my gun when you pry it from my cold dead hands." The artist miscalculated the spacing of such a long phrase on such a thin torso and encircled Ronan by the time he finished the word cold. A compromise between the father and the artist was reached and the words "dead" and "hands" were tattooed, in red ink, on the back of Ronan's warm, live hands.

***

During Ronan McCoy's senior year in college, he watched all too much of Jayden Quinn's meteoric rise in the NBA draft rankings and how calm and cool he appeared to be with the media. Jayden's rigidly straight back and "Yes sir," "Yes Ma'am," during interviews before the draft were enough to make Ronan dislike the guy immediately.

It wasn't until Jayden Quinn and Ronan McCoy met at the rookie NBA Summer League in 2012 that Ronan's opinion of the guy changed. The change of opinion took five minutes.

Those first five minutes of the summer league did not go well for Ronan McCoy. As the new NBA players were stretching and eye-balling their future competition, one of them was also eye-balling the various tattoos Ronan had all over his upper torso, arms, back and neck.

"What's that you have on your back, white boy?" asked one of the other rookies. He was speaking to Ronan McCoy who was shirtless during stretching exercises.

"Could you be more specific? I have a lot on my back."

"That swastika and the words 'White Power' above it. That pisses me off. You some kind of white supremacist or something?"

"Sorry, I didn't mean to offend anyone. It was a gift from my dad. What are you, Jewish?" Ronan asked the six-foot, nine-inch tall African-American man.

The player wasn't pissed off because he was recently bar mitzvahed. He was upset because he was black. He and two other black players took at Ronan. Before Ronan could raise the words "dead" and "hands" to defend himself, they landed several excruciating blows.

The blows stopped when the three players started receiving some themselves. All from the un-tattooed hands of Jayden Quinn and all devastatingly powerful. It was over in twenty seconds. By the time the three offended men regained consciousness, Ronan and Jayden were on their way to becoming best friends.

As the summer league drew to a close, the two new players were inseparable. They remained that way through their entire NBA careers as they were both drafted by the same team. Jayden, number one overall. Ronan, in the second round.

For Jayden, Ronan was everything he was not and he loved it. Spontaneous, funny and lived as if he hadn't a care in the world. Ronan was also fiercely loyal to those he loved. Another traditional characteristic of those of Scotch-Irish descent. Lastly, Ronan had a knack for getting the two in all kinds of trouble. But the fun kind of trouble a couple of 22-year old men enjoy.

***

It was on their first boy's trip to Paris right after the end of summer leagues that Jayden knew he was in for a wild ride with his friend. The two future NBA stars were arrested in the Les Marais district for soliciting prostitution from a pair of undercover cops. Actually, Ronan was the one doing the soliciting, Jayden was the bystander shaking his head in inebriated disbelief.

After spending the night in a holding cell with a dozen of Paris' Les Miserables, the two were arraigned the next morning. Ronan pleaded not guilty. He informed the French judge, by way of an interpreter, that he read on Wikipedia that selling sex in France was legal. The judge responded, again via the interpreter, how much he admired the legal prowess of Mr. McCoy.

Indeed it was legal to sell sex in France. But against the law to pay for it. Since he was the buyer; *coupable* (guilty). Pay the 10,000 euro fine or spend a week in jail. Ronan opted for the fine. The story was all over the US press by the time the young men got home.

"Ronan, come with me to St. Louis. I want you to meet my girlfriend and my family," Jayden said.

"Sure, I have no place better to go but please don't bring up Paris."

***

Five minutes after arriving for dinner at the Quinn's home, Ronan McCoy wished he had someplace better to go. Actually, in hindsight he would have accepted the week in a French jail compared to what was in store for him in Missouri. Also in attendance were all three Gibbs and all three Quinns.

"So, Ronan, what made you think paying for sex was a bright idea?" asked Tracy Quinn.

"Mrs. Quinn, I'm not famous for bright ideas. I go with what feels right. Oddly, that usually turns out to be wrong."

"Well, don't you have someone special in your life to help you with right and wrong?"

"Well, I'm trying. I thought *les deux prostituees* in Paris had potential but who knew they were cops? Right, Jayden?" Jayden shook his head in disbelief of what could come out of Ronan's mouth.

"Well, what about family? Are you still close?"

"Let me think about that. Haven't seen my dad since I was fifteen. Nor will I again. He died of Red Neck Consumption three years ago."

"You mean tuberculosis right?" asked Tracy. "Consumption. That's what doctor's used to call it. When a black person died of TB they would list the cause of death as Negro Consumption."

"No, I mean consumption as in Dewar's and Jameson. Liters of it at a time. My mom, my third oldest brother and my sister are still alive in Milton. I know they're still kicking because they cash the checks I send them every month.

"My fourth oldest brother died of an overdose at eleven. He thought a bag of crystal meth was rock candy. We buried him at center court in our backyard. We were extremely close to him, when we shot hoops. My second oldest brother is in prison for cooking crystal meth. It was his product that killed my fourth oldest brother.

"And my first oldest brother, Jeffery, is buried at Arlington cemetery in DC. He stepped on an I.E.D. in Iraq the day President Bush landed on the U.S.S. *Abraham Lincoln* and told the world, 'Mission Accomplished'. The upper half of my brother landed on the same aircraft carrier a day later but in a casket."

Dinner ended before anyone asked where the lower half of Ronan's brother landed. General Quinn and Coach Gibbs had a pretty good idea. All over the side of an armored personnel carrier crashed in a roadside culvert in Iraq.

"He's not good for Jayden's career, don't you think?" Tracy asked Orlando as they did the dishes.

"Give it a break, hon. They're two young people having fun. Don't you remember how much crazy stuff we did when we were in our twenties?"

Tracy didn't remember. She didn't remember doing crazy stuff until she was in her forties.

***

June 12th, 2014 – somewhere over Texas

"Great game, guys. Way to close it out. You coming to the victory parade on Saturday?" asked one of Ronan's and Jayden's teammates on the flight home. The team was starting the celebration early after a six-game, NBA Finals championship against the team from San Antonio.

The series was nasty. A number of players were thrown out from one game to the next. Including Ronan McCoy. He was suspended for one game after beating a fan unconscious who was sitting behind the team's bench.

"I'm going to Key West. There's a parade every night on Duval Street. I don't know about Jayden," said Ronan.

"I can't. I have somewhere else I'd rather be," Jayden answered.

Ronan loved Jayden for the mere fact that he was the one person in Ronan's life that wasn't a complete and utter disaster. Jayden also treated Ronan as a peer, an equal, a human, even though Ronan realized the first two were untrue and the third, barely so.

Without request from Jayden, Ronan stood up and threw down with anyone that dared to insult or attack his friend. It was during Game Four of the NBA Finals series and while resting on the bench when a fan leaned over to Ronan and whispered, "You're better than that spook."

While he thanked the fan for the compliment, he took his dead hands and made hay on the guy's face faster than a West Virginia cattle farmer. Ronan and the fan were both tossed from the game. Ronan walked out of the arena. The fan was carried out. He was suspended for Game Five.

It was a pattern of friendship that continued for the rest of their lives.

FOURTEEN

June 14th, 2014 – Gibbs' Family Home, St. Louis, Missouri

Melissa and Jayden had the entire home to themselves as their parents were staying at the families' vacation house down at the Lake of the Ozarks. It was a glorious time for the entirety of the families, as Jayden won his first NBA Championship and was named the MVP of the Finals, which his team won in six games.

He couldn't think of any place he'd rather be than spending time at home with Melissa after such an emotional high of his second season. The travel requirements of a professional basketball player were unrelenting and now as an All Star, it was worse.

As they came to reveal every detail of each other's life and while together privately, Melissa asked, "How in the world did you ever end up with the name Jayden Fillmore? Sounds a bit, ahh, unusual. Is it a family name?"

"My dad named me because of his love of Arabic. Jayden is the Americanization of the Arabic word *jayyidin*."

"Go on, what does *jayyidin* mean exactly?"

"Good."

"What do you mean by good? Like good night, good riddance?"

"More like good as in pure or perfect."

Melissa erupted in laughter.

"I know, ridiculous."

"I can't wait to hear how you ended up with Fillmore as your middle name."

"That one is a lot easier and if you ever tell anyone about *jayyidin*, I'm changing my first name to Fillmore. Fillmore is the district in San Francisco where my dad first met my mom. His second favorite place in the world behind Disney World."

Melissa pondered that statement for a full minute. "Holy shi..." She stopped short, not wanting to curse so often as her mother always had. "Please don't tell me your dad's first name was given to him because of Disney World being in Orlando? What's his middle name, Disney?"

"Ahh, yes as a matter of fact, it is."

She laughed so violently she blew snot all over Jayden's shirt. "A highly decorated, combat veteran, world-traveling, polyglot, two-star Army General is named after a place where idiots don mouse ears and ride on Space Mountain?"

"Actually, he's afraid of Space Mountain. He's never been on it. His favorite ride is It's a Small World."

The lack of oxygen to her brain from five minutes of continual laughter almost made her pass out. When she caught her breath, she said, "I can't believe I once thought about marrying into this goofy family."

They laughed themselves through the night until it was almost time for sleep. Jayden didn't stand from the couch but instead dropped to one knee and nervously reached into this pocket. His words and a ring came out at the same time. "Will you still consider marrying into my goofy family if I give you this? Marry me, my love."

"Are you commanding or asking?"

"Begging."

"In that case, yes Jayden."

They looked at future calendars and agreed upon a wedding date; Saturday, August 6th, 2015. A few months after she would graduate from college.

It was during her last seconds before sleep, she heard her love whispering in her ear as her eyes closed, "*Ya Habeebati, Ya Habeebati.*" ("Oh my love, oh my love.")

FIFTEEN

March 6th, 1857 – United States Supreme Court Building, Washington, DC

"I can't wait to bust out of these chains," said the prisoner to his attorney.

"Let's not get ahead of ourselves."

The 57-year old Mr. Scott stood with his attorneys as the judge prepared to read his final decision. Scott was giddy with the thoughts of finally earning his release after such a long time in captivity. All he wanted to do was hurry home to his wife and kids and for the first time as a free man.

"What do you think our chances are?" Scott asked one of his attorneys, named Montgomery Blair.

"Hard to say with these cases. Who knows what some of these guys are thinking. Don't get your hopes too high as they don't like to overrule the lower courts."

"What about you, your brother is one of the inside guys? He's got to have some idea, right?" he asked his other attorney, George Curtis.

Curtis said, "Well, he's not supposed to say anything because these decisions are to be secret until they vote. However, he told me at dinner last night that he's a lock on your side. That's a good start."

"And the main guy, Taney, isn't he from Maryland? I thought Maryland was one of the more progressive states in the country. I mean, come on, the capital of the most free country in the world is right next door. I'll bet you a dollar he goes my way." Scott was certain he'd win and for his sake, he'd better. He didn't have the dollar to pay up if he lost.

"Let's wait and see. Here comes Judge Taney now. He'll be the one that reads the decision. Let's listen," Curtis finished.

United States Supreme Court Chief Justice Roger B. Taney took his seat on the bench and opened his legal portfolio to read the decision. The courtroom was overflowing with every-day, ordinary people both in support of Scott and opposed to him. Almost half in attendance believed that Scott or no one like him should ever be out roaming the streets. Foreign diplomats who happened to be in Washington, DC during the time of the trial attended as well. The outcome of the case was of that much interest.

"Guys like Scott are dangerous, ignorant and a menace to society. Sweetie, do you want to run into him on the street at night?" one man was overheard saying to his young daughter.

"No way, Pappy. Keep that animal locked up."

The media was already in a frenzy and the decision hadn't been read yet. Newspaper reporters from as far away as Missouri, Maine and Louisiana were present. For days they were writing articles and posting them back to their publishers by instant messaging in favor of or against the humble and devoted husband and father of two young girls.

Within minutes of reading the decision, newspaper articles and editorials would be sent instantaneously via telegraph wire services across a network of 21,000 miles reaching as far west as Missouri. A marvel of technological advancement but also one that accelerated the call for war.

"If he wins, someone's going to pay hell for that," said the reporter from Richmond to his colleague from New York.

"Not nearly as much hell if he loses," the New York reporter responded.

The judge was still seated and waited for the crowd to quiet. He began to read and started with quoting from the Declaration of Independence.

"We hold these truths to be self-evident: that all men are created equal; that they are endowed by their Creator with certain unalienable rights; that among them is life, liberty, and the pursuit of happiness; that to secure these rights, Governments are instituted, deriving their just powers from the consent of the governed. "

"This is going good," Scott said to both attorneys.

"Shhh, he's going to say a lot more I promise." Blair was right about that. Supreme Court Chief Justice Taney continued reading for another three hours and finished with, "Negroes are not citizens and have no rights which the white man is bound to respect."

"What the hell did he say? I have no rights? I'm going to bust him up."

When it was all said and done, the man lost his case by a vote of seven to two. It was the landmark case named, "Dred Scott vs John F.A. Sanford." The bottom line for Dred Scott was that he remained a slave and lost any chance to live as a free man with his family. It was his case that angered northern abolitionists to such a high fever pitch that it dragged a country into a war that killed millions, pitting brother against brother; the Civil War.

In Taney's written brief he also employed a legal maneuver called Obiter Dictum meaning "by the way". In effect, the maneuver allowed Taney to express as legal fact his opinion that not only was Scott prohibited from presenting his case because he was not a citizen but that the entire Missouri Compromise of 1820 was unconstitutional and must be repealed.

The Missouri Compromise of 1820 was an agreement between slave and free states in order to keep the balance in the US Senate equal. By admitting Maine as the 23rd state of the union and Missouri, the 24th, the balance remained. Twelve slave, twelve free.

The constitutionality of the Missouri Compromise was never the case before the court. But by claiming such, Taney was throwing coal on the growing flames of the issue of slavery and states' rights.

Dred Scott eventually earned his freedom only after being purchased by a family friend and was set free. He died shortly thereafter of an ailment the local newspaper at the time called, "Negro Consumption". Scott was buried at Calvary Cemetery in St. Louis. His wife Harriet lived free until her death in 1876 and was buried at nearby Greenwood Cemetery for African-Americans.

The Dred Scott decision was a prelude for a city with a long and complicated history of race relations. As recent as 2012, the British Broadcasting Corporation (BBC) produced a documentary on the state of segregation in St. Louis and spotlighted how the city was separated by the locally infamous Delmar Divide.

Delmar Boulevard is an east/west running street that cuts the city in half. Both literally and figuratively. To the north, predominantly low-income, African-American neighborhoods ridiculed by many locals as being drug and crime infested with little more than liquor and convenient stores as the primary industries.

To the south of Delmar, tree-lined streets, high-end shops, restaurants and two prestigious universities. Washington University and St. Louis University.

By 2012, the United States Census Bureau listed St. Louis as the second most segregated city in the country. By 2014, the Delmar Divide was growing ever wider.

***

August 9th, 2014 – Ferguson, Missouri

"Where are they?" the young man asked his friend.

"Right here. Want one?"

"Ah, these are so good. They smell and taste like candy. I love Swisher Sweets."

"Me too. Let's head back home. The Cardinals' game is on at three. You want to watch it?"

"Sounds good. Oh, damn, here come the cops. Stay cool, dude. I'll handle it."

For a period of over two weeks, Ferguson, Missouri, a small town outside of St. Louis, that most of America was unfamiliar with, lost its collective mind. At approximately noon on August 9th, an officer with the local police department shot and killed an 18-year old man.

The officer was responding to a burglary call from a local liquor store regarding the theft of $5 worth of Swisher Sweet Cigars. He saw the young man and his friend strolling down a street and he matched the description of the reported suspect.

Within thirty seconds of the man first being identified, the high school senior cigar thief was shot six times and laid dead in the street. The officer was white. The dead 18-year old tobacco bandit was black.

Eye-witness and police accounts of what actually happened varied greatly. The suspect attacked the officer and he shot the man in self-defense was the official police response. The officer shot the man even though the suspect raised his hands in surrender, was the neighborhood response.

"Hands up, don't shoot," became the rallying cry of a series of protests that brought the town to its knees.

It didn't matter what the correct response was because it didn't take long for the news of the shooting to make its way through the small, predominantly African-American community. Some of those residents decided to take matters into their own hands. Marches and then riots, with various degrees of action, reaction and over-reaction led to another death, many injuries and over 300 arrests. Police use of military-style vehicles, tactics and weaponry came under great criticism.

***

"Call your guy. Now is the perfect time. She's working until 8:30 and there won't be a cop within a mile," Tracy said.

"What are you talking about?" Calvin asked.

"The whole town of Ferguson is going crazy. Cops, protesters, national media. Call your guy now. You promised me this."

"Ok, but after this, we're done with the personal stuff. This is all about business and you need to remember that."

***

"Dudes, how much does that one cost?" asked an 18-year old man of his two friends.

"$15.99," one said, holding up a six-inch hunting knife.

"Man, we ain't got $15.99. Put it in your pocket and let's go. We have to be there by 8:30."

"Why me?"

"Because we're both eighteen. You're seventeen. You get busted and slapped on the wrist. Us? We're doing time. Now grab it."

After stealing the weapon and walking a few hundred yards through a small wooded field between the Walmart and the Ferguson YMCA, the three men spotted a young woman leaving the building, walking toward her car. Like ravenous panthers, they pounced.

"In the car, bitch. Now!" screamed one of the three as he grabbed a fistful of the woman's hair and pressed the six-inch, Mossy Oak hunting knife against her neck.

"What are you doing? Leave me alone!"

"Shut up and get in the car," said the second man as he punched her in the nose viciously, causing her face to explode in blood.

"Marc...!" the woman started to scream as the second man thrust his hand over her mouth and pushed her into the back seat. The third man, a boy actually, stayed outside and watched for anyone that might be coming out of the Y.

"Shut the fuck up. Listen to me. If you think you're getting married, you're wrong. After we're done with you, he won't want to be within a mile of you. Leave that brother alone or we'll be back. And next time, I'll use this."

Both men proceeded to violate her. They were gone in ten minutes. The pain and humiliation were excruciating.

How could this happen? Why would they do this to me?

There was something slightly familiar about their faces but she couldn't figure out what.

The young woman couldn't wrap her mind around the words they'd said either. "If you think you're marrying..." "...next time, I'll use this." And the most vivid, "...he won't want to be within a mile of you." They were right, she whispered as she cried.

Walking out of the Y and locking the doors, Marcus Emerson, Executive Director of the Ferguson YMCA, heard crying and saw the unclothed legs of a woman protruding from the back seat of the car. He knew the car to be that of his volunteer employee, Melissa Gibbs. Approaching the car delicately but deliberately, he was shocked to his core. After a couple of minutes trying to comfort and clothe Melissa, Marcus Emerson carried her back into the building.

"I'm calling the police," Marcus said, while sobbing.

"No, Marcus, please don't!"

"But Melissa, we have to report..."

"I said no, Goddamn it. I can handle this on my own. Marcus, do you even know what's going on in this town right now? Can you please help me to the showers and grab me a shirt and some shorts from the uniform closet?"

As she showered, Marcus started to watch the security video of the parking lot. He stopped it within 30 seconds to throw up. He restarted it. Melissa was showered, dressed and back at the front desk.

"Delete that video now."

"But, Melissa, I can't. I have a duty to report this to the police."

"And then what, Marcus? They're arrested, maybe indicted, maybe convicted. In the meantime, I have to live this shit over and over again. Marcus, you know who I'm engaged to. Think of Jayden and what a media circus this will create."

"The media won't find out. The police protect the name of the victim."

"Please, Marcus, don't be so stupid. This will leak out. I can't deal with it and I'm begging you to delete that video now!"

Marcus felt he had no choice but to follow her wish. He pushed the delete button on the security video computer. It would take nearly thirty minutes to delete the entire day's coverage. Satisfied the video was gone, she said, "Walk me to my car, Marcus."

"No way, Melissa. I'm driving you home. We can come back in the morning for your car."

"Marcus, please listen to me. I love volunteering here and I love you as a supervisor. I thank you for what you've done for me tonight. I need some time to myself. Please do not tell my dad or Jayden and don't call the police. Go home to your wife and kids, Marcus. They need to be with their father, like I do."

Marcus did as he was instructed by walking Melissa to her car and seeing that she drove away safely. With twenty minutes still left before the video was deleted, Marcus pressed pause. He copied the ten minutes of attack footage onto a thumb drive and finished with the erasing of the video files.

He swore to himself he was going to keep a copy for a day only in case Melissa changed her mind about getting the attackers arrested. After the copy was finished, he collapsed on the floor and cried uncontrollably.

"I'm sorry, God. I'm sorry Coach Gibbs, I'm sorry Jayden." After an hour of crying and praying, he attempted to call Melissa on her phone to make sure she arrived home safely. She never answered.

As Melissa approached the intersection at I-70, she pulled mightily to have her car turn northwest, in the direction of her parent's home. But shame, though unwarranted, was now at the wheel and was stronger. It was driving her southeast toward the Mississippi River. Would Jayden ever look at her the same way? Or would he be repulsed and afraid to embrace his love with the same affection? Questions of which Melissa dared not answer.

She drove for ten more minutes. Heading south on the highway, she was within a mile or so of where her love played high school basketball and where she'd first laid eyes on him. The last mile gave her sixty seconds to reflect on the many juxtapositions of the world she now saw.

In front of her were two of the city's greatest iconic symbols of hope, opportunity, duty and love. Sandwiched in between were two more symbols but of failure, false hopes, loneliness and greed. Other city skylines throughout America were constructed or deconstructed similarly but none with such stark contrast as the city of St. Louis.

As the highway slowly turned east toward Illinois she could see the shimmering, silvery glow of Gateway Arch. A 630-foot-high monument built to represent the expansive and seemingly endless opportunities of a young nation. Immediately in front of her, the white-lighted luminosity of the Stan Musial Veterans Memorial Bridge. A tribute to the city's beloved heroes.

Partially obstructing her view were monuments of the city's failed dreams. The Dome at the America's Center and the Lumiere Place Casino. The Dome was home to a failing NFL franchise, the St. Louis Rams who in their last ten seasons were a combined 47 wins, 112 losses and 1 tie. The owner of the team, eight months earlier, had purchased a large tract of land in Los Angeles, California and within two years the team was gone.

The Lumiere Place Casino, across the interstate from The Dome, would be filled with thousands of Rams fans who needed something to do with their retirement accounts. Losing it, one pull of the slot machine after another, seemed as entertaining as watching a one win and 15-loss football team.

Duty and dereliction, opportunity and hopelessness, honor and shame, winners and losers, love and hate, life and death. The lines of these many contradictions were so blurred, Melissa Gibbs could no longer distinguish one from the other.

Now on the bottom third of the Stan Musial bridge, she repeatedly whispered to herself some words in Arabic, some in English. "*Jayyidin*, pure, *Habeebati*, spoiled, *Jayyidin*, good, *Habeebati*, bad."

Reaching the top of the "Stan Span" as St. Louisans called it, Melissa

Gibbs, a 22-year old senior at Washington University stopped, put her car in park, climbed the rail and jumped into the swift and muddy waters of the Mississippi River.

***

"Marcus, where's Melissa?" asked Kenneth Gibbs without the politeness of a hello.

"Ahh, sh-she should be home by now, Coach. Isn't she?" Marcus' caller ID announced the caller as Coach Gibbs, someone he'd known for years.

"I don't know. I got a call from the downtown police station saying they impounded her car and I needed to go there. Where is she, Marcus?"

"Downtown Ferguson Police?"

"No, St. Louis. Marcus, what the hell is going on?"

"Coach, I'll be there in fifteen minutes. I have to tell you something."

"What is it Mar...?"

Marcus hung up, jumped in his car and as promised was at the downtown St. Louis police station a short time later. He had the wherewithal to put the thumb drive of the security video into his pocket.

***

Coach Gibbs and Orlando Quinn were driving home to St. Louis from their shared vacation home in the Lake of the Ozarks when Gibbs got the call from the St. Louis PD. They were hurrying back to the St. Louis area after seeing reports of potential rioting breaking out around Ferguson, Missouri. While they weren't capable of doing anything specific, they thought they needed to be in their city nonetheless.

Their wives decided to stay at the lakeside house through mid-August to enjoy the pending close of summer as they had for the past several years.

Jayden Quinn was still in St. Louis for a few months during the NBA off-season. He was at the Gibbs' house waiting for Melissa to come home from the Y. The two planned on grabbing a late-night dinner after her shift.

***

Marcus Emerson knew both the Gibbs and Quinn families well. Friends, actually. Over the previous twelve years, the two families combined donated nearly $5 million to his YMCA branch and spent thousands of hours volunteering.

Most of those donations came from Jayden, the rising star in the National Basketball Association. With his number one, first-round NBA draft pick guaranteed salary of $21 million in 2012, he donated $3 million to help build a new child education center. Since Jayden's first year in college, he and Coach Gibbs led free basketball camps for thousands of underprivileged kids throughout the region.

Earlier, in the spring of 2014, Jayden and Coach Gibbs in partnership with the NBA started an annual college fund, awarding scholarships of $40,000 each to five high school seniors. Marcus Emerson arranged a big celebration with the press, NBA public relations staff and local politicians and dignitaries.

Both Jayden and Coach Gibbs handed each of the five worthy recipients giant ceremonial checks in the amount of $40,000. It was a fantastic day and one that all the attendees remembered fondly.

Melissa began volunteering years earlier and quickly became one of Marcus' favorites. By his estimate, since high school, she spent over 3,000 hours of her time helping others in the community without receiving a penny in compensation.

***

"Coach, what's going on?" asked Marcus as he sprinted into the lobby of the police station. The general was there as Coach Gibbs paced back and forth.

"I have no idea. They haven't told me a damn thing other than an investigator should be with me in a few minutes. That was ten minutes ago. Marcus, was Melissa at the branch tonight?"

"Yes, Coach. I walked her to her car myself. Maybe 8:45 or 9:00." Marcus tried his best to keep his promise to Melissa but was struggling to do so. Coach Gibbs, in the emotion of the moment, forgot that while on the phone with him earlier Marcus referenced, "I have to tell you something."

Moments later, St. Louis Police Detective Michael O'Hare asked the coach to join him in back. Coach Gibbs insisted General Quinn and Marcus Emerson accompany him.

"Here's what we have. Your daughter's car was found parked at the top of the Stan Musial Bridge. A family is in the other room giving a deposition as we speak. They were driving across the bridge from the Illinois side. All four of them reported seeing a woman get out of her car and..." he hesitated.

"And what?"

"...and jump." The coach, the general and Emerson all let out a verbal gasp.

"There is more, sir, and I'm going to try to be sensitive with my words. All the lab results are not back in yet, but we've found physical evidence of an attack. Ripped clothing, blood, hair and semen. We're still testing."

"Have you found my daughter, is she alive?"

"I'm sorry, sir, but no."

Upon leaving the police station, Marcus grabbed General Quinn by the arm more forcibly than he ever considered before and pulled him aside. "Sir, I need to give you this video and I beg you not to watch it. Please, give it to the police or Coach Gibbs. The footage is from the parking lot and Melissa, she..."

"What?"

"Sir, Melissa was raped. She made me promise not to call the police, call Coach, Jayden or even you. I begged her to let me call the police."

"OK, Marcus. Give me the video. I'll handle it with the coach and Jayden."

General Quinn had much experience handling it with fellow soldiers and families when it came to sharing bad news. He did so over 300 times in four tours of combat over the course of his career.

***

Based solely on video footage from the in-store security cameras at Walmart, on August 11th, two 18-year old men and one minor were arrested for misdemeanor theft. The outside cameras also showed the men entering the woods between the Walmart and the YMCA.

After two days of interrogation and testimony from the minor, the Ferguson Police were able to arrest and press charges against two of the three young men for the suspected rape of Melissa Gibbs. The police had the video from the nearby store, physical evidence to include DNA matches and the testimony of the third suspect. For some reason, Marcus refused to cooperate. He used the excuse that it was against his organization's policy to be involved with legal proceedings that took place on property.

On August 12th, Ferguson police received an envelope with no note or return address, with the sole article being that of a data thumb drive. Upon loading the lone file on the drive and viewing the video of the attack in the YMCA parking lot, the police thought they had a solid case.

***

August 12th, 2014 – City of Ferguson Police Department

"Chief, I want to thank you for letting me do this. I know you have a ton of shit happening right now but I have to see who did this to my daughter," said Kenneth Gibbs.

"OK, but we're going to make this quick. You sit here in front of this glass and we'll bring them into that room. You have two minutes. I got the Feds up to my eyeballs over these riots and need to get back to work."

Coach Gibbs received permission to see the two accused of his daughter's rape on the condition that he wasn't allowed direct access to the suspects. The father felt he had an immediate right to know, given all he did for the citizens of the small town.

Sitting behind the anonymity of a two-way mirror, Coach Gibbs waited vengefully for the charged suspects to enter the holding room. Prior to the teenagers entering, he felt his heart couldn't be in a deeper, darker place. His anger could be no more enraged. He was about to find out otherwise.

The two suspects entered the holding room with their heads lowered, hiding their faces. Upon the order to look straight into the glass, Coach Gibbs looked at the young men, lowered his own head, and tears ran down his cheek. He said nothing. He felt no more anger. Only despair.

There in front of him and close enough for him to break through the glass and strangle the life out of him, was one of the five recipients of the Jayden Quinn and Coach Kenneth Gibbs Scholarship Fund. Both young men had been regular participants in the YMCA basketball camps for years and one of them recently signed a Letter of Intent to come play for Coach Gibbs at St. Louis University.

The suspects were charged with first-degree sexual assault. Upon hearing of the case and the tie-in to the Ferguson riots, the National Association for the Advancement of Colored People (NAACP) Legal Defense Fund sent a team of its most capable attorneys. Upon review of the evidence, the defense attorneys knew the video, a copy of the original, could easily be ruled inadmissible. There was no way to prove the copy had not been altered. The original video was deleted the night of the attack.

Additionally, the DNA evidence of blood from Melissa Gibbs and semen from the suspects could also be challenged. Without a victim, assault, forcible penetration, therefore rape, could not be proved. The defense could also make the argument that if sex in fact occurred, it could have been consensual.

Lastly, the integrity of the entire Ferguson Police Department was called into question. The militaristic-style response to protesters after the shooting of the young man led to a high-level of distrust in the community. The handling of the protests resulted in a ruling by the United States Department of Justice determining the Ferguson Police Department to systematically employ racial profiling and stereotyping. The ruling ended in a clean sweep of the department's leadership and practices. Finding a jury sympathetic to the prosecution in such a volatile climate would be next to impossible.

After several days and on the advice of his own private attorney, Coach Gibbs was informed that any trial was likely to lead to an acquittal. Hoping to avoid the public spotlight and the public viewing of Melissa's last day, the coach conceded to the grim reality that justice was likely to go unserved. He decided to let the matter fade into history.

The unbearable pain that was certain to be inflicted upon her mother and her fiancé Jayden would be too great for them to bear, thought Kenneth Gibbs. He hastily and selfishly decided, along with Jayden's father Orlando, not to tell the remaining Gibbs and Quinn family members of Melissa's assault.

"It's always better if the women don't know what darkness lies in the hearts of men, right General?" asked Gibbs.

"What about the darkness that lies in the hearts of women?"

After three days of around-the-clock searching by local authorities and the US Coast Guard, the effort to find Melissa Gibbs was called off. The police ruled the death of Melissa Gibbs a suicide based largely on the eyewitness accounts of the family of four.

A private funeral ceremony was held with both sets of parents, Colonel Buff Sowers, Ronan McCoy and a Catholic priest in attendance. With no body to bury, the Gibbs agreed to secure a small memorial mausoleum containing Melissa's favorite personal items at Calvary Cemetery in North St. Louis City. Each attendee left an item in the vault to either honor her or as a token to the loved ones she left behind.

Ronan McCoy placed his NBA Championship ring he won a few months earlier as a reminder of the friendship he shared with Melissa's fiancé. General Quinn, Coach Gibbs and Colonel Sowers each laid upon the small altar the Purple Heart medals they had all been awarded, ironically on the same day, in Iraq.

From the love of her life, Jayden placed the wedding ring he'd intended to put on her finger on the day they were to be married. On the inner band of the ring, he had inscribed the Arabic text reading "*habeebati*" meaning, "my love."

And Melissa's mom, a Filipina-born and now naturalized American citizen left the only possessions she ever cared about her entire life. Two sheets of paper that costs less than $1. The first was her Certificate of Honorable Discharge from the United States Army.

The other had been presented to her by an employee of the Citizenship and Immigration Services. The top of the document read "Certificate of Naturalization and Citizenship – United States of America." The bottom read "Theresa Gibbs...having faithfully taken the oath of allegiance...is hereby admitted as a citizen of the United States of America."

As they were leaving the service, Orlando approached his wife who'd arrived late and in a separate car. "Tracy, you told me you were going to leave one of your two gold medals as a token for Melissa. What happened?"

"I changed my mind. I worked hard to earn those."

"Have you been drinking? I smell alcohol on your breath."

"I'm so shaken up by Jayden's loss. She was such a lovely young lady. It shouldn't have turned out this way. He deserved more."

"What shouldn't have turned out this way and don't you mean 'she' deserved more?"

"Yeah right, she deserved more. Sorry, I've been drinking."

***

The Mississippi River has been keeping secrets for millennia. The muddy waters added another terrible secret the night of August 9th, 2014.

What appears to be a gentle, smooth and almost heavenly flowing body of water is anything but. A perfect symbol of the often troubled and misleading current of America's past and present running just under the surface of everyday life.

The Mighty Mississippi is not just mighty, the river is lethal. It starts at a depth of three feet in Minnesota and ends up over 200 feet deep by the time it reaches New Orleans. Cross currents, vicious whirlpools, mud flats, quicksand, giant bottom feeders and even alligators as far north as Tennessee are amongst the many perils awaiting under the surface of "Ol' Man River." With regular flooding and other geological conditions, the river continues to change course, depths, speeds and in some cases, direction.

In 1812, an earthquake, which would have measured 8.6 on today's Richter scale, erupted along the New Madrid Fault south of St. Louis. The quake opened a fissure in the earth so wide and deep it swallowed the entire river and spit it out downstream but flowing in the opposite direction. It took days for the river to find its true course again.

Tremors from the quake were reported to be felt by the occupants of the White House at the time, James and Dolly Madison. Was history about to repeat itself? Did those in power in the nation's capital feel the tremors emanating from Missouri once again in 2014 or were they to be largely ignored as they were in 1812?

The fissure forming in America's heartland in 2014 was not caused by invisible underground seismic forces as in 1812. The dangerous forces in 2014 were above ground and easily visible for all to see. But few took notice, for America was distracted by the much smaller cracks in the surface.

With social tensions escalating, almost weekly mass shootings, growing income disparities, hatred and vile on display almost daily in the media, it seemed the country was heading in the same direction as the Mississippi River did in 1812. The wrong way.

Melissa Gibbs' final resting place was located a hundred yards from the burial site of Dred Scott. The suffering, judicial injustice and premature death of the two set in motion a cascade of events no one at the time could predict. The significance of the two closely-placed memorials of Dred Scott and Melissa Gibbs would one day become two points in history that would be taught to American school children for generations to come.

SIXTEEN

August 15th, 2014 – Quinn home, St. Louis, Missouri

"So, what now?" Ronan McCoy asked of his best friend.

"I have no idea," replied Jayden.

"I say let's get the hell out of here. Like Thelma and Louise."

"Didn't they die in the end?"

"Let's do what guys in their twenties do. We got a couple months before the season starts. When's the last time you went on a guy's trip? Besides Paris?"

"Look how that turned out."

"No, man. It won't be the same."

"That's not going to go over well with my folks, especially my mom."

"Dude, you're twenty-four. You're a multi-millionaire. Do you give a shit what your mom thinks? You need to grow a pair. Your dad up and left his parents when he was eighteen. Joined the Army without knowing a damn thing."

"Where should we go? Have you ever taken off without a plan?"

"I've been taking off without a plan since fourteen. Stole my old man's car. They didn't catch me until Florida. Best three weeks of my life."

The idea of getting out of there sounded pretty good to Jayden after a week of dealing with the death of his soul mate. Before he took Ronan up on his offer, he felt he needed to talk with the one man that had lost as much as he had.

***

August 16th, 2014 – the Gibbs home, St. Louis, Missouri

"Jayden, this is my fault, not Melissa's," Coach Gibbs said. "I never showed the type of emotion a father should share with his daughter. Like I'm sharing with you now. Something must have troubled her so deeply, something Theresa and I never saw in her."

"Coach, do you think it was the attention? The constant pressure from the media. She was always such a private person. People are so damn obsessed with fame. I'm afraid it was too much for her. Even for me. I'm done with this. The press wouldn't leave us alone."

"It could be somewhat related to that but, Jayden, since Melissa was in high school, I shared many stories. Stories I thought helped her understand the many difficulties women face in the world. About women who took their own lives to protect the honor of their men or even their country. The horrors of where, in certain parts of the world, fathers stone their own daughters to death because they were accused of shaming the family.

"I was trying to teach her how blessed we are here, where for the most part, we've made such great progress. Too much I guess for her age and I should have known better."

And to some degree, the coach may have been right. Even up to the night of her death, Melissa struggled to understand how best to play her role of loving and dutiful fiancée to a budding super-star. Public relations, the kind the media and fans expect wasn't in her nature. It seemed no matter what she said or did, she was offending someone.

In the two short months Melissa and Jayden were engaged, she granted one interview with the press. Sara Gujic, with the St. Louis Post Dispatch. The reporter was doing a feature article on St. Louis' newest sports hero and heard about the engagement from Coach Kenneth Gibbs.

***

"Meet with her, Melissa. If you're not comfortable with her line of questioning, leave," Coach Gibbs told his daughter the morning of the interview.

It turned out to be much better than Melissa expected. Gujic was patient and thorough. She wanted to know the facts of what it was like to be engaged to such a popular local figure. She asked about Melissa's parents and what her aspirations in life were. Melissa's answer regarding her father: "...and he's a total history nut. He loves everything about it. He even spent $25,000 on a gun that was used by that famous assassin from Bosnia. Before World War I. What was his name? Princip, I think."

"You're right, Ms. Gibbs. It was Gavrilo Princip. Everyone in the Bosnian community knows of him. Changing the subject, Jayden doesn't resemble his parents very much. Is he adopted by chance?"

"You're right. But no, he's not adopted. I read his birth certificate when we applied for our marriage license. Maybe he's the result of some genetic anomaly. Like when two brown-eyed parents have a child with blue eyes."

The resulting feature story ran a week later and reflected the interview. Straight-forward, honest and not all that interesting. The only controversy was Tracy's reaction upon reading Melissa's physical description of her son. "Great, damn reporter must be the only white person in the world that doesn't think all black people look alike," Tracy said.

"Now that Jayden's in the public spotlight, people are naturally going to be interested in his personal life. But who gives a damn. Let people draw their own conclusions."

SEVENTEEN

August 22nd, 2014 – 7am CDT, St. Louis, Missouri

"Grab your banana hammock. We're heading south, my friend," Ronan said.

"How far south and what's a banana hammock?" Jayden asked.

"The southernmost point. Key West, the Conch Republic. Different country, man. Totally chilled. I've been going there for years and someday after calling it quits, I'm moving there. Anything goes and nothing much matters."

***

Ronan was right. The two friends spent ten days on the tiny island and neither could remember anything other than fishing and drinking.

"Well, La Te Da, look who the pussy cat dragged in," Jayden said to Ronan at eight in the morning on their last day in Key West.

"Give me a break, dude. It was a rough night. Those were no pussy cats that dropped me off, those two were Colombian jaguars. And they were hungry."

"Ronan, for you, sex is like basketball. You've always preferred threes over twos."

***

Back in St. Louis, Tracy, took care of all the demands being asked of Jayden regarding his contract, product endorsements and most importantly, his personal affairs on social media. And she was killing it. The money rolled in by the millions.

She answered his growing base of fans and followers on Facebook, Instagram and Twitter and monetized those followers by product endorsements on Jayden's timeline and by other methods.

After Melissa's death, many of Jayden's fans expressed their thoughts and prayers for the young basketball star. Tracy turned those thoughts and prayers into layers of cold hard cash. A post on Facebook from Jayden read; "In lieu of flowers, please donate to my Go Fund Me account tagged below. Proceeds to benefit underprivileged children being served by the Bi-State Unified Church of God."

That post, of which Jayden knew nothing about, resulted in $2 million.

***

August 30th, 2014 – Disney World, Orlando, Florida

"Wheeeeeeeeeee!" screamed Ronan as he spun the wheel in the teacup faster and faster. "Dude, this fucking place rocks!"

"I can't believe your dad never brought you here when you were kids. Slow down, man. I'm about to get sick."

"What dad? I grew up in a house with eight people. We couldn't afford a second toilet, much less this. Hold on, mofo. I'm taking it up a notch."

"Please don't." Jayden left his Cinderella Royal lunch in the teacup and the two left Disney World and headed north.

***

August 31st, 2014 – Atlanta, Georgia

Jayden and Ronan drove to their next stop of a road trip that would last the entire off season. The hometown of Colonel Buff Sowers and a Unified Church of God Pastor with whom Tracy had arranged housing for the two NBA stars.

"His name is Buster Hicks and he's the pastor at Peachtree Evangelical African Church of Hotlanta. He calls his church the PEACH. My mom said he's a preacher from her church or something. She said we can stay with him at his house in Buckhead. Take the 400 north from I-85," said Jayden.

"Man, I don't want to stay at the home of a priest. Let's book an Airbnb or something. Besides, tell me how a guy who's a pastor of a church in a low-income neighborhood is living in Buckhead? Typical religious BS. Charitable organization, my ass."

"What's Airbnb? Come on man, a little religion isn't going to kill you."

Jayden was right. It wouldn't kill Ronan to have a little religion in his life. But it almost did.

They spent two nights with Hicks, but never got near the PEACH. Hicks was not only a senior fellow at a church, he was also the sole proprietor of some of Atlanta's other popular establishments. Strip clubs.

Pastor Hicks joined Heyward while serving an eleven-year sentence for first-degree assault and battery in Chattanooga. The victim of the crime was one of his ladies as Hicks ran the largest prostitution ring in east Tennessee. The woman got pregnant and to teach the others a lesson about the importance of a healthy workforce, he beat the woman so severely she almost died. The unborn child did.

After Hicks' release from prison, he chose the city of Atlanta to start his operation as it was within a couple hours' drive from where he grew up. Not to mention the city was the Strip Club Capital of America. A perfect place for him to start a second enterprise. Another organized prostitution ring.

When Hicks wasn't tending to his flock in the troubled neighborhood of Harvel Homes where his church was, he was tending to a different one. Hicks was spreading the word mostly at the Cheetah Club and figured two, young NBA players preferred an evening of dinner, bottle service and personal service. Little did the pastor know that strip clubs weren't much of a thing for either Jayden or Ronan.

"Let's blow out of this town. Nothing hot about it except the weather," Ronan suggested on day two.

"No, we've got one more place I want to check out. I called a different church yesterday and they've invited us to attend a meeting with their Youth in Government participants."

"Government? Shit, even worse than religion. All a religion can do is send you to hell if you don't give them money. The government can send you to jail."

Jayden and Ronan spent the entire day with a group of fifty teens in the Youth and Government program at the Ebenezer Baptist Church. They were introduced to the group by Buff Sowers, Jayden's father and NBA All Star Iver Koch who'd all grown up as members of the famous church.

Koch was considered one of the top five players in the league and was nearly Jayden's equal in many statistical categories. He was also the volunteer chairman of the youth program at the church. He personally contributed over $4 million. In nine years, thousands of kids received the opportunity to visit their State Capitol and Washington, DC to learn and participate in the fine art of democracy.

The young boys and girls of the church were engaged, informed and passionate about following in the footsteps of the church's history. Peaceful protest yet civil disobedience when social injustices were evident. Even with their star power, Jayden and Ronan were treated as everyday citizens and welcomed to participate in the practice of democracy and freedom of speech. Both remembered the day for a long time.

***

The two weren't always so welcome wherever they went. They took a side detour on their road trip to see if they could get a guest pass to play a round of golf at Augusta National Golf Club. They were, after all, nationally famous NBA champions and they figured they might be able to take advantage of that.

"Yeah, right. Have a nice day guys," was the only response. They continued to drive north where they found the reception in Southeast Washington, DC was even worse than Augusta.

***

"Hey guys, how do you get to the mall from here?" asked Jayden to two guys standing on a street corner after he got turned around driving into the nation's capital.

"Get the fuck out of here," said the guy standing closest to the car. He lifted his shirt and showed Jayden and Ronan the 9mm Glock he had tucked into his belt.

As they were taking his advice, the other guy said, "Man, I think that was Jayden Quinn and Ronan McCoy you told to get the fuck out of here." Jayden and Ronan didn't go back to tell the guy he was right.

The two were invited to sit in a session of Congress by a representative from Missouri. The only practicing of democracy the two witnessed was congressmen and women voting on which five-star restaurant they wanted to dine at for lunch.

"You believe they're paid for that shit?" Ronan asked. They moved on.

***

Jayden promised his mom to at least visit with the UCG pastor in Baltimore. Kendley Charles was officially titled Bishop Charles as he oversaw two churches in the area. One was in Pigtown, a less than desirable neighborhood west of downtown named after the hog slaughterhouses of the nineteenth and early twentieth centuries.

The other was in Dundalk, a tough, blue-collar area outside the city limits. Between the two neighborhoods alone, they averaged a half a murder a day. Who knew you could kill half a person? Ronan did.

Bishop Kendley Charles, like his colleague to the south in Atlanta, was also a one-time resident of the State of Tennessee penal system. His crimes? Operating a pharmaceutical company without the proper licenses. Namely, meth, cocaine and heroin. By the mid-'90s, Charles liked to brag that his business in Nashville was "a boomin'" and that he had more regular and repeat customers than the Grand Ole Opry. That was until he got "a busted."

He served seven of a 15-year sentence and was to serve ten more on probation. Also, like Hicks, Charles met Pastor Calvin Heyward at the state pen. He converted to Heyward's church after a private ceremonial baptism by buggery in the prison showers. They were both devout followers of each other from that day forward. But for different reasons.

He moved to Baltimore upon his release based largely on the prison gossip that if there was one place in America where criminals don't go to jail, it's Maryland. A perfect state for opening another pharmaceutical company. By 2014, business was once again 'a boomin' with more fans than the Baltimore Orioles. Which wasn't saying much.

***

"The Orioles are in first place. Can you believe it?" Charles said to Jayden and Ronan as the three sat in the club suite at Camden Yards.

"Give them another chance, they'll suck again in no time," Ronan said. He was right. But win or lose, it didn't matter to Charles. He was at every game. He regularly invited young recruits to his crime ring to attend games with him in his private suite. It worked. His crime crew grew to twenty devout followers in their own rights.

***

After each city stop, Jayden spent time recording their visit in his personal journal. By the time they completed their two months of travel, Jayden was on his fourth notebook. Most entries were beautifully written monologues describing a melting pot of citizenry, an unwavering love of country and a land of endless opportunities.

Ronan and Jayden hopped from Airbnb to Airbnb. Staying in people's homes, often sharing drinks and late night conversation about all that was good in America and sometimes what was not. Regular people wanting nothing more than to raise a healthy and happy family, enjoy the company of good friends and if possible, give time to helping others.

A few of Jayden's entries were not so encouraging. He noted a tear here, a break there where the social fabric of the American dream was showing signs of weakness. It disturbed him greatly. Even more disturbing, all the pastors Ronan and Jayden met on the recommendations of Jayden's mom, were to say the least, less than pastoral.

***

For the next three years, at the end of each NBA season Jayden and Ronan went on their annual Hajj. Their star power was at a near zenith as they added two more NBA championships to their resumes. It became more difficult for the two heroes, as they were often called, to travel the country without their fame getting in the way of their desire to let loose and get to know America. There were exceptions.

Each of the three years, they attended the same Youth and Government workshop in Atlanta where they were two voices amongst many. No privileged treatment, no greater influence, no heroes; ordinary citizens.

Most impactful was on their last trip during the summer of 2017. On the suggestion of Jayden's father, they spent a day at Mortuary Affairs Squadron at Dover Air Force Base in Delaware. Even in 2017, armed services members were coming home in caskets. They saw firsthand what the term 'hero' meant. It was also there they decided to do something crazier than spending ten days in the Conch Republic. They were going to spend two years serving the American Republic.

***

September 24th, 2017 – ten miles south of St. Louis on I-55

"Happy Birthday, dude. There it is. The Gateway Arch in all its shining glory. Have you ever been up to the top?" Ronan asked.

"No. No one that lives in St. Louis ever has. Ronan, I can't tell you how much this trip has meant to me. One more stop."

"What's the address?"

"Just head downtown. Been there hundreds of times."

The marquee in the building's lobby had what they were looking for.

"Military Entrance Processing Station – 4th Floor."

Jayden had been there often, with his dad. General Quinn made it a point to visit as often as possible and shake the hands of those men and women who were volunteering to be tomorrow's soldiers, marines, seamen and airmen.

"You ready to do this?" Jayden asked.

"What the fuck? We've got nowhere better to be."

Actually they did. They were both supposed to have reported to NBA training camp two days earlier. But they weren't heading to NBA camp. They had a different camp in mind.

Jayden and Ronan stood side by side, their hands over their hearts and recited the words together.

"I do solemnly swear that I will support and defend the Constitution of the United States against all enemies, foreign and domestic; that I will bear true faith and allegiance to the same; and that I will obey the orders of the President of the United States and the orders of the officers appointed over me, according to regulations and the Uniformed Code of Military Justice. So help me God."

***

"You did what? Orlando, get your ass in here now." Tracy was yelling out an order to a two-star general. He reported as ordered, as he knew when he was outranked.

"Tell your father what you did."

"We signed up."

"For what?"

"The Army. Ronan and I joined together. It was his idea at first but I agreed. We leave in four weeks for Fort Leonard Wood. 11B's, both of us," Jayden said, referring to the Military Occupational Specialty (MOS) code for Infantry.

"Did you hear that? I told you that Ronan McCoy was no good. How ridiculously stupid it is to join the Army? Super star athletes don't sign up for the military in the prime of their careers. You're throwing away millions, hundreds of millions. I won't allow it."

"Mom, ever heard of Joe DiMaggio, Yogi Berra, Jackie Robinson, David Robinson, Chad Hennings and Pat Tillman? These men did exactly that. What makes me different?" Jayden answered his mom, having prepared his response a day earlier.

"Orlando, you have to do something. You out-rank those guys down at the MEPS center. Call someone. I'm not going to let my son ruin his future and maybe get killed for some stupid war in God knows where. Well, don't stand there, what are you going to do?"

"I'm going to congratulate my son and tell him I've never been more proud of him in my life. He's twenty-seven. If he wants to serve, that's his decision, not mine and not yours."

Tracy stormed out of the house and dialed her lover.

"I want him dead," Tracy said after Calvin answered the phone.

"You know we're not to talk about this on the phone. We need to meet somewhere in private. Not my home, not the church. Later tonight, how about seven?"

"No one's listening, Calvin. I have done everything you've asked and I need this in return. I want that fucking McCoy dead. Jayden is not going into the Army. Is that clear?"

"This is not what our organization is about and you've made this way too personal. The girl was one thing and the timing was perfect. No way my guy can handle this and I'm not doing it myself. You want a hit on a popular sports figure? Impossible. You need to calm down and accept it."

"I'm coming over to your house now. I'm not done with this."

"But the Rams are playing the Seahawks at three."

"Fuck the Rams, Calvin. They already moved to LA."

***

Back at the Quinn's, "Dad, we signed up for two years under the National

Call to Service program. Tell Mom when she calms down that I'll be back to the NBA when I'm twenty-nine. Not exactly an old man."

"Son, listen to me. I'm proud of you but I'm scared. You and I have talked about this. You can't tell when or where the danger will come. You could be sitting safely stateside today and gone to the battlefield tomorrow."

"All my life I've watched you and those under you go off to defend our country. Some of your men didn't come back. Ronan and I have spent three years traveling around the U.S. and we both agree on one thing. It's worth defending."

Jayden left his father standing there and retired to his old bedroom. Before doing so, he ripped out a page from one of his journals and placed it in his father's hand. It read: "America is a great dam, built from stone as solid as the Rockies. Behind which, a deep and endless reservoir of opportunity is available for all to tap into. But a near-invisible crack has developed in that dam and at its most vulnerable and dangerous location. At its base, at the bottom, where the pressure is always the greatest.

America is uniquely better than other places I have lived and in so many ways. But she is not unique in her sins. No person, no nation ever is. We must acknowledge these sins and strive for forgiveness through our actions and through the good fortune of which we are blessed.

As a nation, we must complete our patriotic penance by serving others in whatever capacity a person may. If not, that hairline crack will continue to grow, the pressure will continue to mount and one day all will burst.

I hope I may live so long as to see the day where status, fame and money are but the results of good fortune and not a measuring stick of one's value. I fear I may not. For there is an anxious nausea that has crept over the land. An illness without an immediately identifiable cause or remedy.

I will honor my Melissa, my parents and my country nonetheless. I will serve as they have, selflessly.

Jayden Fillmore Quinn – August 9th, 2017 – the 3rd anniversary of Melissa's death.

Orlando finished the letter weeping. If his son only knew the story behind his own history. Would his son still honor him? Would he still want to defend a nation that killed his parents?

In an age where the loudest voices in America were screaming "What's in it for me?" "Where's mine?" Were there those out there with no other desire than to serve?

In a country where reality TV stars, professional athletes, corporate executives, even politicians were raking in the millions while millions of others went without, were there men and women willing to serve and risk everything for a greater good? Yes there were. Jayden and Ronan were two more willing to do just that.

General Quinn didn't interfere with his son's decision to join but he made one little concession to his wife's unreasonable request. With one phone call to the MEPS Army commander in downtown St. Louis, Jayden Quinn and Ronan McCoy were no longer classified as infantry. They were reclassified to MOS 13B – Cannon Crew Member.

"Let them have some fun blowing stuff up," General Quinn said to the MEPS commander.

***

November 3rd, 2017 – Army Basic Combat Training, Fort Leonard Wood, Missouri

"Pick up your shit, off the bus and put your ass on that yellow line over there. Shut your pie holes and hurry the fuck up. What's taking you so long? Move it, Goddamn it," yelled Drill Sergeant Messina.

"Why do they keep telling us to hurry the fuck up? We get some place and stand around for four hours," Ronan asked Jayden.

"Shut up, Ronan. For once, keep your mouth shut."

"I heard that, Recruit Quinn. I hear everything. I see everything. Men, for the next ten weeks I'm your fucking father and mother. Not your friend. You'll follow my rules and they are final. Keep your mouth shut and do exactly what the fuck I tell you to do. Is that clear?"

"Yes, Drill Sergeant Messina."

"Forget whatever the fuck you read in the brochure. I'm not here to teach you to be killers. That's up to you. I'm here to teach how to take care of the soldier next to you. To do your duty and keep your sorry ass alive.

"And I don't give a damn what gender pronoun you go by out there in the world. Here, they don't exist. You will call everyone by their title and last name. If I hear a single 'he' or 'she' out of any one of you, I'll have your ass.

And speaking of asses, there'll be no grabbing them in the barracks' showers, if you know what I mean. Not while you're under my roof. Is that clear, too?"

"Yes, Drill Sergeant Messina."

Jayden and Ronan cruised through Army Basic Combat Training with relative ease. As professional athletes, they were more than up for the physical part. Even the yelling, cursing and motivation by humiliation were nothing they hadn't dealt with before from numerous coaches.

But like all recruits, each had their moments and questioned what it all meant. Jayden missed Melissa tremendously and he silently wept himself to sleep on numerous occasions. When it came to weeping, Ronan wasn't so silent.

"Which one of you cocksuckers is crying in my barracks now, Goddamn it?" an exceptionally loud Messina yelled after turning on the lights and waking everyone.

"I'm sorry, Drill Sergeant, thinking of a loved one," said Ronan.

"Well, Recruit McCoy, since you woke everyone up, tell us which one. Your mom, your sister or your girlfriend? Oh, wait, you're from West Virginia. They're all the same person." Messina had a way of seeming merciless.

"No, Drill Sergeant Messina, my oldest brother. He went through this training over ten years ago. Killed in Iraq in 2005."

"Sorry to hear that, Recruit McCoy. Iraq, FUBAR. Try to sleep, son. Oh, and recruit McCoy... Hooah."

"Hooah, Drill Sergeant."

Messina had a way of being merciful.

***

January 15th, 2018 – Graduation Day, ABCT, Ft. Leonard Wood, Missouri

"Excuse me, Drill Sergeant Messina, I think a mistake has been made here. Our recruiter said we'd be in the Infantry but these orders say 'Artillery – Cannon Crew'," said newly-minted Private Ronan McCoy to the most foul-mouthed human being he'd ever met.

"Son, I don't give a damn what your recruiter said. So much shit comes out of a recruiter's mouth, you'd think it was his asshole. Now, I'm looking at your orders and it clearly says, '13-Bravo, Cannon Crewmember'. Are you asking me to disobey an order, son?"

"No, Drill Sergeant, but we both signed up for Infantry. Maybe you could talk to Private Quinn's dad. His name is Major General Orlando Quinn. He's right over there in the grandstands." Ronan pleaded his case to someone who kept referring to him as son, even though Ronan was four years older.

"Private McCoy, I'd love to talk to the general. Heard great things about the man. But I don't care if you and Private Quinn are the twin afterbirths of General Dwight D. and Mamie fucking Eisenhower. Besides, the last thing you should be in is the Infantry. After ten weeks you still haven't figured out the ass-end from the working end of your M-16. You think I want our brave infantry soldiers dying by friendly fire?"

"No, Drill Sergeant."

"What you two limp dicks signed up for was the United States Army. And if my Army orders you to shovel the mountain of shit that comes out of the Pentagon for the next two years, then that's where I'm sending you.

"My suggestion to you, twinkle-toes, is that you and Private Quinn here pick up your shit and di di mau your asses over to the transport terminal. Your bus leaves in twenty minutes. You're both going to Field Artillery School, beautiful Fort Sill, Oklahoma. Enjoy the rest of your miserable fucking lives...Hooah!"

"Hooah, Drill Sergeant."

***

Jayden and Ronan did not end up shoveling excrement coming from the ass-ends of high-ranking officers, but their jobs weren't much better. They shoveled 95-pound high explosive projectiles into the ass-end of a 155mm Howitzer. After basic training and artillery school they had multiple duty assignments throughout the States.

The highlight of their entire two-year Army career was that no matter where they were assigned, they were blowing stuff up and playing basketball. Each Army post, big or small, had organized inter-post sports teams that competed against each other. And they competed fiercely. Football, baseball and basketball were the money sports. Post Commanders wagered hundreds and sometimes thousands that their squad could whip the tar out of the squad from some other post.

When commanders learned that two of the best basketball players in the world were coming to play for so-and-so Army Post, all bets were off. "Not even a high-ranking officer is dumb enough to bet against you two," said several teammates. Ronan and Jayden never came within 5,000 miles of a combat zone. But wherever they traveled in uniform, people were "thanking them for their service."

"I hate that phrase," said Ronan after hearing it for the thousandth time. "What am I, a damn coffee barista at Starbucks? If America wants to thank its military members for their service, why don't they pay them a decent, living wage?"

By October 2019 and their enlistment term coming to an end, they both decided it was time to get back to the world of professional basketball. In the NBA, they were paid slightly more than an Army E-3's monthly salary of $1,800. Calculated accordingly, Ronan's monthly salary playing a game was $1,985,500. Jayden's was closer to $3 million.

Ronan wanted to commemorate his time in the Army by adding a couple more tattoos but he had a hard time finding any available epidermal real estate. On a suggestion by the artist, he had a 155mm Howitzer inked on his left butt cheek and a basketball hoop on his right.

Scrolling across the few available inches right above his ass crack was the rendering of a 95-pound, high explosive projectile in mid-flight heading toward its target. A range indicator was added to show distance. Twenty-four kilometers the indicator read. A three-pointer.

"I'm in the best shape of my life. Some of those guys we played against were as good as we are. Especially that team from Fort Leonard Wood. They should start their own NBA franchise. They kicked our ass," Ronan said to Jayden as they boarded their flight back to the civilian world.

They both appreciated the opportunity to wear the uniform of the US Army and would miss the days where their bodies were tested and exhausted from the physical labor of practicing war. Their hands were black from the spent gunpowder but their hearts were filled with the red, white and blue pride of teamwork and country. Which was good.

Because in August of 2020, they were going to need to test their bodies again. Their patriotic hearts would be tested as well. And lastly, the time would come to make war, not practice it, and they would do so with their black hands.

***

PRESENT DAY

August 9th, 2021 – 4:51pm, Russell Senate Office Building, Washington, DC

"Ladies and gentlemen, fellow Americans, that concludes our briefing for today," starts Sara Gujic. "We will be picking it back up tomorrow morning starting promptly at 8am. While this commission is in no position to issue homework assignments to the American people, we would like to make two suggestions that will aid in understanding our presentation tomorrow.

"There are two movies available by streaming on our website that we encourage everyone to watch even if they have done so before. *The Dirty Dozen* and *Saving Private Ryan*.

"Also, on our website page at www.89.gov is a downloadable copy of the United States Constitution. We will be discussing a number of provisions contained within our greatest document and a refresher on its contents will be invaluable. Are there any questions from the Senate or House Chairpersons before we dismiss for the evening?"

The Senate Chairman on Homeland Security starts, "Madam Gujic, I commend you and your team on such a thorough yet interesting perspective on the people and events of August 9th, 2020. Your use of historical references, metaphors and might I say, colorful language, has made the day go by very quickly. This style of down-to-earth communication is often lacking in the chambers of Congress. Is this a technique you've used throughout your career in journalism?"

"First off let me say that everyday language is infinitely more 'colorful' than what I've shared with you today. I said at the beginning of this briefing that as it relates to dialogue, we took some artistic liberties. In other words, I cleaned it up. If I were to repeat the sort of language that was most likely said, we would spend the day cringing with apprehension.

"What I've used today would never make it to copy in normal reporting but my editor-in-chief insisted it be put into our presentation to add context to the story. I was outranked."

"And who was your editor, if you don't mind me asking?"

"The Vice President of the United States."

As she's leaving the Russell Senate building, the Capitol Police officer states to her kindly, "Please don't bring another gun with you tomorrow, Ms. Gujic."

"How about an A-10 Warthog instead?" she answers with a smile.

Part III
"The Crna Ruka and the Black Hand"

EIGHTEEN

PRESENT DAY

August 10th, 2021—8 am, Russell Senate Office Building, Washington, DC

Sara Gujic, the same attendees from the previous day, and now 200 million Americans are ready and eager for her to begin the second day of the briefing. Another 4 billion people are watching worldwide, making it the single largest television audience in history and surpassing the lighting of the Olympic flame in 1996 by world-renowned sports hero Muhammed Ali.

"Good morning, ladies and gentlemen. Thank you for being on time. We will forgo the formalities and start right into today's briefing.

"I want to begin this morning by turning the tables for a moment. A question for both the Senate and House chairpersons on Homeland Security. Sir, ma'am, did either of you see the movies we recommended?"

Sara knows the answers already, as the two leaders organized a series of national watch parties held across the country at empty stadiums and arenas.

"You first," the Senate chairman said.

"Yes, *The Dirty Dozen*," began the congresswoman. "Twelve guys sent on a mission from which they were unlikely to return. Only two or three survive. I did a little research. That movie was mostly based on an actual event that took place the day before D-Day.

"On June 5th, 1944, a group of commandos from the 101st Airborne Division called the Filthy Thirteen parachuted behind enemy lines. Their orders were to blow up as many enemy-held bridges and communications antennae as possible before the main invasion of Normandy. I think only two of them lived.

"In the movie *The Dirty Dozen*, I love the actors. Lee Marvin, Jim Brown, and Charles Bronson. Dreamboats all of them." Checking to make sure her HDMI cable isn't plugged in, Gujic searches the three men from the 1967 film. So do 50 million young women and 2 million young men who couldn't watch the movies the night before. The congresswoman is right. Dreamboats.

"And what was the main plot of that, ma'am? And was the mission successful?" Sara asks as a follow-up question.

"The mission was to infiltrate an enemy stronghold and kill as many Nazi officers as possible. Even though most of the twelve men ended up dying, their mission was a success.

"They were able to penetrate the fortification by pretending to be enemy officers themselves and by knocking out the communication systems. Once inside, they killed hundreds. The premise was to cut off the head of the German war machine. Wipe out their command and control capabilities in preparation for the bigger objective, the full-scale invasion of Europe and the defeat of the evils of Nazi fascism."

"Thank you, ma'am. And you, Senator?"

"I saw both of them for the umpteenth time. *Saving Private Ryan* is as realistic a production of the horrors of war as there is. The main theme is how a squad of eight men risked everything to save the life of one. I think a total of six died, but Private Ryan lived. A cinematic tribute to the sacrifice soldiers make for their fellowman. Great acting as well.

"The film is loosely based on the true story of the four Niland brothers. Three were presumed killed in action, and the remaining brother was thought to be still alive during the first few days of the Normandy invasion. The army sent a squad of men to find this brother and bring him home safely so that at least one lived on. Why do you ask, Ms. Gujic? Why is this important?"

"Great acting, a heroic suicide mission, and one man worth saving is what this morning's briefing is about. Thank you both for sharing and for playing along."

The two leaders of Congress look at each other, not knowing they and much of America had just been played.

***

NEARLY TWO YEARS AGO

October 1st, 2019 – Madic's Café, Little Bosnia, St. Louis, Missouri

The door to the café opened, and the two bells attached to the top of the door alerted the owner of a patron's entrance. The owner, Hamza Madic, rarely, if ever, had customers during the dinner hours. He never had breakfast or lunch patrons either.

To now see a stunning African-American couple standing in his restaurant's foyer took him totally by surprise. These two, who were draped all over each other, made for an impressive sight. The man, a giant, was someone Hamza concluded instantly he didn't want to mess with. The woman, a Nubian queen, beautiful and built. If ever given the chance, he would mess with her a lot.

"Two for dinner?"

"Yes, please," replied Calvin Heyward. Tracy had recommended the small café as she had visited it numerous times with her husband quite a few years ago. The place was always empty, and the Bosnian community had a reputation for minding its own business. A perfect place for privacy. But now, the café owner was staring at Tracy a moment too long for her comfort.

"Is there something wrong?"

"You look familiar. I saw you on TV. Yes, you are the mother of the Crna Ruka," Madic said, implying Tracy somehow spoke Bosnian.

"The what?"

"Crna Ruka. The 'Black Hand' in Bosnian. It is spelled C-R-N-A R-U-K-A. Jayden Quinn, three-time NBA champion—he is the Black Hand. You are his mother, no? You were with him on television during NBA draft."

Now Tracy was downright irritated. She hated any type of nickname for her son, and one that drew attention to his skin color was an insult of the worst nature.

Hamza could see the disturbed look in her eyes and he figured out why. "No, no. I'm sorry. Crna Ruka, the Black Hand, it is not about the skin. Crna Ruka is a secret organization in my country. Heroes. Dragutin Dimitrijevic was Supreme Commander. He was Apis. The Holy Bull. Gavrilo Princip was shooter. Killed that Austrian bastard Archduke

Ferdinand and his wife in Sarajevo in 1914. You know, the event that started World War I."

"What the fuck are you talking about?" Calvin asked.

"Her son, Jayden Quinn, is most famous shooter in basketball and also hero, like the Crna Ruka. Everyone back in my country, we are crazy about basketball. We call Jayden Quinn, Crna Ruka. The Black Hand."

Neither Tracy nor Calvin had any idea what the guy was talking about and wished he'd shut his mouth and take their order.

"Please, say it with me. *Tschirna*; you must pronounce the *T* and the *S* before the *C*."

"But you said the word was spelled C-R-N-A in English. Where's the *T* and the *S*?" Tracy Quinn replied, confused.

"In English you have no same letter but I'm telling you the way to say the word. Keep trying, I'll get dinner ready." The tiny, near-hairless man giving the language lesson went to the kitchen to try to find something for them to eat.

"I love that phrase, Crna Ruka. The Black Hand." Heyward searched Crna Ruka on his phone. "It has history and meaning," stated Calvin. "I want to name our little enterprise something. The Italians are the Cosa Nostra, the Japanese the Yakuza, the Russians, the Bratva. I'll be the Supreme Commander," he said seriously.

"It says here the leader of the Crna Ruka had a nickname. He called himself 'Apis,' and it means the Holy Bull. I love that, too. You can call me Apis from now on, and I'll call you my *consigliere*."

"*Consigliere* is Italian, Calvin, not Bosnian. No more stupid nicknames. That one sounds gay. Your friends will call you 'Apith,' with a lisp...Tirna Ruka...Sirna Ruka...Chirna Ruka. Fuck it. Can't we call it the Black Hand in English?"

"No, I like it the way it is," demanded the newly appointed Supreme Commander of a crime ring now named the Crna Ruka. Heyward relished the idea of being known as something more than the boss of bunch of gangsters. He wanted a legacy.

"My plans are bigger than you can imagine. The country's a goddamn mess. That's a good thing for us. The divisions in this country are getting worse, not better. Shit, even the cops are on the defensive. We can leverage that."

"This whole line of thinking of yours isn't normal, Calvin."

"Neither are you. You're the mother of one of the wealthiest athletes in the world and you're with me. And you're stealing state secrets from your husband."

With Tracy's years of help in providing real-time, satellite imaging of targets of opportunities as well as access to police departments' response protocols and targets of investigations, across the country Calvin's group benefited from a tactical advantage that other crime groups did not. His power, wealth, and criminal influence over his men grew accordingly.

Calvin spent the rest of the evening scribbling on a Bev-Nap. His writing would become the Crna Ruka's new secret oath. Actually, it was the old oath of the Crna Ruka, and he got that from Google as well. He modified it only slightly for currency of language. He handed it to Tracy for her signature.

She read it, rolling her eyes. "There; you happy? I signed your stupid, juvenile oath."

For the previous nineteen years, Heyward had arranged for the five other crime bosses to come to St. Louis to discuss their operations. Calvin was excited about introducing the new name at their upcoming meeting, scheduled for January 2020.

***

Like Tracy and Calvin, the café owner, Hamza Madic, wasn't normal either. Yes, he was Bosnian by country but not Bosniak as he claimed, not of Muslim faith. He was a Bosnian Serb, as they were called ethnically. His was born of Eastern Orthodox faith. He'd immigrated to the United States under the false pretense of being Bosniak, as his sister married a Muslim man.

Originally, Madic was on the murdering side of the war. He was part of a Serbian Army unit responsible for killing over 8,000 civilian men and boys in the small town of Srebrenica, Bosnia, in 1995. He personally murdered his sister's husband (father to Davud Novak, the NBA star).

Madic found faith in Allah after an international war crimes tribunal started chasing down the Eastern Orthodox murderers. He left Bosnia under the sponsorship of his sister. She never knew it was her own brother who had killed her husband.

Madic opened his small café in St. Louis in 2000 not knowing much about food. He was more a procurer of hardware, software, and vaporware -

specifically guns, human trafficking, prostitution, and crack cocaine. Whether a customer wanted to kill or enslave someone while being whacked out of their mind, Madic could get the appropriate product.

Weapons came from Russia and the war-torn nation states of southeastern Europe. Young men and women came from the same region. Lured to America on the pretense of "jobs" by Madic and his associates back in Europe, they became modern-day slaves. Sex and drug-dealing were the products of their labor, not cotton.

***

"Boss, you go see the little Bosnian when you need guns or girls, not food. He's a small-time player but he never fails to deliver. You could use a guy like that on your payroll," said Calvin Heyward's main right-hand guy. On his second visit, Calvin ordered something not on the menu.

"Hamza, I heard you might be able to sell me something I need for work," Calvin said.

"And I was told you might be asking. One of my regular customers said to expect a visit. What do you want? Boy or girl?"

"I'm looking for guns, two AKs and a 9mm."

"This is America, my friend. Much easier than boys and girls. Come back next week. $10,000 for the two AK-47s, full automatic. Made by great grandson of Kalashnikov himself. I have big contacts in Russia. They love Serbs. The 9mm is free."

"Okay, but I thought you're Bosniak?"

"Same thing."

Madic was excited about his new customers and never challenged why the family of one of the most successful sports superstars in America needed guns. He didn't ask many questions. It was bad for business, and he preferred to do all the talking. The little criminal also thought he could continue to grow his enterprise by having such important customers. And he could have, if he'd kept his big mouth shut. He didn't.

***

November 1st, 2019 – Madic's Café, St. Louis, Missouri

"Coach Gibbs, good to see you," said Hamza as the coach entered the restaurant. "How long has it been?"

"Quite a while, Hamza. The last time I was here was to pick up that pistol you sold me."

The only reason Coach Gibbs ever went to Madic's café was to practice his Bosnian and to see if the licensed gun dealer came across any military items of historical note. The last time he'd met with Madic was in 2014. He'd purchased the exact pistol used by the famous killer Gavrilo Princip of the Crna Ruka to shoot the Archduke Ferdinand in 1914. He'd paid $25,000 for the gun and thought it a bargain considering its historical significance.

Gibbs never challenged how Madic came into possession of the weapon. He thought that as long as the gun came with all the documents of authenticity and provenance of chain of ownership, he was fine with it.

What the coach didn't realize was that the gun was stolen. The thief who'd stolen it was Hamza Madic himself when he was in the Serbian army. His unit sacked the city of Sarajevo, and many of the soldiers helped themselves to the artifacts of many of Sarajevo's museums. Madic was smart enough to take all the accompanying papers of authenticity with him from the museum.

"It should be the pride of your collection. Princip was Bosnian hero. Speaking of heroes, I met the parents of Jayden Quinn, the NBA star."

"Yeah, I know who Jayden is. He is a close family friend and he played for me in college. Where did you meet his parents?"

"Right here. Few weeks ago. During Rams and Cowboys game. They are so, how you say, lovey-dovey. Always kissing. Best-looking black couple I ever saw."

"Great; glad you met them."

"Yes. Giant man! If you're friends with Jayden, you must know his dad as well."

"And what did they talk about?"

"My English is still not the best, and I mind my business. They did say something about her son's old girlfriend. About being reaped."

"You sure they didn't say 'raped'?"

"Yeah, yeah. What does that mean?"

"Everything."

Coach Gibbs asked for the check. He left with his plate full, both literally and figuratively speaking.

***

"If what that café owner says is true, then it couldn't have been Orlando with Tracy," Ken said to his wife.

"How certain are you? Did you talk to the general?"

"I didn't need to talk to him. I was with him. We watched the Rams game on TV together."

"I'm sure it was an innocent mistake. Probably two friends having a bite to eat."

"Theresa, I need you to sit down. We need to talk, and before I start, I'm begging for your forgiveness. I believe Tracy is somehow involved in Melissa's death."

"What did that son-of-a-bitch do?"

NINETEEN

November 17th, 2019—Madic's Café, St. Louis, Missouri

During Jayden's two-year stretch of military service, Calvin Heyward proved to be right about his prediction he made to Tracy. Without the distractions of family and basketball matters, Tracy and Calvin grew his organization to unprecedented levels of success. Under his immediate command were the five former inmates that controlled most of the organized, illegal activities within their respective markets. All under the guise of operating a church.

With the "tithing" each man was expected to pay to Calvin, he became one of the more powerful crime lords in the country. The success went to his head. Hamza Madic went to his head as well.

"Calvin, when the Soviet Union and my former country Yugoslavia collapsed under the weight of communism, it was the most profitable times. Entire industries became the personal property of the men with the power to grab and grab quickly. They are all now billionaires and leaders of their countries. Imagine if something like that happened in the United States."

"But those men had armies. Maybe we have 200 men across the country. Mostly boys who think this is some type of game."

"They had ball, not armies. With small groups of men, they took control of, how you say, *elektri•na kompanija?*"

"You mean electric companies?"

"Yes, and mines, oil, banks. No one knew what the hell was going on. The people were scared. Many in government abandoned their people, stole from treasury and left. Why do you think there are so many rich Russians in this country? Now is the perfect time. My guys can join you. Maybe fifteen or twenty.

"Look at how people live. Isolated and scared shitless in their stupid gated communities way out in the suburbs. Their Facebook posts where they 'Marked Myself Safe' during a fucking rainstorm. We need to show them, they're not."

"How so?"

"Hit where it hurts the most. At the top. Make a statement to America's aristocrats that there's a new order in this country. A new Crna Ruka."

Since he was a young man, Calvin had always felt destined for something more than life had given him. Here was a chance for him to take it. He talked it through with his five associates. They weren't so convinced their boss and a former war criminal knew what the hell they were talking about. But they were too frightened and isolated themselves to challenge the man.

***

Calvin Heyward had been right about something else two years ago. By the start of the 2019–2020 season, Jayden Quinn was five years into his basketball career and had won three NBA championships. He added as many NBA Most Valuable Player awards. A relatively unknown kid from nowhere and everywhere at the same time, Jayden became the league's biggest star. The two years in the army had only brightened his star power.

Fortune 500 companies, sneaker manufacturers, and movie producers all loved the squeaky-clean, worldly, and patriotic image that Jayden exuded. Advertisers grew tired of superstar athletes and Hollywood actors and musicians who couldn't keep themselves out of trouble. Jayden Quinn was the antithesis of trouble. He was good.

His personality reflected his upbringing and military service, and it was as American as apple pie. During post-game interviews and everyday conversations, he stood at attention, answered questions abruptly and honestly, and finished every sentence with "sir" or "ma'am," a habit he was taught by his father and reinforced by the Army.

Jayden Quinn, by way of multiple successful contract negotiations by his mother, product sponsorships and investments, had an estimated net worth of nearly $250 million by 2020. Tracy Quinn's sports agency had a clientele of one and pulled in over $3 million a year in commissions. Jayden insisted his mom keep the money. She earned it. She worked tirelessly to protect the image of her son and was ruthless with anyone who tried to damage it, including—and especially—the media.

She was particularly intolerant of those who tried to hijack her son's name and assign some ridiculous nickname to him. To her it was lazy, hurtful, and indicative of a media that couldn't care less about the wishes of her family. They were trying to leverage a brand they had assigned to him for their own pleasure and benefit. She and General Quinn had chosen their son's name for a reason, and she expected people to use it accordingly.

At the start of the 2019 season, one particular tone-deaf reporter by the name of Frank Unnerstall felt her wrath. Unnerstall continued to refer to Jayden as "J.Q.," a nickname too stupid to be considered evenly remotely cute. Tracy was sick of it and coached her son how to prepare for the next post-game interview.

"J.Q., you didn't look your best today. What happened?" asked Unnerstall.

"F.U., I think I played okay," Jayden said. "F.U., this game is harder than most realize."

F.U. was turning red.

"If I didn't meet your standards of play today, well, F.U., let me close with saying, F.U., F.U."

Mr. Unnerstall never said the letters "J" and "Q" together again.

Even with all the success, endorsements, and book deals for Jayden, Tracy still hadn't come up with a proper and legal name for her agency. She didn't think she needed one. The IRS not so subtly encouraged her to do so. A name was eventually suggested by her husband, and she instantly loved it. IASW, LLC filed its corporate papers in 2019.

Her friends, including the Gibbs, the media, and Hollywood producers tried to get out of her the meaning of the acronym.

"International Athletic Sports World?" guessed one. Nope.

"Individual Athlete's Secret Weapon," said another, referring to her single client and her ruthless negotiating skills. Nope. Finally, most gave up guessing and asked her.

"She could tell you, but then I'd have to kill you," General Quinn joked.

To NBA brass, Jayden was the face, voice, and image of professional basketball. He had unmatched global recognition, social and economic influence, and between the four leading social media platforms, Jayden's followers topped 300 million. The Pope had 200 million.

Jayden never understood how his social media following could be so high. He never posted or tweeted in his life. He had no clue that his official and only post on Facebook about winning his third Most Valuable Player award was: "Humbled, honored and undeserving." That is, until his mother told him. The post received 45 million "Likes," and not surprisingly there was a static advertisement of a popular shoe company displayed next to the post. That one post earned him $250,000.

In Jayden's future, there was little doubt in people's minds that with his upbringing, talent, and universal influence and appeal, one day he might even become President of the United States. If that were to ever happen, people thought, he would be the first president to be born outside of the country, as he was born in a hospital in the Middle East. Those same people would have been wrong by a multiple of ten.

The first nine presidents of the United States were all born prior to the ratification of the Constitution on December 7th, 1787. They were, until that date, citizens of the British Empire. George Washington was no more a naturally born citizen of the United States at birth in 1732 than Jayden Quinn was in 1990.

And by 2019, Jayden and Ronan were not just teammates and road-trip mates, they were roommates. They shared an apartment in their NBA city during the season and a home in St. Louis during the summers. Their time together, which was always, gave them ample opportunity to discuss everything from basketball to politics.

"What do you think's going on in this country?" Ronan said.

"How so?"

"Is it me or is everyone angry about something?"

"You got a point. There was some bullshit in the Army, but for the most part, we all got along."

"Roger that. But read the paper, man, or check out the news sites online. Everyone's trying to own each other or destroy their opponent in the simplest of disagreements. Social media has created an instant and anonymous way to go off. Could you imagine if we talked the type of crap people put online to somebody on the basketball court or in our army unit?"

"We'd get our asses kicked."

The mass media as well as users of social media were becoming increasingly intolerant toward any position not a hundred percent in alignment with that of their own. The verbal and written threats were more frequently manifesting themselves into actual hostilities. People blackballed from their careers or from college campuses for voicing their First Amendment rights. Mass shootings occurring almost weekly. Open physical clashes in streets across the country.

"Do you think there could ever be another civil war?" Ronan asked Jayden.

"That sounds crazy. But when both sides of an argument believe it could be the end of the world if the other side wins, then yes, another civil war is possible."

"How could something like that even start? When is the 'zero hour' or that flashpoint when neighbors decide to hell with it and pick up arms against each other?"

"Maybe when a white guy wins an NBA MVP award," Jayden joked.

"Dude, this year I'm shooting for your title, my friend. Of course, then I'll retire and move to the Conch Republic. No one wants to kill each other down there. All they want to do down there is fish, drink, and other things."

"Yeah, I know, Ronan."

TWENTY

"*One bag of otters' noses please. Wait, make it two,*" *Reg said.*
"*Are you the Judean People's Front?*" *asked Brian.*

"*Fuck off. The Judean People's Front? Huh. We're the People's Front of Judea,*" *Reg answered angrily and continued.* "*The Judean People's Front, bunch of wankers.*"

"*Can I join your group?*"

"*No. Piss off. Listen, if you wanted to join the PFJ, you'd have to really hate the Romans.*"

"*I do already. I hate the Romans as much as anybody.*"

"*Oh yeah, how much?*"

"*A lot.*"

"*Right. You're in. But the only people we hate more than the Romans are the fucking Judean People's Front. And the Judean Popular People's Front. Splitters.*"

***

Buff Sowers pressed the "Off" button on the TV remote. No matter how many times she watched the 1979 Monty Python classic *Life of Brian*, she couldn't help but nearly wet herself laughing. Members of the comedy troupe were visionaries as well as hilarious. The movie was a simple script about the chronicles of a historical case of mistaken identity. Little did she know, she would also one day be written into a script of mistaken identity with historical significance.

Earlier in her career, during three tours in the Middle East, Sowers often marveled at how hysterical yet prophetic the brilliant group of comedians from England were.

Between Al Qaeda, Iraqi insurgents, Bosnian and Chechen fighters, ISIS, Hamas, Hezbollah, and other various splitter groups, she had a hard time distinguishing the good guys from the bad. So like any good airman, she did as ordered and blew up every target assigned. No questions asked. She thought someone higher up figured out the good from the bad. No, they hadn't.

Back home in the States things weren't much different. Buff still had a hard time figuring out who the good guys were and who were the bad. Again, she assumed the higher-ups had it figured out. No, they hadn't, either.

At least Buff knew a few of the good guys. Kenneth Gibbs and Orlando Quinn. They saved her life; therefore they must be good, she deduced. Since they'd become friends, they often spent long weekends together doing nothing more than telling war stories and getting rip-roaring drunk.

She was about to do the same with one of the bad guys. Or in this case, bad girl.

***

November, 2019—Sean Bolan's Irish Pub, Bel Air, Maryland

"$F2 = G\frac{m_1 m_2}{r^2}$" declared the ringtone on Colonel Buff Sowers' phone. Newton's universal law of gravitational force was her favorite mathematical formula. Mostly in that she spent the majority of her life defying it. Sowers answered her phone.

"Colonel Thowerth here. How can I help you?"

"Buff, it's Tracy. Sorry I'm running late. I'll be there in twenty minutes."

"No problem, Trathy. Thee you in a bit."

"Fuck, she's drunk already," Tracy said while hanging up. Buff heard every word.

***

"Trathy..." said Buff, lisping badly upon completing her sixth pint of Guinness. The severely burnt and damaged muscles of Sowers's lower left jaw weakened even more every time she drank alcohol. The combat injury and booze caused her to have a major speech impediment. Tracy Quinn cringed at the very sound of Buff speaking. Buff noticed.

"At firth I wath upthet the boyth couldn't make it, but I underthand how buthy they are. I'm glad itth juth uth girlth. Whereth Theretha? We thould FaythTime her."

"No. Let's not, please. We don't see each other much anymore. She's not as much fun as she was before Melissa died. I like to party. Fifty is the new thirty."

"No itth not. Fifty ith old ath thit."

"Not with these." Tracy was alluding to the fact that her husband now referred to her as "the Quadruple D's" after a second boob job.

"Good luck not tripping over thoth when you're thikthy. Thpeaking of Melitha, howth Corporal Quinn?"

"His career is where I planned it to be. I was at a meeting this morning with the marketing department of Under Armor in Baltimore. We signed a ten-million-dollar endorsement deal over the next three years."

"What about Jayden'th planth?"

"Buff, I'm sorry to hear you were turned down by the promotion board again. Orlando told me about it." A nice deflection by Tracy.

"I'm not giving up. With thome exthepthion, I've had a good career in the Air Forth. I juth don't have the money to retire yet. One more promothion interview in two weekth and if that happenth, I'll do two more yearth and retire at O-theven pay. If not, I'm done."

Tracy saw an opening for a possible conversion. "What if I told you a church I'm involved in is looking for new leaders. People with different skills, different connections. There is a branch right here in Baltimore. The opportunity is much more lucrative than you can imagine."

"I'm lithening."

"Let's wait until tomorrow when you can talk more intelligently. When you're sober."

"I'm thorry if my lithp botherth you. I'll try not to get half my faythe burned off nekth time I crath."

The next day, Buff shook off her hangover and lisp and wanted to talk to Tracy again, more intelligently. Tracy, likewise, was ready to put it all out there with a woman she believed was ready to join the Crna Ruka.

"Black women are always lowest on the totem pole in this country, Buff. Here's a chance for you to rise to the top. Come to St. Louis and meet my pastor, Calvin Heyward, and the other brothers. Talk to them. Let them get to know and like you."

"Just get to the point. I'm done trying to impress men."

"As a senior ranking officer of the National Guard, I would guess you have access to information about domestic emergency response protocols, guard unit strengths, police tactics, and potential weaknesses."

"Okay, and...?"

"There are those who would pay handsomely for that information."

"What you're asking me to do is commit treason. To go against everything I believe in. What's stopping me from calling the cops now?"

"Because you know in your heart you deserve more. In your career you've been passed over, ignored, ridiculed for who you are and spied on by your own government. Join me, Buff. Let's show the world what two strong black women can do together.

"There's something else I should tell you. I have unrestricted access to the entire intelligence community's networks. Courtesy of the man you love so much. My husband. By scores of army and civilian laws, he will be found guilty of espionage. He gave his wife access to our nation's systems. If you turn me in, you turn him in. Would you want that to happen to a man who saved your life? I'm leaving him, Buff. I'm with Calvin now."

"Tracy, I'm a PhD in mathematics, but I'm nothing compared to you."

"How so?"

"You're one calculating thlut."

***

"Hello," Tracy said after recognizing Colonel Sowers's number.

"What the fuck did you say to the general about me?"

"What are you talking about? I didn't say anything."

"Bullshit. I was turned down again for promotion. The board said the general gave me a less than favorable personal recommendation. Said I'd been unstable since Adrian died. What the fuck did you say to him?"

"Buff, I swear I didn't say anything. I was afraid you might tell him about our conversation."

"Well, whatever. I'm in. I want to earn some big money and fly the hell out of this country forever. I'm done with this crap. I've got an idea – give me a few weeks to work out the details."

TWENTY-ONE

January 23rd, 2020—North End Zone Club, Dome of America, St. Louis, MO

Pastor Calvin Heyward called to order the 20th Annual Convention of Pastors of the Unified Church of God and the first-ever convention of the Crna Ruka. In attendance were leaders from individual churches across the country and officials from the headquarters, located in St. Louis. People came from as far west as Oakland, California, and from as far east as New York City. Prior to 2020, the convention had been held at various venues and on different dates based mostly on the availability of affordable space.

In celebration of twenty years of fellowship and felonious activity, Heyward decided to host this year's convention someplace special. The former home of the St. Louis Rams football team: the Dome at America's Center.

The date, January 23rd, 2020, was chosen, as it was also the 20th anniversary of the St. Louis Rams defeating the Tampa Bay Buccaneers in the NFC Championship Game in the very same building.

Heyward had been in attendance at that game, and the Rams went on to win their one and only Super Bowl two weeks later. Sixteen years later, the owner of the Rams told the world, "Fuck St. Louis. This city is rotten. I'm moving the Rams to LA."

The team had vacated the 60,000-seat venue after the conclusion of the 2016 season and the building was now being used to host Comic-Con conventions, concerts, and Monster Jam events. It was Heyward's delusional dream that one day his organization would grow to a size that required every last one of those 60,000 seats, but for 2020, he settled on renting the North End Zone Club instead.

After taking into account the two other local church officials in attendance, Heyward accurately tallied the number of attendees for this year's convention to be eight.

A complete list of attendees as well as an agenda was provided to start the convention.

Pastor Heyward - Unified Church of God, St. Louis and National Director

Pastor Hicks - Atlanta, Peachtree Evangelical African Church of Hotlanta

Bishop Charles - Baltimore, Pigtown and Dundalk Presbyterian

Pastor Smiley - Los Angeles, Unified Church of Compton

Pastor Morton - New York, Bronx Assembly of God

Pastor George - Oakland, Golden Gate Order of God

Tracy Quinn - Chief Financial Officer, HQ, Unified Church of God

There was an eighth attendee, an administrative assistant at Heyward's church, and he was there to take notes for the meeting. His name was not printed on the agenda.

The cost of the venue was extraordinary compared with years past, but 2019 had proved to be a blessed year for the church. Large amounts of funding were provided by ongoing operations and by an anonymous benevolent benefactor in the way of multiple six- and seven-figure cash donations. The benefactor was so anonymous, even he didn't realize he was being so graciously benevolent.

Jayden Quinn was being robbed, one large wire transfer after another, by his mother and Heyward. It was easier than passing around the collection plate, armed robbery, and murder. It was also quite a bit more lucrative. In total, Tracy had stolen over $7 million from Jayden's accounts in the previous six years, and the basketball star never realized it was gone.

Most of the money went to upgrades to Heyward's private pastorium, transportation, and funding of international mission trips. He was now living in a $3.5 million home in Ladue, driving a BMW 8 Series convertible, and leading church missions to places like the south of France, Oahu, and Dubai.

The convention, like most, had its traditions, and it commenced with a new oath of allegiance, followed by a short prayer from Pastor Heyward. He concluded his opening remarks with passages from his favorite book of the Bible, Exodus.

"At midnight on the ninth of the month, the Lord killed all the first-born in the land of Egypt, from the first-born of Pharaoh who sat on the throne, to the first born of the farmer, who profited from the toil of slaves. Pharaoh got up in the night, he and his servants and all the Egyptians. And there was a loud cry in Egypt. For there was no home where there was not someone dead...then Pharaoh called for Moses and Aaron at night.

"He said, 'Get up and go away from my people, both you and the people of Israel. Go and worship the Lord, as you said. Take your flocks and your cattle, as you said, and go...the people of Israel had lived in Egypt in slavery for 454 years.'"

The agenda for the meeting was typed up by Calvin's assistant and was presented in the proper and professional manner of an organization that knew what it was doing. At least one member of the Crna Ruka had had experience in a regular office job at one time or another.

Plans for Coordinated Spiritual Retreats for August 9th, 2020, 12:01 pm CDT

Proposals from each of the five visiting pastors

Anticipated number of fatalities

Financing requirements

Communications and Information Technology

Public Policy Position paper

Action plans for next six months

"Gentlemen, you've had the agenda for some number of weeks and each of you were asked to develop a plan for the events you will be leading on August 9th. You were all instructed to design those plans based on your local area and with three criteria.

"Identify targets of opportunity likely to be heavily populated with affluent individuals.

"Targets must be considered 'soft' in regards to levels of security and police presence.

"Attacks should be less than thirty minutes on station and result in 200 casualties or more.

"You will present your plans today. We will discuss and approve financing requirements and our communications protocols. You will be in charge of local logistics and operational execution.

"We'll finish the meeting discussing our demands which will be delivered to Washington, DC, within days after August 9th. Are we good with the agenda?" Heyward asked.

All nodded affirmative.

"Good, now who wants to go first?"

Pastor Smiley from Los Angeles raised his hand. "I'll start. I'm leaving early to catch my flight at six."

"Always one at every meeting who has to leave early. What makes him so goddamn special?" whispered one of the other attendees to his table-mate.

"My twenty soldiers are ready to go. They are 100 percent committed. My first lieutenant will lead the attack. They're going to meet at the church and take a school bus we intend to steal the night before. We're going to a rally point at a golf course in Beverly Hills. We'll split into two groups.

"There is an annual fundraiser at the Playboy Mansion scheduled for the second Sunday in August. Half the men will go there. The other half will head to Rodeo Drive as people are having breakfast and prepping for a day of shopping. Both sites are less than one mile from the rally point, and my men will have to double-time it to the attack locations.

"We estimate we can kill at least 200. The total elapsed time we will be at the club is scheduled for thirty minutes. Back on the bus and back to Compton. With Tracy's maps and real-time police response routes, we are confident in our ability to pull this off.

"We'll need somewhere around 550 grand for the weapons, safe houses, hush money, bail if needed, and something for my guys. I think there should be a little left over for my pastoral coffers so to be safe, I'm asking for 600 grand."

"I like the 30,000-foot plan, but you'll need more details than that to carry it off without getting caught. In your presentation you casually mention you won't be personally leading the event. Do you mind sharing with the group why not?" Heyward asked, curious.

"Guys, I'm not a soldier, a killer. I'm turning seventy-one next year and I am not physically up to the challenge. My main guy is more than capable of leading the group."

"Pastor Smiley, do I need to remind you of the new oath of allegiance you affirmed an hour ago?" Heyward rose up from his chair, his massive body blocking out the entire PowerPoint image that was being projected on the wall behind him.

"You will be attending the event or you can leave now." By leave, what Heyward was telling Smiley was that it was unlikely he would make it to the airport before being gunned down in the parking lot.

"Okay, I understand. I'll be there. Am I green-lighted to go with this?"

"Yes. Who's next?"

Bishop Charles from Baltimore spent twenty minutes presenting his plan of attack. After he clicked through his last PowerPoint slide, which was a picture of the Red Eye's Dock Bar on Kent Island, Maryland, Pastor Heyward had some follow-up questions.

"Brother Kendley, I like the concept, but I'm concerned about your escape route. From the maps provided by Tracy, it shows one way off of Kent Island. You need to drive back over the Chesapeake Bay Bridge. Intel shows that traffic volumes, particularly heading west back toward DC on a Sunday afternoon, will be heavy enough to cause a bottleneck. How do you intend to get off the island?"

"We've already figured that out," said Charles. "Two of my cell members are newly minted Maryland State troopers. Each will position himself at opposite ends of the Chesapeake Bay Bridge. One on the west side, one on the east. A third member will be dropped off at the top of the bridge, pretending to be a jumper. My cops will close the bridge in both directions so they may also pretend to be attending to the troubled man at the top.

"We plan on purchasing a used fire truck from a national dealer outside of Baltimore. My shooters will be inside. We can pack fifteen, many even twenty, men into the cabins in the model we want.

"The truck will proceed across the bridge as if in response to the jumper but continue on for a few miles to the target, complete their mission, and travel freely back across the bridge. We're going to the Red Eye's Dock Bar. There is a bikini contest every Sunday, and rich, power boaters from across the entire state will be there. We'll kill everyone in sight.

"The cops will pick up our jumper and the truck will head back to Baltimore but now with the two state police escorts. We've already calculated it all out. From the moment we first close the bridge and reopen it again after the attack will be less than twenty minutes, total. The fire truck alone is going to cost me between $75,000 and $100,000."

"Now this is the type of detail I like to hear. And this fire truck dealer? They'll sell a truck to anyone with the money? No questions asked?"

"Sure they will. Especially if you own a Firehouse Sub franchise, like I do."

"Good, let's move on."

It took less than four hours for all the presentations of the planned attacks for August 9th, 2020, to be completed. There were other items to address, but Heyward asked the admin assistant taking notes to do a quick recap of the meeting of what had been presented.

Atlanta Cell: Augusta National Golf Club, 250 dead and $400,000

Baltimore Cell: Red Eye's Dock Bar, Kent Island, 300 dead and $750,000

Los Angeles Cell: Playboy Mansion and Rodeo Drive, 200 dead and $600,000

New York Cell: South Hamptons, 300 dead and $450,000

Oakland Cell: Menlo Park and Pacific Heights, 200 dead and $500,000

All told, the group was going to need $2.7 million and had set a combined goal of over 1,000 fatalities.

"Not bad," Heyward said. "Hell, the government spends billions on killing a few thousand rag heads in Iraq. We're more efficient than the damn United States Marine Corps.

"I'd like to add one bit of exciting news. For each of you who hits your goal, there will be a $1 million bonus to you personally. Courtesy of our esteemed benefactor, Mr. Jayden Quinn." The crowd of eight let out a roar that could be heard for yards. Much like the final game the Rams played in St. Louis.

None of the attendees bothered to inquire about Calvin Heyward's plan. He was, after all, the guy who secured the funding from the sweet-looking Chief Information and Financial Officer sitting right next to him, and they wouldn't dare challenge his authority.

Calvin and Tracy were impressed with the plans. The group took a play right out of Osama Bin Laden's Al Qaeda playbook. Centralize the functions of financing, communications, and approval of overall strategy. Decentralize operational planning, execution, and staffing. Heyward also followed in OBL's lead by specifically not telling the others his own plans.

Compared with the Al Qaeda attacks in the United States of September 11th, 2001, on the USS *Cole* in October 2000 and the two US embassies in Tanzania and Kenya in 1998, these plans by Heyward's men were going to be a breeze. Soft targets, all of them. Not some bunkered, heavily-guarded or reinforced buildings like the Pentagon, World Trade Center, a ship of war and US embassies.

Done with the planning and financing aspects of the meeting, the group moved on to communications, information systems, and intelligence. They would finish with the most important part. The big reveal. The final solution. Calvin turned the meeting and the PowerPoint presentation over to Tracy.

"Good afternoon, gentlemen. We're going to discuss our communication plan in great detail. You'll receive the same information in a summary email that will be sent to your personal email address. You must put the plan to memory as that email will auto-delete in two days. Do not share any item in this plan with anyone in your organization other than your immediate lieutenants.

"Okay, item one. You'll all be given a new phone before you leave here today. These are for communicating with each other on the day of the attacks. Do not store any numbers in the phone and do not text unless using WhatsApp. You will also be given a new GoPro video camera.

"The phones will be loaded with three apps: Facebook, WhatsApp, and the mobile app for the National Geospatial Intelligence Agency. Facebook is to be used only for streaming of Facebook Live and must be paired with your GoPro in order for it to work. WhatsApp is what we will use to communicate. Phone calls, text messaging, video conferencing—all through this app. I have preloaded your profiles into each.

"Lastly, the NGIA app. It's preprogrammed to go live on August eighth and deactivate on August tenth. Each of you has your respective cities entered into the app. This is your best chance of avoiding cops and first responders. You'll be able to see the routes they're taking to the attack sites.

"I'm going to say it one last time: DO NOT text or call anyone from these phones! Once you use this phone on a telecom network, you are on the open grid and can be tracked immediately. At least with Facebook and WhatsApp, it would take days for the cops to get a FISA warrant. Am I clear?"

All heads are shaking yes with the exception of Smiley from Los Angeles. "What's the matter, Pastor Smiley?" Tracy asked.

"I told you: I'm old. I'm not good with this technology stuff. How am I supposed to pull this off?"

"I'm happy to have Marcus spend time training you. We have seven months to be ready. Are there any questions?"

"Yes," said Edwin Morton from New York. "Why seven months? Why can't we do this now? My guys are ready to go."

"We picked August ninth for a number of reasons. The sixth anniversary of the Ferguson riots is the ninth. A major Hollywood movie release is scheduled for that same week. It will be top-of-mind for everyone. That could play very favorably to our overall objectives.

"The date is also positioned right between the two political parties' national conventions. One is in late July. The other, in late August. Hitting these towns during that time of political uncertainty is, again, to our advantage.

"It's a Sunday, when our target areas will be the most crowded. And lastly, it gives me the liberty of being able to provide you with the information you'll need out of the NGIA system. I know for certain my husband will be out of the country. He'll be attending the Olympics with my son. Jayden has already told me he intends to play. He wanted to in the 2016 games but was coming off an injury at the time. He'll be at these games. I guarantee it."

Tracy Quinn was correct in her assessment of August 9th being the perfect date. There were other reasons, but she didn't feel the need to share. One, she didn't want her son anywhere near St. Louis on August 9th. Two, she had devised an attack plan of her own and it had to happen in August.

"I got a question, and it is for the table not just you, Tracy," Pastor George from Oakland said. "What do we see as our chances of success? I'm not talking about the actual attack. I think we're going to catch most of these targets by complete surprise. I'm talking about getting away with it."

Tracy jumped back in. "While you were presenting, I loaded as much information as I could into the NGIA's Battlefield Scenario Assessment software, and collectively it generated a projected success rate of under sixty percent. Some of your plans are less than fifty percent. You need to work on them, and I can recalculate the data once you provide it to me. This brings me to my last point. The big reveal, the final solution as I like to call it.

"When you leave here tonight, you'll be given a small cooler with bottles of a clear, blue liquid in them. You need to take the cooler back to your home towns, and for God's sake keep the contents cool. Never anywhere near room temperature."

"What's in the cooler, and how are we supposed to bypass airport security with it?" George asked.

"The contents of these coolers are your final escape route if your original one doesn't work. It will, 100 percent, guarantee success. If you and your teams are in the process of getting caught, each member needs to drink about three ounces of what's inside. Hydrogen cyanide. You need to keep the liquid cool, as it turns gaseous at room temperature. Let them warm up, and if the bottles aren't perfectly sealed, you're dead. Put them in your freezers back home.

"As far as airports, you won't need to worry about that. Each of you has a brand new Ford conversion van waiting for you out in the parking lot. Title and tags for your home state included. You'll be driving these back home.

"Each of your vans has been loaded with a cache of weapons for the day of the attack. AK-47s, Uzi's, hand guns. Around fifty each. If you need more, go out and buy them in your local markets. I'm sure you know people. I've even put a dozen grenades in there for each of you."

"Thanks, Tracy, that was very instructive. Gentlemen, one more item before we dismiss you. Our demands after our success. There are two. A half-million dollars for every African-American man, woman, and child alive on August 31st.

"Reparations for centuries of oppression. Based on our success on August 9th, they'll have no choice but to pay. The second demand, release of every African-American held in federal, state, and local prisons and jails. We're talking over a million people. Any questions?"

"Why didn't we know about this? Who the hell is going to count every single black person in this country? And what is the definition of black? That sounds like a lot of money," said Pastor Hicks from Atlanta.

"Let me address each, one at a time. First, who said anything about this being a democracy? No one. Clear? Good. Second, the government's going to count for us, and the people will decide whether they are black or not.

"By July 31st, the first summary report of the 2020 census is due to Congress. If someone declared themself and their family as African-American, they're in. If not, tough shit. They don't get a second chance to change their race, like some of those fucking politicians.

"Lastly, on the question of how much are we asking for, and can the government afford it? To be honest, I don't care. The last census estimate of the number of black people in the country was around 42 million. I tried to multiply that by half a million dollars, but the calculator on my phone doesn't go that high. It doesn't matter. The government will find a way to pay. They always do."

Immediately, all five men entered 500,000 times 42,000,000 on their phones' calculators. The answer came back as $2.13e + 13$. *What the heck does that mean?* they wondered.

"You're going to let a million criminals out on the street? What! Are you crazy?" asked the absent-minded criminal out on parole from Baltimore. Calvin didn't answer the question.

Calvin wrapped up the meeting a full hour early with another prayer and some parting words. "Gentlemen, I thank you for coming today, and if God wills it, in seven months we'll set a course for all the world to notice. You are all dismissed, and God bless you and God bless the Crna Ruka," Heyward said without pronouncing the *T* or the *S* in front of the word *Crna*.

"God bless the Black Hand," they all said in English.

After the meeting, Calvin, Tracy, and the church administrative assistant stayed around to gather their work materials and talk about the meeting. "So, what did you think of these guys?" Calvin asked Tracy.

"Well, most are Okay, I guess. The guys from Baltimore and New York seem to have their shit together. But..."

"But what?"

"The LA guy? A disaster waiting to happen. You couldn't find anyone else?"

"I'll keep an eye on him. He has a capable lieutenant. You two ready to go?"

"You haven't heard my plan yet," Tracy said. Calvin's assistant continued packing up the meeting supplies.

"I didn't know you had one of your own. How many do you plan on killing, and what's your budget?"

"Just one. And it will cost us $2 million. The whole amount goes to my lieutenant," Tracy said without a hint of hesitation.

"One? Better be someone worth it."

"It is."

Tracy sent a quick text message. Seconds later, Colonel Maretta Buff Sowers walked into the conference room.

"Pastor Heyward, good to meet you, sir. Colonel Buff Sowers."

"Jesus Christ, what's wrong with your face?"

"Calvin! What's wrong with you? She has a war injury. Don't talk to her like that. I'm sorry, Buff," said Tracy.

"I'm sorry. You said Colonel? Are you in the Army?"

"Don't worry about it. I'm in the Air Force."

"And how do you know Tracy?"

"We've been friends for a long time. A couple months ago, when we were both drunk as sailors, she told me about an opportunity to make a lot of money. I figured it was two sisters talking shit. Well, after another time of being passed over for promotion, I said what the heck and gave her a call. Long story short, I'm here now."

"I'm not sure what Tracy told you, but maybe it was the liquor talking. We're not hiring those with military experience at this time." Calvin gave Tracy a contemptuous look.

"She hasn't told you what she intends to do. Hear her out."

"Not before that guy leaves," Buff said, pointing to the one person yet to speak.

"Take a walk," Calvin ordered the guy.

"Who the hell is that? I thought this was an operation run by black brothers and sisters. How did a white guy get in here?"

"I never said that. Besides Calvin, the only other 'brother' is our guy in Atlanta. The rest are white. The brother in LA is Latino. Calvin calls them 'brother' because of the church, not their race. And the guy you saw? He's a direct descendant of a slave owner by the name Dr. John Emerson. He's a byproduct of a time when rape was legal. Which is what Dr. Emerson did to his female slaves. You must know of him. He's infamous in African-American history."

"Never heard of him, and I don't give a shit. I'm the daughter of Lucy the Missing Link 3.2 times 10 to the fifth power removed. That doesn't make me an Ethiopian ape. I can't believe I had to become a criminal to find an organization with a legit diversity and inclusion program."

"Just tell him what you're going to do, Buff."

"I'm going to shoot him."

"Shoot who?"

"The president."

"Impossible. This is a waste of my time. First off, you'll never get close enough. I'm certain even an Air Force officer will be screened for weapons at any event where the president would be in attendance."

"You haven't heard the plan. Buff, tell the man."

"Actually, it's better if I show him. Play the video, Tracy."

Tracy pressed "Play" on her computer. For the next two minutes the three watched footage of the destructive power of the A-10 Warthog in various training exercises and live firings. Tanks, bunkers, and buildings being obliterated within a matter of seconds. Tracy pressed "Stop."

"Well, what do you think, Mr. Heyward? How close to the president do I need to be to kill him with one of those?"

"I've never seen anything like it. Okay, great; you have that death machine. I'm assuming you plan to hit the president either at the White House or his summer home. How can you be sure he'll be at either on August 9th."

"Who said anything about August 9th? You're right, though. Difficult to know where the president will be at any one time. Especially if your plans for the 9th are any success. My guess is he would be bunkered down somewhere while he deals with the shit.

"There is, however, one date, one time, one city, and one target at which we can pretty much guarantee he will be in attendance."

"Where's that?"

"The Spectrum Center, Charlotte, North Carolina, August 26th, 7 pm EDT, the scheduled time of his acceptance speech for a second nomination for the 2020 elections. His party's national convention and the date and time of his speech are set.

"Even if by some chance he's not there, I can promise you the consolation of scores of party leaders, delegates, congressmen, and press. Washington's going to be a mess. A no-lose situation."

"Does that plane carry enough firepower for the convention center?"

"Let's just say that in about one minute, I could take out this piece-of-shit stadium, that godawful casino across the street, and that loopy thing you all love so much down by the river. What do you call it, The Arc?"

"But August 26th? It's two weeks after the 9th. Our demands will have a deadline with the president prior to that."

"If you think the president or his security council is going to agree to your ridiculous demands because you've killed a few thousand people, you're nuts. Tracy told me about your reparations demand. Do you know how much money that is?"

Tracy and Calvin both shook their heads.

"My calculator doesn't go that high," Calvin said, feeling a bit stupid.

"What, are you on the spectrum or something? Level Three – total fucking retard? Take the number forty-two, multiply it by five and add eleven zeros. I knew how to do that shit in fifth grade. It's $21 trillion. They don't have the money."

Heyward didn't understand what "on the spectrum" meant and was feeling more than a little bit stupid.

"The government is going to stall long enough to hunt your ass down and kill you. Way before paying you or anyone else a dime. I'm not even going to address your demand to free all those felons. Did you include the rapists, child abusers, and murderers in that group?

"And what's your comeback when the government doesn't do as you ask? Not a damn thing. You're done. Blew your wad on the 9th. Well, now you have something to hit them with again: me. If this all works, I'll take the half-million in reparations on top of the $2 million you're going to pay me. Let me convert my cash to some other currency before you make them pay. The dollar won't be worth shit after."

"Ok, let's run with this some more. After the 9th, don't you think the airspace over the convention center will be made a no-fly zone?"

"Yeah, it will. No doubt. There will be a no-fly zone for all civilian aircraft. Not for military and police aircraft assigned to provide air cover. As a matter of fact, my unit and an A-10 unit out of Moody in Georgia would be tasked to provide low-altitude patrols.

"I'm the highest-ranking officer in my unit. Guess who's going to be providing cover during the president's speech? I designed the entire plan a hundred times. It'll work."

"Okay, but no money until after the job is done."

"Bullshit. The chances you and the idiots under your command survive the 9th are for crap. You'll deposit the money on the 8th into my account or no deal. If it doesn't go in, I'm bringing my A-10 to St. Louis."

"How do we know you'll go through with it on the 26th, and what the hell is your escape plan?"

"The mere fact that I'm here today means I've already committed about a half dozen felonies, including treason and conspiracy to assassinate the president. I have nothing to lose. My plan is to enjoy my cash somewhere other than this place.

"I'll complete my run on the convention center, fly my A-10 straight west to the Smoky Mountains, and bail out. Ever heard of S.E.R.E training, Mr. Heyward?"

Tracy had, but not Calvin.

"No, what is it?"

"It stands for Survival, Evasion, Resistance, and Escape. Best damn training I ever went through. Air Force taught me how to escape and evade enemy capture. Eat nothing but bugs and bear shit and navigate my way out of any terrain. I'll be fine.

"I can make it for a couple weeks without getting caught. By mid-September, I'll be sitting in a beautiful hamlet in Port au Prince, Haiti, courtesy of a friend of mine who runs private charters of food to the island every week. He flies out of Pidgeon Forge, Tennessee. Extradition agreement between Haiti and the United States is over a hundred years old and nonsense. *Babay* as they say in Creole. Goodbye."

"Ok, what do you need from us?"

"First, I'm going to need a couple of guns. An M-16 and a 9mm would be nice. I'll need to hunt for food and defend myself. I also need to know what cities you plan on hitting between Georgia and Maryland. I need the exact details, down to the minute."

"We can get you the guns. Today. I'll send you to my guy. Hamza Madic. What do you need our attack plans for? Tracy, didn't you tell her we don't divulge cell plans to anyone other than the leaders?"

"I did, but hear her out."

"Look, if you go and kill hundreds of people in Charlotte, Atlanta, or as far north as Maryland, the deal's off. NORAD and the southern bases of the Eastern Air Defense Sector are going to shut down the entire region, including military aircraft not on immediate ready alert.

"Hell, the president might move his party's convention altogether and at the last moment. If, however, cells in those areas are somehow brought to justice on or before they complete their attacks, we'll be flying normal patrols around Charlotte as expected. I can't have those cells be successful, or I'm screwed.

"What do you want, Mr. Heyward? A thousand no-name dead civilians or possibly the president, the new vice president nominee, and a large number of party leaders? This deal is too good to pass on and almost guarantees reparations will be paid."

Heyward thought more on it and finally saw the opportunity to be worth the sacrifice of two of his cells. It all made sense to a guy who was losing any ability to understand what made sense and what didn't.

"Tracy, I'm putting you in charge of this with the colonel. Make sure she has what she needs. One last item, Colonel. I need you to take the oath of allegiance to the Crna Ruka."

"Fuck your stupid Black Hand oath and your black ass for that matter. I'm in this for one reason. The money. I took an oath of allegiance once already. Look how that turned out.

"This is payback for my own government spying on us. The money? Not payback, but back pay. I calculated ten years of increased salary at a general's pay grade. With interest, $250,000."

"And the other $1.75 million?"

"Flight pay."

"One last question, Colonel. Why?"

"If you want the clinical answer, talk to my therapist. My answer: Hell hath no fury like an A-10 pilot scorned."

All three concluded the meeting in agreement with the "Buff" plan. Heyward decided it was the most well-thought-out of the entire bunch. He also decided that although she was more than a foot shorter and 150 pounds lighter than him, Colonel Maretta "Buff" Sowers was not someone he would want to mess with.

Tracy asked Buff to stay another hour so she could provide her with as much detail as she had on both the Maryland and Atlanta cells and their plans. Once they finished, each agreed to weekly calls with any updates or changes.

Buff Sowers drove away from the Dome at America's Center smiling and talking aloud to herself. "Damn, I'm not just a great pilot and mathematician, I'm a pretty good actress, too."

The "Buff" plan was actually more the bluff plan. She had no intention of killing the president or anyone else for that matter. She would make some exceptions for Calvin Heyward, Tracy Quinn, and the entirety of the Crna Ruka. She would gladly kill them. That was a lot of exceptions. But she wouldn't get the pleasure of doing it alone. She conference-called her Best Man and Maid of Honor.

"They bought it. I'll be there in fifteen minutes," Buff said to General Quinn and Coach Gibbs. She was thrilled with her performance and wouldn't change a thing. Okay, she would change one thing. She wouldn't disparage those who suffer from autism or use the "R" word again when calling someone stupid. She knew better than that.

***

August 10th, 2021—10:00 am, Russell Senate Office Building, Washington, DC

"Ms. Gujic, we've received a question via text from a young lady named Shannon Conlon in Seattle. The gist of her question is concerning the racial and ethnic composition of both the cell leaders and young cell members.

"Apparently, Miss Conlon is sight-impaired and is unable to see the profiles we included in our report. She asks the commission to spend a moment summarizing this data," said the phone bank manager.

"Thank you, and my apologies on behalf of this commission for failing to take into account those with limited or no access to our full report. Photos and brief biographical summaries were provided for each cell member in the appendix. But I can address that now.

"Across the country, all six cells were exclusively men, with the notable exception of Tracy Quinn. Over ninety-five percent were under the age of twenty-five. From a racial or ethnic perspective, the Crna Ruka was as diverse as America. The Bronx cell was equally divided between non-Hispanic whites, Hispanics, and African-Americans. The Baltimore cell was two-thirds white, the other third black. Kendley Charles, the Baltimore cell leader, recruited heavily from the Dundalk area of Baltimore.

"Atlanta was all African-American. St. Louis split between young African-American men from the north side of the city and young white men of Bosnian descent from the south side. Los Angeles was predominantly Latino, and Oakland exclusively Asian, of Cambodian and Vietnamese descent. The Oakland group all came from a notorious gang called the Asian Street Walkers. Are there any questions before we go on?"

"I have one," said the Chairman of House Subcommittee on Crime, Terrorism and Homeland Security. "Sara, I'm still not 100 percent clear on how we define an organization like the Crna Ruka. Were they a terrorist group or simply an organized crime gang?"

"Sir, I'm no expert on this topic. I believe you know my colleague Steve Herrington. Steve is a former chief of police in New York and was the chairman of the counterterrorism task force for the entire New York, Connecticut, and New Jersey region."

"Sir, we would label the Crna Ruka as a hybrid. Very common these days across the globe. Not too dissimilar from what you might see in certain Central American countries, like the FARC in Colombia. Their intent was murder, hysteria, and paralysis. Like Al Qaeda, ISIS, and others. But not because of some political, social, or religious ideology. Their goal was to enrich themselves and consolidate power in the illegal markets in which they operated.

"They believed that by focusing their attacks on the wealthier, more affluent population, they could send a shock wave of fear so strong as to evoke immediate overreaction by our government. In that sense, ironically, they were successful.

"Our government, for a short few weeks, was flying blind and without a rudder. It so happened that a counterterrorism group, employing the same factor of fear, was able to countermand the efforts and objectives of the Crna Ruka."

"And the name of that organization was…"

"The Black Hand. Same words, different language. A perfectly accurate translation but a completely different interpretation. Same objective of creating an overreaction by the government, different desired outcomes."

"Thank you, Mr. Herrington. Sara, please go on."

TWENTY-TWO

January 24th, 2020—DeLux Motel, East St. Louis, Illinois

Kenneth Gibbs, Orlando Quinn, and Buff Sowers arrived at the motel within a few minutes of each other. The three had arranged to meet after Buff called the general weeks earlier and told him about Tracy's trip to Maryland. From that call forward, the two spoke daily about how to proceed from there.

It was with the general's guidance that Buff was able to create the "bluff" plan. Orlando asked Buff to attend Heyward's meeting in St. Louis and then be prepared to discuss what to do regarding the Crna Ruka.

"Buff, before we start, Ken and I need to tell you something. Ken?"

"Both the general and I have suspected for a couple of months that something has been going on with Tracy and this guy Heyward. What I'm about to share with you very few people know. My daughter was raped the night of her death. We now have absolute proof that Tracy and Heyward were behind the attack.

"At the time, the general and I thought it was three deeply troubled kids who had committed a horrible crime. We now know differently. They were ordered to do it. I only recently told Theresa about this. I'm sorry to lay such a heavy, personal burden on your shoulders."

"Ken, I can't imagine the pain you've been suffering all these years. And now, Theresa. Let's put that at the top of the reasons these bastards need to die...What's the master plan here?"

"How's your knowledge of World War I history? Specifically, its origins."

"I'm not good with the dates and names but I know the math...incalculable."

"So you've probably never heard of a Serbian colonel by the name of Dragutin Dimitrijevic. He led a secret paramilitary group, including a number of assassins who shot and killed the heir to the Austrian-Hungarian Empire. It was that lone assassination that lit the spark for World War I.

"Most of the group never knew his true identity until years later. He went by the code name 'Apis.' It means 'Holy Bull.'"

"Where the hell is this going?" Buff asked.

"We want to introduce you to the man who has drafted the blueprints for our master plan. We want you to meet our Apis."

"General, you never mentioned this guy. I'm not here to get involved with someone I don't know. I agreed to this for you two. Not some bullshit dude code-named Apis."

"You're going to meet him now... Apis, you want to join us?"

From the door adjoining the room, an army major in full dress blues walked in. Several medals adorned the uniform, including the Bronze Star.

"Holy shit. It's you! Come here and let me hug some love into you. When was the last time I saw you?"

"At your wife's funeral. I was one of the pallbearers, remember, with these two. Thank you for the honor, Colonel Sowers."

"The hell with that. It was my honor, and you know better than to call me Colonel. Call me Buff. Okay, what is going on here with you guys?"

"I'm not just one of the guys. You can call me Apis or sir. Is that clear?"

"Yes, sir," said Buff.

"All right, we're all reacquainted, but we need to work. We're not leaving until we have this plan is all worked out," said General Quinn. "What did you learn at the meeting of the Crna Ruka?"

"General, they have access to your NGIA system. They've been using it for years. Tracy believes she has a trump card of being able to turn you in to the authorities if I were to say anything to the cops. Something about you giving her access."

"I did. Sandbox access only, but she's clearly taken it to the next level. I guess we could go to the cops, but you said the Baltimore cell has men inside the police department. What makes us think the same isn't true in every city they plan to hit? The local and state cops are out. We don't know if they have inside guys there as well.

No, they need to be taken out. We have the strategic plan of Apis's. We need to focus on the details. Recruitment, operations, logistics, and timing. Buff, you mentioned the guy you saw with Tracy and Heyward at the start of your meeting. Did you get his name?"

"Not completely. They said he was the descendant of some historically famous guy named Emerson. And he was white. Took me by surprise."

"What did he look like?"

"Thin brown hair, tiny nose, no lips. Wearing a polo shirt and khakis. Maybe thirty-five or forty."

Coach Gibbs and General Quinn stared at each other for a moment. Could it be him?

Around-the-clock for the next two days, the three best friends and their new commander relied on decades of experience and strategizing to work a plan so broad in its objective yet so intricate in detail; they each concluded the odds of success bordered on the impossible.

The general yawned deeply. "So, Buff, your thoughts? Can you do this? How much do you love your country?"

Her yawn followed his. "General, depending on the time of the month, I love my country more than anything. Even more than I love the three of you. But one week a month, I am a bit emotional about the crap the NSA does to our own people. It makes me want to blow shit up."

"What kind of mood are you going to be in during the week of August ninth? In six months?"

Buff did some quick math and biology calculations in her head. "I'm definitely going to be in my 'blow shit up' mood. And you, General? How do you feel?" Buff asked.

"I've been ordering the sons of this country to be prepared to die in its defense for nearly thirty years. I can order one more. Even if it's my own son. Ken and his team have the most to lose. Coach?"

"I'll say it for him. He's going to do it. That's what fathers do for their children, right?" said Apis.

"Yes it is."

"So, what do we call our little unit?"

Ken jumped in. "We don't have a choice. History and fate has chosen our name for us. We will use the name Crna Ruka openly in our communications to the public and the government.

"Everyone will think we're part of Heyward's organization. We want that. It will cause greater confusion and fear. But when speaking privately, among ourselves, we will use the name Apis gave us. Eventually the world will come to know the truth."

"And what's that?"

"The Black Hand. We're Americans. We're going to speak English for shit's sake."

***

February 14th, 2020—St. Louis, Missouri

"*But back home he'll always ruuuuun...to Sweet Melissa,*" Jayden Quinn's ringtone sang. He always answered when this man called, who, not by coincidence, had the same ring tone on his phone.

"*Marhaban Mudarib.*" ("Hello, Coach.")

"Jayden, *Kaifa Halika, sawdeequi?*" ("How are you, my friend?")

"*Jayyidin jiddan. Shukraan.*" ("Very good. Thank you.") Jayden hoped that was the end of speaking in Arabic. He hadn't practiced much. Not to mention that starting a conversation by referencing the origin of his own first name was embarrassing.

"Thanks for coming into town. Your dad and I are excited to see you. How long are you on break?"

"The All Star game's on Sunday. Up in Chicago. Tonight's some celebrity game or something. It was an easy trip. Where are we going for dinner, Coach? And please god, don't say Madic's. Last time you took me there, that creepy owner kept calling me the Crna Ruka, the Black Hand."

"We're going to Madic's. There's someone there we want you to meet. I have practice until eight. I'll swing by and pick up your dad. How about 8:30?"

"Can't we eat on the Hill or White Castle?"

"Nah, do this for me and your dad. I know the food is terrible, but we haven't been there in years. We both want to practice our Bosnian."

"Alright, I'll see you at 8:30."

***

Later that night, Jayden arrived at Madic's a few minutes early; he wanted to wait in the parking lot for his former coach and his dad. The less time he had to spend listening to Hamza Madic talk about his nephew being the best player in the world, the better.

But nature was calling, and, second best player in the world or not, Jayden had to go. He figured he could sneak in, use the restroom, and sneak back out to meet his dad and his coach in the parking lot.

Coach Gibbs and General Quinn arrived five minutes past the 8:30 meeting time. A total of three cars were in the lot besides theirs. Two high-end sports cars and one late model coupe with a bumper sticker that read: "Enterprise Rental Car." Jayden's rental, the two men concluded.

"A busy night at Madic's," Orlando said to Ken. "Let's wait here. It won't be long."

Thirty seconds after Jayden entered the café, he was back out and headed to the parking lot where his two dinner companions waited.

"We need to leave, now."

"We know, Jayden. Get in the car. We'll drive down the street and grab some burgers at White Castle," his dad replied. The men were silent for the five-minute ride.

"Dad, I need to tell you something."

"Son, you don't have to tell me anything. I know what you saw. You were probably in too big of a hurry to notice that one of those cars in the parking lot was your mother's. She has been coming here with that man almost every Friday night."

"How long have you known, Dad?"

"Jayden, that's a bigger question than you realize. But let me start by saying I'm sorry. Coach and I set you up to see that. That was their little rendezvous place. They figured no one ever goes there and they wouldn't be discovered."

"But, Dad, why didn't you talk to me about it? Why don't you leave her? You deserve better than that."

"Actually, I don't. Jayden, I can't begin to tell you how hard it is to be the spouse of a career soldier. Your mom and I have been married for over thirty years. By my guess, I've been away from her and from you for almost twenty of those. It's too much to ask of a person. I don't blame your mother for seeking the companionship of another person. But there are other things to blame her for, and it's been a long time coming that you and I are having this conversation."

"Dad, is this appropriate with Coach here? Can't this wait until we're alone?"

"There is so much we have to tell you, son. So many secrets, so many lies. I'm going to let Ken tell you the truth about Melissa. Something so terrible about her final night that we both thought you would be better off not knowing. We were wrong, and we're going to ask you to forgive us."

Jayden didn't wait for the coach to start talking. "What are you talking about? What could possibly add to the pain of her killing herself?"

"Jayden," Coach Gibbs said, "I have to tell you a story that has no happy ending. It's tragedy on top of tragedy. Do you remember what other event happened here on August 9th, 2014, besides Melissa's death?"

"Of course I do, Coach. It was the day a young man was shot and killed by a Ferguson police officer. The town erupted in protests, riots. What does Ferguson have to do with Melissa?"

"Everything."

***

By the time Coach Gibbs finished his story, not only was Jayden in tears, so was his coach and his father. How could those young men, with such promising opportunities, do what they did to the love of his life? His mind was racing too fast to comprehend. It was about to race even faster.

"Jayden, your mother and Calvin Heyward ordered the rape. We have the proof," Orlando said to his son.

"How can that be? What proof do you have?"

"At work the past couple of weeks, I checked the archived satellite imagery from Ferguson on August 9th, 2014. We provisioned three separate satellites that day due to the protests and eventually the riots. Look at this photo. Who do you see?"

"That looks like, oh, what was his name? Marcus. Marcus Emerson. The guy from the YMCA. Where is he, and how does that prove Mom did this?"

"He's coming out of the apartment of one of the rapists. Look at the time stamp. August 9th, 2014, 6:19 pm. Two hours before the attack. I contacted one of the other agencies I work closely with. I gave them Marcus's cell phone number and at 4:31 pm he received a call from a number with a Tennessee area code. That number belongs to Calvin Heyward, your mother's lover. Except it was issued in the name of Archie Heyward shortly after he got out of prison. He changed his name but he never changed his number to a Missouri area code."

"That doesn't prove anything. Maybe he knew Marcus. A coincidence."

"Maybe. But this picture three days later proves it. Your mom is coming out of the Ferguson Police Department with the three young men. She paid their bail."

Jayden sat in disbelief once again. Finally, he said, "I'm going to kill them. All of them."

"No, son, you're not. I've never given you an order in your life. I'm giving you one now. Please listen to what Ken and I have to say. There's more, so much more that you need to know. You'll get your revenge and then some."

After another two hours in the White Castle explaining the strategy devised by the Black Hand leaders, Orlando asked his son the hardest question of his life. "Will you do this? And the other men will do this?"

"Dad, when we all took our oath of enlistment, it included enemies foreign and domestic. Yes, sir. We will do this and so will the others. But honestly, sir, how can this ever work? They outnumber us twenty to one."

"This is not just about taking down the Crna Ruka. We told you that. That's our secondary objective. That'll be relatively easy. We have better command, control, better intel. We'll have coms, they won't. And we'll know who they are. They won't know us, at first anyway.

"Besides that, we'll have the power of hundreds of millions of Americans and all of social media right behind us. Lastly, we have something no else does. We have Jayden Quinn. One of the most recognized and influential people in the country, if not the world. We have the Black Hand."

TWENTY-THREE

March 28th, 2020—St. Louis, Missouri

"Hello, Kenneth Gibbs here."

"Coach Gibbs, this is Richard Pues with the United States Olympic Committee. We would like to invite you to Colorado Springs to interview for the job of the men's basketball coach for the 2020 games. If the interview goes well, we'd like to make the announcement within a few days. Are you interested?"

"I was expecting your call. I'm happy to accept the job."

"One second, Coach Gibbs."

The chairman put the coach on mute. "What an arrogant bastard. Accepting a job we haven't even offered him yet. Does this guy not realize why the committee was interested in him in the first place?" the chairman said to his assistant.

Coach Gibbs knew why. Jayden Quinn.

"Great, a private plane will be waiting for you at Lambert tomorrow morning. We'll see you at our offices around noon."

By 3 pm the Olympic Men's Basketball Team selection committee offered Coach Kenneth Gibbs the job. He accepted.

The selection committee initially wanted a much higher-profile coach from the NBA, and whomever they were to hire would certainly want Jayden Quinn and Ronan McCoy on the team. But it was a phone call from Jayden to the head of the committee that made the decision an easy one. Jayden told Mr. Pues that if he had any interest in having him, Ronan, and seven other NBA stars that Jayden listed playing on the Olympic team, Coach Gibbs from St. Louis University would lead them or they wouldn't play. Ronan never knew Jayden was speaking for him, but he would have been perfectly comfortable with it. The seven others knew who Jayden was speaking for.

The Tokyo Olympics were scheduled to begin in four months' time. Several negative developments since the 2016 games made the prospects of a successful Olympics in 2020 for the United States team look bad.

The US Olympic Gymnastics team was a shell of its former self after it was discovered that the United States Gymnastics Association allowed a serial sex abuser to remain the team's doctor even after hundreds of athletes reported abuse over many years. Many parents pulled their talented children out of the sport and decided to pursue other interests.

Almost the entirety of the US Track and Field team was under investigation for drug-doping after a few of the athletes tested positive. A final decision from the US and International Olympic Committee's Anti-Doping division was still a month away. And for the first time in twenty years, the US Olympic Swim team would not have the gold medal factory that was Michael Phelps. He finally retired his banana hammock after twenty-three gold medals.

The US Olympic Selection Committee had to have Jayden Quinn on the team or 2020 was going to be a complete disaster. It stood to lose hundreds of millions of dollars in lost sponsorships if they couldn't guarantee the most popular athlete in the world would play for his country.

***

April 1st, 2020 – Chaifetz Arena, St. Louis University, St. Louis, Missouri

"The US Olympic Men's Basketball committee could think of no better coach to represent our country and bring home the gold than Coach Gibbs," the chairman lied.

"Coach Gibbs possesses both an impeccable professional and personal reputation. He is an accomplished teacher of the game and holds both a bachelor's degree and a master's degree in World History from the United States Military Academy in West Point, New York." Truth, this time, from the chairman.

"His demeanor is quiet and confident, and we know he can easily handle the pressure of such a high-profile position. He is also a former Army Lieutenant Colonel who served his country proudly and courageously for sixteen years." Again, all facts.

"Please join me in welcoming the new head coach of the 2020 US Olympic Men's Basketball team, Coach Kenneth Gibbs." The chairman finished where he started, by lying. He had no intention of welcoming the coach.

"Thank you, Mr. Chairman. I am excited to lead this team. Without too much delay and fanfare, it is with great honor to announce the 12-man roster of the 2020 Olympic Men's Basketball team. There will be a brief 10-minute question period after the roster is announced, so please hold all your questions until that time.

"Born in Saudi Arabia, he speaks multiple languages fluently. He is a former corporal in the United States Army and a generous donor and board member at the St. Louis Region YMCA. He is co-chairman of the Jayden Quinn and Kenneth Gibbs Scholarship Fund. Please join me in congratulating a close personal friend to my family, Jayden Quinn."

The press and fans present gave an unenthusiastic round of applause. They were a bit dumbfounded about why the coach was reciting more of a public service announcement and not basketball stats.

"Andrew Beutel, at six feet two inches and averaging fifteen points a game in the NBA, playing guard from Bloomington, Indiana."

Great, the press thought. Some basketball stats, but not much.

"Our next player, from Cleveland Ohio, served two tours of duty in Afghanistan with the 1st Infantry Division. He is executive director of the 'Carey it Forward' Institute, teaching business and life skills to disadvantaged teenagers throughout northern Ohio. Please join me in congratulating Darnell Carey on being selected to the US Olympic Men's Basketball team."

Again, the media was confused and now irritated. They were, after all, sports reporters. They were beginning to feel as if they had been invited to a charitable event. *When is the "big ask" coming for donations?* many thought.

Coach Gibbs continued on with each of the players he introduced. He made it a point to talk about their many selfless contributions, including the military service of nine of the twelve players. It was clear to anyone watching the press conference that Coach Gibbs had selected these men for reasons not exclusively related to their abilities on the court.

"Coach, Bobby Payne with ESPN. You've spent the better part of thirty minutes telling us some great personal information about the team. What can you tell us about your choices from a basketball perspective? It's this reporter's opinion that there were some more talented players left off the roster. This should be about the game, right?"

"No, the game is not what this is about. Next question."

"Coach Gibbs, Soppy Powell, CBS Sports. Are you prepared to state here today that this team you've chosen will guarantee the US a gold medal?"

"No, I'm not guaranteeing a gold medal. As a matter of fact, I'm not guaranteeing we'll win even one game. Next question, please."

"Coach Gibbs, Joey Kuhn with Nookiebookie.com," Kuhn said quickly, hoping the coach didn't hear his introduction. Nookiebookie.com was an online porn and gambling site founded by Kuhn. The value proposition of the online startup was to eliminate the need for 30-year-old men still living with their parents from having to open two separate web browsers while entertaining themselves.

"Coach, your first game in four months is against Vietnam," Kuhn continued. "Vegas has the opening line at 79.5 points. I'm advising my clients to take the over. Safe bet?"

"Son, I wouldn't bet a penny on anything that was predicated on the United States beating Vietnam."

The question-and-answer session of the press conference was over in three minutes. None of the other reporters dared to ask their prepared questions and weren't light enough on their feet to come up with new ones.

The Olympic Committee public affairs office distributed a quick bio for each player so the reporters could at least be accurate in naming the squad. They were listed in alphabetic order and with minimal information.

Jayden Quinn, 6' 6", Forward. Born: Riyadh, Saudi Arabia. 30
Andrew Beutel, 6' 2", Guard. Born: Bloomington, Indiana. 35
Darnell Carey, 6' 3", Guard. Born: Cleveland, Ohio. 29
Alphonso Detandt, 6' 1", Guard. Born: New Orleans, Louisiana. 31
Iver Koch, 6' 8", Forward. Born: Atlanta, Georgia. 31
Daniel Kreinbrink, 6' 5", Guard. Born: Salt Lake City, Utah. 25
Mattox Jabbur, 6' 8", Forward. Born: Oakland, California. 29
Ronan McCoy, 6' 3", Guard. Born: Milton, West Virginia. 30

Charles Mwangi, 7', Center. Born: Los Angeles, California. 27

Russell Norcross, 6' 11", Center. Born: Detroit, Michigan. 28

Davud Novak, 6' 10", Forward. Born: Srebrenica, Bosnia and Herzegovina. 37

Carl Wilson, 6' 9", Forward. Born: Memphis, Tennessee. 32

The national sports media talk show hosts were apoplectic that evening. Who was this guy? Upon googling "Kenneth Gibbs basketball coach," all they could find was a two-sentence reference on Wikipedia.

"Head Coach of the St. Louis Billikens. Former college coach of NBA Champion and MVP Jayden Quinn." Now they knew why he was selected. There was no reference to his years in the military. His team was much older than Olympic teams in the past, with the youngest player being twenty-five.

"Where were all the one-and-done, 20-year-old studs?" asked the Sports Center host to an audience who couldn't respond. "And a 37-year-old immigrant from Bosnia? Hell, he's not really an American. Probably in this country for the money."

In actuality, the "not really American" 37-year-old Bosnian scored a perfect score on his naturalization test and donated tens of millions to local charities in his adopted home of St. Louis. Coach Gibbs introduced Davud Novak stating that. None of the reporters took note of it. They were too busy on their laptops taking Vietnam +79.5 points on Nookiebookie.com.

"Gentlemen, congratulations on your selection to the team. You should take great pride in having the opportunity to represent your country.

"Our first formal practice will be in two weeks' time on April 16th, the day after the NBA regular seasons ends. That gives us 116 days before the Games end on August ninth.

"During these next months, we will work hard on our game. We will work harder on becoming not a team, but a single entity. Yes, made up of different parts but serving one purpose. That purpose will be to represent our country in the spirit of which the United States has come to signify to billions around the world."

Ronan McCoy got his first taste of Gibbs's coaching style and he whispered to Jayden, "This guy is going to be a pain in my ass."

"We will convene, practice, and reside as a team here in St. Louis. All practices will be at this arena, and you'll be staying in the student dormitories while you're here. Practices twice a day, Monday through Thursday. Friday through Sunday is free time to go home to your families or stay here in St. Louis and do as you please."

How was Ronan supposed to do as he pleased in a college dormitory? In his first years in the NBA he always stayed at a local high-end hotel, ordering room service. The past year he'd been Jayden's roommate in a house the size of a mansion. Now he'd be in a jail-cell-sized room with two single beds and a mini-fridge.

"Are there even TVs in these rooms?" he asked Jayden.

"No, shhh. Coach is still talking."

"During your time in dorms, you'll have a roommate. If you can't decide on who that will be, I'll choose one for you. You will also be roommates with that same person during our stay in the Olympic Village in Tokyo.

"I recognize a majority of you still have commitments to your professional team, but the moment your team is eliminated from the playoffs, I expect you to arrive in St. Louis to join the squad full-time."

Ronan seriously thought of leaving the team. He was making millions of dollars a year and at thirty years old, he was going to have a roommate in a dorm? At least it will be with Jayden, he concluded. He remembered reading that the 2004 US Olympic Men's Basketball team stayed aboard the *Queen Mary* in Athens. Why didn't they get the same sort of first-class treatment?

"Before we leave here today, you will also choose a team captain. I'll cast the tie-breaking vote if need be. The captain's duties will be to represent the team in public appearances and press conferences. There will be no exceptions. No interviews, no social media posts, no phone calls or emails to loved ones discussing team business until after the games. Everything we discuss as a team will remain confidential."

"Control freak," Ronan said.

Coach Gibbs handed out pieces of paper and pens. Each player cast their vote, folded the paper, and handed it back to the coach. McCoy knew it was going to be Jayden in a landslide.

"Charles, please keep the tally," Coach Gibbs instructed Charles Mwangi.

"Jayden Quinn," read the first ballot.

"Jayden Quinn," read the second.

"I knew it. Landslide."

"Ronan McCoy."

"Jayden's being nice, everyone," Ronan said sarcastically.

"Jayden Quinn, Ronan McCoy..." On the next seven ballots, three more votes were cast for Jayden and four more for Ronan. It was a tie, six to six.

"I cast my vote for Ronan McCoy," the coach said without hesitation.

"Coach, something's wrong. You don't want me being the spokesperson for this team. I'm a complete fuck-up, and I hate public speaking. I get so nervous. My head rains with sweat and my mouth dries up like a bale of cotton."

"It wasn't up to me. It was up to the team, and we chose you. You'll be fine, Ronan. Now men, take five minutes and figure out who your roommates are going to be. I'll step outside, but when I come back in, you need to be done."

"Jayden, me and you, right?"

"Sorry, pal, I already chose a roommate and he agreed. I'm bunking with Mwangi," Jayden said, referring to the big man from LA. Ronan looked around and everyone else was paired up, with the exception of the forward originally from Bosnia, Davud Novak.

"Well, looks like the two of us *mi amigo*," Ronan said to Davud, thinking everyone with even the slightest accent spoke Spanish.

"The way to say 'my friend' in Bosnian is *'moj prijatelj,'* you idiot. Either way, I am not your friend. Leave me alone or I will kill you with my bare hands."

"I wonder how you say 'fuck off' in Bosnian," Ronan whispered to himself, but too loudly.

"Jebi se."

Jayden's roommate, Charles Mwangi, was born in Los Angeles but raised by his paternal grandfather in Kenya after both his parents were killed in a car accident in the United States. The parents originally moved to America to avoid a decades-long civil war that tore the northern region of the poor African country apart.

Mwangi returned to the United States after being drafted number one in his rookie season in the NBA. His grandfather moved to the States with him. Every off-season they returned to Africa. The Mwangis had over 300 direct family members in a small, 15-mile radius of each other in southern Sudan and northern Kenya.

Coach Gibbs concluded the meeting with one last item on the agenda.

"There is a complete list of team rules on the table by the door. Please pick one up on your way out. I have also typed up a team homework assignment that will begin today. Questions?"

"Coach, are we playing basketball or joining a cult?" asked none other than Ronan McCoy.

"You're joining a mission, men. You should consider it an honor that you've been selected to be a part of this.

"There are tens of thousands of men out there of every age that would love to have the opportunity to be in the position you are now. If, at any time, you wish to leave this team, of course you are free to do so."

The homework assignment the coach wrote up for each player read as follows:

Gentlemen, there are 116 days that we will be together as a team, from our first day of practice on April 16th until the close of the Olympics on August 9th.

Not by coincidence, that is the exact number of days the United States Constitutional Convention met in Philadelphia in 1787. The result of that convention was the finished US Constitution, the document that is on display in the Rotunda of the National Archives in Washington, DC.

You men, for this assignment, will pretend to represent the delegations of the twelve states that convened that conference. Your assignment is for each of you to propose a new bill, constitutional amendment, or addition to the Bill of Rights you would like to see enacted. You may also choose to select a law currently on the books that you would like to see repealed or changed.

As such, the twelve of you will be given equal time to discuss and debate your proposed bill at team dinners I will host at my home here in St. Louis, twice a week starting on April 16th. On August 6th we will vote on which bills will become law. I will serve only as a tie-breaker, and we will all celebrate our work during our final team dinner together.

Lastly, for those who are interested, I've arranged a tour of some historical sites here in St. Louis and invite you to join me."

***

Everyone with the exception of Ronan joined the coach on the tour. They stopped at multiple sites, including the final burial spot of Dred Scott and the famous courthouse of his original trial. They also visited the Gateway Arch with a ride to the top.

One of the most memorable stops was at the Jefferson Barracks National Military Cemetery, and the mass grave site of the Palawan Massacre. Coach Gibbs provided the narration.

"Palawan is a small island in the Philippines. With World War II drawing to an end, Japanese prison guards forced American soldiers to dig trenches throughout the prison camp. Once completed, the men were ordered into the trenches, where they were summarily murdered.

"One hundred and twenty three of those soldiers' remains were moved here to Jefferson Barracks in 1952."

The tour ended with a final stop at a small park with an ornate water fountain in the Little Bosnia neighborhood of St. Louis.

"This fountain, called a *sebilj*, is an exact replica of the water fountain in downtown Sarajevo, Bosnia. It was donated to the city by the president of Bosnia in 2013. For those of you not from the area, you may not know that St. Louis has a Bosnian population of over 70,000. Most came to the United States after fleeing war and even genocide in the mid-'90s. St. Louis is now considered the largest Bosnian city outside of Bosnia itself.

"I have one other historical item to show you." Coach Gibbs displayed an unloaded handgun to the men. "This gun, the Browning FN 1904, may be one of the most significant pistols in the history of the world. And it has Bosnian roots as well. It is the exact gun used by an assassin by the name of Gavrilo Princip. Does anyone know who Princip was?"

"I do, of course," said Davud Novak. "Princip was a member of a secret organization named the Crna Ruka. The Black Hand. Princip was the shooter who killed Archduke Ferdinand in Sarajevo in 1914. That one murder led to World War I.

"The leader of the Crna Ruka was a man so secret that, for years, no one but his two closest lieutenants knew his true identity. He was always referred to by his code name: 'Apis.' It means the 'Holy Bull.' Apis's identity finally became known publicly after World War I. His real name was Colonel Dragutin Dimitrijevic. He is considered by many to be the great unifier of what became the country of Yugoslavia.

"It wasn't until the fall of communism in the early '90s that all-out civil war erupted in the region, killing millions. Neighbors killing neighbors. Intermarried families killing each other. One of those killed was my father. He was murdered and dumped into a ditch on the side of the road outside my hometown. I swore an oath that if I ever discovered the man who pulled the trigger, I would kill him with my bare hands."

The team sat silent and prayed for Novak's father and his country. They also prayed for their own fathers and their own country.

TWENTY-FOUR

July 22nd, 2020—Los Angeles International Airport, Los Angeles, California

Coach Kenneth Gibbs, best friend General Orlando Quinn, and the NBA players boarded the private jet for a direct flight from Los Angeles to Tokyo, host city to the XXXII Summer Olympiad. This was the second time Tokyo hosted the summer games, as the city had done so in 1964.

The '64 Tokyo games were deemed a success from a standpoint of international good will, athletic accomplishment, and technological advancements. The torchbearer who lit the Olympic flame to open the games was a 19-year-old Japanese runner named Yoshinori Sakai, born in Hiroshima on August 6th, 1945, the day, for the first time in history, a nuclear bomb was used against mankind. Choosing Sakai for the honor was a successful display of world harmony.

And for the first time ever, the 1964 games were broadcast on live television around the world using two geosynchronous communications satellites operated by the National Aeronautics and Space Agency (NASA), founded six years earlier.

For the 2020 games, the Tokyo Olympic Bid committee had originally proposed they be held in October, as they had been in 1964. The proposal was based on an attempt to avoid the annual typhoon season that runs from July through October, with most storms occurring in August and September.

While the International Olympic Committee was impressed with the overall bid, it insisted the games be held in the summer months and prior to the starts of both the European Premier Football League and the National Football League in America. The US television sponsor, investing nearly $1.5 billion in broadcast rights, insisted the same.

On July 24th, 200 countries and 11,000 athletes marched into the National Olympic Stadium with 60,000 spectators and 3 billion television viewers watching worldwide.

***

August 1st, 2020—Olympic Arena, Tokyo, Japan

The team had their way with every opponent in the Group A stage of the tournament. General Orlando Quinn was as giddy as a schoolboy watching his son Jayden run circles around the international competition, much like he had done when he was a young boy.

Their first game was against Vietnam. The Americans were beating the Vietnamese this time, and were up by eighty-one points with a few seconds on the clock. Somehow, accidentally, Jayden Quinn tipped a defensive rebound into his own basket, making the final margin of victory seven-nine points. The well-funded start-up Nookiebookie.com would be bankrupt and shut down by the end of August.

***

August 6th, 2020—International Olympic Official Press Conference, Tokyo, Japan

Japanese and International Olympic Committee officials announced that the scheduled 8 pm Closing Ceremonies in three days' time would be moved forward four hours. The day before, the Japanese National Weather Service announced an alert of a category-two typhoon that had developed in the central Pacific, and several projections had the storm, now named Typhoon Ignacio, tracking toward Japan. Forecasters were predicting landfall within a week, possibly sooner. The country needed the time they could to prepare for the pending storm.

Once again, the US television broadcast sponsor protested vehemently. A 4 pm start time in Tokyo would mean the ceremony would be live on the East Coast of the United States at 2 am. The ratings for such a late start time would be abysmal, and the broadcaster would be expected to refund tens of millions of dollars to advertisers.

Japanese officials politely expressed their acknowledgment of the network's concern but refused to alter the new start time. As a concession, they agreed to change the basketball tournament schedule so that the finals would be played at noon on August 9th, the day of the Closing Ceremonies versus the traditional day before. The logic went that since many Americans would be watching the Gold Medal game at 10 pm on the East Coast in the United States, many would stay up to watch the Closing Ceremonies a few hours later.

What Japanese officials wanted to say was to impolitely remind the American TV executives that today, August 6th, 2020, was the 75th anniversary of America's decision to murder 120,000 Japanese civilians in the city of Hiroshima, and they couldn't give two shiitakes what they wanted.

TWENTY-FIVE

August 6th, 2020—The home of Colonel Maretta Sowers, Savage, Maryland

Did Superman and Wonder Woman have heroes? Doubtful. Your typical United States Air Force fighter pilot is like a superhero. They don't have heroes either. Or at least they think they're like superheroes. Colonel "Buff" Sowers was not your typical Air Force fighter pilot. She didn't have a hero; she had five.

Her first two were her parents. Their tireless work ethic and sacrifice for the purpose of advancing Buff's opportunities in life ultimately killed them both but Buff learned the importance of sacrifice and a hard day's work.

General Orlando Quinn and former Lt. Colonel, now Coach, Gibbs were heroes number three and four. They'd risked their lives to save hers. She survived the helicopter crash in Iraq because of their bravery.

And Buff's final hero was a mathematician she met late in the woman's life, Katherine Coleman Johnson. Johnson was the first African-American woman to work in the highly segregated fields of science and mathematics at NASA starting in the 1950s, ending her amazing career decades later. Johnson's office door at NASA never had her name on it. It read: "Colored Computer." Johnson was a computer, a human one. And, as referred to during that time, she was "colored."

Colonel Buff Sowers had received an email five days earlier from Coach Gibbs. It contained a single, simple question. Simple in asking, incredibly challenging in answering. She needed to call on the spirits of her five heroes in order to be up to the task. Hard work, personal sacrifice, and mathematics.

"Could you please calculate an appropriate payment amount for reparations of descendants of peoples wronged over the course of American history? Apis needs your answer by 11 pm JPT, August 6th, 2020."

"Really, Coach Gibbs? Is that all Apis needs? Shit," Sowers said to herself.

She called General Massie at the National Guard immediately. "Sir, I need to take five days of emergency leave."

"I'm sorry, Buff. Was there a death in the family?"

"No, sir. I have to figure out how much you owe me." She hung up the phone.

Only five days to solve a problem that had been debated by politicians, civil rights leaders, and philosophers for decades. No one could ever agree. Their problem? They never did the math. Neither had Buff.

To get in the mood for the task ahead, Buff opened her first bottle of Pinot Noir. She dimmed the lights to a mere glow and synced her phone with her Bose speaker. When working with numbers, Buff's playlist always started with a few minutes of her favorite serenade from Barry White called 'Love Makin' Music'.

Feeling relaxed and into the moment, she began to slowly and softly massage all the right buttons. Those buttons being the keys representing the numbers and arithmetical operations of her Texas Instruments NSPIRE CX II Graphing Calculator.

She broke the problem into multiple parts and began to apply the complex mathematical computations needed to develop her recommendations. The staggering number of variables would need to be calculated one at a time.

How much for descendants of slaves?

How much for butchered Native Americans?

How much for Japanese Americans interned during World War II?

Her list would go on and on. Hundreds of variables. She even included, "How much for that son-of-a-bitch Calvin Heyward who was planning on killing hundreds of Americans because he got pulled over by the cops when he was eighteen?" She had an immediate answer for that. "Nothing."

She needed every minute of the next five days until her conclusions were tested, retested, and finally proven. There were two possible solutions and Sowers's response provided both.

"Infinity or zero." She hit send on her email. Confirmed receipt.

***

Coach Gibbs checked his phone once more for texts. There was the one he was looking for. He opened it. It read: "Infinity or zero."

He, General Quinn, and the team had settled into a luxurious tatami room at one of Tokyo's most exclusive hotels. Gibbs and General Quinn were both staying there while the team stayed at the athletes' dormitories at the Olympic Village.

The team completed their semifinal match against Serbia and came away with the victory. The men played well as a team, but Davud Novak played like a man possessed. Originally born in Bosnia before his family immigrated to St. Louis, Novak gave every ounce of energy he had to teach the Serbs a lesson. He led the team in every statistical category, with thirty-one points, thirteen rebounds, eleven assists, and ten blocked shots. A quadruple-double in basketball parlance.

"Look at this," Ronan said as he and the others sat comfortably on goose-down pillows. "Now this is living."

After a spectacular meal and numerous servings of sake, the men moved to the business at hand. Their homework assignments.

"Gentlemen, when we first met, I gave each of you the same assignment. The homework was an opportunity to propose a new bill, a constitutional amendment or a repeal of an existing law. We've spent the last four months discussing what was submitted, and I can't tell you how thoroughly I've enjoyed our debates. I know it wasn't always pretty and sometimes the process broke down, but here we are today, ready to vote."

Without actually saying it, Coach Gibbs was referring to incidents back in St. Louis in which teammates argued vehemently and, one time, violently. Two of his players ended one particular dinner with a knock-down, drag-out fistfight over the subject of reparations for slavery. It was Charles Mwangi and Ronan McCoy.

McCoy lost the battle. He'd received a broken nose and tooth from the fight. Mwangi didn't receive so much as a scratch. Ronan couldn't get his dead hands high enough to land a solid blow to the giant's face.

"Any item we vote on tonight will be done openly with simple 'Yeas' and 'Nays.' If a majority is reached on 'Yeas,' it will become our new bill. If there is a tie in a vote, I will vote to break that tie. Are we clear on the process?" A nod of all heads indicated yea.

"Who wants to go first?" the coach asked.

"I will," said Andrew Beutel, the point guard from Indiana. "The capital city of the United States needs to move. The original site, Washington, DC, was chosen at the time because it was near both the geographic and population center point of the country. That was over 200 years ago when we had only thirteen states.

"Many countries have moved their capitals and some fairly recently. Brazil, Australia, and India are a few examples. The nearest sizable city to the center of the continental United States is Kansas City. Two hundred miles west of the population center, and 220 miles east of the geographic center.

"I believe and have argued before this body for the past three months that where a nation's capital resides does matter—even during an age when boundaries, borders, and a sense of place are becoming more and more obsolete. Economic development, political influence, and jobs can be attributed to its location relative to the seat of government. The flyover states of our nation's heartland have been ignored long enough.

"Many a politician has promised to 'drain the swamp' of the Potomac if elected. I don't believe we need to drain the swamp. We need to move its inhabitants to newer, cleaner waters. The confluence of the Missouri and Kansas rivers."

"What is the government and the Pentagon going to do with all that real estate?" asked one of the players.

"Keep DoD in DC. The farther we can get congressmen and generals away from each other, the better. That way they won't be declaring war after a couple of martinis in Georgetown.

"As far as the rest of the city? Who gives a fuck? Turn it into an amusement park for all I care."

"All in favor, say 'Yea.'" There were eight positive responses. The Nays were players mostly from the eastern states and one from the West Coast. "The Yeas have it. Congratulations, Mr. Beutel, your measure passed."

"Next?" asked Coach Gibbs.

"I'll go, Coach." Iver Koch, the forward from Atlanta stood up. "We need to get rid of political gerrymandering. Voters are no longer choosing their politicians, politicians are choosing their voters. It's ridiculous.

"We have the knowledge of population densities to easily redraw these maps to be in sync with where people live. In some cases, there are congressmen and senators who have been in office for over forty years. The demographics of their states have changed but so have their congressional maps. Ones more perfectly suited to ensure their reelection.

"By changing congressional districts to match population heat maps, we can assure Americans that they are being represented by politicians who actually represent their local and regional issues."

"All in favor, say 'Yea.'" Koch's proposal passed unanimously. The bill voting process continued. Davud Novak went next.

"Article II, Section 1, Clause 5 of the Constitution states three conditions of eligibility to become President or Vice President of the United States. Candidates must be natural-born, at least thirty-five years old, and have been at least fourteen years a resident of the United States. I contest that these qualifications are unjust and were a product of the times in which they were written. The natural-born requirement originally excluded those born prior to the adoption of the Constitution, as there was no United States.

"The first nine presidents, including the father of our nation, George Washington, were all born before the United States became a country. In effect, they were not Americans by birth but citizens and subjects of the British Empire.

"I see no reason to exclude an entire population of Americans today because of their country of origin. There are millions of Americans who have taken an oath of allegiance to their new country but cannot become president. Why is that? Many of those same millions have donned the uniforms of our Armed Forces, serving (and sometimes dying) in defense of our nation. They should be entitled to the opportunity to lead it."

"What a fantastic argument, Davud. Well thought out. Let's vote on Davud's proposal," Gibbs said.

The vote for repealing the clause of the Constitution regarding having to be native-born was tied at six to six. Coach Gibbs was expected to be the tie-breaker and he was. "Yea," is all he said. In the game of democracy this group was playing, any American, regardless of country of origin, could become president of the United States.

Seven more submissions followed, with four more being affirmed and three being voted down. The team had a total of seven new bills.

"Mr. McCoy and Mr. Wilson, we have yet to hear from the two of you. Who would like to go next?"

"Ronan, let me go last. Okay? We're going to be debating it for some time," said Carl Wilson.

"Well, to be honest with you guys, up until tonight I couldn't care less. Coach, when you first gave us this assignment, I thought it was bullshit. But I do want to propose something.

"I believe each and every American should serve in the military. Minimum two years. When Jayden and I were in the army, I was blown away by the spirit of brotherhood and, yes, sisterhood we were fortunate to be part of. A collective spirit of sacrifice and duty that we talk about in sports but the men and women of our armed services live.

"There are plenty of jobs in the military that don't require combat service. Take the general as an example. He was a linguist. He probably never killed anyone. That's my proposal, and I appreciate the opportunity to present it."

Ronan's quickly drafted submission was approved. Eleven to one. Jayden Quinn was the only player who voted against it without giving a reason to his best friend.

Then it came time for the last and most contentious bill. The matter of reparations for African-American citizens. The bill's sponsor, Carl Wilson, a forward from Memphis, presented his argument in favor of reparation payments, and all agreed it was well thought out and compelling.

His proposal came with reasonable ways to fund payments, including spreading them over the course of a decade. When asked what the appropriate payment amount should be, Wilson deferred. "We need to hire our best and brightest economic and mathematical minds to answer that," he said. No number was submitted. It proved fatal to his argument.

The vote took thirty seconds. Six were in favor, six were opposed. Surprisingly, Ronan McCoy voted in favor of the measure, and Charles Mwagi, a guy with deep African roots, voted against. They had engaged in fisticuffs back in St. Louis and for the same reason.

"Coach, you're the tie-breaker. What's your vote?" asked Alphonso Detandt.

"Men, obviously this is a sensitive issue, and strong opinions exist both in favor and opposed. But ultimately, it is a debate in futility. I find it impossible to equitably come to any type of agreement on the payment of reparations. It's not the money. It's the determination of the aggrieved.

"How can a nation account for every sin, every atrocity committed? We simply cannot. While we owe a mighty debt to our history, we cannot bankrupt our future in order to pay that debt. It must be forgiven. I am, therefore, opposed. I vote Nay."

The evening ended quietly. With each man thinking deeply. Not of basketball or themselves, but of their country. Coach Gibbs's exercise in democracy was meant to teach the men to think and feel a connection to a history, a future and a spirit of what a great privilege it is to call themselves Americans. The lesson was learned well.

Coach Gibbs closed out the night by settling one last question. "I will type up our new bills and have a copy for each of you before the end of the games. But gentlemen, what shall we call this document? It must have a name, wouldn't you agree?"

"The Bill of Heights," blurted out the seven-footer Charles Mwangi. The table of giant men laughed wildly.

"Twenty-Twenty Vision, you know, like the eyesight thing," said Alphonso Detandt.

"Yeah, we get it. Nice, I like it," said Gibbs with others nodding their heads in approval.

"Since the capital would be moving to Kansas City, we should call it The Missouri Compromise of 2020," Davud Novak said with pride. Coach Gibbs thought for a moment.

"It is perfect," he said. And he was right.

"Davud, what are we compromising as a nation, what are we willing to sacrifice so that our laws may move forward?" asked Beutel from Indiana.

"We can sacrifice the status quo. Our elected officials, the ones meant to represent the people, have become entrenched, disengaged, and self-serving. I suggest, for these bills anyway, that we put it out to the people to decide. Not our politicians.

"I, for one, am going to copy all of these on my Facebook page. I'm going to ask my friends to vote on them. A simple Facebook poll of yes or no. I'm interested to see my voter turnout."

The Missouri Compromise of 2020. They agreed with their coach. It was perfect, and the vote was unanimous in favor of the document's name. Each man loved the idea of putting it on their social media pages and letting friends vote.

Daniel Kreinbrink, the point guard from Salt Lake City, said he knew of ways to create groups that could be filtered by location. That way, anyone voting has to have a United States IP address. Between the players, they had a combined 115 million unique friends and followers who lived in the United States.

The Missouri Compromise of 2020 was posted onto the social media platforms of all the players on the morning of August 7th. By the morning of the eighth, over 50 million had voted. Many of those 50 million shared with their friends, and when the online polling finally closed on the morning of August 9th, over 130 million had cast a vote. Four million more than the 2016 presidential election. The United States Men's Olympic team's exercise in democracy was a successful one. Every bill passed. But the whole exercise was a game. Like basketball. Or was it?

***

August 8th, 2020—the Kotokuin Temple, Kamakura, Japan

"In ancient Japan, Samurai warriors were treated as heroes of their country. It is on this site that many a Samurai warrior took his last breath." Coach Gibbs started his history lesson to eight of the team's basketball players and General Quinn. "After a defeat in battle or to protest against injustice, they came here to perform the sacred ancient rite of Seppuku.

"Seppuku is a ceremony of assisted suicide. The Samurai begins the ritual by slicing open his belly across the entire width of his body using a traditional warrior knife called a Tanto.

"But standing behind the Samurai was his trusted comrade or mentor, officially called a Kaishakunin. The Kaishakunin, with one violent and accurate swing of his Samurai sword, ended the suffering of his friend. A final act of mercy. It was considered the greatest of honors to be asked to be Kaishakunin.

"One of the most famous Samurai in Japanese history wasn't even

Japanese. His name was Yasuke. Yasuke was an African slave, possibly from Ethiopia or Sudan. His exact origin could never be verified. He was brought to Japan by Catholic Jesuits in 1579 and was taught Italian, Portuguese, and Japanese. He escaped from his enslavers and was accepted into the Samurai shortly thereafter. The Samurai marveled at the man's incredible height and strength.

"He fought in countless battles beside his mentor, Oda Nobunaga, the unifier of modern-day Japan. Nobunaga adopted Yasuke as a son after it was determined his wife Nohime was barren and could not have children. Oda Nobunaga is considered the number one Samurai in Japanese lore. Today there are numerous statues of him all around the country.

"At one point in Yasuke's life as a Samurai, and after his clan was defeated in battle, he considered committing Seppuku himself. The men under him volunteered to take his place as the thought of losing their most fierce and capable warrior was too much for them to bear.

"Legend has it that Yasuke lived on and eventually made his way back to his homeland. Again, that could not be verified." Coach Gibbs finished his history lesson, with the men sitting in silence.

***

On the ride back to Tokyo, the coach had one more point for discussion.

"Men, we have one last resolution to vote on, and we will do so now. We've discussed this measure for months; you know the details, so no further debate or presentation is necessary. But unlike our votes from two nights ago, this one must be unanimous, and both I and General Quinn will vote as well. Jayden, it was your resolution. You vote first."

"Yea," said Jayden without a second's delay.

"Yea," said the other seven players.

"Yea," said the coach and the general, but with a long minute of silence in between.

"Then it's passed. Thank you, men, and I will see you tomorrow. God bless the Black Hand and God bless America."

"God bless the Black Hand and God Bless America," everyone said in unison.

TWENTY-SIX

August 8th, 2020—home of Sara Gujic, St. Louis, Missouri

P *ing*, sounded the smartphone of Sara Gujic at 6 am, indicating she'd received a new email to her work account. As a Pulitzer Prize–winning newspaper reporter, she'd learned early on to read her work emails immediately as opposed to during normal business hours. Besides, as an investigative reporter, her normal business hours were 24/7/365.

Some of her best stories came from unidentified leads she received at all hours of the night and morning. She looked at this one. It was from gprincip@gmail.com. She had a vague remembrance of the name *Princip*, but on waking, her mind was too foggy from sleep to know exactly who that was. In the text of the email were the words *Crna Ruka*. She opened the attachment.

"Oh shit, what the... I'm going to be sick," she said as she ran to the bathroom to throw up. She watched the rest of the five-minute video. The email subject line read: "The rape of Melissa Gibbs – Jayden Quinn's fiancée. Marcus Emerson and Tracy Quinn guilty. August 9th, 2014."

Gujic got up, dressed, and was out the door to work. She needed to access all the archived newspapers from the period around the Ferguson riots, and she needed to do so quickly. She also remembered interviewing the victim a few months before the riots, a fluff piece of meaningless drivel about what it was like to be engaged to a budding superstar.

***

Gujic wasn't a sports fan, but she knew who Jayden Quinn was. Everyone in the world did. At this moment he was over in Japan with Coach Kenneth Gibbs getting ready to play in tomorrow's gold medal game of the men's basketball competition. Gujic wrote up some questions and an outline of a leading story. She knew whatever story she wrote would go global. But first she had to get the story right.

Her search of the archives of the papers from the days and weeks following August 9th, 2014, produced little insight into the assault. There was a brief mention in the Metro section about three young men being arrested and charged. No specific details of times or location were in the mention.

Three days later, there was a two-column story about Melissa's suicide with a brief interview of one of the witnesses who saw her jump off the bridge. But no mention of an assault.

Too much column space of the paper in those days was dedicated to all that was happening around Ferguson and the country. Most of the front page and main stories for the week had been written by Gujic herself. The victim's name was not mentioned anywhere, as it was the policy of the police not to reveal it and of the paper not to report it.

Gujic called the Y.

"Ferguson YMCA, how may I help you?"

"Marcus Emerson, please."

"Who may I say is calling?"

"Sara Gujic, *St. Louis Post-Dispatch*."

"One second please..."

"Hello, this is Marcus; how can I help you?"

"Hello, Mr. Emerson, my name is Sara Gujic from the *Post-Dispatch*. What can you tell me about the assault and rape of Melissa Gibbs on August 9th, 2014, in your parking lot?"

"Wha...What are you talking about? What assault?"

"Is your official answer, Mr. Emerson, that you know nothing of the events of August 9th, 2014?"

"August 9th, 2014? Ah, well, yeah, that was the day that young man was shot and killed here in Ferguson. A lot was going on at that time."

"Mr. Emerson, I watched a video of Melissa Gibbs being assaulted in your parking lot. Minutes later, you are carrying her back into the Y. Thirty minutes after that, you escorted her to her car. Are you sure you don't know anything about this?"

"Ms....Gujic, is it? That was six years ago. It was a horrible tragedy. But it was Melissa and her dad who didn't want the rape to become public knowledge. It wasn't my idea. Can't you please leave this alone?"

"Mr. Emerson, I pulled the public records at the Ferguson Police Department, and I believe you. I know they attempted to prosecute these young men. But as you had a duty to report the crime, I report the news. And this is news. I expect it will be picked up nationally, and I'll be on the major networks by tonight. If you prefer to go off the record and tell me more, I promise I will not quote you as one of my sources."

"I appreciate that, Ms. Gujic. I did try to do everything I could. The video shows that clearly. But I'm afraid I can't talk about this. It's against my organization's policy of not discussing any events that happen on our property without clearing it with our attorneys first."

"I understand, Mr. Emerson. One more question and then I'll let you go. I received this video of the assault via email from a source I don't know. The subject line read: 'Melissa Gibbs raped. Marcus Emerson and Tracy Quinn guilty.' What does that mean to you?"

For five seconds Gujic heard nothing. Then she heard Emerson crying.

"It was her idea, not mine." Marcus Emerson hung up the phone.

"Holy shit," Gujic said to no one on the other end.

***

"We have to run with the story now. If we wait too long, someone else is going to get it. I want to post your story on stltoday.com now," said Gujic's editor.

"No, I need to talk to the Gibbs, the Quinns, and the police. I want to get this right. This is the problem with journalism today. You want the sensationalism now. Who gives a damn about the truth?"

"I'm sorry, Sara. We're going with it. I'll write the damn story if I have to."

"Go ahead, do it. And I quit."

Twenty minutes later Sara Gujic was packing her personal things, including her Pulitzer Prize. She headed out the door of the paper for the last time. The story went live at 9:30 am, St. Louis time. The story's byline had the editor's name.

As Sara walked to her car, she dropped her box of belongings and started thinking. She had completely forgotten to tell the editor about the email address and the subject line. The only information the paper had was the name of the victim and that she was Jayden Quinn's fiancée. Her editor was in too big of a damn rush to ask the most basic of questions.

"gprincip@gmail.com?" Sara said to herself. She often talked to herself aloud as if interviewing someone live. "Melissa Gibbs, Coach Kenneth Gibbs, the $25,000 gun, Gavrilo Princip, gprincip?" Her brilliant, investigative, chain-of-custody and connecting-the-dots mind was working overtime.

She recalled a passing statement Melissa Gibbs made to her during their one-on-one interview years ago. Melissa mentioned that her father owned the exact gun used by Gavrilo Princip. The Bosnian assassin of 1914.

Gujic had the mind of an elephant and never forgot details. Which was good for a reporter. Her last name, translated from Bosnian, meant snake. Which was also good. She could slither her way into stories unnoticed until it was time to strike.

"Damn it. It was Coach Gibbs who'd sent me the email. He wanted that video to be released to the general public, and he got me to do exactly as he wanted."

"But why now and why the cryptic email address? He must have known I would figure it out." Sara looked at her phone. It was 10:05 am in St. Louis. She typed, "If 10 am in St. Louis, what time in Tokyo?" The result said 1:00 am, the next day. It was August 9th.

She also searched "Gavrilo Princip" and read the search results: "Member of the Crna Ruka. Secret para-military organization led by Colonel Dragutin Dimitrijevic, also known by the code name Apis. Responsible for the start of World War I." What message was the coach sending to Gujic?

"Of course he wanted it out on August 9th. The anniversary of the assault. 'Crna Ruka,'" she said a few more times. The Black Hand, Melissa Gibbs, Jayden Quinn. "Everyone in my neighborhood calls Jayden Quinn 'Crna Ruka'...The Black Hand." Gujic was born to be an investigative reporter.

After arriving back home, some more Google searches, Facebook searches, and property records research produced her next lead. She jumped in her car and began the two-hour drive west. To the vacation home of the Gibbses and the Quinns.

Sara read a post on Theresa Gibbs's Facebook page about spending every

August 9th at the Lake of the Ozarks. The anniversary of her daughter's assault and death. But where was the house? She couldn't locate a house anywhere in the Lake of the Ozarks listed by the last names of Quinn or Gibbs. She dug deeper.

She searched for any of the two family names that might be listed as a resident agent, the person responsible for executing a purchase under the name of a limited liability corporation. She found it:

Tracy Quinn, Resident Agent, TOTK, LLC.

"Pretty clear that stands for Tracy, Orlando, Theresa, and Ken," she said aloud. She now knew the address. She was hopeful no one else would, for some time to come.

***

"Good evening, America, welcome to the evening news. We have an important developing story. A story that began six years ago. A warning for you parents out there. We will be broadcasting a disturbing video of an assault on a young lady, and you may wish to refrain from having your children watch tonight's program. We will be showing the video multiple times and having our experts discuss its implications.

"On August 9th, 2014, in Ferguson, Missouri, a young lady by the name of Melissa Gibbs was brutally assaulted in the parking lot of a local YMCA. In case you don't recall, August 9th, 2014, was also the day a young black man was shot and killed by a police officer from the Ferguson Police Department.

"The father of Melissa Gibbs is Coach Kenneth Gibbs, now coaching the United States Olympic team. Her fiancée at the time was Jayden Quinn. Yes, *that* Jayden Quinn. We will now show the video..."

***

News stations, both local and national, all went with the same story for the rest of the day. The ratings for the news outlets were off the charts. Tens of millions turned off the Olympic coverage on one station and watched the others.

There were no interviews with the Quinns, the Gibbses, Emerson, the Ferguson Police Department, or any of the relevant parties. It wasn't that the national press didn't try. Hordes of reporters showed up at the homes of the

Gibbses and Quinns in St. Louis, but no one was there.

The reporters left, but not before a compelling piece was aired on all the major networks. The lead story that evening was how both families most definitely needed to cut their grass. One of the on-air, talking-head experts presented an explanation of how 12-inch-high zoysia in the year 2020 could lead to rape in 2014. Something about the Butterfly Effect combined with the Broken Window Theory but in reverse time.

The men, of course, were in Tokyo for the Olympics. Theresa Gibbs was at the summer home at the Lake of the Ozarks, and Tracy Quinn was nowhere to be found. In Tokyo none of the men were talking, at least not to the press.

TWENTY-SEVEN

August 9th, 2020—the Imperial Hotel, Tokyo, Japan

"How is this coming out now?" Ken was overheard yelling at his best friend, Orlando, as they exited the elevator into the hotel lobby.

"I have no idea."

"But you had the only copy. I thought you gave it to the Ferguson Police Department. Did you make another copy for yourself? Why, Orlando, why would you do this to me? On the anniversary of her death no less...answer me, Goddamn it!"

The major news networks and reporters from hundreds of newspapers mobbed the lobby of the exclusive hotel and picked up every contentious moment of the two as they exited the hotel elevator.

"Did the coach accuse Jayden Quinn's father of giving the media a video of his daughter being raped?" a beat reporter in the Tokyo hotel lobby asked another.

"Probably because he hasn't been playing Jayden enough. I know sports parents pull some crazy shit regarding their kids and their coaches, but this is over the top."

"Totally unbelievable," responded the reporter, who filed an article an hour later with the headline "Totally Believable."

***

August 8th, 2020—Madic's Café, St. Louis, Missouri

"Totally unbelievable, Tracy. How is this happening now? How did that video get out? Oh, and one other little, startling note. My right-hand man, Marcus Emerson, is dead," Calvin said.

"What? How?"

"He lost his shit when some reporter called him about the video. He pulled a copycat of the girl and jumped off the Stan Span. I have a cop on the payroll. Said divers dragged a mangled body out of the fresh water intake at the Anheuser Busch brewery downriver. It was Marcus."

"Can I get you two a couple ice cold Emerson-infused Buds? Sorry, just working on my English humor," interrupted Madic.

Tracy gagged. "Get the fuck out of here, Hamza. You must be the only Bosnian in this town who doesn't mind his own business."

"Not true. That bitch reporter Sara Gujic. Prints nothing but lies. Got me arrested, but cops couldn't prove shit."

"The same reporter who called Marcus," said Heyward.

"Whatever. Just go away, Hamza... So what are we going to do? Is everything still a go for tomorrow? What about the other guys? They must be losing their shit right about now."

"Everything's a go. No reason to panic now. By tomorrow afternoon, no one is going to give a damn that your son's girlfriend was raped six years ago or that a guy turned up in a drainage pipe."

"I'm going with you tomorrow. Only two people ever had their hands on that video besides the Ferguson cops. Marcus and Orlando. Obviously Marcus didn't send it. Orlando did. He's sending some kind of message."

"How would he know?"

Tracy put her computer-like mind to work. "That bitch."

"Who?"

"Sowers. If she told him, that means he knows everything. You and me. Atlanta. Maryland. The national convention in Charlotte."

"Tracy, if that were true, the cops would have been here months ago. You're being paranoid. Who knows, probably some record keeper at the Ferguson Police Department sold the video for thousands of dollars. Focus, bitch."

"At least tell me you didn't wire the $2 million to her account?"

"It went through two hours ago."

"Damn it, Calvin. That's all the money we have. For some reason, I can't access Jayden's accounts anymore."

Calvin Heyward's life story of bad timing was adding another chapter. With only a day left before his dream of becoming an important and respected man came true, he thought a few minor setbacks were not going to stop him. But he was wrong. There were those that cared about a woman who was assaulted six years ago. One of those was Marcus Emerson, Calvin's right-hand man.

Marcus never forgave himself for being an accomplice to the attack. He loved Melissa Gibbs, and to witness her suffering and to be the cause of her death was a sin of which he knew he could no longer forgive himself.

As penance, his final act before sending himself and his cell phone off the Stan Musial Bridge was to send a text message to a former YMCA board member. Coach Kenneth Gibbs. The text read: "Calvin Heyward, Tracy Quinn, Kendley Charles, Tyrell George, Buster Hicks, Edwin Morton, and Antonio 'Smiley' Hernandez—the Crna Ruka. You'll understand tomorrow. Please forgive me."

TWENTY-EIGHT

"THE COBRA AND THE SNAKE"

August 8th, 2020—Gibbs and Quinn's vacation home, Lake of the Ozarks, Missouri

"I love you, Theresa. I am going to miss you so very much. But I'll see our daughter and I'll hug her for the two of us. Please forgive me."

"I don't have to forgive you for anything. You are my brave American soldier. I wish you would come home. I want to hold you one last time. I love you, and have since the first day I saw you."

"Goodbye, my love. My beautiful Cobra."

"Goodbye, my Nubian Prince. I love you."

Kenneth and Theresa Gibbs both disconnected from the video call. It was the last time they set eyes on each other.

An hour-and-a-half later: "Good evening, ma'am, my name is Sara Gujic, and I'm with the *Post-Dispatch* in St. Louis," said Sara after knocking on the door of the Gibbses' vacation home.

"I'm sorry. Who are you again?" Theresa asked as she wiped her eyes. It was obvious she had been crying for some time.

"Sara Gujic. I'm a reporter for the *St. Louis Post Dispatch*. Would you have a minute or so to talk?"

"Ok, but about what?"

"Have you not seen the news, ma'am?"

"Come in, please. I don't follow the news. Why, what's happened?"

"Do you have a Facebook account?"

"Yes, but I don't do much on it. I've posted once or twice."

"Mrs. Gibbs, I'm going to ask a strange request of you, but it is imperative that you do this for me now."

"What's that, Sara?"

"Open your computer, sign on to Facebook, and without looking at your newsfeed, please let me deactivate your account. I know you just met me, but you have to trust me on this."

"What? I don't even know you."

"Actually, ma'am, I met your daughter years ago. I did an article about her and your family. As well as her relationship with Jayden Quinn."

"I remember that article. You brought out a side of my daughter I rarely saw. What do you want me to do with my Facebook account?"

"Shut it down. Trust me on this. If you value your privacy, let me help you shut it down now."

"Whatever."

Sara knew it would only be a matter of time before other reporters figured out where Theresa Gibbs was. They would be on their way to the Lake of the Ozarks in no time. She needed this story to be hers. Exclusively hers.

Sara thought hard about her next move. She assumed Theresa was crying about the video of her daughter. What question was most appropriate for the moment? Sara decided to turn off her journalistic instincts and turn on her human ones instead. Try to get the woman talking. To build some rapport.

"Mrs. Gibbs, do you have some tea?"

"Call me Theresa, and to hell with the tea. Let's open a bottle of wine. Then we'll talk."

The two women spent the next three hours and three bottles of wine talking. Not about the recently released video. And not about Melissa's suicide.

They talked almost exclusively about America. Each was an immigrant, albeit from different countries, but both had left their homeland under similar circumstances. Theresa came to the United States during the Ferdinand Marcos era. Corruption, widespread poverty, unemployment as high as fifty percent, and political rivals being incarcerated or, in some cases, murdered.

Sara came to the United States as a young girl during the Yugoslavian civil war. Part of the Bosniak diaspora after hundreds of thousands of her kind were murdered. Genocide.

America was good to both of them. Yet consistently, their hometown of St. Louis and their adopted country had violent crime rates as much as ten to twenty times greater than those in the Philippines or Bosnia. How was that possible in a country with such great resources? What could be done to change that? Questions for which Sara did not have answers.

As far as Theresa? That was a different story. She had answers.

"I can't let you drive back, especially if you're as drunk as I am. You're spending the night," Theresa insisted.

"Okay, Theresa, thanks. But I'm setting my alarm for five. We need to talk about why I'm here."

"I'll set the alarm for four, and I'll tell you why a man named Apis sent you here."

"What are you talking about? Apis sent me here? Who is Apis? No, I figured this out on my own. That's what I do. I'm one of the best investigative reporters out there, Theresa."

"She knows you are, Sara. That's why we sent for you. We'll talk in the morning. Good night...why are you smiling?"

"I couldn't help but hear; you used the wrong pronoun. You said '*she* knows you are.' Talking about this guy, Apis. I had the same problem when I came here as a little girl. My native language is Bosnian. It has gender-specific pronouns, but we don't use them in everyday conversation. Our verbs conjugate to indicate gender, as do many other words. If I were to say in Bosnian, 'She went to her house,' and used pronouns, it would translate in English as 'She, she went to her, her house,' which would sound ridiculous. Aren't languages fascinating?"

"All I know is English is bullshit...and cowshit. I sometimes use the wrong pronoun to mess with people. Especially with people I don't like."

"Is that why you said 'she' to me?"

"No, that was a mistake. I like you, Sara."

"Theresa, I have to know before I go to bed. Who is 'we,' and who is this guy Apis?"

"We are the Black Hand, and Apis is our supreme commander."

***

Theresa Gibbs went to bed the night of August eighth, but she did not go to sleep. She thought about her life with her husband and daughter. And she prayed. All night. Her professed atheism over the years was a deflection, a diversionary tactic, like the events unfolding before her.

She believed strongly in her God. She never felt a need to tell anyone. Her relationship with God, like with her husband, her daughter, and her life in general, was private and sacrosanct. It was no one's business who she prayed to or loved. A principle by which she'd lived her entire life.

Her privacy was so important to her she had, at first, refused any attempt by her husband to get her to use social media, text messaging, or any other type of electronic communications. She only created a Facebook profile to aid in tracking down old friends and people she'd served with while in the military. She'd only posted once or twice in her life.

The tears she'd shed moments before Sara Gujic knocked on her front door were for her daughter and her husband. Her sorrow was also private. Over the course of the previous months, Theresa and Ken had talked for hours each day. But the conversations had little to do with basketball. The subject was war. One coming in the future and two from the past. Theresa recorded their conversations. Ken insisted there be an oral history of the lead-up to August 9th, 2020.

***

"Theresa, it was November 2004. My final tour in Iraq. I was assigned as an advisor to a Marine Corps unit planning a large-scale attack on the city of Fallujah. The city was known for harboring Islamic extremists, including insurgent fighters from multiple countries. I was there in 2003 and knew the terrain and the enemy's tactics well. Or so I thought.

"Before we knew what hit us, over a hundred Marines were dead. The single bloodiest battle of the entire campaign. The unit I was assigned to was going house to house. Killing those even remotely considered insurgents. We did other things to those who happened to be caught in the cross-fire.

"By the tenth day we were tired, scared, and lost six men in my small squad alone. The Marines were looking for some payback. They found it. As I and another Marine guarded the door to a house, five others went in. After five minutes, I grew concerned. There was no gunfire, no orders being issued. I went in to investigate and found the men raping a mother and her daughter.

"I did nothing. I turned around and walked back to my post. I had a duty to report the men but said nothing. I don't know why I froze, but I did. I'm sorry, my love. That is why I left the Army. I failed as an officer to do my duty. I failed my country."

"Ken, you don't have to apologize. You weren't involved. You weren't even their squad leader. People don't understand what war can do to someone. Besides, each person is responsible for his or her own actions. I'm sure those men are dealing with this in their own way."

"That's not it. Something very similar happened almost ten years earlier. In Bosnia, 1995. My first time in a combat zone. I watched hundreds of fathers and sons executed. Buried in mass graves. We were there as a peacekeeping unit, and yet all of us stood by and let it happen."

"I'm with you, Ken. I understand what you must do, and I will do my best to honor you for your sacrifice."

Part IV
"Hooah!"

TWENTY-NINE

ONE YEAR PRIOR

August 9th, 2020—Joint Base Pearl Harbor, Hickam, Honolulu, Hawaii

"Chief Baeztel here," said Mr. Scott Baeztel.

"Mr. Baeztel. Major Green. We need you on the flight line ASAP."

"What's up, ma'am?"

"We have an inbound flight arriving approximately zero three hundred," said Major Annie Green. Both she and Chief Warrant Officer Four Baetzel were assigned to the Army Criminal Investigation Division Major Cybercrimes Unit at Joint Base Hickam.

"Possible multiple homicides on board. Major General Orlando Quinn is on board and believed to be the shooter. He's deputy director NGIA in St. Louis."

"Holy shit. Ahh, sorry, ma'am. I know the general, but why are you calling me and what does that have to do with cybercrimes? I'm retiring in three weeks. Shouldn't this be turned over to the MPs at Schofield Barracks?"

"Mr. Baetzel, get dressed. That's an order. There is a lot more going on than what's happened on the plane. I'll explain when you get here."

"I'll be there in thirty minutes."

Chief Warrant Officer Four Scott Baetzel arrived to the flight line at Joint Base Hickam in Honolulu in twenty-five minutes. He was staying in nearby temporary quarters. Mr. Baetzel was wrapping up a 32-year career in the Army and had relinquished his permanent on-base quarters weeks earlier.

Prior to becoming a lead investigator with the Army Criminal

Investigation Division (CID) he was a helicopter pilot with multiple tours of duty in the Middle East. His first was during Operation Desert Shield and Desert Storm in the early nineties and from 2003 to 2005 in Operation Iraqi Freedom.

He exchanged his wings for a badge after witnessing firsthand the human rights violations committed by his fellow soldiers at the Abu Ghraib prison compound in Iraq in 2003. Detainees at the prison were frequent victims of sexual abuse, torture and murder.

Baetzel loved flying. He loved his army more, like a father, actually. And in 2003, it was clear some of the children needed an ass-whoopin'.

For the past three years he'd served as the lead investigator for the Major Cybercrimes Unit based at Hickam. It was an unfulfilling end to an otherwise meaningful career. The most serious of cybercrimes he investigated were of some soldiers running an illegal gambling site.

He missed the days of investigating actual crimes. Prior to joining the Cybercrimes unit, Chief Baetzel successfully investigated felonies to include arms trafficking, drug smuggling and murder. His most troubling case was that of a group of four GIs returning from Afghanistan. They were caught attempting to smuggle millions of dollars' worth of freshly-produced opium. Upon their arrest, they each committed suicide by drinking hydrogen cyanide. They'd procured the poison from Afghan farmers who used it as a pesticide.

But now, with such limited time left in his career, to be called into a case involving multiple murders when he no longer was assigned to that unit? What would be expected of him? Probably not much, he concluded.

"Damn," Baetzel said to himself while driving onto the flight line. "Orlando Quinn. Poor guy's been on the shitty end of an Army mule train since I've known him. When was that?" Baetzel slammed on his brakes and looked at his watch again. "August 9th? Are you kidding me?"

It turned out Mr. Baetzel wasn't kidding himself. He was the Black Hawk pilot on August 9th, 1990, and had flown the-then Lieutenant Quinn and the new-born Jayden Quinn to the hospital in Riyadh. He was one of three people in the entire world who knew the truth about the general and his son.

Baetzel never said a word about the shooting incident mostly on the premise that he didn't believe the young officer had done anything wrong. Quinn received direct orders from a superior officer, of which Baetzel was a witness. The shooting fell within the parameters established by command in Riyadh.

Also, unless saving a new-born infant's life and raising him as his own could be considered wrong, to Baetzel, it was none of his business and it was better that no one knew. The Army way.

***

Upon arriving at the flight line and before stepping a foot out of his car, the investigation had its first major breakthrough. The general wasn't the shooter and there were witnesses to prove it. Hundreds of millions of them saw the entire incident on Facebook Live. Kenneth Gibbs was the shooter. Baetzel heard the news report on his car radio.

"Good, I'll be off the case before noon."

***

"Chief Baetzel, thanks for coming so quickly," said Major Green as the chief was joined by multiple teams. "We have a much bigger problem than the plane that's landing in five minutes. We received communication from NORAD and directly from the Pentagon over regular coms.

"All of our systems are down. NGIA, NSA, NRO, everyone. All have lost operating capabilities. A major virus and no one knows what the hell is going on. When that plane lands, get the Forensics done quickly. I'll get the remaining passengers over to the VIP quarters for interviews. This is going to be a shit show. I promise."

"Ma'am, I'd like to interview the general directly. I know the man. Served with him multiple times."

"That's fine. Oh, and by the way, I've put in a request to extend you for another three months. I know you're sorry to hear that, but we're moving your retirement to November."

Chief Baetzel wasn't sorry. He was excited to be involved in such an important case. He would have gladly put in for the extension himself and for however long necessary.

Twenty-four hours later, the major would be right. He would be sorry.

"Here's what we're going to do when they land. Your squad of men are going to escort, not arrest, the passengers and crew. Take them over to the Distinguished Visitors Quarters. Get them fed and I'm sure they're tired. We'll keep them here for twenty-four hours for interviews. Got it?" ordered Baetzel.

"Yes sir. Do we confiscate their personal effects, phones and computers?" asked the lead MP.

"Just the coach's. Let the FBI handle the investigation with the other civilians. They'll probably be here in a few hours."

"And the general's?"

"I'll handle that."

***

"Oh my god, what is that smell?" asked one of the team members as they boarded the Bombardier Global Express minutes after touching down.

"What are you talking about? I don't smell anything," said Baetzel as he boarded the plane.

"Chief, you can't smell that? It's not normal. Smells like bitter almonds."

Baetzel's mind raced for a moment. "Sergeant, forget what you said. Do you understand me?"

"Sir?"

"I said forget it. That's an order. You and your crew get over to the hangar and bring two air handlers here. Get them hooked up and running. You got it?"

"Yes sir."

Four hours later, Forensics had all they needed from the aircraft and the victims. The squad from the morgue was called in to take the dead. But before releasing the bodies, Baetzel removed the watches from each of the dead men and put them on his wrist one at a time.

"Just what I thought."

He then tagged them with the victims' names and put them in separate evidence bags. The watches were all the same brand and model – Apple series 5.

Chief Warrant Baetzel began issuing orders again.

"I want a full autopsy performed on every victim. You got that, Lieutenant? And call in a tech from Toxicology."

"But Chief, that will take days. They all have a bullet hole in their heads. Everyone saw what happened on Facebook. Case closed."

"Start with the last man to get shot besides Gibbs. You should be able to determine that from the Facebook video. I want that victim's autopsy results first. Do it and bring the results to me and only me. That's a direct order, son, and if you violate that order, I'll have your ass."

"Sergeant, come here," Baetzel ordered the ranking MP.

"Yes sir."

"Call the FISA court. I need a warrant immediately."

"Who are we issuing the warrant for, sir, and what do we need?"

"Apple Corporation. I want the health-related data of each of these watches for the past twelve hours. They keep all that shit on iCloud. I want the results sent directly to me electronically. Get on it. I'm going over to talk to the general."

***

"Good morning General Quinn," said Baetzel as he entered the general's temporary quarters.

"Holy shit, Scott, is that you? My god man, how long has it been? Five, ten years?"

"Five, sir. The last time I saw you was at the 25th reunion of our unit from Desert Shield. How's your wife, Tracy? How are the old war injuries?"

"I'm fine, but I didn't think I'd ever say this Scott…today is worse than Somalia and Iraq."

Baetzel picked up on the fact that the general didn't answer the question about his wife. "I can't imagine, sir. What the hell happened up there?"

The general gave his full account of Coach Gibbs' death walk down and back up the aisle of the plane. Included in the account was a second-by-second description of how Jayden was able to knock the gun from the coach. The general then grabbed the gun. Seeing Coach Gibbs reaching into his coat pocket, he had no choice. He killed his best friend, firing once, striking Gibbs in the head.

"Tell me again, General. Exactly how did these men die?"

"What do you mean? Didn't you see the Facebook video? Didn't you see me shoot and kill my own best friend? It was self-defense. Jesus Christ, Scott."

237

"I did see it. I saw it all, along with hundreds of millions of Facebook subscribers. Compelling visual evidence. But a good investigation relies on all the senses including smell. One of my assistants smelled bitter almonds. Hydrogen cyanide. One of the quickest and deadliest poisons there are.

"The smell originates from a dead body a few hours after ingestion. Did you know forty percent of all people do not have the gene required to smell that? I guess I'm in that group because I couldn't smell shit. We're going to be conducting full autopsies including toxicology reports.

"I've also requested FISA warrants for Apple. Specifically, heart-rate monitoring history on all the victims. I'm going to find out the exact minute and second those guys died. Do you have anything you want to add to your account, General?"

The general did have something to add.

"Article Five – The Code of Conduct of the United States Fighting Force. When questioned, should I become a prisoner, I am required to give name, rank, service number and date of birth. I will evade answering further questions to the utmost of my ability. I will make no oral or written statements disloyal to my country and its allies or harmful to their cause."

"Dammit, General, I know the Code. You are not a prisoner. I am not your enemy. I'm your new best friend again. Remember what I did for you during Desert Shield and Gothic Serpent? Now tell me what the fuck happened up there or I'm going to get pissed. Sir."

"Let's wait a week, Scott. Then tell me if what you said about us being friends is still true."

***

August 9th, 2020 – LAX Airport, Los Angeles, California

As it turned out, the first hours after the plane touched down were not as much of a shit-show as Major Green predicted. At least not in Hawaii. The same could not be said about LAX International Airport where the flight was originally scheduled to land.

Thousands of members of the media, basketball fans, mass-murder fans and the police were waiting for the most watched shooting in human history to touch down. It was the OJ Simpson-in-the-white-Bronco scene all over again, times eight. Except there was no Juice. No one knew Flight 9 8 7 had landed thousands of miles away.

NORAD was suddenly unable to connect with the FAA database to inform controllers of the new landing location of the plane. Without specific guidance from the Western Air Defense Sector, all other scheduled inbound flights to LAX were rerouted to other area airports so that security could be put in place.

Outbound flights were canceled as well. At least those flights on the tower's schedule. By seven in the morning over fifty unauthorized and privately piloted drones were hovering the tarmac hoping to get a glimpse of Flight November 9 8 7. There would be no glimpse but there were five mid-air collisions watched by thousands.

"Yay!" all the adoring spectators screamed when one of the drones crashed into another.

As shit-shows go, the made-for-television and the internet mess occurring in Los Angeles was like watching a mouse squeeze out the tiniest of turds. The cinematic epic that would be August 9th, 2020, was starting to play in theaters everywhere and it was a hot, steaming, giant pile of elephant excrement.

***

Hours later another amateur drone crash landed. But not at LAX. At 1600 Pennsylvania Ave. Its pilot was hiding behind a statue of Andrew Jackson on the grounds of a former slave market. Lafayette Park. The drone barely cleared the fence around the White House and crashed hard on the North Lawn.

"Sorry, Dad, I need to work on that," said Colonel Sowers as she looked skyward and drove away.

***

The FBI never showed up at Hickam as Chief Baetzel predicted. It was dealing with more pressing priorities. Cities across the country were under attack. St. Louis, Long Island and Silicon Valley were hit particularly hard with hundreds murdered at a country club, a populated public beach and the headquarters of social media giant, Facebook.

Additionally, incidents of mass protests, riots and a number of individual fatalities occurred in cities not directly threatened by the Crna

Ruka. Hundreds of thousands took to the streets in towns across the country enraged over the killing of seven all-star basketball superstars. The protests and riots that occurred in Ferguson, Missouri on August 9th, 2014, were but a blip on the radar compared to August 9th, 2020, and the days immediately following.

Less than ten hours after landing at Hickam, Chief Warrant Officer Baeztel, General Orlando Quinn, the rest of the team and the flight crew were on another private chartered aircraft. This one, a C-17 Globemaster destined for Scott Air Force Base. Thirty minutes east of St. Louis. Ground zero of August 9th, 2020.

THIRTY

August 9th, 2020 – the Gibbs' residence, St. Louis, Missouri

"Open up! St. Louis PD," yelled the SWAT team leader at 5:45am. After five seconds without a response: "Break it down, now."

Two members of the St. Louis Police Department Special Weapons team rammed the front door and entered the home of Kenneth and Theresa Gibbs with a squad of four behind them. Three more cops covered the home's sides and back doors.

Theresa Gibbs did not hear the order as she was in the shower at that time. She was also 120 miles away at her summer home at the Lake of the Ozarks. Within twenty-four hours her front door at the lake house would be knocked on again, as in St. Louis. Except this time it wasn't the black-gloved hands of SWAT members. It was the members of the Black Hand.

***

August 9th, 2020 – Lake of the Ozarks, Missouri

"So when do we talk about why I'm here?" Sara started as the two women sat down for coffee.

"Sara, yesterday and last night was a test. You passed or you wouldn't be here now."

"A test of what, Theresa?"

"A test of your journalistic skills as well as your personal integrity. You passed on both fronts."

"How so?"

"My husband and I were well aware of your background. We knew you would find me. The question that remained was could you first get to know your subjects or was it all about the sensation of the story?

"Last night, you could have been yourself, a reporter. But you showed you could put aside that instinct and sit with me and talk. I can't tell you how much that meant to me. Now, we need you to be a reporter again and tell the story that is being written as we speak."

"And what story is that?"

"The story of the Crna Ruka and the Black Hand. Forty-five minutes ago, eight men gave their lives for this country. Their deaths were broadcast on Facebook Live. What appeared to happen was my husband killed them and then was shot by Orlando Quinn, Ken's best friend. Jayden Quinn's dad. That's not what happened at all."

"I need to see it. I need to see the Facebook video."

"I saved a copy to my laptop. Watch it if you must. I haven't and I won't. It's now irrelevant. I'll give you fifteen minutes." Theresa Gibbs hated watching people suffer and die. Once a nurse, always a nurse.

Sara Gujic did watch it. She had to. It was her duty as a reporter to know and report the facts. To confirm from multiple sources before jumping to conclusions.

"Theresa, I have to go to St. Louis, and you need to go with me. The police, the media, everyone is going to be looking for you. I'm sorry for your loss but this is bigger than a news story. This is murder."

"We'll go, if that's what you insist. If that's the extent of the story you wish to go with. But then you'll miss out on so much more, and I'll never share another word with you. That's your choice, Sara. You'll miss out on the story of a lifetime."

"The cops are going to find you, Theresa. I found you in less than eight hours. They'll be down here before the day is over."

"No they won't. And by the end of today, I won't even be on their primary list anymore."

"Who will be?"

"The Crna Ruka."

Six hours later, Sara Gujic watched another video. It was the attack on the St. Louis Country Club. A terrorist group calling itself the Crna Ruka murdered hundreds of innocent people. She received the video via a text sent to her by someone with a 615 area code. She didn't know the number of the sender.

It would be over a week before she would find out. Would she share the video with the media? Would she show the world what the faces of hundreds of innocent people look like the moment before they are slaughtered? The ratings and views would be off the charts. *No, not in a million years*, she concluded.

THIRTY-ONE

"Let's look at this only from a position of status. I don't want to hear about suspected global conspiracy theories and gut feelings. Only what we know," said FBI Special Agent-in-Charge Donald Scheck.

Scheck was assigned as lead investigator into the events of the day before. However, given the scope, other investigative teams were formed in the cities across the country where either the attacks had been successful or thwarted for one reason or another.

Authorities arrested the entire group from the Atlanta cell with the exception of Buster Hicks, the cell's leader. Likewise, the leaders in Los Angeles and Oakland were not among the attackers in their respective cities. Scheck and his teams across the country didn't know who the leaders were anyway and wouldn't for many days.

With the obvious exception of the NSA facilities and the death and destruction that occurred on the Chesapeake Bay Bridge, Scheck also didn't know there was a separate attack planned in Maryland. Or that the guys killed on the bridge were the entirety of the Baltimore terrorist cell. Not actual first-responders.

All he knew was a crazy A-10 pilot did more damage to the NSA than the hijackers of 9/11 did to the Pentagon. And she walked away free. The hunt for the new Osama Bin Laden was on.

His immediate job and that of the others in the room was to focus on three targets of investigation. The incident on the plane, the attack in St. Louis and the lone pilot attack in Maryland. He concluded that the first two were obviously connected. The coach and general both called St. Louis home, and the coach used the name Crna Ruka. The same name the group in St. Louis spray-painted on the walls of the country club. But how was the pilot of the A-10 connected?

In the briefing room with Agent Scheck was Chief Warrant Officer Four Scott Baetzel. Additionally, agents and analysts from the National Geospatial Intelligence Agency, the Central Intelligence Agency and the National Security Agency were in attendance.

Overnight, the intelligence-gathering capabilities of the country were coming back on line. The virus that had infected the entirety of the network was dead. However, many of the agencies were far from full capacity. NSA systems administrators worked feverishly to reroute electronic and signals monitoring to other facilities around the world, but their first priority was to get their massive database of archived intelligence back on line.

"Let's start with the pictures. NGIA. What can you tell us of the St. Louis attack?"

"Well, our satellite images for August 9th have produced some mixed results. Let me put the photos on the screen," said the analyst from NGIA.

"We had a good amount of satellite time for St. Louis yesterday before everything crashed. Someone, we don't know who yet, provisioned it right before the attacks. The bus carrying the attackers is seen taking a return route that avoids any of the first responder routes to the club. As if they knew exactly from where the cops and fire trucks would be coming from.

"We lost our imaging before the bus was located back at the rec complex. That's all we have. There are no clear pictures of the perpetrators themselves."

"And how could they possibly have known what routes to avoid?" asked Scheck.

"Well, there's only one place to obtain that specific information."

"And where's that?"

"From my office here in St. Louis, I'm afraid. Someone in their group must work at NGIA."

"General Quinn maybe?"

"Not likely. Our friends at NSA said the IP address of the hacker was here in St. Louis. The general was thousands of miles away at the time dealing with his own shit."

"What about the pilot in Maryland?"

"Again, same problem. Only a few moments of satellite time. Nothing

245

substantial other than the location of the plane which the local cops found within an hour anyway. Oh, and there is a photo of the pilot. Let me put it up on the screen."

There, standing next to the A-10, was Buff Sowers. She was looking up to the skies with her middle finger extended directly above her. Colonel Sowers was well aware a spy bird was flying above, as she had requested and received provisioning of satellite time from General Quinn hours before taking off. Flipping the bird at the satellite was a pilot's way of saying...well, everyone in the room knew what she was saying.

"You must know more about her?" Scheck asked the NSA employee.

"We do. We know quite a bit." He went on with five minutes of biographical information on the colonel. To the best of his knowledge, the woman was a true blue All American right up until August 9th.

"We were able to access her personnel file and it turns out she, Gibbs and General Quinn all received their Purple Heart citations for an incident in which Sowers was a passenger on a helo that went down in Iraq. Gibbs and Quinn rescued her and were injured themselves. We believe they've been friends ever since.

"Nothing more surreptitious of note other than she's a dyke. Her wife was a target of ours for having a known association with an ISIS member in Iraq. That's why she blew up our offices. Some bullshit statement of revenge.

"I specifically said I didn't want to hear any nonsense about motives or theories without the supporting facts. The fact that they all knew each other is key. What the fuck were these three up to?" Scheck responded. "Any COMINT or ELINT?"

"A little of both. We've had a few hours to get many of our assets back on line so our results are limited as well. We have a few text messages back and forth between Coach Gibbs and Colonel Sowers referencing some guy code-named 'Apis'. Supposedly, he's someone Gibbs considered to be some type of commander. We cross-referenced all duty assignments between Gibbs, the general and the colonel and with the exception of Iraq, they were never stationed together or near each other. We have no idea who Apis is or where he's from."

"What about the relationship between the general and Sowers? He has to be involved somehow," asked Baetzel.

"We don't think so. They must have fallen out as friends. Twice, when

Sowers was up for promotion, the general gave her rave references. On the third try, this past December, he sent the most scathing of reviews to the promotion board. Something about her being mentally unstable after her wife was killed in a car accident. Turns out, he was right.

"Back to the hacker. As was mentioned earlier, we've narrowed down the access point of the virus that started at the National Reconnaissance Office. It was an IP address of a computer registered within twenty-five miles of downtown St. Louis. Oh, we also have a clear index finger print of the hacker."

"Wait, what did you say? We have the fucking hacker's fingerprint? Maybe you should have led with that."

"Well sir, we ran the fingerprint in your IAFIS and there's no match. We figured that until we found a person to match the print, what's the point of pursuing it?"

"Just out of curiosity," Chief Warrant Officer Baetzel asked, "how did you get this fingerprint? You're not field agents. It's not like you're out there collecting them."

"Well, it's actually easier than you might think and we don't have to go anywhere to get them. People just, kind of, give them to us."

"Go on."

"You start with basic cyber-cryptographic hash functions and by spear-phishing the users..."

"Stop with computer lingo please. Get to the point," ordered Scheck.

"We steal them. It always starts with the users, either at home or in the office, who are paranoid about security. They insist on using the fingerprint optical reader on their computers for their log-in verification versus a good old-fashioned username and password.

"We created a software program that allows us to lift that scanned fingerprint right off of the user's hard drive when they're online. The scanned images go into our database. There you go."

"Well, of all the PCs out there, how do you know which ones to lift the fingerprints from? Which ones are a threat to national security? You can't possibly check every single computer in the country?" the CIA agent asked.

"Ahh...yes we can, and that's exactly what we do. Isn't it funny?" No one was laughing. "People think they are being super-secure with their fingerprint and they're actually making their personal information less secure. We can't match the print with the actual identity of the person behind it because that would be against the law. We aren't supposed to collect that type of data on American citizens."

"Oh, but hacking into their systems and lifting their fingerprints are fine?" asked Scheck, again taking the lead.

"Sure, there were never any restrictions entered in either the Patriot Act or the US Freedom Act. No one knew it was even possible, much less something that should be illegal."

"So, no FISA warrants required?" Scheck asked.

"FISA warrants? Who the hell do you think really approves those...the 9th Circuit? It's my bosses upstairs."

"Maybe it wasn't such a bad idea for that pilot to blow the place in half after all," Scheck whispered to the CIA agent. "Is there anything else that you guys at NSA have decided isn't important?"

"Just confirmation that Gibbs was the shooter. Remember, the camera was being worn on someone's head. There's no way to see the face of the shooter as the camera lens is pointing away. We ran a voice analysis of the words spoken on Facebook against the archived audio of the press conference where he announced the team. It's him. It's Gibbs."

"And what about the CIA?"

"We're working on the group arrested in Atlanta. We have a few of them at one of our facilities nearby for interviews. They haven't shared anything of note but it should only be a day or so before that changes.

"The weapons they had we believe came from an illegal arms operation out of Bosnia and Russia. Our agents in the region confirmed increased shipments were sent here to St. Louis months ago. We informed your offices about it back then and left it at that."

"Interviews?" asked Scheck. "It's that what you guys call them now? Anything else?"

"The Middle East is having a field day with this. Our assets in Damascus, Baghdad and Kabul are saying that if we can't control what's happening in our own back yard, now's the time to strike at our troops overseas. It's the Arab Spring all over again. The rest is domestic. What about you, Agent Scheck? What's the FBI got?"

"Like the rest of you, not much. We started with the A-10 attack. We were able to get film from the gun camera and it shows her blowing up two state troopers, a jumper and a fire truck on the Bay Bridge. We checked with the locals and no 9-1-1 dispatch was ordered for the bridge that day until after the attack.

"Local fire authorities have no one missing from their ranks and the two troopers were new officers. One from Dundalk, Maryland, the other from west Baltimore. Cops found a floater late last night on a beach covered with crabs. Probably the jumper and we're still waiting on his identity.

"We interviewed the players and crew from the Tokyo flight and released them. Same goes for General Quinn. His shooting of the coach was clearly an act of self-defense. St. Louis PD has little other to share with us other than that one of the attackers was a woman. Here's a picture of her. Everything but her upper face is covered.

"And what about the general's wife?" asked Chief Baetzel.

"We can't locate her either. She hasn't reported home or attempted to make contact with her husband or son. Very odd. Maybe she's traveling and trying to get back to St. Louis. Still too early to know what's happening."

"What about the witnesses from the bus company, the valets? There must be some descriptions?" asked the NSA guy.

"The main guy, you can see him here on the security cameras. Very large African American man. Supposedly he was some type of church leader. We ran his description through our database and no hits. We have over 150 thousand registered black preachers across the country. We focused our search on St. Louis and the other cities under attack. Nothing."

"Why the files on black preachers only?" asked Baetzel.

"Just old habits. Goes back to the J. Edgar Hoover days. He was convinced if there were ever to be a national uprising of a serious nature, black church leaders would be reasonable candidates for leading it. Looks like Hoover was at least partially right," Scheck finished.

"Chief Baetzel, what did you find during the initial investigation on board the plane?"

"I have reason to suspect the shootings on board the plane were not as cut and dry as we saw on Facebook. Something isn't quite right. I want to polygraph the general and I want to ask the questions."

"What the hell are you talking about? Everyone has seen what happened up there. The press has been reporting non-stop the exact second-by-second details of the shootings. Are you saying what we saw was some kind of a hoax?"

"I'm waiting for some information and autopsy results, but it may be possible that the players did not die from gunshot wounds. I'll know more, hopefully, by the end of today."

"Chief, I began this meeting saying let's keep it to what we know and work from that. You know as well as I do that investigations of this scale can go completely sideways if we start entertaining all manner of speculation. By all means, work your theory, but I have to provide an initial report this evening. I won't be including anything not substantiated by fact."

"But there's one other item..."

Scheck cut Chief Baetzel off in mid-sentence and called the meeting to a close. Going forward, the investigative team would meet twice a day. As the others were gathering their belongings, Scheck pulled Chief Baetzel aside.

"Chief, I'm going to unofficially take you off the investigation. I'm aware you're a short-timer and I've received your initial report from the plane. Thank you. I'll keep you up to speed on any developments, but I don't need my teams chasing down some wild theory.

"I'm also not going to question General Quinn for the moment. Don't get me wrong. His office is under suspicion due to the cyber-attack, but not the man himself. In other words, back the hell off. Am I clear, Chief Warrant Officer Baetzel?"

"Yes sir. You are."

***

Baetzel retired to his hotel room and opened his laptop. There were two emails of the highest importance. One from the medical examiner at Pearl Harbor-Hickam Hospital. One from the FISA court labeled 'Apple Corporation – Results of FISA Warrant Request'.

He opened the medical examiner's email first. It was the toxicology and autopsy report for Carl Wilson. Wilson, as was shown on the Facebook video, was the last person shot by Coach Gibbs. Cause of death: Cyanide poisoning. Time of death: Undetermined.

The second email contained an attached spreadsheet listing the names of the seven players and heart rate data beginning at 4pm on August 9th in Tokyo. Within a range of a few minutes, not a single player registered a heartbeat on their Apple watch thirty minutes prior to the time of Coach Gibbs' shooting spree. There it was. The men were dead before Gibbs "killed" them.

Baetzel continued his own investigation through the night. He found police reports of two murders, one filed in Los Angeles and one in Oakland. Pastor Antonio "Smiley" Hernandez had had his throat sliced open. Pastor Tyrell George was gunned down on his own street. The suspects turned themselves in within hours of the crimes. The murderer in LA was Simba Mwangi. Grandfather of Charles Mwangi. The two in Oakland. Twins with the last name Jabbur. He crossed-referenced the names against those of the players. "Shit. What are these guys up to?"

The other critical item he wanted to share with Agent Scheck but had been cut off; it was the picture of the terrorist group in St. Louis that included the woman. Even with the lower part of her face covered, Baetzel was fairly certain he could identify her. Eyes, ears, body-type, bust-line and the perfectly-centered mole right between her eyes.

He remembered seeing those exact features five years ago at a military reunion. He and his wife spent the better part of the weekend with the general and Tracy Quinn. It was her. He had no doubt.

Baetzel called the general. "Sir, I need to talk to you right away. It's about your wife."

"Are you going to arrest me, Scott?"

"No sir, a conversation."

"Get in your car. I'll text you the address. It's a two-hour drive. Oh, and Scott? Come alone or we're back to Article V of the Code. Is that clear?"

"Yes, General."

THIRTY-TWO

August 10th, 2020 – Drury Hotel, St. Louis, Missouri

"*Brazil, an intense dream, a vivid ray of love and hope descends on earth...*" sang the Brazilian National Anthem on Ronan McCoy's iPhone. While in Tokyo, the beautiful volleyball twins had hijacked his phone and changed his ringtone to remind him of their nights together.

He couldn't figure out how to change it back nor did he care. He quickly tried to silence it as he didn't want to wake the two flight attendants who were lying on either side of him, naked. Too late. They got dressed and left. The call was from Jayden but Ronan didn't answer.

Immediately after arriving in St. Louis on the 9th, the entire flight crew, surviving players and General Quinn were guests of the Federal Bureau of Investigations in St. Louis. After multiple hours of interviews they were all free to go. The city was still reeling from the attack at the country club and those not from the town were quickly escorted to military hops out of Scott Air Force Base and back to their respective hometowns.

Ronan didn't have a hometown, so staying in St. Louis at a shared home with Jayden seemed like the best idea he could come up with. They met in the hotel lobby to discuss what to do next. His decision to stay turned out to be a bad idea.

"Ronan, are you ready to raise your right hand and defend your country again?" Jayden asked his best friend.

"What the fuck you talking about, dude? I'm not going back into the Army. I did my stint. I'm good."

"I'm not asking you to join the Army. I'm asking you to join the Black Hand."

"The Black Hand? That sounds cool. What the hell is it and do I get to kill someone?"

"Hopefully. Let's get in the car. I'll tell you while we drive. We have two hours."

***

August 11th, 2020 – vacation home, Lake of the Ozarks, Missouri

"Scott, that's everything. You now know exactly what we know. I've shared every detail of what we did and will be doing," General Quinn said to Chief Baetzel.

In the room with the chief and general were Jayden Quinn, Theresa Gibbs, Ronan McCoy, Sara Gujic and one of the new ten-most-wanted people in the country: Colonel Maretta "Buff" Sowers.

"I knew that was your wife in the photo from the country club. Jesus Christ, General, why did you tell me this? What do you expect me to do?"

"I expect you to join us. Do you think it was a coincidence that we staged our little charade knowing we would be forced to land in Honolulu? No. We waited four hours after takeoff. We did so because I knew you would be assigned to the case. I also knew you would figure it out pretty quickly.

"Help us track down the cell leaders and kill them. Most of the junior-ranking members are either dead or in jail. That leaves four guys, Atlanta, Baltimore, New York and St. Louis. If you report this, these guys get busted and might incite more violence while sitting in prison. You remember the Blind Sheik, Omar Abdel Rahman? He was Al Qaeda's inspiration for 9/11. This will be the same. We have to kill them."

"And what if I say no? I don't think you have it in you to kill me, General."

"No, I don't. But she does." General Quinn pointed to Buff. "You probably heard of the pilot who killed the state troopers and a truck full of firemen in Maryland? The press is referring to her as the 'Savage Warthog'. Colonel Sowers, meet Chief Warrant Officer Baetzel."

"Scott, let me ask you a question. How's the investigation going with the FBI? Let me guess. The NSA, CIA and FBI are up to their usual tricks. Violating dozens of laws as if this is their country alone, and not ours as well. Hell, even my own agency has been spying on Americans without giving it a second thought. It's time for a change, Scott."

"I guess I can understand your motives. But the seven men and Coach Gibbs? Why did they kill themselves? How would they even get their hands on the hydrogen cyanide? It's not like they could buy it at the local pharmacy."

"Coach Gibbs got all they needed from the university. Monsanto has a research lab at St. Louis University and one of the products they study is cyanide. The stuff is one of the more popular pesticides out there.

"We don't see it as them killing themselves and neither did they. Our first and foremost tactical objective was to cause a nationwide panic. The staged video of the coach putting a real bullet into their heads did just that. Fear is a powerful weapon if used correctly. More powerful than guns and bombs.

"The eight men saw it the same way you and I have seen it for decades. Willing to do what was necessary for freedom and for justice. A way to go out with honor. The Japanese actually have a word for it. It's called 'Seppuku'."

"I know what Seppuku is, General. There's a half-million people of Japanese descent that live on Hawaii. I've seen the results. A case with a small group of Yakuza members. They all committed Seppuku."

"Then you understand. I was Kaishakunin of Seppuku for Ken Gibbs.

"Every last one of those men on the flight, gave their time and treasure endlessly. The more they gave, the worse the divide in the country became. Increased violence, incarcerations, more hatred, and more death.

"They saw this plan as their last-ditch effort to change a system that seemed to be working against us. Please don't use the word *suicide* to describe their actions. It was a mission of sacrifice. We'll find out in the coming weeks and months whether or not that mission was successful."

"General, you can't convince me to kill someone. I won't do it. What good am I to you and your little team here?"

"We can use you to run interference, provide logistical support and get the clearances we need to get from point A to point B. Also, we need an airplane. As a senior ranking investigator, you can get one. Buff here will be the pilot. She'll also be the shooter once you're on the ground."

"And Jayden and this guy. What's your name? McCoy? What are they supposed to do? They have no experience in these types of ops."

"Well, Ronan's the bait. He's going on a goodwill mission and he wants to donate millions to charities in the names of those that perished on the flight. He specifically wants to give to the churches of the cell leaders who like to call themselves pastors. Atlanta, Baltimore and New York.

"Jayden and Ronan met these guys years ago. They know Ronan's crazy enough to give away millions of dollars. And these guys might be crazy enough to accept. They're going to be desperate for cash as their funding source has been turned off.

"Jayden, he's going along for the ride. Obviously they know he's Tracy's son so it's unlikely they would come within a hundred miles of him. They would be instantly suspicious.

"Unlike the guy here in St. Louis, for these guys it was always about money. When Ronan McCoy calls wanting to make a sizable donation to their churches, we're hoping at least one or two of them will take a meeting. In a public place. They'll feel safe. They won't be."

"And what about St. Louis? Who's taking out Heyward, not to mention your own wife?"

"They're mine. I'll find them."

"And Ms. Gujic?"

"She's going with you to tell the story. That's why we want to hit them in public. We want her to record the events. Successful or not, people will know what we tried to do. If we fail, she'll give her full report to the police like you suggested. If we succeed, she'll have a best-seller."

Forty-eight hours earlier, Chief Baetzel was looking forward to a quiet retirement. It had been years since he was involved in any case of note and now he was presented with the opportunity to be on the other side of the case, not the investigator.

"Fuck it, General. I'm in. But when this shit goes south and it will, I want it on the record with Ms. Gujic that I didn't have a choice."

"You have a choice, Scott. You can leave right now if you want. The colonel isn't going to do anything."

"Like I said, fuck it. I'm in."

***

PRESENT DAY

August 10th, 2021 – 1:35pm, Russell Senate Office Building, Washington, DC

"Ms. Gujic, let me start by saying that up until the past hour or so, I have been absolutely enthralled with the account that you and your team have prepared for the American people," said the elderly senator from Arizona.

"However, this latest revelation, that these eight men knowingly sacrificed themselves, their fortunes and their futures for some kind of suicide mission is beyond the realm of believability. This doesn't happen in this day and age. What other possible theories exist that could explain how they died from cyanide poisoning? Is it possible the coach somehow spiked their drinks?"

"Senator, with your permission, I'd like to ask my colleague on this commission, Dr. Christopher Schwanger, to respond to your questions, if that's Okay?"

"That's fine."

"Dr. Schwanger is the head of the National Institute of Mental Health in Bethesda, Maryland. He holds both an MD and PhD in psychiatric medicine and research. Chris?"

"Senator, before I answer your questions, may I respectfully ask you a few of my own?"

"Sure, go ahead."

"Sir, prior to becoming a senator, what did you do for a living?"

"I think most of America knows. I was CEO of a Fortune 500 company."

"And prior to that, before climbing to the top of the corporate ladder?"

"I was a Marine Corps pilot. And not a very good one. I was shot down on my third combat mission. In Vietnam."

"Yes sir, most of America knows about your military experience as well. Including the fact that you spent five-and-a-half years in a prisoner of war camp in Hanoi. You are a Marine, Senator. What's that saying you Marines share so proudly?"

"Well we have two sayings. *Semper Fidelis*, Always Faithful. It means a Marine lives by a code of duty and honor forever. The other is 'Once a Marine, always a Marine.' Okay, Dr. Schwanger, where are you going with this?"

"Sir, I remember a speech of yours when you talked about that experience. You shared how scores of American POWs gave up their own meager rations so others might live. All of the POWs at that time were forced to endure horrible physical and psychological torture when they refused to provide sensitive information about their fellow servicemen. In many cases those selfless men, your brothers in conflict, succumbed to starvation and their wounds. Did they not?"

"Yes," the senator said as his eyes begin to well up. He pictures in his mind the many faces of the men left behind.

"Why, Senator? Why would those men, in the youthful prime of their military careers, knowingly sacrifice their own lives for such a desperately hopeless situation?"

"It was their duty."

"Sir, even with all your fame and wealth, all of your success, would you give it away if you could go back in time to that prison and change places with those men that didn't come home?"

"Dr..." The senator is now openly sobbing. The two senators sitting next to him are consoling him.

"Sir, you don't have to answer that. The entire nation knows you would. You are a hero and anyone that says otherwise is a damn fool. Senator McGinn, the men of the Black Hand are heroes too. They once lived as soldiers and marines and they died that way. Not as basketball stars or a coach. They did their duty.

"Let us all celebrate your sacrifice, the sacrifice of the men and women we've lost in all our wars as well as the eight on Flight 9 8 7. Let us do so without questioning their motives as we would dare not question yours."

The entire audience stands and gives the senator, his fallen colleagues and the dead members of the Black Hand a 10-minute ovation. There isn't a dry eye in the place. Or across America, for that matter.

THIRTY-THREE

August 11th, 2020 – Vacation home, Lake of the Ozarks

"Ok to recap, here's what we have so far," General Quinn said. "Chief has a plane waiting for the team at Fort Leonard Wood. An hour south of here. The first stop has to be in Atlanta. Jayden, what do you have about the cell leader down there?"

"His name is Buster Hicks. Ronan and I met him years ago. I still have his cell number. Ronan called and he answered. Tell the group what you two talked about, Ronan."

"I told him I was donating a million dollars in the name of my slain friend and teammate from Atlanta, Iver Koch. He was hesitant but he agreed to meet for breakfast tomorrow near the airport.

"My guess is that he's trying to skip town since tomorrow will be the first day commercial flights are scheduled again. All these guys were expecting a large payout from Heyward based on stealing from Jayden's personal accounts. Those have all been shut down, so they'll be looking for other ways to get cash and get out of the country."

"Do you have the cash to take with you?" asked Chief Baetzel.

"We have a hundred grand because Ronan here always carries that much with him. Hicks won't have time to count it. I promise," said Buff. "Sara, you go in early, grab a seat and watch and record the show. Chief, you're going to drop off Ronan. He'll start the meeting. I'll end it."

"What about Baltimore and New York?" the general asked his son.

"Again, we know the guys. Kendley Charles is as stupid as he is greedy. Probably whacked out on his own stuff he sells. His entire cell is dead, thanks to Buff. The only lead we have is that the Orioles are back to playing on the 14th and he's at every game. The game from the 9 was canceled and they'll be playing the makeup at home on Friday. He's stupid enough to be there and we know where his suite is. We'll get eyes on him until he comes out. Buff, you and the chief will have to get him on the drive home.

"New York, Morton is the cell leader and the smartest of the group. We haven't figured that one out yet. Getting him out in public will be difficult. He's likely to hear of the hits in Atlanta and Baltimore and try to run. Dad, we're going to have to adjust on the fly with this guy."

***

August 12th, 2020 – Waffle House, College Park, Georgia near Hartsfield International Airport

"I need two over-easy, bacon, smothered, covered and diced...and a side of grits," yelled the server to the kitchen as Buster Hicks entered the Waffle House.

"Good morning, Pastor Hicks. Good to see you again," said Ronan. Across the aisle, reading a newspaper and sitting by herself nursing a cup of coffee was Sara Gujic. She discreetly had her phone video recorder on, pointed in the direction of the booth with the two men.

"Good morning, Ronan. I'm sorry to hear about the team. What was that lunatic coach thinking? I've never seen anything like it."

"FUBAR. How's the church, Pastor? How's the PEACH?"

"Well, we've run into some difficulty but that's not stopping us. I'm leaving on a mission trip this morning. I can't thank you enough regarding your donation. Did you bring it?"

Ronan opened a bag and showed the man stacks of hundred dollar bills.

"Let's have some breakfast first and then we'll take care of business," Ronan said as the waitress approached.

"Fair enough, I'll have two eggs scrambled, ham and I want my hash browns smothered, covered and chunked."

"I'll have the same. Excuse me, I have to take a poop. I'll be right back."

Just as the food was being delivered to the table and Hicks was about to take his first bite of hash browns, Jayden walked in and added 'splattered' to the man's breakfast plate. With two quick shots from a 9mm Glock into the back of his head, exploding gray and red matter exited from the front. The disgusting glob of fried potatoes, cheese, onions, brains and blood looked remarkably similar to the meal being eaten by the startled patron sitting in the booth opposite to them.

Jayden grabbed a stack of hundreds from Ronan's bag, handed it to the waitress on the way out the door and apologized for the mess. Ronan exited the restroom and he, Jayden and Sara all calmly walked out. They got into the car with Baetzel and Buff waiting and headed back to the airport.

"What the hell, Jayden? I thought Buff was going to do the shooting. Now the whole world knows it's you."

"Sorry, but I wasn't going to let her have all the fun. She got to kill the guys in Maryland. It was my turn."

Sara sent the video to the media and the Atlanta news station as well as national broadcasters were live at the Waffle House reporting the story about the shooting within 20 minutes. The news feed at the bottom of the TV screen continuously scrolled with the headline, "Beloved minister gunned down by the world's best basketball player while dining with the world's second best basketball player. Whereabouts unknown."

"That's bullshit," said Ronan. "I beat you out for the MVP this year."

***

"We need to go to New York first then Baltimore," said Baetzel. "Since Monday, there's been a rash of murders up in the Bronx. One was confirmed last night as the helicopter pilot from the National Guard. Sounds like Pastor Morton is tying up his loose ends."

"Like Joe Pesci in *GoodFellas* after the Lufthansa heist," said Ronan.

Baetzel ignored him. "I checked with the State Department. He has a passport. The guy in Baltimore doesn't. If someone's going to run, it will be Morton. What do we know about him?"

"The only lead we have is that the entire cell stayed at the Bruderhof outside of New York City on Sunday and Monday nights. I talked to the Head Elder and he mentioned Morton has a mission in Nicaragua," Jayden responded.

"Number one staging area for processing cocaine out of Colombia and into the United States. My guess is Morton has an operation there, or at least a safe house. Bullshit extradition laws so we need to get him before he leaves."

"Let me call his home and see what happens – it worked last time," Ronan suggested.

"No, he's not here, Mr. McCoy. I want to thank you for the generous offer of a donation but he's leaving on a mission trip this afternoon. I saw the news at the Waffle House in Atlanta. You must be traumatized...second best player?" the wife of Pastor Morton informed Ronan.

"He's bugging out," Ronan told the group.

Chief Baetzel immediately went to his phone and laptop. His investigation on Edwin Morton started with searching for flights to Managua from any of the New York area airports. The only one he could find was from JFK on COPA Airlines. He called TSA and confirmed Morton purchased a ticket.

"It's leaving in four hours at 2:30. Open it up, Colonel, we need to get to JFK in three hours," Baetzel instructed Buff.

"In this? Top speed is three hundred. It will take every bit of three hours and maybe more. You need to radio ahead and get direct clearance to land or we're screwed."

***

August 12th, 2020 – John F. Kennedy Airport, Queens, New York

"When we land, I've arranged for a car to shuttle me across the field and into Terminal Four. You all need to stay in the plane. I can bypass security. I'll arrest him, bring him back and, Colonel, you're going to kill him before this plane takes off again. Throw his ass out on the tarmac for all I care," said CW4 Baetzel.

Once Buff touched the Beechcraft C-12 down, she quickly taxied to the private charter terminal. Baetzel's ride was waiting. It was likely Morton was already boarding his flight to Managua, so the race was on.

***

"Sorry sir, the flight departed early. Every passenger was here and ready to go so the flight was cleared to take off," said the gate agent for COPA Airlines. *Since when did a flight ever leave on time from New York, much less early?* thought Baetzel.

"Well, this is a matter of national security. I'm ordering you to bring the plane back."

"American national security or Colombian national security? Sir, we're not an American airline and the flight is already over international waters.

You cannot order us to do anything."

He would have given her a piece of his mind except he knew she was right. He immediately placed a call back to his office in Hawaii. In ten minutes he had the answer he was hoping for and hung up. He made a few more calls. He made his way back to the plane with Ronan, Jayden, Sara and Buff waiting.

"Where is he?" Buff said impatiently.

"He's on his way to Nicaragua but he'll be back in ten hours. I took care of it." Baetzel was smiling.

"What's so funny, Chief? The son of a bitch got away."

"No he didn't."

His phone call to his office confirmed what he had hoped to be true. It appeared the smartest member of the Crna Ruka had read on Wikipedia that the Nicaraguan government does not extradite suspected felons from their country back to the United States. They do, however, extradite convicted felons. And Pastor Morton was indeed that. He was released from prison years ago but was still on parole. His sentence was not completely served out and by legal definition, he was considered to be a convicted felon and he was on the run.

With a couple more calls, Baeztel informed the Nicaraguan authorities that a convicted felon would be landing in four hours. "*Enviarlo de vuelta*" ("Send him back") ordered the Immigration Officer in Nicaragua after the flight landed. And he was sent back. On the first flight to the US, which happened to be to Atlanta.

Ronan McCoy couldn't help but chuckle to himself that the fugitive possessed the same legal prowess he had displayed years ago after a solicitation of prostitution charge in Paris. "Never trust Wikipedia," he said to the group.

"Well, how am I going to kill the bastard if he's in custody?" Buff asked, sounding disappointed.

"I told you. I took care of it."

***

There were nine members of the Atlanta cell of the Crna Ruka being held in a state police lockup in downtown Atlanta. Baetzel requested the U.S. Marshals' office meet and arrest Morton at Hartsfield and lock him up with the other nine.

He also asked the marshals, if they wouldn't mind, to inform the young cell members that Morton was apprehended trying to get out of the country and was now ready to testify against the entire Crna Ruka organization in an exchange for a plea bargain.

By the next morning, as a cop was delivering breakfast to the cell containing the ten Crna Ruka members, he found Edwin Morton's arms extended beyond the steel bars. No, he wasn't reaching for his breakfast. His arms just happened to be dangling free. The rest of the man was wrapped around the poles. Like a Christmas garland around a lamp post.

The nine other cellmates, after hearing of Morton's plans to leave and turn witness, figured out how to tear Morton into four, fairly-equal pieces. Once drawn and quartered, they pulverized the body to such a degree of malleability they were able to decorate the cell with the man. It was the most upsetting scene the Georgia state cop had ever witnessed in his life. That included the time the Atlanta Falcons blew a twenty eight to three lead against the New England Patriots in Super Bowl L.

***

August 14th, 2020 – Orioles Park at Camden Yards, Baltimore, Maryland

"Welcome to tonight's game with the Baltimore Orioles playing the World Series Champion Washington Nationals. The Orioles enter the game with thirty-eight wins and eighty-two losses. An improvement of four games over this same time last year. Ladies and gentlemen, let's hear it for Yooooour, Baltimoooore Orioles."

The 1,900 fans in attendance largely ignored the public announcer and drank their first Natty Boh instead.

"Throwing out the first pitch tonight, five days after the horrible attacks on our country, we welcome the President of the United States. Please, let's all stand and give the president a round of applause," read the announcer. Only a few people stood and clapped for the president. The other fans cheered loudly from the comfort of their seats when the beer salesman showed up with a full tray.

Among the few cheering was none other than Kendley Charles. With the entirety of his men wiped out five days earlier, the whacked-out and dim-witted criminal could think of nothing he'd rather be doing than watch his team once again lose from the comfort of his private suite.

"Let's go over the plan again, Ronan," Jayden said. "We keep eyes on the guy. When he gets up to leave, we call the chief. They'll follow and Buff will hit him at a stop light."

"Shouldn't we have a gun?"

"Did you see the security? The president's throwing out the first pitch. No one but cops and secret service are getting in here with guns. Keep your hat and glasses on so no one recognizes us."

Jayden was wrong about no one else having guns. Kendley Charles had a small arsenal in his private suite. Over the course of the year, he'd successfully smuggled a dozen hand guns into the stadium without so much as a question from the bored security staff. His intention was to leave the stadium with at least two of those guns tonight, given all that had occurred in the last five days.

***

"What did you think of my work?" asked Buff of Sara and Chief Baetzel as the three waited in the Ride Share parking lot of Camden Yards.

"What are you talking about?" asked Sara.

"When we came into BWI. Didn't you see the NSA? It was right in our flight path. I did that. Blew the shit out of the place. Fucking Peeping Tom perverts."

Baetzel had no comment but knew she was right.

"Can we go over this one more time, Colonel?"

"It's simple. We get word from the two boys that Charles is heading out. We tail him. Pull up next to him at a stop light. I get out and shoot him. It's classic drive-by. Happens once or twice a day here in Baltimore. No one will bat an eye over it. What's there to discuss?"

"Shit never goes that easy. Does it?" The chief was right.

***

Two hours later, fourth inning score, Nationals 12-Orioles 2, Kendley Charles left as did most of the fans. But he did not proceed to his car. He didn't bring one. He headed straight to the Ride Share lot to catch an Uber home.

"He's coming right at us. What do we do? I can't risk killing an Uber driver," said Buff.

"I got him." Baetzel exited the car and began to draw his service weapon, thinking the man couldn't possibly be armed with so much security.

"Kendley Charles, you're under arrest. Hands up."

"Fuck you," the drug kingpin said and pulled a .38 caliber pistol from his belt. With two quick shots, he hit Baetzel both times. One in the stomach, the other in his shooting shoulder. Baetzel dropped his weapon immediately.

Charles grabbed the nearest Uber driver, threw him from his seat and sped off in the direction of the Inner Harbor.

"Tap on the 'Start Drive' icon. I want to get paid for this bullshit," the Uber driver yelled to the carjacker as he drove away.

"Jayden, you and Ronan get in your car and look at the Life 360 App on your phone. I loaded my number and you can follow me. I'm chasing Charles but I'm a few cars behind. He shot the chief. I got him in the back seat with Sara."

"Chief, you okay? Sara, how is he?"

"I'm fine. Keep after him."

"He's bleeding bad, Buff."

"The dumb shit is turning on Fort Avenue. He doesn't know it's a dead end. Stops at Fort McHenry. We got him. Jayden, where are you?"

"We're passing a neighborhood pub. Barfly's. Looks like we're two minutes behind you."

Three minutes later, the four were on foot and laying chase to Kendley Charles on the grounds of Fort McHenry. Baetzel remained in the car, unable to move. Buff offered Sara Gujic a gun for self-defense but she at first declined.

"Sara, the guy doesn't care if you're a journalist. He'll kill you if he gets a chance. Now take this. All you have to do is point and shoot."

Charles was desperate for a place to escape or make his last stand. He was ready to run or kill. He ran into an open entrance to the Fort's outer redoubt and nestled into a dark, two-foot deep bastion that would put his pursuers in a defenseless position as they ran by him.

Two accurate shots from Morton's gun as Jayden and Buff passed in front of him first. They both went down immediately. Jayden took a slug to his right hip. The bullet, once hitting the hard bone took a 90-degree right turn and exited a millimeter from his femoral artery. The bleeding was slight but the damage to the hip was disabling.

Buff felt the hot metal hit her right thigh and pass straight through. She was surprised by the lack of pain. *It must be the adrenaline*, she thought. Her powerfully-built legs were still strong.

Ronan heard the shots, saw the two fall and with the stopping skills of a star basketball player, hit the brakes. He stopped on a dime, a yard short of the shooter's line of sight. Ronan held in his *Dead Hands* a .38 of his own, but he was shaking uncontrollably. Sara was behind him, doing the same.

Charles, thinking he had downed the only two people chasing him, quickly raced out from his hiding spot and stood over Buff and Jayden, ready to finish the job. But Ronan and Sara were a few feet behind the man and each quickly pulled their triggers. Ronan four times. Sara twice. Each bullet hit Charles square in the back, knocking him forward and on top of the two Black Hand teammates.

"Is he dead?" asked Ronan.

Buff was the first to rise and with the force of a jack-hammer, she raised her powerful leg and stomped on the man's junk with all her might. He didn't move. "Yep, he's dead."

"Ronan, stand next to me, clench your right fist and raise it up. Like me," Buff ordered as she stood atop Kendley Charles, as if the dead man was an Olympic podium. "Sara, take our picture."

The photo reminded Buff of the iconic one of Tommie Smith and John Carlos. Two African-American track stars, raising their black hands in protest at the Mexico City games in 1968. Except in Buff's photo, one of the hands was white.

"Why do you get to be on the top? I'm the one that killed him." Ronan looked sad.

"Shut the fuck up, Ronan. Pick up Jayden and let's get out of here," Buff ordered again. Ronan couldn't do it. He wasn't strong enough. With her leg screaming in pain, Buff squatted and using her proper power-lifting technique, clean and jerked Jayden onto her shoulders. "This is why you're not on top. Men, weak-ass shits."

The four made it back to the car in a minute.

"Here, you want to be on top? Take these two flags and run them up that flagpole. You pick which one goes first."

Ronan did as requested. First was the American flag; the second looked like a rainbow. It was. Buff had packed the two flags in her flight bag before leaving St. Louis. She always prepped thoroughly for a mission.

"Now we're good. Let's go."

***

August 14th, 2020 – Baltimore/Washington International Airport

"General Quinn, its Ronan, sir. We just took off from Baltimore and we have three casualties on board. Sir, Jayden was shot in the hip. Buff took one in the thigh but it's clean and she's flying the plane. Tough broad. We're worried about Chief Baetzel. He was shot in the stomach and he doesn't look good. We need to get them to a hospital."

"Ronan, bring them here. There's a small airport called Lee Fine and it's twenty minutes from the house. Theresa and I will meet you there and get everyone back. She'll take care of their injuries and if the chief needs to go to the hospital, I'll take him myself."

"Sir, I don't know if we have that long."

"Bullshit, I'm fine. The mission comes first," said Baetzel as he overheard the conversation.

***

For the next hour, the five Black Hand members sat silently contemplating what had occurred over the previous five days. It wasn't over. There was still Heyward and Jayden's mom, Tracy, to deal with. The first to speak after the long silence was Chief Baetzel.

"Jayden, I have something to tell you and I want the entire squad to hear this." For the rest of the flight he shared a detail-by-detail account of how Jayden Fillmore Quinn had been brought into the world. The four others sat stunned by the story.

"Your father's a hero Jayden, not a killer. He did what he was ordered to do and without hesitation. You wouldn't be alive today if it wasn't for him. I'm telling you this because the general would never share what I know to be the truth. Your birthday is August 9th, Jayden. Not what was written on your birth certificate. That was the day your father received the approval to adopt you. I agreed to this mission for one reason only and it was because of him and you. Tell him that for me."

"Chief, you can tell him yourself. I know how hard it must have been to keep that secret all these years but in many ways, I already knew I was adopted. Look at me. How does a person turn out as black as I am with a black mother and a white father? Did you know my real mother and father's names?" Jayden asked.

"Only their last name. Mwangi."

"Thank you Chief...Chief? Chief!"

Chief Warrant Officer Four Scott Baetzel was dead. He entered the army as a soldier and he went out as one. Once a grunt, always a grunt. Not an investigator, not a retiree, but a casualty of war and a hero to his country.

THIRTY-FOUR

"THE COBRA VERSUS THE MONGOOSE"

August 16th, 2020 – St. Louis, Missouri

"Buff, how's your leg?" Theresa Gibbs asked.

"I'm fine, Theresa. Let's get on with this thing."

Five members of the Black Hand made the drive from the Lake of the Ozarks to St. Louis starting long before sunrise. It was a week after the tragic events of August 9th and all but one of the Crna Ruka leaders were dead – the one from St. Louis.

Buff, Ronan, Theresa and Orlando had one final mission. Find and kill Tracy Quinn and Calvin Heyward. Sara was again along to document exactly what was to go down. Jayden stayed behind at the lake house as the gunshot wound to his hip was too serious for him to walk. Theresa stabilized the injury, but except for a few hobbled steps on crutches, he could not move.

The five discussed the possibilities of where Tracy and Calvin could be hiding out. They also inventoried their weapons.

"We have one nine millimeter, one .38 and these two that Theresa's grabbed from the lake house. They were part of her husband's collection. A .22 and a .357." Buff listed off the guns.

"General, you said they got their weapons from Hamza Madic in Little Bosnia. Madic was a player in my story on human trafficking years ago and I know of at least two or three safe houses he maintains in south St. Louis. There are lots of young women and men working so if Calvin and Tracy are there, you'll need to smoke them out somehow. I have the addresses in my contacts on my phone."

Orlando logged onto the NGIA system for an immediate live feed from a satellite he provisioned for the day. He entered the addresses. On the second house, he had his bogie. Clearly pictured was Tracy's car. She knew no one official was looking for her at the moment. She felt comfortable enough parking the vehicle on the street in plain view. Orlando dialed her cell number on the small chance she would answer it. She did. Tracy Quinn had something to say.

***

August 16th, 2020 - St. Louis, Missouri

"I can't believe that genetic freak, blue-eyed, nigger husband of hers fucked this all up. Where is that slant-eyed cunt? Hiding out at the lake house, I bet? I should go down there and put a bullet in her head."

"Yeah, she is as a matter of fact. She's hoping you'll come down. She feels the same way about you. We know where you are, Tracy. I have the address. Here are your choices. You two turn yourselves in immediately or I'm coming for you and I'm not alone. It's over, Tracy."

"Yeah, so I saw on the news. What a team you've got. Our own son, that dirt bag from West Virginia and the dyke pilot. Tell the last two of them, I can't wait to kill them as well. Where's my son? Is he with you?"

"Why do you care? He knows everything. Melissa's attack, all the money you stole from him. Even about his real mother and father. You're nothing to him anymore. Tracy, where's Calvin?"

"I don't know. He left after hearing that the last of his friends got whacked by your team. He's crazy, you know. Thinks he's Rosie Greer, some fucking boxer and Tony Soprano all rolled into one. Why don't you call him? I'll give you a hint. His phone number starts with a 615."

Tracy hung up the phone, left the safe house and started driving to the lake house. She had no plans of turning herself in. The idea of spending the rest of her life behind bars was worse than dying. Tracy was going to kill the woman whose daughter was raped on her own orders. Somehow this all made sense to her.

***

"General, the video of the St. Louis Country Club massacre was texted to me by a 615 phone number. I still have it on my phone. Can you track it in the NGIA system?" Sara asked.

"Damn right I can. Give it to me." Sixty seconds later: "He's at the Dome."

Ten minutes later: "Look at the door. It's shattered. He's inside. Theresa, I can't let you go in there. It needs to be Ronan. You two girls stay here."

"Orlando, I said I'm going with you and that's an order. You know I am capable of using this," Theresa said as she held up the .357 magnum. "I was in the fucking army. Keep Ronan and Buff here in case he gets by us, or worse."

"No, I want to go too," said Buff.

"Buff, you're not going. That leg of yours just slows us down. Ronan, if we're not out in ten minutes, call this number. This is Scheck with the FBI. Their offices are five minutes away. He can bring an army," ordered the general.

"Theresa, after you shoot the son-of-a-bitch, kick him in the balls to make sure he's dead. Like that scene in *Trainspotting*," Buff said loudly as Theresa and Orlando were leaving.

"Have you noticed Ronan and Buff live their entire lives through the movies?" Theresa asked.

"This would be a good one except I don't know anyone who could play Apis. I don't know any actors from his country."

"What about Le..."

"Come on, let's go already."

***

Theresa and Orlando entered the stadium through what was the mid-field section of the former football field. They could hear someone and he was shouting out commands, to no one.

"I've got A gap, you got B. Check that, stunt left, stunt left," said Calvin Heyward as he took a three-point stance on an imaginary football field one yard line. He was playing defense. "Hut, hut." Now he was on offense. Heyward burst through the line and dove at the feet of an invisible running back. Defense again.

Wearing his #76 Rosie Greer Rams jersey, Heyward tackled the non-existent ball carrier from the Tennessee Titans short of the goal line. The

60,000 fans seen only by Heyward's eyes let out a mighty roar. "Yea!" Heyward was now one of those fans.

"Ladies and gentlemen, he did it. Archie Heyward has single-handedly won Super Bowl XXXIV for the St. Louis Rams!" Heyward was now the play-by-play announcer. He may have won, cheered for, and announced the game being played in his head but in his mind, he lost everything else. He was a raving lunatic.

"Stay here, Theresa. I'm going to kill him," said Orlando as he pulled the weapon from his back pocket. He looked at the gun as he was running toward the field. "Shit, I've got the .22. Better make these head shots," he said to himself. He was on the field and yards away when Heyward saw him.

"Heyward!"

"What the fuck are you doing here and with that little thing? You're not man enough to kill me. I'm Archie Moore, the Mongoose, I'm Rosie fucking Greer," said Heyward as he slowly moved toward Orlando.

Two quick shots from the small handgun. Both to the chest, not the head. The small bullets didn't faze the giant killer as he quickened his gait and approached five yards from the general. Two more shots; one to his lower jaw, one missed. Still nothing slowed the man. He was at full speed and rammed into Orlando.

The two tumbled, Orlando back, Heyward forward. He was on top of the general. The gun fell a yard away. The murderer's massive hands engulfed Orlando's neck. He squeezed and the overpowered soldier began to turn blue. Heyward was killing him.

"Get the fuck off of him now," ordered Theresa Gibbs.

"What the hell are you going to do with that cannon, you little cun..."

"Goddamn you!" Theresa screamed as she pulled the trigger three successive times. The first two hit him in the chest as well, but with much more effect. He was knocked back into the invisible end zone. The third entered his open mouth and blew out the back of his neck. That bullet put him down. Theresa wasn't done. She took Buff's advice.

With the leg power of Adam Vinatieri kicking the winning field goal to beat the St. Louis Rams in Super Bowl XXXVI, she drove her right foot into his groin with all her might. The behemoth let out an audible moan.

Standing over him, Theresa, one-third the man's size, rested the muzzle of the .357 magnum on his forehead. "Fuck the Crna Ruka, let 'em rot in hell." She pulled the trigger. His head exploded. She didn't need to kick him again. He was dead. Theresa sat down next to Orlando and began to cry.

"Theresa, you did it. You killed that monster."

"Orlando, all my life, I've tried to save lives. Even my enemies. I don't like the feeling of taking them. It feels too...too good."

Orlando hugged his best friend's wife for five minutes. Buff and then Ronan were there quickly after hearing the shots fired.

***

Gibbs/Quinn vacation home, Lake of the Ozarks

"Where are you, bitch?" screamed Tracy as she entered the lake house looking for Theresa Gibbs. She gripped a pistol in her hand.

"She's not here. We're alone. Theresa's with Dad in St. Louis. He was hoping you would come here so you could face me one last time. Are you going to kill me?" said Jayden as he struggled to stand.

"Jayden, what happened? You're hurt."

"Your friend in Baltimore shot me. He was about to kill me when that redneck you hate so much saved my life. Why, why did you do all this? For a piece of ass?"

"You have no idea what it's like being a black woman married to a white man. Everyone, including your father, always treated me like his bitch slave. Dragging me from one country to another like I was his property. Never asking what I wanted. You can't imagine how humiliating it was. With Calvin, I was treated with respect. Like the successful woman I am. Like a champion again."

"That's bullshit and you know it. Dad shared with me your favorite saying. 'Tell a lie often enough and people will believe it.' You've told so many lies, even you believe them now. We had everything. Dad loved you, me and Coach Gibbs more than life itself. News-flash – we're all black. Hell, since Dad was a kid, Grandpa taught him how to treat everyone equal regardless of their damn skin color. He took Dad to Butler Beach where they were the only white family. They were even members of Martin Luther King's church. Dad donated tens of thousands of hours and dollars. You took all shit for granted from Dad, and you took Melissa from me."

"She wasn't good enough. You're Jayden Quinn. You're famous, rich. You could be president someday. I'd do anything for you Jayden, you know that."

"I don't care about that crap. I don't want to be rich and famous or the president. What a crock of shit you're talking about. You ordered the rape of the woman I loved."

"I'm sorry. I'm so scared. Please let me hold you like a mother does to her son."

Jayden paused. He slowly approached Tracy with his posture in a submissive, almost child-like manner. Head down, shoulders slumped. As the two began to embrace, he made a move with his right hand to the pocket of his pants. Out came a hunting knife, purchased for $15.99 at Walmart. His black hand thrust the six-inch blade into Tracy Quinn's neck.

As blood erupted from the wound, a small dollop of the bright red fluid landed on Jayden's lips. The metallic taste of the life-giving liquid gave him a sense of courage he'd never felt before.

He looked into her dying eyes and whispered, "*Habeebati kanat jayyidin,*" ("The woman I loved was good"), "*Ante sharira,*" ("You are evil"), "*Itheb illa jaheem,*" ("Go to hell"). "*Ante lestu umi,*" ("You are not my mother") were his final words to the woman who was not his mother.

***

PRESENT DAY

August 10th, 2021 – 2:20pm, EDT, Russell Senate Building, Washington, DC

"Ms. Gujic, we have a swarm of recorded messages coming in and there is one we'd like to play for you and have you respond. Is that okay?" asked the manager of the phone bank center.

"Please."

"Good afternoon to all and my congratulations to Ms. Gujic and her team for an outstanding presentation over the past two days regarding the events of August 9th, 2020.

"However, Ms. Gujic used a word that many Americans believe should be stricken from our language. I would like to ask a question directly to her.

Does Ms. Gujic, as a journalist, believe the 'N' word should be banned?" asked the Executive Director of the NAACP.

"Ms. Gujic, your response?" asked the Speaker of the House.

"First off, I did not use that word. It was a direct quote from Tracy Quinn. I heard the conversation between her and her husband and made a note of it. Now, that being said, I am in no official position to answer a question of that magnitude on behalf of our nation.

"But since it was asked of me personally, I'll answer it, personally. I am not speaking for the president or the vice president and certainly not for the American people.

"No, the word shouldn't be banned. No word should ever be. Period. The word, as despicable both in its intended meaning as in its very sound, is a part of our history. We cannot change that.

During World War II, in Nazi Germany, to be called a Jew was a death sentence. Imperial Japan banned its soldiers from uttering the word 'surrender' and untold tens of thousands died. Even going back a couple thousand years, the word Christian meant a date with hungry lions. Yet those are words we still use today and they do not carry the stigma they once did.

"Let those that use the word in hatred be the ones who suffer in their own repugnancy and ignorance. But there are occasions, especially very personal situations, when the word takes on a different meaning. A term of endearment, an honorific almost. Let those that use it as a term of affection and of love, continue to do so without judgment.

"Colonel Sowers shared a story with me once. It was about her father. A man who grew up in Atlanta in the '50s and heard the N-word more often than the word 'peach'. Most of the time, it was directed at him in the vile manner in which it was intended.

"But privately, he cherished the moments when his only daughter, who he loved more than life itself, would look up at him and say, "Daddy, you're the wind beneath my wings. You're my nigger."

The entire gallery and most people watching at home gasp at Gujic's audacity. But not Buff Sowers. She's enjoying her fourth strawberry daiquiri with a garnish of tropical fruit and a little umbrella. She's sitting and watching the briefing from the pool deck of a hotel where fifty years ago, a racist owner had a sign in his window stating "No Niggers Welcome."

Hearing Gujic's last comments and moderately drunk, Buff jumps up from her chaise lounge, looks around and lisps to anyone within earshot, "I told her to thay that! I told her to thay that!"

Buff yells back at the TV screen and to Sara Gujic who is hundreds of miles away, "You go my nigga!"

Part V

"August: To be held in high regard, respected"

THIRTY-FIVE

August 16th, 2020 – St. Louis, Missouri

"Agent Scheck, it's General Quinn."

"Where the hell are you? And where is Baeztel? I've been trying to locate you two on your phones for days."

"We used burner phones when we had to. Chief Baetzel is dead."

"Goddamn it. I need you to come into the office immediately. The chief was right. The players didn't die of gunshot wounds. I read all the autopsy reports. Poisoning, and it looks like suicide. Through a FISA warrant I was able to gain access to each player's email accounts. Every one of them sent a final letter to loved ones. Like soldiers did in wartime. I need you in my office now."

"I'm already coming in. And I'm bringing a few folks with me. Theresa Gibbs, Ronan McCoy and..."

"And who?"

"Colonel Maretta Sowers. I think the media is referring to her as 'The Savage Warthog'."

"I know who she is."

***

"Down on the ground now!" screamed Agent Scheck as he and four other agents ran toward Buff, their service weapons drawn. The general and his team had just exited their car at the FBI field office.

"I said down now." Scheck put a knee to the back of Sowers as she did as he requested. He cuffed her and while yanking her to her feet, she let out a groan of pain. The leg with the bullet hole was on fire with inflammation.

"Take it easy on her. She needs medical attention," demanded Theresa Gibbs.

"Shut up. We've been looking for you as well. Put the colonel in the holding cell," Scheck said to an assistant as he re-holstered his weapon.

"Agent Scheck, get her some help now or I swear you'll pay for it someday."

"Shut up. General, when I couldn't reach you, I had no choice but to search your house. We lifted numerous fingerprints including your son's and your wife's. Where is she? It was her fingerprint that logged onto our secure networks and planted the virus. She did the same to Facebook. And where is that son of yours? The whole world saw him murder a man in a Waffle House in Atlanta."

"My wife is dead as well. My son killed her too. He's at our lake house in the Ozarks."

"Holy shit. What is going on? You're all under arrest."

***

There was a lot of shit going on Agent Scheck didn't know about. Starting with the fact that the Black Hand team, both directly and indirectly, killed six men who liked to refer to themselves as holy men. They weren't. They were Crna Ruka cell leaders. Additionally, Scheck incorrectly believed that Tracy Quinn was responsible for hacking into the nation's intelligence agencies and Facebook. Yes, it was her fingerprint, but not her.

Jayden had used the same programming method as NSA and was able to lift a digital image of his mother's print from her own laptop hard drive. He then shared the image with his dad. Orlando planted the virus by logging into his computer as if he was Tracy.

Hacking into Facebook was a lot easier than that. The virus was originally traced to a Facebook account of Petar Princip. The dead father of the 1914 famous assassin Gavrilo Princip in Bosnia. Davud Novak, under the instructions of Jayden, had a family member in the country create the fictitious Facebook account and planted the virus in his timeline. When hundreds of millions of Americans clicked on the hyperlink on the post that was shared to the dead basketball players' profiles, the virus was let loose.

***

August 17th, 2020 – Honshu Island, Japan

If a butterfly flaps its wings in Brazil, can it cause a tornado in Texas? A famous question posed among chaos theory mathematicians for decades. Or was it a typhoon in Japan? If so, thousands of butterflies must have been flapping away for the seven days of August 10th through the 16th, 2020.

The main island of Japan was pummeled by a Category Five super-typhoon named Ignacio. Two hundred-plus miles per hour winds, the equivalent of an F4 tornado, ravaged the island relentlessly for a week.

Coupled with what had transpired in the United States, thousands of "thoughts and prayers" from foreign embassies, media outlets and religious leaders rolled into executive offices. Thousands of fatalities, millions cut off from communicating with loved ones, countries hit with catastrophic effects.

Only a small number of those official communiques ever reached the desk of the President of the United States. That's because most weren't sent to the president. They went to the Prime Minister of Japan.

The storm made landfall in the early morning of August 10th, a full day before forecasters predicted and ripped the island-nation into pieces. A monster of over 1,000 miles in diameter, Typhoon Ignacio encompassed the entire island of Honshu where more than 100 million Japanese lived.

Within two days, the Cat 5 storm killed thousands and millions were without their homes, electricity or other life-support basics. The storm parked itself over Tokyo Bay and inundated the surrounding area with tornado-strength winds and relentless rain.

Nearly a hundred of the fatalities were Olympic athletes from multiple countries housed in hastily and poorly-constructed Olympic dormitories that collapsed from the wind and flooded foundations. The world was busy mourning the loss of life in Japan, not in the United States.

Back in the United States, it seemed the world wanted no part of America's domestic problems. American authorities requested, from their closest allies, access to intelligence-gathering assets, but all requests were denied.

Even the tiny nation government of Sierra Leone, a reasonably cordial friend of the US, sent a rather ambiguous official communique from their embassy. It read, "Our heartfelt sympathies go out to our American brothers and sisters and we pray for a speedy victory against the oppressors of freedom."

Economically, America suffered its worst month in modern history. Most stock exchanges closed until the following Friday, August 15th; the longest period since 1933. A bad idea given the modern stock markets' ability to correct even when trading floors aren't trading.

By the time the markets did open, a week's long backlog of sell orders hit Wall Street like another F5 tornado. Stop-Loss orders flew everywhere yet there were no buyers. There was no stopping the losses. On the first day of trading the Dow Industrials lost over 15,000 points from the high on Friday, August 7th of 29,750.

Leading the market's crash was Facebook's face plant on the trading floor with the company losing almost eighty percent of its value in one day.

THIRTY-SIX

August 17th, 2020 – 7am, EDT, The White House, Washington, DC

"Wake up Mr. President, it's Agent Chalk."

"What time is it?" the president asked, wondering who Agent Chalk was.

"It's seven, as you requested sir. Your meeting with the National Security Council is in one hour. All your senior military staff members will be there as well."

"Where's the First Lady?"

"Sir, ah, she passed away three years ago."

"Right, I knew that. I'm a bit foggy from the sleep."

***

The president, his national security council and all the chiefs from the military began their meeting on the Monday morning with one objective in mind. Stop arguing and make a damn decision.

A week earlier, an amateur drone landed on the North Lawn of the White House. The unmanned aircraft contained an SD card with a letter and list of demands from the terrorist organization known as the Crna Ruka. For the past week, the White House was lit up 24/7 as the leaders of the free world debated what to do.

Whoever sent the message effectively neutralized billions of dollars' worth of intelligence-gathering equipment around the globe, yet delivered their terms on a retail drone purchased for $400 at the local electronics store. The White House communications director once again distributed a copy of the terrorists' demands to each of the meeting's attendees.

The letter, in its entirety, read as follows:

August 10th, 2020:

To the President of the United States, the National Security Council, Members of Congress and the United States Supreme Court,

We are the Crna Ruka. An organization and a disciplined force of tens of thousands of citizens, decades in the making. From this day forward, we represent the millions of people of all colors, ethnicities, and backgrounds who will be denied our rights no longer. Within every community, governmental agency, and military installation and at every elected and appointed level there are those who have joined and support our cause.

We all swore an oath of allegiance and are prepared to give our lives and take others, as was demonstrated yesterday.

The events of August 9th were not rogue attacks but a sampling of our abilities. It is in the best interest of our nation that the bloodshed stops now. But only if our demands are met. If not, the entire nation will again witness a lethal response the likes of which has not been seen on American soil, ever.

We are a trained and experienced force in the art of making war. We have fought in every American conflict since Vietnam. We are prepared to continue to fight and die for our country once again.

There will be no safe harbor, no target of opportunity off-limits, no restraint of our actions. Every man, woman and child snuggled safely in their homes, gated communities or guarded facilities will be considered enemy combatants of our mission. You and you alone are empowered to put both the fears of a nation and the loss of life to rest.

We present to you our demands requiring immediate action of all three bodies of government prior to the president's national convention on August 23rd. If our demands are not met by this deadline, a second wave of attacks will commence on day one of the convention. The convention headquarters themselves, in Charlotte, will not be a safe-haven for the president's party and will be considered a potential target for attack.

Where necessary and possible, our demands are to be implemented by presidential executive order, Congressional amendments to the United States Constitution and judicial rulings from the Supreme Court. Our demands and subsequent ratification of such will from here on be referred to as The Missouri Compromise of 2020.

Our demands are to remain classified and are not to be released to the media. Any attempt to do so or grandstanding by politicians will result in the media themselves and those politicians becoming an immediate target of the Crna Ruka.

The entirety of the United States Constitution was written by our Founding Fathers in less than five months. This, of course, was at a time before electronic communications, air transportation and 24/7 media access. Every modern convenience we take for granted. These were leaders who put themselves to work and refused to quit until their mission was accomplished. We are confident in those in power today to do the same. Except, you have two weeks.

As a sign of good faith, contained on this SD card is the computer code for an anti-viral software that will kill the virus infecting your intelligence-gathering assets. If, however, our demands are not met, another virus, modified slightly, will be unleashed on your systems once again and no anti-virus will be provided by this organization ever again. God Bless America and God bless the Crna Ruka!

***

The Missouri Compromise of 2020

Citizens' Rights:

The capital of the United States will be moved to Kansas City, Missouri. Kansas City is the nearest large, metropolitan city seated in between the geographic and population center of the continental United States. The three bodies of government will be moved with completion set for September 2021. The Department of Defense will remain in Washington, DC.

Demilitarization of state and local law enforcement agencies. Immediate cease of Department of Defense – Program 1033 that allows for the direct purchase of military-grade equipment by law enforcement.

Cease all intelligence-gathering activities on United States citizens by America's spy agencies. Investigations of domestic criminal activity will be conducted strictly by federal, state and local law enforcement agencies. Directors of intelligence agencies found to be in violation of this requirement will be held criminally responsible for their agency's conduct.

Immediate presidential executive orders of clemency and pardon will be granted to citizens involved in the activities of insurrection against the government of the United States that did not result in innocent civilian casualties between the dates of August 8th, 2020 and the date of full implementation of this list of demands.

Voters' Rights:

Presidential elections to be moved to January 3rd, 2021. The inauguration will be held on April 1st, 2021. Early voting must be available beginning December 3rd, 2020. Presidential and Vice Presidential candidates will no longer be restricted to those born on American soil. Every citizen, whether born or naturalized through an oath of citizenship will be eligible to become President or Vice President of the United States. Future elections will be held on the first Monday of January.

The immediate overturning of Citizens United vs Federal Election Commission Supreme Court decision of 2010. Elimination of Political Action Committees' contributions and advertising. The FEC will establish campaign finance ceilings not to exceed $100 million for any individual candidate including for the office of the President of the United States.

Federally mandated and managed congressional and state government voting districts using geographic heat maps of equally distributed population concentrations provided by the 2020 Census. Implementation will begin with the 2023 mid-term elections.

Term limits of members of Congress of a maximum of twelve years combined service in both houses of Congress. Two six-year terms for Senate, six terms for the House of Representatives or any combination thereof.

Citizens' Duties:

Mandatory military service for a minimum of two years for all citizens between the ages of eighteen and twenty-six beginning within three months of high school graduation. Elimination of all medical deferments. Those physically incapable of performing combat service requirements will be placed in non-combat, administrative and logistics roles.

Publicly-funded educational institutions will include United States Civics as part of its core curriculum including post-secondary colleges and universities. Students must attend four years of civics classes while in high school and two years while in college.

***

"There it is, for the tenth time. We only have less than a week left to respond. Solutions this time, men, not suggestions," ordered the president.

"Mr. President, we cannot so much as entertain the notion of succumbing to these demands. If we do so, we establish a precedent that will be impossible to reverse. We need to hunt these people down and kill them," advised his National Security Advisor.

"Mr. President, I respectfully disagree," said the Secretary of Defense. "If our intel systems are disabled again, we are exposed to other threats on a global level that make the events of last week look trivial.

"In the week since the attacks, China has quickly accelerated its presence in the South China Sea threatening the Philippines. Russia stepped up military support of Iran, Syria and Yemen. Saudi Arabia is now exposed to attack on three sides. We've also been tracking a possible narco-terrorism organization with origins in Mexico. We must at least consider to be in cooperation or I'm afraid we could be in for something much worse if we can't monitor what these countries are doing."

"And how would we cooperate? We don't know who they are or how to contact them," asked the president.

***

The arguing and disagreement between the members of the National Security Council continued for the entire day and into the evening, again. The president, exhausted from the debate decided it best to sleep on it and get a fresh perspective the next morning. But not before talking with his most trusted advisor.

"Agent Chalk, your opinion on all this?"

"Sir, I'm here for one reason. To protect you from harm's way. That's my duty. By the oath of my office, I am not afforded an opinion. However, this group was brazen and organized enough to pull off the attacks and bring down our systems. If members are at all levels of government and the military, as they claim, I'm afraid they might be able to get to you. There's no way to know who to trust. What do you think you will do, sir?"

"My National Security Advisor says we should kill them. But who exactly are they? I'm not going to declare war on our own people."

***

By the start of 2020, the president had enjoyed the highest approval ratings of his presidency as well as that of the previous three administrations. The economy was growing steadily and with record low unemployment rates. After nearly two decades fighting the War on Terrorism, most American troops were home. Not in some foreign battlefield.

Then, seemingly overnight, everything seemed to go south in a big way and exceptionally fast. The Butterfly Effect.

The New Year started out with a bang, literally. On January 1st, 2020 an overzealous Coast Guard skipper opened fire on a boat of fifty-five Bahamians within sight of the US coastline near West Palm Beach. The refugees were trying to escape the ravaged nation after Hurricane Dorian destroyed many of that country's islands the previous September. Thirty of those were shot dead or drowned, and several were children. It was a humanitarian and public relations disaster for the president.

In February, three US Senators, all of the president's party, were forced to resign due to corruption allegations regarding military equipment sales, bribes and kickbacks. The three happened to be from states where the governors were authorized to appoint a replacement until the next general election.

Those three governors were of the opposition party and appointed interim senators of their liking. Combined with the vacancy of a senatorial seat due to the murder of Senator Green in Missouri, the balance of power in the upper house of Congress switched from one party to the other. Now both houses were controlled by the president's opposition.

In May 2020, the entirety of the U.S. Men's and Women's Olympic Track team was disqualified from competing for their home country in the games by the International Committee and the World Anti-Doping Agency. Five athletes tested positive for using performance-enhancing drugs, but the IOC wanted to show a position of zero tolerance.

The athletes not involved with the scandal were offered invitations to compete for the sparsely-populated African nation of Sierra Leone. Seventy of the U.S. team's 130 track and field athletes accepted the invitation.

In June, the vice president resigned on short notice because of an illness in the family. The nomination of a new running-mate was going to be made at the upcoming national convention, but that man, the Governor of Missouri, was dead. The president was back to square one.

Even up to the day of the attacks, there was talk in the House of Representatives about a potential impeachment inquiry. It was discovered that over a year ago the president accepted a box of cigars from the president of Cuba, and forgot to report it to his staff in charge of official gifts. Apparently, half of Congress was under the impression the president was going to turn communist because he loved Cohibas.

And now this. August 9th, 2020. The president stopped thinking about all that had gone wrong in his final year of his first term and started thinking about everything that was still to come. He looked at the man he most trusted with his life and said, " I'm done with this shit."

***

August 18th, 2020 – U.S. Naval Hospital, Bethesda, Maryland

"Agent Chalk, thanks for coming on such short notice. Especially with everything that's happening right now," said the president's doctor. "I wouldn't have bothered you but this is too important to delay.

"We've received the test results back from two weeks ago and I'm afraid your suspicions are correct. There are seven distinct stages of the disease and based on the cognition tests administered, it is my diagnosis that the president is somewhere between stage three and four."

"What does that mean from a timing perspective, doctor?"

"It's so hard to tell with Alzheimer's. He could be relatively stable for the next year or two or his condition could accelerate much quicker. At stage three, the president is more than capable of carrying out the duties of his office but if it gets much worse, to stage five or six, I will make my recommendations to Congress."

"I'm sure you can appreciate the sensitivities around this and your oath of office requires complete confidentiality. I'll share the outcome of the tests with him later today."

"Yes, I understand."

***

August 19th, 2020 – The Oval Office, White House, Washington, DC

"My fellow Americans," said the president. "I am honored to have served you these past three-and-a-half years. In all my decisions I've made in my public and private life, I have always tried to do what was best for America.

"But with America's sons and daughters in fields of conflict far away, with our cities under direct attack right here at home, with our hopes and the world's hopes for peace in the balance every day, I do not believe that I should devote even one more day of my time to any duties of this office – the presidency of this country."

Tens of millions of at-home viewers suddenly came to full attention.

"What did he say?"

"Accordingly, I will not accept another nomination from my party at the upcoming National Convention. Furthermore, and with a heavy heart, I will tender my resignation to the Congress of the United States effective at noon tomorrow. The Speaker of the House will be sworn in as the President of the United States at that same hour.

"God bless you all, and God bless the United States of America."

Upon uttering the last word of his 60-second speech, the president left the oval office accompanied only by Secret Service Agent Chalk. The president briefed Chalk that he would be leaving the country the next day. Chalk needed to arrange a security detail as the president was planning to take some time and travel abroad with his children and grandchildren.

"Thank you for your selfless and brave service to our country, Agent Chalk. I will do everything in my power to never forget your name again."

"Thank you, Mr. President. It has been an honor to serve you."

Agent Chalk was not the first person to know the president would be resigning his position. Eight hours earlier, the Speaker of the House was summoned to the White House. The president informed her, that by way of the line of succession of the office, she would be the next President of the United States.

***

August 20th, 2020 – The White House, Washington, DC

After a brief swearing-in ceremony, the appointed president called a private meeting with the minority leaders of the House and Senate. They were both from the previous president's party. She was not.

"Gentlemen, thank you for your show of leadership during this tumultuous time. To cut to the chase, I shared with you all I know of the organization known as the Crna Ruka, including their demands."

"And your intentions, Madam President?"

"I'm going to accept them. You're here to agree to accept them as well. We need to appear unified on this. Are you willing to do this for your country?"

"Madam President, please. We go along with this and we're going to destroy our party. It makes us look incredibly weak. We've yet to even find a new candidate. We understand where you're coming from. Over half of the demands are part of your party's platform that you decided in July."

"Your party will be my party. As soon as I get my current party to sign off on the demands and openly support the changes, I am going to switch parties and run for president as your new candidate. The country is ready for a woman president, but I can't run with my current party. They chose their candidates already.

"Whoever wrote these demands knew a thing or two about this country. If I join you guys, we can count on my home state of California going our way. New York does whatever California does. On top of your strength in places like Texas, Florida, Ohio and Georgia, the election is two-thirds in the bag with those states alone."

"And all these Crna Ruka or Black Hand, whatever the fuck you call them. What are we to do with them?"

"Like their demands say. We're going to let them go. I'm talking about the five American 'heroes' the media is all a rage over. Didn't you see the video? The general, colonel, the reporter and those two basketball stars. Let them out. Now. It took thousands of lives and ten years to kill Bin Laden. Every bit of evidence suggests these guys did our work for us in two weeks."

"The capital in Kansas City? Really? I have family that have spent decades working in Washington, DC, and have some of the largest lobbying firms in town. I don't think I can sell it."

"Trust me, I'm no fan either. I live in California, work in DC, and grew up in Maryland. The closest I came to the state of Kansas is 37,000 feet above it," responded the president, not knowing the new capital city would be in Missouri.

***

The leaders from both parties fell for the new president's plan. She was correct in her assessment of their reactions. Her existing party believed ratification of the demands would bolster their election prospects by showing swift, decisive and compassionate leadership.

While they remained against a number of the individual provisions, her party was willing to concede as they were certain their candidate would win the election in a landslide. Once in office, they could manipulate, stall and fail to fund those new laws to which they were most opposed.

The party, without a nominated candidate, had no choice whatsoever. By ratifying the demands, they could at least buy some time as the elections would be moved to January. This would give the party a chance to regroup and identify strong senatorial candidates for the additional three open slots that came available due to resignations earlier in the year. Theoretically, when the president switched parties, they could retain the White House and regain the Senate.

By August 23rd, 2020, all the demands written by the men of the Black Hand were enacted into law. The signing of a document known as the Missouri Compromise of 2020 became official. On August 24th, the president did in fact change parties and ran against her former one.

She deduced that it was high time the country elected a woman into the highest office, and she was going to see to it that it became a fact. She was nominated for president on the first ballot of party delegates. The president chose as her running-mate the former Lieutenant Governor, but now active Governor from the State of Missouri. The president selected the man largely for symbolic reasons and with the hope his newly-elevated status would secure the open Senate seat from that state as well.

THIRTY-SEVEN

September 1st, 2020 – Gibbs' and Quinn's vacation home, Lake of the Ozarks, Missouri

"Dad, the four of us have been talking. We want to run a crazy idea by you," said Jayden. Buff, Sara, Ronan and Jayden were sitting in the kitchen after staying up all night discussing politics.

"I can't wait to hear this, son. What's up?"

"First, a few questions. Think about the history of America. In your opinion, who would you say was the least likely person to become President of the United States?"

"Ok...I can think of a few but top of the list? Obama. Where's this going?"

"Tell us why?"

"Well, he came from a humble background. Not a political family like many presidents before him. Actually, a broken one with a foreign-born absentee father. And then of course, there was the fact that he was black."

"And how was it he was able to win the election?"

"Well, mostly because of the political climate at the time of his rise to power. Coupled with a confident personality which resonated with voters. His first election came at a time of national crisis. The deepest recession since the Great Depression. Not all that different than when Lincoln, Truman and Carter got elected. Before the Civil War, at the end of World War II and, of course, Watergate. The media loved him. They promoted and endorsed a new face for a new time. So, now that I've given the four of you a presidential history lesson, what's up?"

"We want Theresa and you to run for office," Ronan blurted out.

"Run for what office?"

"President and Vice President," said Buff.

"Guys, the jobs of these offices are next to impossible. Far too many people are looking for a couple of people to have all the answers. It's a nice thought but there's no way Theresa is running for president."

"We don't want Theresa to run for president. We want you. She would be your running-mate. The country not only needs a strong commander, it needs a trauma nurse."

"Go on. I'm sure there's more."

"It could work. Your popularity with the press is off the charts. You can thank Buff and Sara for that."

***

TWO WEEKS EARLIER

"Shouldn't I get Theresa's approval before we post these?" asked Sara.

"I talked to Apis, and he said do it. That's all the approval we need," the general responded.

Unbeknownst at the time, Buff Sowers followed Theresa and Orlando into the Dome at America's Center the day she killed Calvin Heyward. From the stands, she recorded the entire deadly scene on her iPhone. Buff posted the video to her Instagram account. She tagged the post, "David vs. Goliath 2.0". The post went viral.

Sara also posted videos and photos of the shooting in the Waffle House and the picture of Buff and Ronan standing on top of Kendley Charles.

Overnight, the members of the Black Hand became media sensations. Sara Gujic wrote a detailed, full-length feature article that was picked up by the national news wires and was published in newspapers and online media outlets around the country.

***

"America loves you and Theresa more than Oprah," Jayden continued. "The two of you make a perfect combination of strong, experienced leadership and competent compassion. You're both apolitical yet you know everything about our system of government and its history. The other two parties are a mess. Since the election has been moved to January, we have some runway to work with."

"What about campaign financing, choosing a party name and platform? Who knows anything about running a national campaign?"

Buff jumped into the fray. "Between Jayden and Ronan, they have hundreds of millions. We talked about it last night. They are willing to either outright give or lend funds as needed. Our platform was pretty much signed into law over the past week. The amount of work needed to get those new laws into practice is going to take years. We think Sara would be a perfect campaign manager. Her writing is truthful, direct and well-respected. She knows the national media and how it works."

"Not to change the subject, Buff, but where's the $2 million that was wired to you in Haiti? I'm pretty sure those funds came out of my accounts," said Jayden.

"That wasn't my account. It was the account of an organization called the Kore Foundation. They build chicken and egg farms all over the countryside in the poorest damn region of the world I have ever seen. Your $2 million will feed 10,000 kids for a year. You need a receipt for your taxes?"

"No, I'm good."

"Can we stay on topic please? We've even come up with a party name. The Unification Party," said Sara.

"Do you really believe we could win a majority of the voters?" Orlando kept asking questions. He was becoming a little more intrigued with the idea.

"We don't need to win a majority. There'll be three candidates at least. Both parties nominated old career politicians. We could steal the Millennial and Gen Z vote based on age alone. Both of you served in the military so there's a possible solid bloc of veteran voters. The president's numbers are horrible after a week. After she switched parties, the public is viewing her as a power-hungry opportunist and nothing more."

"Now the big question. Have you mentioned this to Theresa?"

"No Dad, that's your job. And that's an order."

"Let me talk to Apis and get his thoughts on this first. Then I'll talk to Theresa."

"Who is this dude, Apis? Tell him to grow a pair and come out in the open," finished Ronan.

"Oh, he's got a pair already. Trust me," said Buff.

Later that evening, after the group finished a fifth bottle of Pinot Noir:

"Me? Orlando, are you bat-shit crazy?" Theresa asked seriously. "I believe anything in this country is possible, with the exception of that. What the hell do I know about politics?"

"Theresa, you don't have to know politics. I agree with the others. Americans are tired of career politicians. I can handle the defense and intelligence affairs and I know how Washington works."

"And what about these ass-clowns? What are they going to do?"

"Jayden has his own plans. Buff and Sara have jobs in mind if you win. And Ronan...?"

"Let me guess. Secretary of State."

"Hey, why's everyone always picking on me? I could do the job. Just don't send me to Paris."

THIRTY-EIGHT

January 3rd, 2021 – Unification Party election night celebration, the Dome at America's Center, St. Louis, Missouri

With 55,000 adoring party supporters in attendance, jumbo screens throughout the stadium continually posted election night news. The early results were encouraging for the Unification Party in as much as the results were non-existent, at least at the Dome.

"Ladies and gentlemen," said the anchor from a news agency founded by Sara Gujic. The startup company was funded by private equity firms in Silicon Valley. The unique value proposition of the new company was reporting nothing but the news. Sara named the company Cronkite 2.0.

"The first precincts are beginning to tally their results. In the interest of those who have yet to vote, we will not be predicting or sharing results until they are final. However, we can share with you that voter turnout numbers indicate the highest on record. Over seventy-five percent of registered voters have already voted. Please stay with us as we will announce the winners after the polls have closed."

Theresa Gibbs and Orlando Quinn were not among the thousands of adoring fans at the stadium. They were at their vacation home in the Lake of the Ozarks adoring each other.

"You know this isn't going to go over well on social media," Orlando said to Theresa as they hugged on the couch.

"Who gives a shit about social media? Is it too early, Orlando? Should we let more time pass before this goes any further? It's only been five months."

"We'll take it at whatever speed you're comfortable with, Theresa. You probably don't remember but years ago, you made a comment about how

Tracy and you could switch husbands and not much would change. For a moment, I thought about that. The idea was tantalizing."

"Well, don't become too tantalized. I don't want to have to pour cold water on you."

They kissed and hugged again. By 10 p.m. on election night, they were both fast asleep. In their own bedrooms. They wouldn't know the results until the next morning. It was Jayden who delivered the news.

"Dad, you won! Can you believe it? You and Theresa won. You crushed it. You two should have been at the party. No one's gone to bed yet. It's crazier than the party after the Blues won the Stanley Cup two years ago."

"Where's the rest of the crew?"

"No idea. Last time I saw them was about four this morning. Ronan was heading out somewhere with Davud Novak. You know, the guy from the team. Buff and Sara were looking for any bars that were still open."

Indeed, the Unification Party ticket of a two-star general and a nurse did win. And big. While they were only able to eke out a small, overall majority of the popular vote, the electoral numbers were a landslide. Three-hundred-and-seventy-three compared to the other parties' totals of a hundred-and-one and sixty-four respectively. The sitting president's party came in third. She was right about the country being ready to elect a woman. She was wrong about which woman and to which position.

Orlando and Theresa captured every state which members of the United States Basketball team called home and in states where the Black Hand happened to kill a cell leader of the Crna Ruka. That included the big electoral states of California, New York, Michigan, Ohio and Georgia.

They also easily won their respective home states, Missouri and Florida. In Missouri, the majority of St. Louis voted for the two and in Kansas City, the majority voted against the sitting president for agreeing to allow the nation's capital to be moved there.

They won Florida not because of a few thousand hanging chads. It was the three Championship banners hanging from the ceiling of the Amway Center in Orlando. The city where Jayden Quinn and Ronan McCoy played the entirety of their NBA careers. In central Florida, the two basketball stars were more popular than Mickey Mouse.

In Texas, they didn't win a majority of the popular vote but they did win a plurality. With thirty-six percent of the popular vote, compared to thirty-four and thirty by their opponents, they won 100 percent of the state's thirty-eight electoral votes.

"Now what are we supposed to do?" Theresa asked her president-elect.

"Pack lightly. We'll be in DC for a year and then onto Kansas City."

"Kansas City...really? I hate that city. Jayhawk fans, all of them. What the hell are we going to do with all those leftover government buildings and real estate in DC?"

"How does 'Disney-DC' sound to you?"

***

April 1st, 2021 – the Presidential Inauguration, the Gateway Arch National Park, St. Louis, Missouri

On a grandstand underneath the shadow of the Gateway Arch in St. Louis, the nation was ready to watch the swearing-in of the 47th President of the United States. To the right of Orlando Quinn stood the sworn-in vice president. Among the guests of honor positioned within a few seats of the president-elect was a 'Most Valuable Player in the NBA', a Pulitzer Prize winner, an Air Force pilot and the president's son.

President Quinn walked to the podium and stood in front of the Chief Justice of the Supreme Court.

"I do solemnly swear..." Orlando paused while smiling at his vice president.

Theresa lip-synced out the words, "Please don't swear."

President Quinn's inauguration speech lasted only three minutes. Hundreds of thousands of citizens attending the ceremony roared in appreciation of his brevity. The St. Louis Cardinals had their home opener scheduled for later that evening and everyone wanted to get to the pre-game party. The new president threw out the first pitch. He missed the plate by 10 feet left and hit the Cardinals mascot, Fred Bird right in the head.

***

President Quinn's first Executive Order, with the permission of the families, was to move the bodies of the nine fallen heroes of the Black Hand and have them buried together at the Jefferson Barracks National Military Cemetery south of St. Louis. With a bagpiper playing 'Amazing Grace' and a bugler calling Taps, the men were buried side-by-side. The memorial plaque laid upon their final resting place listed their names and read, "America's Dream Team." It wasn't a reference to basketball.

***

April 2nd, 2021 – Madic's Café, Little Bosnia, St. Louis, Missouri

Davud Novak pulled his car into the near-empty parking lot. The only other car there he recognized as his uncle's. Novak was dressed in formal attire, as today was his wedding day and he couldn't be more excited.

"I'll be right back, my love. I have a gift for my uncle as it's customary in my culture for the groom to give small presents to family members on their wedding day," Novak said to his future spouse. The couple had only dated officially for seven months, but had lived together since the first day they met back in April of 2020.

"Hurry back, sweetie, the wedding starts in forty-five minutes."

The bells on the front door of Madic's Bosnian Café in St. Louis rang, announcing a visitor.

"A lunch customer?" Hamza Madic asked himself. "Impossible. I have a wedding to attend." As he walked to the front door, he instantly recognized the gigantic shadow being cast on the floor.

"Davud! My nephew, how are you? It's your big day. Please tell me you have brought your gold medal. I need to see it. I want to wear it."

"I'm great, *Ujak* (Uncle). Of course I brought it. May I put it on you as I received it in Tokyo?"

"Please, nothing would make me happier. I can't believe I will wear the gold medal."

Novak pulled the medal from his pocket. He'd replaced the traditional Olympic lanyard with a heavy, 14-karat gold chain as thick as a dog collar. Madic loved it. He lowered his head, bent over forward, with his nephew standing in front of him. He loved the feel of the heavy gold chain as Novak placed it around his skinny neck.

"Sing, *Ujak*, sing your national anthem as I congratulate you on your Olympic triumph."

"*Oh say can you see, by...*Davud? Davud! What are you doing?" His six-foot, ten-inch nephew was lifting the tiny man off his feet by pulling on the gold chain with every ounce of energy he had. Novak was strangling the life out of him.

"I said sing your national anthem, not mine. You know the words, *Ujak. God of Justice; Thou who saved us, when in deepest bondage cast...*" Novak was singing the Serbian National Anthem.

"How many have you cast into their deepest bondage, my dear *Ujak?*"

Madic was losing consciousness but he could still squeeze out a few more words from his dying lips.

"Davud, we are both Bosniaks, both Americans."

"No, you are a fucking slave trader, a murderer and a Serb. You are not Bosniak and you are not American," were Novak's final words to his uncle. The human trafficker and arms dealer was dead and would never again see, *'the dawn's early light.'*

As it turned out, Sara Gujic had researched her archived stories and photos from her Pulitzer Prize-winning articles on human trafficking coming out of Bosnia into the United States. She found one photo of a squad of Serbian soldiers standing near a road-side ditch with hundreds of bodies of men and boys. The killers were smiling.

Clearly identifiable was Hamza Madic. She showed the photo to Davud Novak and while he couldn't confirm Madic had killed his father, to him, it was close enough.

"How did your uncle like his gift?" asked Davud's bride-to-be, back in the car.

"He got all choked up."

***

The betrothed couple arrived at the Bosnian Islamic Center with fifteen minutes to spare before the start of the ceremony. There were 500 guests in attendance. Four-hundred-and-ninety-five sat on the groom's side and five on the bride's side. A very odd wedding.

The ceremony began as most weddings did. First the flower girl, followed by the wedding party and finally the bride being escorted down the aisle as Pachelbel's 'Canon' played over the mosque's PA system.

Buff Sowers looked slightly uncomfortable in her flower girl dress. But then again, not many flower girls could bench-press 225 pounds. Ten times.

Then came the maid-of-honor. The Vice President of the United States, Theresa Gibbs. She was as shapely and beautiful as ever. Lastly, came the bride and a stand-in for the father as the real father had passed away years ago.

The bride was dressed in pure white. "Yeah, right," whispered many of the guests. He wore a white three-piece Armani suit, white shirt, white tie and white shoes. The bride looked gay. He was.

Ronan McCoy, arm-in-arm with President Quinn, walked slowly up the aisle as the music continued to play. The president was in his Army dress blues. Ronan's future husband, Davud Novak, was waiting at the front of the mosque.

Ronan scanned the rows of people in attendance. On Davud's side of the mosque, it seemed the entire Little Bosnia community of St. Louis was there. But where was his uncle?

On Ronan's side, he smiled to his mom and remaining siblings. It had been so long since they were a family and his heart was warm. They'd finally accepted who he was. They tried to accept him when he was a young boy, but Ronan's father routinely beat the acceptance out of them.

The other two guests on the left side were his best friend, Jayden Quinn and United States Army Drill Sergeant Anthony Messina. He held a large, life-size portrait of Ronan's dead brother, Jeffery, taken after he graduated from basic training. He was photographed in Army blues of his own. Jeffery had been killed in Iraq.

"Hooah," whispered Messina as Ronan passed.

"Hooah!" Ronan shouted to everyone in the mosque.

***

During the four-and-a-half months Ronan McCoy and Davud Novak were roommates, it didn't take long for the two to discover each other's born preferences. The physical closeness of staying in such tiny dormitory rooms led to other types of physical closeness.

Davud overlooked Ronan's indiscretions in the early stages of their relationship. Besides, Novak could hardly fault him. The twin Brazilian Men's volleyball players were exotic creatures. Both six-foot, six-inches tall, tan, muscular and could cook up Brazilian delicacies in the dorm kitchen like there was no tomorrow. "Those two gorgeous flight attendants. How are

Michael and Steven doing these days?" Davud teased Ronan often.

"And what about the French under-cover cops who were posing as prostitutes. Remember when you got arrested with Jayden in Paris? What were their names?" Davud would not stop teasing him.

"Hell, I don't know. Who asks hookers their names? I'm guessing Jacques and Pierre or something like that."

"So all those years traveling with Jayden. You two never, you know?"

"No, Jayden's weird. He likes girls."

***

Davud and Ronan settled in the Little Bosnia neighborhood of St. Louis. Davud took over his uncle's café as it was his mom who actually owned the building. After changing the name, he changed its reputation. After a year, a table at Davud's Bosnian Bistro was one of the most sought-after in all of St. Louis.

Ronan launched a non-profit academy. Its mission was to provide training, counseling and physical fitness programs to high-school-aged children preparing them for their mandatory military service once they turned eighteen. He funded the organization with a $50 million gift out of his own pocket, a match of the same from Jayden and another $25 million donated by the families of the deceased basketball players. Tens of thousands of young kids would benefit greatly from the tireless work of Ronan and the staff of the Black Hand Foundation.

***

FOUR DAYS AGO

August 6th, 2021 – the South Lawn of the White House, Washington, DC

Vice President Theresa Gibbs and President Orlando Quinn were married on August 6th. The same date Melissa Gibbs and Jayden Quinn were to be married seven years earlier. The couple enjoyed a small and private wedding with only four guests; Buff Sowers, Jayden Quinn, Sara Gujic and Ronan McCoy. Sara was Theresa's maid of honor and Buff, the president's best man.

The remaining two guests sat on the bride's side. On the groom's side were nine empty seats, each with a properly-folded American flag. On the flags sat a Purple Heart medal. Awarded for being killed in the line of duty. There was a second medal on each of the chairs as well. President Quinn would present the Medal of Honor posthumously to each of the fallen men's families the next day. Theresa would also accept the nation's highest honor on behalf of her hero and deceased husband, Lt. Colonel Kenneth Gibbs.

Later that night, the president and vice president celebrated their honeymoon in the presidential bedroom of the White House.

"Get those fucking knickers off and get in this bed right now, my Celtic Warrior," ordered the vice president as she lay atop the blankets naked. "I want some ice cream. I've only had chocolate my whole life and I'm excited about trying vanilla."

"I love it when you talk dirty."

"I hope that stereotype about the difference between black men and white men isn't true."

"Wait until you see my cobra, my Cobra," he bragged, as the important part of the soldier stood at attention.

"Oh...it's true."

***

Immediately following the military medal ceremony on August 7th, Jayden Quinn jumped on a flight to St. Louis. He spent the majority of the next twenty-four hours visiting the mausoleum of Melissa Gibbs. A full day talking to her, holding her pictures, placing her wedding ring on his smallest finger. He would have stayed through the ninth but he didn't want to miss his first birthday party.

At 7am on the eighth, the first of a many-leg journey began for Jayden. A flight from St. Louis to New York. Then a 12-hour flight to Jeddah, Saudi Arabia. His watch automatically updated to reflect the eight-hour time difference. It was now 8am on the 9th. He hoped to make it on time. It took an hour to clear customs and another hour to get to the port from the Jeddah airport. The ferry left at eleven sharp. In calm seas, the ferry took twelve hours. In rough, up to fifteen. The seas were calm.

At 11:30pm local time on August 9th, 2021 at Port Sudan, Jayden Quinn came home for the very first time. He looked over the rail and saw a crowd of hundreds waiting for him. They were easy to spot. Collectively, they were the tallest group of human beings Jayden ever laid eyes on.

Uncles, aunts, cousins, all with the last name Mwangi. Even three of Jayden's four biological grandparents were still living. As fate and a DNA test would have it, Jayden was a second cousin to his former teammate, roommate and now Medal of Honor recipient, Charles Mwangi. It was a small world indeed, thought Jayden.

Charles Mwangi's immediate family was from a village in Kenya, a few miles south of the Sudanese border. Jayden's side of the family lived a few miles north of the border. The patriarchs of both families were brothers. The grandfather on Charles' side of the family was Simba Mwangi. The same Simba who killed and drank the blood of the bastard pastor in Los Angeles. Which made sense. Simba means 'lion' in Mwangi's tribal language. And lions drink blood.

Everyone on the dock waved signs reading, *Marhaban illa watanik. Eid almelad assayida, Jayyidin.* (Welcome to your homeland. Happy birthday, Jayden).

Jayden planned on staying for two months in Sudan and then he would be off to Officer Candidate School. His plan, not anyone else's, once receiving his commission was to attend the Defense Language Institute in Monterey, California. His language of choice? Modern Standard Arabic.

***

PRESENT DAY

August 10th, 2021 – 4:45pm EDT, Russell Senate Office Building, Washington, DC

"Ms. Gujic, I'm sorry for hurrying this along but we're scheduled to end this briefing at 5pm sharp. We only have fifteen minutes left and we have yet to hear the reason why the men of the Crna Ruka committed such atrocities. You opened this briefing yesterday explicitly saying this was one of the shortcomings of the 9/11 commission report. Can we expect the same shortcoming?" asked the House Chairperson on Homeland Security.

"Ma'am, we are prepared to discuss that now. It won't take more than a few minutes, I promise. I'd like to turn over the microphone to my colleague on the commission who is an expert on this subject. Ronan, can you share with the American people your expert opinion on why the young men of the Crna Ruka did what they did?"

Ronan McCoy has been sitting next to Sara Gujic for the entire two days. He has yet to say a word. He's wearing the only suit he owns. A white Armani, a white shirt, white tie and white shoes. He is also wearing a white tennis headband around his long, shoulder-length, dark-red wavy hair as he was prone to sweating profusely when nervous. He has a raggedy mustache and beard. A tear-drop tattoo under his left eye and a sun-tanned glow to his face round out his appearance.

He's yet to appear solely on television as well. The cameras did catch a brief moment of him earlier in the day during a break. As he was leaving to use the men's room and not knowing the cameras were still filming, he stood right behind Sara Gujic, his red-inked hands on her shoulders. He leaned over her to excuse himself, but whispered too loudly, "I gotta go take a poop." The microphone picked up what he said. The whole room erupted in laughter.

***

In Des Moines, Iowa, after finishing her twentieth Hail Mary for sneaking a second cookie at lunch, legally-blind and hard-of-hearing 92-year-old Sister Esther from the Villa Jesus Retirement Convent watched the briefing on a color TV built in the '70s. She saw and heard something different.

"Was that my Lord and Savior we saw crying and comforting Ms. Gujic? And did he say he has to go talk to the Pope?" she asked on one of the recorded phone lines. Possibly, to Sister Esther's first question. Definitely no, to her second.

***

Ronan has been rehearsing for this moment for months. Nervously, he looks at his many pages of notes even though he's memorized every word he intends to say. He takes a long drink of water to moisten his cotton-dry mouth and lips.

He stands, pulls the cordless microphone close. Billions of people are watching and waiting to know the answer to the question 'why'. Ronan's tries to convince himself that public speaking is no different than taking the winning free throw at the end of a game. Ignore the crowd, focus. He speaks.

"Dad!"

Ronan drops the microphone confidently. He lets out a loud sigh of relief, pumps his hand in the air and does a victory lap around the table. Nothing but net. He stops, puts his notes into his briefcase and starts to leave the room.

"Wait, what?" asks the House Chairwoman. "What did you say, Mr. McCoy? 'Dad'? That's it? Where are you going? Please stay and talk to us, Mr. McCoy."

"Ronan, stay. It will be alright," says Sara.

Ronan stays. He picks up the microphone and begins walking around the room. He starts talking again. This time it's to everyone in the room and to everyone in the world. He is doing so completely unrehearsed.

"I said 'Dad.' Maybe I should have said 'no dad.' The men of the Crna Ruka; I'm talking about the young men, not the cell leaders. Not a single one of them had a real father in their lives. The cell leaders? Fuck them. They were in it for the money and power. But the 18-year olds, 19-year-olds – they were fatherless.

"I don't have any advanced degrees in sociology or psychiatry, but the calculus on this is simple. A son needs a dad.

"I know it is fashionable these days to bash fathers. Look at our entertainment and media industries. Every day on television, in the movies, dads are portrayed as bumbling idiots or worse. But dads suck it up and take it. That's what dads do. Until they don't...and decide to become absentee dads instead. Those sons of absentee dads can become marginalized young men. And marginalized young men can turn into radicalized killers.

"I did my research on Wikipedia. The nineteen hijackers on 9/11? With rare exception, almost every one of those young men grew up either without a father or with an abusive one. They found a new father. His name was Osama Bin Laden.

"It's not video games or the internet turning our young men into drug dealers, school shooters and Crna Ruka. It's a lack of positive male role models willing to deliver a good old-fashioned ass-chewing if the boy deserves it.

"Over the past two days we've heard many titles, honorifics, nicknames and a word used for both hate and love at the same time. The words general, coach, mentor, hero, even the N-word can all mean the same thing. I didn't need to look it up in the dictionary to know what that word is. It's 'dad'."

"Mr. McCoy, I must say, for being unrehearsed, your perspective on this is enlightening. But that hardly qualifies you to represent yourself as an expert. Wouldn't you agree?"

"I absolutely agree. I never said I was an expert. Ms. Gujic did. Maybe the word 'example' is better. Maybe Sara, Jayden and the men who voted me as their team captain saw me as the 21st century equivalent of Lucy, the Missing Link.

"Except I'm not the dead, singular personification of biological evolution. I'm a living example of social evolution. I was once on my own path of destruction. Alcohol, drugs and sex were my weapons of rebellion. Not bullets and guns. As a species I was an ape, an animal interested only in my immediate pleasures. But after I met men like my coach and the general, I believe the lessons they taught me made me a better man. A better human.

"But if it wasn't for having those strong adult men in my life, it is within the realm of conceivability that I could have ended up like the young men of the Crna Ruka. Over forty percent of today's households do not include a father. I'm telling you today, if that doesn't change, we can expect more days like August 9th to happen."

"Mr. McCoy, that is as profound and understandable as anything I heard over the past two days. But that doesn't explain why Tracy Quinn and Calvin Heyward did what they did. She didn't need money or power, she had it. Calvin grew up with a dad. Even gave him his nickname, the Mongoose. What happened to them?"

"Like boys, girls need dads too. For different reasons. Take Buff Sowers as another example. She grew up in a desperately poor household but she grew up with hard-working and loving parents. Two of them. We know the rest of her story. She's an American hero.

"But Tracy Quinn never had a father. He died three months before she was born. Killed in Vietnam. Like far too many other fathers during that time. FUBAR."

"And what was his name?"

"United States Marine Corps Lance Corporal Tracy Beckette. Once a marine, always a marine, right, Senator McGinn? Yes, Tracy is both a boy's and a girl's name. Turns out the reason Tracy Quinn never liked any nicknames was because she learned from her mother that her father was ridiculed as a boy. Other boys would mock his name by pronouncing it as 'Trathy', with a lisp. As if he was gay. He wasn't. The dead soldier's daughter was named after him."

"And Mr. Heyward?"

"There's no sound reason for his actions other than insanity. Maybe eleven years locked up in a cage for smoking pot at the age of eighteen will do that to a man. But like fathers, we all need our mothers too, don't we? That's my whole point. What is it that we all don't understand?

"Heyward grew up in a single-parent household as well but with no mom. His mother was murdered in front of his very eyes when he was three years old. A victim of a drive-by shooting in Memphis as she and her son walked home from the grocery story."

"And what was Mrs. Heyward's name? Did we find that out?"

"Yes, ma'am. It was Rosie...Rosie Heyward."

The audience is dead silent for one very long, thought-provoking minute.

"One last question, Ronan. What should we do about it? How do we change?"

"Ma'am, that's up to you to decide. I'm talking about our elected officials. We didn't put you in office so that you can all sit around and debate which bathroom someone can or cannot use. Or what letter I call myself. Me? I'm a G. Buff Sowers? She's an L. Last I heard, Jayden Quinn's still a virgin. I guess that makes him a V. But who gives a flying F? Our house is on fucking fire and everyone's arguing about what color to paint the baby's room. At the end of the day, we're all P's. People.

"Our sons are dying before our very eyes and what are we focused on? BS. Congress spent nearly two months last year investigating a president because he smoked a cigar with a man named Castro. Do us a favor in the future. Unless a president commits a serious crime, like insulting Oprah Winfrey or something, let the American people choose who runs the country. Go to work on the shit that matters. Pardon the obviously sexist phrase, ma'am, but it's time to man the fuck up.

"I challenge every member of Congress, the president and vice president and all Americans to jump in your cars and drive through our cities and towns. No, not to a stadium to watch a game or to go antiquing on a small-town Main Street. But to the inner-city neighborhoods and the edges of those small towns. Drive down Monument Street in Baltimore or Livernois Avenue in Detroit. Document what you see. Jayden and I did that for three years during our off seasons.

"There is a Delmar Boulevard Divide in almost every major city in the country. Unfortunately, the name of that street is far too often named after our greatest Civil Rights leader, Martin Luther King Jr. If he were alive today and drove down some of the hundreds of streets named in his honor, he would fall to his knees and cry.

"Take a trip to my hometown; Milton, West Virginia. Take a hike in the woods. Our teenagers aren't shooting squirrels and stealing kisses. They're shooting poison in their veins and turning tricks.

"Let's stop fighting enemies around the world when the most dangerous enemy is in our own backyards. Those same backyards where a little boy is holding a basketball, looking to play a game of one-on-one. But he has a problem. There's no one to play with. There is no dad. That's all I have to say. I'm sorry. I don't like to speak in public." Ronan drops the microphone again.

Now two minutes of silence.

Sara Gujic begins, "And that concludes our report before this body and the American people. It is with a heavy heart, knowing this will be the last time this room, this building will be used to convene the senators elected to represent the will of the people.

"When the Senate returns in September, they will do so in the newly constructed Senator Green Building in Kansas City, Missouri. For those who don't recall, Senator Green was killed on August 9th, 2020, at the St. Louis Country Club.

"The House of Representatives will convene at two WeWork locations in downtown Kansas City until their new offices are completed.

"Thank you all for coming and God Bless the United States of America."

Everyone in the Russell Senate Office Building and across the globe stand and give a roaring five-minute ovation. The meeting ends at 5pm as promised. A first in the halls of Congress. The President of the United States is also roaring even though he's nowhere near Washington, DC. He's 1,000 miles away and he is scared shitless.

THIRTY-NINE

THIRTY-THREE HOURS AGO

August 9th, 2021 – 8:00am, EDT, Air Force One, Andrews Air Force Base, Maryland

"Congratulations again, Madam Vice President, Mr. President. It was a lovely wedding. Where to this morning, the usual?" asked the Brigadier General pilot of Air Force One.

"Well, you were a stunning best man, Buff. No, somewhere different. No barbecues and go-fast boats at the lake this time. St. Augustine, Florida. My home town," ordered President Orlando Quinn.

"Let me call Director Chalk, sir. He'll need to get an advance detail down there. They left for Missouri thirty minutes ago. Sorry, I thought we were headed to the Lake of the Ozarks."

"Is Scheck on that detail?"

"Yes, ma'am. I believe he is."

"Good, we're going to run his ass ragged again. Tell him he's got two hours to get to Florida." The three friends laughed out loud.

"Sir, I'd like to take a quick detour north after takeoff. Today's the grand reopening of the Chesapeake Bay Bridge. I'd like to see it. It's going to be named after my deceased wife. Thanks for your help with that one."

"No problem, Buff. She deserves the honor."

The four-engine 747 roared off the runway at Andrews Air Force Base. Buff climbed to only 500 feet. As the plane passed over the crowd and Colonel Adrian Foster Memorial Chesapeake Bay Bridge, Buff began to wag the aircraft's wings back and forth. The crowd looked up and waved back.

Painted on the bottom of the president's plane for all to see was one name but spelled in a manner so as to phonetically draw out its first letter. "Aaaaaaadrian." An Air Force One pilot's way of saying, "I love you."

Two-and-a-half hours later, Air Force One touched down at the St. Augustine Municipal Airport. General Maretta Buff Sowers rolled to a stop with over 2,000 feet to spare. It would be a much more difficult take-off from the short runway, but she had done the math. No problem. As long as the president didn't gain 4,432 pounds while on vacation.

After landing, husband and wife jumped in a rental car and headed south on highway US 1. The newlyweds refused to take the presidential limousine that had arrived seven minutes before them.

"Dammit," said Agent Scheck. "Here we go again." Former FBI Agent, now Secret Service Agent Scheck was about to have another one of those days. The vice president seemed to take great pleasure to make him "pay for this someday," as she'd promised a year ago.

Their first stop was Fort Mose Historic State Park a few miles south of the airport. They spent two hours walking the grounds and reflecting on the site where black men and women had become the first free Africans to live in the United States.

They then checked in to the Historic Bayfront Hilton Hotel overlooking the Matanzas River downtown. The new hotel was built on the exact site of the former Monson Motor Lodge where decades ago, protestors were having acid poured on them. Orlando and Theresa quickly changed and ran down to the pool.

"Last one in is a rotten egg," Orlando yelled as he belly-flopped into the pool.

"Let's play Marco Polo," said Theresa.

"You can't play with two people. We need someone else."

"Agent Scheck. Go change into your banana hammock and get in here," ordered the vice president.

"Goddamn it," Scheck said quietly so the vice president didn't hear.

"I heard that."

Two hours later, the couple was bicycling their way to St. Augustine Beach.

"Don't be a salmon!" screamed a stranger on his bicycle as he rode past Theresa and Orlando.

"What does that mean?" Theresa asked her husband as the middle-aged guy in way-too-tight bicycling shorts passed them.

"I think it means we're on the wrong side of the road. He's telling us we should be going with the traffic, not against it."

"Fuck her."

Agent Scheck and his squad were ten yards behind the two and were also swimming upstream on their bikes. They stopped the bicyclist and gently reminded him not to yell at the president and vice president of the United States ever again. And to buy some looser shorts.

"Where are we going now?"

"Butler Beach. All are welcome. Even gender-neutral Filipinas. Only ten miles."

The next day, Theresa and Orlando were off to Orlando's favorite city. Orlando. During the drive, he downloaded the app for Disney World, purchased tickets and reserved a spot in line for his favorite ride. Within an hour he received a text. He read it aloud to Theresa.

"Your seat at IASW will be available in thirty minutes. Please report to the ride's location within this time."

"IASW?" Theresa asked. "Wait, I've heard that name before. It was the name of the agency Tracy owned when she was representing Jayden. What does it mean?"

"You'll find out."

Once inside the park, they sprinted at top speed to make sure they didn't lose their seats. Even the president and vice president of the United States had to get a Fast Pass.

"There it is. Like I remember." Theresa caught up to him, looked up and read, "It's a Small World." I.A.S.W. She finally got it. They took their place in line. An hour and fifteen minutes later they completed the ride.

"Wasn't that remarkable? I'm sitting my ass on this ride the rest of the day."

"Oh no you're not. We're riding Space Mountain. Or are you scared? "

***

"Sorry to cut the honeymoon short Madam Vice President, but there's been an attack on our border. We're refueling now and we'll be ready to takeoff in ten minutes. Where's the president?" said General Buff Sowers.

"He'll be here in a minute. He's wrapping up a call in the limo. Which border?"

"Both of them. A separatist group out of Quebec raided a Department of Homeland Security regional office a few miles south of the Canadian border in New York. A similarly-named group is holding 300 hostages at the Alamo in San Antonio. They came over the border from Laredo."

"What do they want?"

"The group from Canada wants sovereignty from Ottawa and claims northern New York to be historically their territory. The Mexican terrorists want Texas. All of it."

"Well, we only got thirty-six percent of the vote in Texas. Let them have it. I'm teasing, Buff. What are the groups' names?"

"The French Canadian group goes by *La Main Noire* and the Mexican group calls itself *La Mano Negro*."

"Speak English for shit's sake, Buff."

"The Black Hand."

"Jesus Christ. Not again."

"You know, ma'am, they should make a movie about all of this. A blockbuster for sure."

"You think so, Buff? Who's playing you?"

"I love Kevin Hart. He's hilarious. He just needs to hit the weights and grow some tits. What about you, ma'am?"

"I guess...Lea Salonga. You probably know her. She was the lead in 'Miss Saigon'."

"Hey, let me in on this," said the president as he joined the two. "I think Oprah would be a perfect Tracy. We just need to catch her at low tide."

"Sir, please don't insult Oprah again or we're going to have you impeached," smiles Buff. "And Apis? Who do you think, ma'am?"

"Like I said, Lea Salonga. Buff, I told you months ago. I'm to be called Apis or sir, when we're alone. Orlando, we need to get the National Security Council on the line. I'll meet you in the communications room." Theresa leaves.

"Mr. President, I have to say, the first time I saw Theresa walk into that hotel room in her dress blues, I about lost it. It's funny how we form certain perceptions without knowing the truth. I wouldn't have guessed her to be

Apis in a million years. Especially after you and Ken kept referring to her as a man. "He planned this…" "He needs to approve that..." Totally shocked my hair straight."

"Buff, you know in the vice president's native language you could say, 'She planned this, she needs to approve that.' It's all the same. No gender pronouns. People are just people, remember? She's Apis, the Holy Bull. Or the Holy Cow, if you want."

"We should try going without gender pronouns in English some time. See how that works in this country. When was the last time the Philippines declared war on anyone?"

"A hundred and twenty years ago. Against us...Ken and I first used 'he' as a little joke because Theresa was always getting it wrong. But we realized it added another level of secrecy. We needed to protect her. She was our superior officer. She outranked us. Always has.

"I first met Theresa in 1993 during the battle of Mogadishu. I met her by way of having a bullet pass through my lower back. The bullet nicked my femoral artery on the way out and I was bleeding to death. Theresa was the flight nurse on the medivac.

"She reached her hand up into my gushing wound and clamped off the artery. If it wasn't for her, I wouldn't be standing here today. The pilot at the controls of that Blackhawk was a man by the name of Chief Warrant Officer Two Scott Baetzel. At the time, I was a captain. Ken was a captain. Theresa was a major. She outranked us then and she has ever since."

"Man, it's a small world."

"When it comes to making war it sure seems like it. Doesn't it?"

"And Ken knew this story about Somalia as well?"

"Yes he did. The three of us have been friends since long before I moved to St. Louis. I never told Tracy. I never shared any of my battlefield experiences with her. The Army way. The Gibbs were the reason I accepted the job there. They were also the reason my son decided to play for St. Louis University. I told him the story on his 18th birthday. On August 9th, 2008. The day he became a man."

"But why, why would she order her own husband's death? Why order his best friend to kill him?"

"Buff, you should know this. Since the beginning of time, officers have ordered sons and daughters to kill or be killed countless times. All of us saw it the same way. But with a husband and a best friend, instead of a son or a daughter.

"The plan she created was out of a love for her new country. And out of love for a daughter. Hell has no fury as a patriot mother scorned."

***

PRESENT DAY

August 10th, 2021 – 5:45pm, the Missing Ink and Chink Tattoo and Massage Parlor, Chinatown, Washington, DC

"I want to be very specific with you. I want a single black hand, making a fist, tattooed right here over my heart. Is that clear?" says Ronan.

"Yes, brack hand tattoo over heart. Got it," replies the elderly Chinese shop owner.

"Then I want the words 'Black Hand' written over the hand and 'Foundation' under it. Is that clear? And I'm in a hurry. I gotta catch a flight to St. Louis in two hours."

"Yes, yes. I unnastan. Brack Hand words over hand. Found Nation words underneath. Prease sit, must hully. You catch a fright. St. Rouis. You want happy ending? $10."

"Ten dollars? Damn, DC's more expensive than Tokyo. No thank you."

And that's exactly what the artist/masseuse inks. The words "Black Hand" above the rendering of a hand and "Found Nation" underneath it. First upset, Ronan stares at it in the mirror for a few minutes, then he says aloud, "Black Hand...Found Nation. It's better, much better. Thank you, sir. Great job."

For America, it is a happy ending and it is free because of The Black Hand.

The End